DAILY GRIND

THE TAKEOVER SERIES BOOK FOUR

ANNA ZABO

Second Edition

First edition published by InterMix (Berkley Romance), 2017-2021

Cover Design: Cate Ashwood, www.cateashwooddesigns.com

Print ISBN: 978-1-947550-08-7

To those who struggle to find the space to be who they are. It can happen and you will be.

CONTENT NOTES

This novel contains descriptive on-page consensual sex, including light bondage and toy use.

Characters consume alcohol socially.

Biphobia, misogyny, and homophobia are discussed.

Burnout from stress is discussed and depicted, including disordered eating, mood swings, and physical collapse.

Rob's previous relationship involved a large age-gap and blackmailing (of Rob) with business consequences.

The deaths of Rob's parents are discussed, including one by suicide (prescription drug overdose).

CHAPTER ONE

Bright sunlight from the first warm spring day in Pittsburgh drove cheerful customers looking for a tasty jolt of caffeine into Grounds N'at. Brian Keppler wiped his brow with his forearm while two shots of espresso dripped into glasses for an order, then set about frothing the milk.

One cappuccino. One Americano. Both easy drinks, thank goodness.

He needed to down a shot or two of espresso himself. This morning had been *cruel.* He'd barely made it to the shop in time to open, and the flow of customers had been nonstop since he unlocked the door at eight AM.

A sunny Saturday always meant business would be brisk, and he was grateful for all his customers, but man, he needed about three more hours of sleep.

Coffee would have to do, as usual.

He finished crafting the drinks and handed them over, with a smile, to the high-school kids who had ordered. They set up their papers and laptops at a table near the window.

The line had died down to nothing and everyone in the shop had what they needed. For a moment, he had a reprieve from slinging bean juice. Good. He started brewing a much-needed shot for himself and leaned against the counter.

He knew better than to sit down, though he kept a stool under the counter. The instant his butt touched wood, a flood of customers would pour in.

He did check his phone and found a text from Ethan—the barista who *should've* been working this morning.

Hey, am I still on for Monday?

Brian twisted his lips and pondered that same question. He hadn't enjoyed being woken up by a phone call from Ethan at seven thirty to be told he couldn't make his shift—not after a rare night out for Brian with his brother and sister. He'd fallen into bed after two in the morning.

Normally, he'd have let it slide. Things happened, sometimes. But this was the *third* time Ethan had called off on short notice for no other reason than "I'm just not feeling it today, man."

Brian clicked the phone screen off and tucked it into his pocket before collecting his much-needed espresso.

He *hated* firing people, but didn't see much choice in Ethan's case. He needed dependable baristas, not dudes who came into work only when the moon was in the right house or whatever.

The bell rang on the door and Brian downed his shot and prepared for another round of slinging drinks.

A guy walked in. Tall. Red hair. Sunglasses. Not a regular customer—he'd have *remembered* this guy. Freckles and a bright-ass smile while he took in the shop.

Brian swallowed and set his espresso cup down. He usually didn't dig dudes. But sometimes... sometimes he did.

This was one of those sometimes.

Sunglasses walked farther in and took the glasses off—and that really wasn't any better. He had pale eyes—hazel or blue or green—and cheekbones that went straight up to heaven as he stared at the drink menu.

Brian's usual line was "What can I get started for you?" That's not what came out of his mouth, though.

"See anything you'd like?"

Sunglasses stepped forward and met his gaze. Hazel—his eyes were hazel and they had little lines around them that matched his smile. "Lots of things." The melodic words slithered through Brian, all wrapped up in a British accent. "What do you recommend?"

He completely forgot what drinks were even on the damn board. "Well, what do you *like*? Light? Dark? Bold? Something with a bit of cream?" Did he *really* just say that?

A huff of laughter. "I'm fond of bold. And cream."

"Chili Mocha?"

His smile deepened. "Bold, hot, and spicy?"

Yeah, he was in trouble. "With cream."

"Of *course*." He tucked his sunglasses into the neck of his t-shirt. "Sounds *exactly* like what I want."

Shit. "For here or to go?"

"For here, for now, I think." Each word was enunciated with humor.

That meant ceramic—and no name. "I'll get that started for you." Brian turned away and stared at the espresso machine. He didn't flirt with men. Except he just had. Hard. Every bit of his skin tingled.

Good thing making coffee was pretty much muscle memory by now, because his mind was spinning like a fucking bean grinder. What was he doing?

Making a drink for a British redhead with one hell of an

amused voice. He pulled out the Mexican chili chocolate and crafted the man's drink with hands that were mostly steady. Brian caught glimpses of Sunglasses while he worked—and each time, the man met Brian's gaze.

Oh yes, he was being watched. Heat rose from his toes to the top of his whirling head. He finished the drink, added a dollop of whipped cream and a dusting of cinnamon, and set it down on the counter.

"That looks lovely." Deep, appreciative voice with all those round vowels. Brian could get hard from listening to this man.

Hell, he already was.

Brian shifted to the register and rang him up. Cash—which meant he still didn't know the dude's name. "New in the area?"

"No—and yes. I've been in Pittsburgh on and off for about two years. Things have finally calmed down enough for me to explore a bit." He picked up the drink but didn't go far—taking a seat at the bar top next to the register rather than at one of the tables.

"On and off?" Brian didn't need another espresso. Started making one anyway.

Sunglasses took a sip of his mocha, leaving behind a smear of whipped cream on his mouth, which he licked off with a slow swipe of his tongue. "This is quite spectacular." Those eyes met Brian's again. There was a dusting of light freckles over his nose and cheeks.

Brian couldn't move. Could barely breathe. "Glad you like it."

Another swipe of tongue over those lips. "The company I work for moved its headquarters here from Chicago. I spent quite some time going back and forth while we were co-located. But we're here now—and so am I."

The end of that sounded far too much like an invitation.

Maybe he did need the espresso after all. He took the cup and, despite tempting a flood of customers, pulled a stool over and sat. "Welcome to the neighborhood."

More whipped cream on that mouth, and a smile. "Thanks." A dart of tongue. "I'm Rob, by the way."

Rob. *Rob Rob Rob Rob.* The name rang in Brian's mind like a bell. "Brian." He held out his hand. "Nice to meet you."

"Likewise." Rob's grip was firm and warm, and Brian was glad he was sitting, because touching the man was a bit like sticking his finger into a socket. The handclasp lasted a little too long before they both pulled back.

What was he *doing*? Every nerve sang.

"And you?" The whipped cream had melted into the mocha, but foam from the milk still touched Rob's lips. This time, Rob didn't lick it off.

It was distracting as fuck. "What?"

"Are you from around here?" An almost knowing smile formed on his frothy lips before he took another sip.

"Yeah. Born and raised." He drank some of his espresso —it hadn't gone tepid, but it was bitter as hell. "Well, not *this* neighborhood, but in Pittsburgh."

"I've noticed all the little neighborhoods. The bigger ones, too. North Hills. South Hills." He waved a hand at the windows. "There's places to explore everywhere." He looked down into his coffee. "Gems to discover." His eyes flicked up and met Brian's.

That— Yeah, this was *definitely* flirting and Rob was interested. Only... Brian didn't date men. Didn't do *anything* with men but admire them from afar.

For all intents and purposes, he was straight. Even if he wasn't.

Rob tipped his head and raised an eyebrow. There was a hint of silver at Rob's temples, which likely placed him close to the same age as Brian. He had gray too, but it blended in with the blond.

"I—" He was completely at a loss for words and his hands were shaking. He pulled something out of his brain. "What have you seen of Pittsburgh so far?"

"Not as much as I'd like." He eyed Brian and sat back. "Well—very little, truthfully. Point State Park. Downtown. Some of the execs took me on one of those Ducky tours last summer. Went to a Pirates game."

"Tourist stuff."

He nodded. "And now I must fend for myself."

So, single. "How'd you end up in Squirrel Hill?" Did he live here?

A laugh and that fascinating smile. "A coworker recommended some restaurants to me—and this shop. His husband works in the company above."

Only one person that could be. "Todd Douglas."

Rob sat up straighter. "Yes." He sounded surprised.

Brian chuckled and finished his espresso. "Fazil Kurt's husband."

Rob glanced at the ceiling. "Do you know everyone up there?"

"Well, it's a small office and I'm their coffeepot, so yeah." He pushed his cup to the side. "Plus, Sam Anderson's assistant, Justin, was my best barista until Sam hired him away." He missed Justin's competency and work ethic. The shop had run smoothly then. Unlike now.

"This is *your* shop? You own it?" Rob leaned in, his face bright. "That's fantastic!"

"Most days." This one had started out as shit, but with Rob sitting in front of him, he couldn't say that now. "So you must work at that robotics place down in Bakery Square."

"CirroBot," Rob said. "Yes." His cheerful demeanor vanished into thoughtfulness.

That was odd. "Don't like it there?"

There was something raw and unguarded about Rob's reply. "No, I *love* it there." The smile returned, but a bit more restrained. "Problem is, I'm somewhat of a workaholic if left to my own devices. Hence—" He gestured at the shop.

That Brian understood. "Get out of the house, see the sights, and not work yourself to an early grave?"

"Exactly." The grin dropped away. "You as well?"

The bell on the door rang and Brian slipped off the stool. "This place *is* my life. Just ask my ex-girlfriends."

Rob's brows knitted, but Brian couldn't say anything more—not with three customers bearing down on him and another two ringing the bell on the door a second time. "Gotta go."

"Of course," Rob said. He didn't move, just sipped his coffee and watched Brian as he waited on the flood of customers.

Oh, the confusion when he'd mentioned girlfriends. He didn't know how to explain himself to Rob. Then again, he didn't know how to explain himself to *himself*, so that was nothing new.

He was thirty-eight years old and *tired.* He'd known since high school that he was bisexual—except guys weren't bi. They were either gay or straight. If they *were* bi, then they were just on their way to being gay. Or liars.

He whipped up a triple caramel macchiato with two pumps of chocolate and winced—more at himself than the drink.

He was *thirty-eight*. Why did he still give a fuck what other people believed?

Two cappuccinos followed, then an iced latte.

Rob finished his drink, but he remained at the counter, idly running a finger around the lip of his cup.

During a small breather between customers, Brian leaned over. "Would you like another?"

"Yes." Crisp and clear, and the force of that word made Brian shiver. "But finish up with your customers, and then we'll talk."

Brian nodded and got back to work.

SADLY, ROB ANCROFT COULDN'T LEAN BACK IN HIS chair, cross his arms, and just *watch* Brian, the barista and shop owner, since the barstool he was sitting on that made such displays impossible. Probably a good thing, in hindsight. He'd likely teeter over onto the floor.

What a curious and handsome man Brian was! Full of wit, innuendo, and charm. No doubt Brian knew exactly what he was doing, the flirty thing that he was. Not a naive young man—he wanted Rob. That had been apparent from his *cream* comments.

And yet, ex-*girlfriends*.

But no negative quips about Todd or his husband. Or Sam Anderson's little queer consulting firm above his head.

Bi? Pan? Not that it mattered. Rob hadn't come here to pick up a date—just a cup of coffee. He examined Brian's back. Powerful shoulders, *very* nice arms, and a trim waist. Went well with his lovely long face, sandy hair, and pretty brown eyes.

Brian was very much like the coffee he'd drank. Bold

and spicy. And yes, a taste of that cream, too, please. He hadn't had a date, let alone a roll in bed in... far too long. CirroBot had eaten his relationships along with his life for the last few years.

But now they were in Pittsburgh, and the company was settled. He'd handed over much of the responsibility—and part of the ownership—to a board of directors.

He certainly *could* have more than one cup of coffee, especially since what he wanted was a taste of that nice tall Americano.

Even if Brian proved elusive as a bedmate, the man was witty and easy on the eyes. He also knew this city, which Rob decidedly did *not*. Recommendations on new and interesting non-tourist attractions would be most welcome.

Perhaps they could help each other with the whole workaholic problem.

Rob shifted on the barstool and watched Brian work his business. He smiled at each of his customers. Conversed as he made their drinks. Most topics were inoffensive—weather, sports—but Brian also knew several of the people in line, and well, too. His manner changed subtly, then. His grin became open and light played in his eyes. He had a delightful exchange of witticisms with a bearded gentleman, a more serious discussion with a younger woman about her college classes, and an animated chat with a mother and her little boy.

Rob turned in his seat and examined the shop and patrons more closely. In a way, it reminded him of a pub but without the beer and sports. Lots of locals. Younger people working on school assignments. Couples having chats. An older gentleman reading a newspaper.

The mother and son sat down nearby and the child proceeded to devour a cookie while reading a library book.

He was very good not to get crumbs on the pages.

"Still interested?"

Rob turned back to the luscious man that was Brian. "Very."

"In another drink?" Breathless voice, and a hint of nerves pinched Brian's eyes.

"That, too." Rob slid the cup back over.

Brian took it and swallowed, his Adam's apple bobbing. "Coming right up."

That, too.

Brian was efficient, but also careful and precise. That showed pride in what he made, be it a simple coffee or something complicated. Oh yes, the man was the owner. Rob saw that now. Couldn't be anything else.

In short order, Brian deposited another cup in front of Rob. Fresh ceramic.

"Cheers," Rob said and took a long draw. Great espresso, a hint of pepper and the sweetness of the cream.

Brian was staring at him, his lips parted, his cheeks flushed. *That* was the look of a man who needed more than a nice *conversation*. Unfortunately, the same expression was coupled with another that looked like fear. Closeted? Hard to believe, given the people he knew.

So, press on.

Rob eyed Brian. "You said you weren't from this neighborhood. Which one, then?"

Brian sank onto the stool behind the counter. "I grew up in Bloomfield."

Rob nearly choked on his next sip. "I live in Bloomfield."

A white flash of teeth. "Close to work."

He nodded. "I bike in, believe it or not." In a suit, even.

Because why not? Though his fellow execs warned him that would end once the summer heat kicked in.

"Nice!" Brian straightened. "Do you like to bike? There's a ton of trails in the area, now."

"So I've heard." Another taste of the coffee. He dabbed his finger at some cream that had dripped over the edge, sucked it off, and watched Brian squirm. Fucking *delightful*, that. "I'd love to check some of them out."

"I can..." Brian hesitated. "Well, if the scheduling works... I could show you some."

"I think I'd like that."

"And more." Brian reddened. "I mean, of Pittsburgh sites."

"I'd like that, too." *And more.* He reached into his back pocket and pulled out his phone. "Number?"

Brian started, looked around, and then rattled off a phone number.

Gotcha. Rob typed it in and hit send. Once again, Brian jumped. He whipped out his phone.

"Now you have my number, as well."

"That a Chicago area code?"

Astute. "It is. Didn't make sense to change it, not for my personal number."

The damnable bell on the door rang, and Brian was off his seat and moving to the counter. But that *was* the nature of his business. After creating some drinks and some pleasant small talk with his customers, Brian came back to Rob.

"I'm sorry I'm not the best conversationalist."

Rob waved the words away. "You're working. I'm the one imposing by sitting here and distracting you."

There was a small pause and then quiet words. "I don't mind."

Rob studied Brian. A little red on that neck. A little heat in those cheeks. "Good."

Poor man looked so conflicted. If only Rob could deduce *why*. The attraction was *obvious*. Probably to everyone else in the shop, too.

Brian collected the forlorn espresso cup. "I should go do some dishes before they pile up."

"Don't let me keep you."

Brian snorted, strode to the sink, deposited the cup, and strode right back. "Not like the boss will yell at me." He took a seat.

Nice. Oh so nice. "It's good to be the king."

He laughed. "Something like that." An all-American flash of teeth in his grin. "So you like biking. What else do you do with your free time?"

"Well, back when I had free time, I liked to hike. I'm also handy with a camera."

"Photographing the outdoors?"

"Yes—but not just the countryside. I like this—" He waved at the shop. "Cities. Urban areas. Industry." In fact, he should have brought his camera today. Rob craned his neck around. There were some interesting shots he could have taken in here. Brick and wood. Brian's machinery.

He'd been itching to get back into photography. And hiking. And men.

When he looked back, Brian met his gaze. "Squirrel Hill's an interesting place to explore with a camera," Brian said. "There's both old and new. Different cultures. A mix of everything."

He'd noticed. Synagogues. Men in hats and suits with tassels from their shawls hanging below the bottoms. But also college kids. In the short walk from the top of Murray Avenue to Grounds N'at, he'd heard Russian and Chinese.

Passed a Thai restaurant. A multitude of colors, sites, and sounds.

"Todd mentioned a few places I should try for lunch." From pulling out his phone earlier, Rob knew it was nearly noon.

Brian glanced at his watch. "Which places?"

He brought up the notepad app on his phone and slid it across the counter.

Brian pursed his lips. "Well, they're all good. What are you in the mood for?"

A tall, sandy-haired American. He didn't say that though. "I'm remarkably easy to please."

Deep brown eyes. They lingered on Rob for quite some time. "Well, I already know you like bold and spicy."

"And cream."

Brian inhaled. "Thai, then. Bangkok Balcony." He slid the phone back over. "Or Silk Elephant."

"What's the difference?"

"Do you like to nibble, or have a full meal?"

Brian just kept *handing* Rob opportunities on a fucking platter. "I'm fond of nibbling, but I certainly wouldn't object to being full." He smiled across the counter.

As if Brian only now realized what he'd said, he sat bolt upright, cheeks flaming red. "Silk Elephant," he stammered. "For nibbles."

Time to probe a bit deeper. "And what about you?"

Brian shivered. Oh yes, he'd gotten to the man. "I'm—full of steam. Just hot water."

He didn't quite know how to take that. About ready to blow his top? Hot—but no substance?

Brian looked down at the counter. "And I'm working all day."

"How long is that?"

"Eight to eight."

The businessman in him took over. "That's a hellish shift!"

"Yeah." Brian snorted. "My boss is an asshole."

Brian *was* the boss. If there wasn't anyone else, you did what you had to. Rob had lived that, in the early days of CirroBot. "I hope you don't do this often."

A pained smile. "I try not to, but if someone calls off..." He shrugged.

Brian needed a backup, then. Someone else to spell him for emergencies. A manager or... something. Rob's brain whirled through options. Except he didn't know shit about this industry. "Don't burn yourself out."

That got him a chuckle. "Burning coffee beans is bad. Slow roasting is the way to go."

Both lead to toasty things, though. That, in a person, wasn't good. This man? He definitely needed someone to drag him off the job once in a while.

Brian tapped the counter near Rob's phone. "You should try to get in to Silk Elephant soon, or you'll have to wait until after the rush."

Rob picked up his phone and slid off the stool. "Then I'll head out."

"Nice meeting you, Rob." Soft words.

"Likewise." He placed a hand on the counter and leaned in. "And I'll be back for more."

He held Brian's gaze, indulging in that flushed and nervous look once more before he headed for the door.

Outside, he slipped his sunglasses back on. Oh yes, that was one drink he wanted to sample again.

CHAPTER TWO

After Rob left the shop, the rest of Brian's day was like one long exhale. His skin tingled and he couldn't get his pulse back down to something normal. Pretty sure *that* wasn't from the cups of espresso.

Worse, every time the bell on the door rang, he hoped it was Rob coming back in. It wasn't. Didn't stop his body from tensing with anticipation, nor the cold wash of disappointment he shoved aside so he could serve his customers with a smile.

Been a long time since he'd been turned that inside out by anyone, let alone a man. Rob pushed all Brian's buttons at once. Red hair. Freckles. British accent, coupled by a sly charm, intelligence, and common interests. If he'd been a woman, he'd have gotten his number.

Except he *had* Rob's number. Holy shit.

Brian leaned against the back counter, ran a hand through his hair, and checked his phone. Yup. There it was, Chicago area code and all.

Only *he* hadn't gotten Rob's number. No, Rob had

asked for Brian's and given his own in return. A clever move —one Brian had used in the past.

He was being picked up.

A warmth spread out from his belly. Well, that was different. And strange. But it also felt entirely normal and natural.

Maybe that's because it was.

Something fluttered in his chest, and if he didn't know better, he might have labeled it *hope*.

Brian pushed off the counter, collected all the used dishes and utensils, and headed to the sinks. While cleaning up, he tried not to think too much about doors and bells and ginger anything.

Halfway through the following week, Brian stopped looking for Rob when the bell on the door sounded. He'd gotten no texts or calls, either. Was he supposed to make the first move? Had the encounter actually happened? Other than the number in his phone and some stunning daydreams of Rob's lips moving on his—he didn't have much to prove Rob existed.

He didn't even know his last name. Rob might as well have been a dream.

Today, Miranda was working the shift with him, for which Brian was grateful. He'd ended up firing Ethan this past Sunday. Not a conversation he'd enjoyed.

Ethan had been mildly upset, but not regretful. He'd thought Brian unfair. "It's just coffee, dude."

"It's my *business*, Ethan."

He'd rather be short another barista and work long shifts that he knew about in advance than stagger into his own shop without sleep. Of course that was happening anyway. Too many shifts, not enough downtime.

The morning rush thinned, so he turned to Miranda. "Mind running solo for a while? I need to catch up on the paperwork."

She shook her head. "Hell, if you want to get out of here, you can. I'll be fine."

She would be, too. One of his best employees. If only she could work more regular hours, but taking care of her grandmother had become her full-time job. Family always came first—he'd told her that months ago. She came in when she could for the extra bit of money and Brian rejoiced each time she asked to be scheduled.

"Nah, I'll stick around a bit." He slipped in back and grabbed a stack of mail he'd been meaning to sort through and his laptop. "Duty calls."

She chuckled and he settled in at one of the tables near the coffee grinder. It was a spot the fewest people took, due to the noise. He'd rather leave the prime real estate for paying customers, but if he sat behind the counter, he'd itch to serve people drinks.

Most of the mail was junk. He ripped the envelopes in half and tossed them in a pile to recycle. The rest were bills and catalogues. The latter he set aside for last—after he knew how much was left from paying his suppliers. Maybe he could afford something a little extra this month.

He opened up his laptop and got to work.

Deep into it, he completely missed the tinkle of the doorbell. It was familiar voices—one deep, the other smooth and sweet—that jolted him from his work.

Justin and Eli, come down from on high. Eli's cane tapped against the hardwood floor and Brian glanced at his watch. The morning had flown by in the midst of seeing his profits shrink. Nearly eleven thirty. "Time for the office coffee run already?"

Justin smirked the way he used to when he'd been a brash barista behind the counter. "*Someone* is like clockwork." He gave Eli a pointed look.

Eli's smile was not the thin thing it once had been. His grin was large and full of teeth. "*Someone* needs his caffeine fix." He pulled out a slip of paper. "Several someones, actually."

Pretty normal for Sam's cohort. If one person came down to get a drink, chances were they came with an order for more. And judging by Eli's presence—the whole office must have ordered. They'd need more than Justin's hands to carry all the cups.

They headed to the counter and placed the orders with Miranda. Yup. Seven. Brian closed his laptop and rose.

She waved him away. "I can handle it."

"Oh, I know. But I *like* these guys." Sam's team had been supporting him since they'd moved in above. They could have bought their own coffee service—there were enough corporate ones running around Pittsburgh—but Sam had very specifically not done so.

I like supporting local business, and you can't get more local than this!

Sam also bought a good deal of the coffee for his workers either on his own or the company card, so he wasn't shocked when Eli handed that over to pay.

"How's business?" Justin bounced on the balls of his feet and peered behind the counter.

"Good."

Miranda rolled her eyes and bumped his shoulder. Justin raised both eyebrows at that.

"Well, it could be better. I had to fire Ethan."

"The lazy kid with the diamond earrings?" Eli perched himself on a stool and rested his hands on his cane.

Yeah, that pretty much described Ethan. "That's the one, though I'm sure they weren't real diamonds."

"Oh, they were," Eli said. "Figured he wouldn't last long because of it."

Brian thought back to Ethan, then shook his head. "So, maybe he has some money. Didn't mean he wouldn't work."

A huff of laughter. "I know that. But it struck me that this was a hobby to him—not a job."

"It's not a job for most people." Brian's good mood shattered when the reality of Eli's words stabbed in. He finished Sam's cappuccino and set it in the drink carrier. Thinner margins every day. "No one takes it seriously."

"I did," Justin said and there was a touch of longing in his voice. "It was a job for *me*."

"You're about the only one." Two pumps of peppermint syrup for Fazil. "You know, I really—" He stopped himself.

Justin looked down and Eli rolled his eyes. "It's fine," he said. "Sam knows. I know. We did steal him away rather handily."

Especially Eli, who had up and married Justin.

And damn, hadn't Justin been a catch? Not that Brian would ever have made a move on an employee.

Unlike Eli.

But the whole affair had worked out in the end. They were all in a better place. Eli, Justin, and Sam.

Everyone but Brian. He missed Justin as an employee, and not just for his snark and spiked hair, but for his work ethic and reliability. "I wish I could find another you."

Miranda placed the last of the drinks in the two carriers and Justin picked one up. "You can," he said. "You will."

Eli grabbed the other and Brian said his good-byes. Justin opened the door for Eli, and they were gone.

"Shit." Brian scrubbed his hands on his jeans.

Miranda snorted, but it wasn't a happy noise. Nor was her stare when he met her gaze. "None of us are ever going to stack up to him, are we?"

Embarrassment ripped through Brian. "I didn't mean—"

"Of course you didn't. Not with me *just standing here.*" She kept her voice soft, but there was heat there.

His stomach dropped. *Way to go, Bri.* "You're the best barista I have."

"And yet..." She stabbed a hand at the door Eli and Justin had vanished through.

"I—" He hadn't been thinking. At all. "I'm sorry, Mir. I just—the Ethan thing has me rattled."

Her shoulders dropped.

"I'd make you a manager if—" That was a sore point too, with all the baristas—no one worked quite the hours he needed for that. "Anyway, I apologize. That was a shitty thing for me to do."

"Yeah, it was." She grabbed a towel and set to wiping down the milk steamer. "You doing okay? I mean, aside from the Ethan thing? You seem... out of sorts."

"Lots of hours," he said. "That's all." No need to mention the drop in profits.

"Well, don't kill yourself. We need you, too."

"I know. It'll right itself when I hire some new folks."

Except he'd been saying that for how many months? Ethan was supposed to have helped fix the issue. And now? Brian washed his hands and headed back to his laptop.

He kept his own salary at the median of everyone else's, mostly so he could see what a full payroll would run him. Made figuring out the money easier.

There was less each month. He'd been ignoring that fact because he threw his own overtime back into the pot.

The extra hours were wearing on him. Hiring more baristas, which he needed to do, would cut things tight if he kept or raised their pay.

He plopped down in front of the laptop, opened it, and sliced open another bill. He winced at the number. He'd figure it out. No one said any of this would be easy, even after years of running the shop.

CHAPTER THREE

Another fine Saturday. Rob locked his bike up and headed down the street to Grounds N'at. The past week, the weather had been a mix of rain, wind, and chill, but the skies had finally cleared and spring warmth had returned. Perfect day for a bike ride.

He needed the exercise after the week he'd had in the office. Juggling customers, prospective customers, and releases during the same week never mixed well. Sales wanted one thing—or, rather, everything—and engineering knew they could deliver only a fraction. You had to be on your best behavior, meanwhile everyone was stressed trying to get the product out on time.

Made for some tense meetings at times.

But it was Saturday and all of that was hours behind him. He'd biked off all his stress climbing to Squirrel Hill from his house in Bloomfield. The "hill" part of the name was very *very* apt.

Right now, he wanted a cup of coffee, a glass of water, and another shot at flirting with Brian. Hopefully that lovely man was working today. He ought to have texted, but he enjoyed the element of surprise.

He pushed open the door, stripped off his sunglasses, and Brian was there, thank goodness. He wasn't behind the counter though, but sitting at one of the tables, opposite a nervous-looking young man who had a balled-up napkin in front of him.

Brian's arms were crossed and his expression was shuttered—though it opened a fraction when he met Rob's gaze.

Brian raised his eyebrows, then focused on the young man.

A strange flare of heat rose in Rob's chest before the situation made sense. He *knew* that look, in both the young man and in Brian. This was an *interview*. Despite the surroundings, grilling a candidate was a universal thing.

Rather than bother Brian any more than he had by walking in the door, Rob strode to the counter and ordered a latte from the barista—a black man with tribal tattoos around his arms. He found a table about as far from Brian as he could get, but from where he could watch Brian's back—and waited for him to finish.

A tiny regret for not texting, but he'd wanted to see what Brian did with his number. Couldn't quite put his finger on the cause of the hesitations embedded in Brian's flirtations. It was curious.

He liked a challenge, though.

Even though Rob couldn't see Brian's face, he knew from his tension and the posture that this particular candidate wasn't impressing him. Rob studied the kid—couldn't be much older than nineteen—and wondered what Brian saw that Rob didn't.

Sure, he was young, but this was a coffee shop. Didn't young people thrive in jobs like this? A supplemental income for college? Goodness knows, he'd done some odd jobs while at university. Working in a coffee shop would've been a blessing.

After ten minutes or so, Brian rose and shook the kid's hand in a friendly way. The kid nodded, said something in response, then took off through the front door, the bell ringing in his wake.

Brian deflated once the kid was out of sight. For a few moments, he stared out the window, his hands on his hips, t-shirt stretching over those shoulders and across his trim back. The pose framed his arse beautifully.

So very nice. Rob shifted in his seat.

Brian swung around, scanning the shop until he found Rob. The smile that lit up Brian's face was warm and inviting and tightened Rob's chest, along with his dick.

Seemed he'd made an impression after all.

Determined strides brought Brian to Rob's table. "You came back."

"I said I would." Rob waved a hand at the other seat. "If you're not busy."

He pulled it out and sat. "I am, but I can take a breather."

For him. The words weren't there, but they hung in the air. Rob smiled across his latte. "You were right about Silk Elephant. Plenty to nibble." He took a sip.

That earned him a blush from Brian. "Were you satisfied?"

"Mostly." The coffee was warm and smooth in Rob's mouth. No whipped cream to play with, though. "I would've enjoyed company."

A calculating look from Brian. "There are other days to the week besides Saturday, you know."

"True. But I'm a workaholic, as well." He put the cup down. "Were you free any of them, anyway?"

That wince spoke volumes.

"I'm guessing you're interviewing to fix that?" Rob took another swallow of coffee.

Brian ran a hand through his hair and leaned back in his chair. "Trying to, anyway."

"That kid not the right person?"

"That kid is a kid."

"So?" Kids. Coffee shop. Rob didn't see the issue at all.

"I need someone for weekends and mornings. Most college students have classes during the hours I'd want them here during the week—and they want their weekends free."

That made sense. Of course there would be scheduling conflicts in a business like this. "So why interview him?"

"Because they often *say* they can work those hours in e-mail—then let me know they can't during the interview." He huffed a laugh. "I need an older grad student or someone who wants a part-time job. But grad students have a tendency to be busy and..." He shook his head. "It's been rough, finding the right people."

"You have some good staff already." He gestured at the barista behind the counter.

Brian gave the man a nod. "Mark's great, but he usually can't work weekends. He's doing me a favor so I could interview. I should take over so he can go home to his kids."

Mark watched them from the counter, and his smile was interesting. So was the way his gaze flicked between the two of them.

Someone had put one and one together.

"He makes a mean latte," Rob said, letting his gaze linger on Mark, before focusing on Brian.

Brian eyed him, a nervousness pouring tension back into his frame. "Better than my spicy mocha?"

"No." A simple answer.

Brian took a breath. "Your latte's almost gone."

Rob deliberately drank the rest before setting the cup down. "I guess I'll have to order something from you, won't I?"

Brian swallowed, and rose. "I guess you will."

He stood and they both headed to the counter. Rob stuck his cup in the dirty dish bin. Brian ducked behind and conversed while Mark untied his apron. A hit of red touched Brian's cheeks when Mark chuckled and said something Rob couldn't catch in a low, deep voice.

On the way out from behind the counter, Mark clapped Rob on the shoulder once—then he headed for the door.

Brian eyed Mark's back—then stared at Rob when the bell rang. "He knows."

"Knows what?" Rob took a seat and laced his fingers in front of him on the counter.

Brian didn't answer that, though his eyebrows rose into his sandy hair. He rotated to the sink and washed his hands. "So, what are you in the mood for today?"

"Whatever you want to give me."

Brian damn near jumped out of his skin. "What are you... why are you... what is this?"

Ah, so he was conflicted. "You tell me."

Narrowed eyes.

Time to dig. "What do you think it is that Mark knows?"

Brian shook his head and headed for the coffee grinder. The next several minutes, Rob watched Brian craft some kind of drink, his movements sharp and precise. Chocolate—dark, from the looks of it—and some kind of syrup.

Cinnamon. Other spices. Frothed milk. Whipped cream with little chocolate shavings on top.

Brian slid it in front of Rob, his face a mask.

It was almost too pretty to drink and he had no idea what to expect. Only one way to find out.

When the coffee hit his tongue Rob closed his eyes. A mocha—a very dark, bitter one with a hint of spice and orange. Exquisite. Tantalizing. He licked the cream off his lips and opened his eyes.

An extraordinarily satisfied look greeted him.

Rob put down the mug. "What is this?"

"You tell me." Brian lowered himself to his stool.

Well, he deserved that. "This," he said, "is two men seeing how the other reacts."

Brian swallowed a chuckle. "That's what I thought."

Maybe he'd misjudged Brian's intentions. "Does it bother you?"

That question seemed to catch Brian off guard. "No, I just—" The fucking bell on the door rang and Brian started. "Hang on."

One customer seemed to bring a flood of more and kept Brian moving around behind the counter. How he managed to keep everyone's orders straight, especially the more complex ones, Rob didn't know. Brian didn't write anything down, and yet he managed to turn out beautiful drinks either in ceramic or paper cups.

When he finally served the last of the customers, he came back and plopped down. "Look, I'm not used to this." He gestured between the two of them. "I don't know what to expect—or what's expected."

Brian's hands shook a bit, which was intriguing. Worried? Turned on? Hard for Rob to tell. "Right now? Coffee. Chatting. I'd like to pick your brain about this city."

He sipped the dark chocolate–orange creation. "I also wouldn't mind your company, but that's entirely up to you."

Brian was exactly the kind of man Rob wanted as a friend. More would be exquisite, but he knew better than to expect it.

He'd been wrong about men and their desires before.

The tension in Brian melted. "Okay." He drummed his fingers on the counter. "My schedule sucks, though. It's—well. There are a lot of shifts I'm covering at the moment."

"Hence the interview."

Brian nodded, his focus on the door.

Rob rolled the coffee in his cup to gather the bits of froth clinging to the sides. "You know, I have some background in business. Maybe I can help you?" He had no idea how. "At least be a sounding board?"

Brian stared at him. "I thought you were an engineer?"

Yes, and no. Guilt pricked at his pride. "I am, but I've been involved in a few startups. You learn the business side of things."

A thin smile graced those lush lips. "Pretty sure running a coffee shop isn't anything like a high-tech whatever."

No, but business was business. He gave a light shrug. "An offer, nothing more."

"Thanks." There was honest warmth in that. "I've been through this before, though."

"What, the flirting or the business issues?"

Brian's laugh and his ruddy cheeks were things of joy. He rocked on the stool, his whole body shaking. "The business issues."

Not the flirting. "How'd you fix it last time?"

"I hired a non-traditional MBA student named Justin White."

Right. Sam Anderson's assistant. Married to the CFO of

the company. Todd had mentioned the name a few times. "He created a hole you can't fill."

Brian's smile slipped away. "Something like that."

There was so much more Rob wanted to ask about the business. His brain itched to solve this problem, find the perfect solution, and make the company work—but Brian was right. This wasn't like CirroBot or any of the other tech firms he'd help start.

Brian was tensing again, too. Time to change the subject. "So, if you had Easter Sunday free and the option of going kayaking on the rivers downtown or hiking out at Settler's Cabin, which would you do?"

That was all Rob needed to say to make the stress vanish from Brian. "Your camera waterproof?"

Good god, no. "I don't *need* to take photographs."

Brian rested his forearms on the counter. "But you *want* to."

They were close. He only needed to lean in to shorten the distance between them to mere inches. He did just that and murmured, "There are *many* things I want."

Brian parted his lips, shock reddening his skin, but he didn't move back. "Kayaking's better with a friend."

"So's hiking." And more private, because the things he wanted to do to Brian's lips would be very difficult in a kayak.

A quirk at the corner of Brian's mouth. "But I have to work tomorrow."

Both disappointment and elation twined through Rob and goosebumps rose on his skin. Brian *wanted* to go with him. "You work on Easter?"

Brian laughed. "People want their coffee fix. Especially those who gave it up for Lent."

That made sense, from a business perspective. Still, it stung. "So, you're saying I should go hiking."

Brian nodded. "Then come back and show me what you shot."

Definite interest. "Then that's what I'll do." He opened a bit of space. "Assuming you'll tell me your schedule."

"I will." Brian pushed off the counter and straightened. "That's one of the bits of paperwork I need to do today."

"Don't let me keep you from your work." Though what he wanted was Brian *away* from the shop and in his bed. Or Brian's. Didn't matter.

"You're not." Brian tugged his shirt down, stretching the material over his shoulders and pecs. "Mind me working next to you?"

Never. Not in a million years. He shook his head. Brian vanished into the back of the shop, and reappeared with a laptop and paperwork.

"You never did tell me what you call this drink." Rob tapped the saucer.

"Doesn't have a name. I made it just for you." Brian's grin and the sound of the shop door's bell zipped through Rob, making him shiver.

Brian was a fucking *delight.* He might not know how this would end, but he was going to have so much fun finding out.

More than half of Easter Sunday passed before Brian finally got all of the next week's schedule worked out. Lots of customers clamoring for coffee, plus firing Ethan had certainly thrown a wrench into everything—he was covering more than he wanted to. Again, but at least he could text Rob to let him know when he was free.

After making drinks, he leaned against the counter and pondered the screen of his phone. A tightness in his chest and an ache in his balls. Time to admit that he had one *hell* of a crush on Rob.

Was he even allowed to have crushes at thirty-eight? Staring at Rob's number on his phone, he felt fifteen again and calling the first girl he ever asked out on a date.

Why *now*? He'd ignored his desire for men for so long. Not flirting, not dating, not *anything*. He had no time for a relationship—yet here he was, in the first steps of that dance.

Anita, his last girlfriend, would be laughing so hard right now if she knew. Not at him dating a guy—but contemplating dating at all.

I care about you, Bri. You're a great guy. You're also fucking married to that shop of yours.

True. Above anything else, he had a responsibility to his employees and the shop. He shouldn't be flirting with *anyone*. Or making plans to meet up.

But Rob did things to his head that no one else—man or woman—ever had. It wasn't entirely lust, either—though certainly that was there.

Someone he could banter with. Someone he could talk to.

The screen went dark, a fine indication that he was overthinking. He unlocked the phone and typed in a text.

> Hey, I'm working every night except Friday, if you want to stop by with your photos.

He jabbed send before he got cold feet. There. He'd

figure out what he was doing later, probably after he'd done it. *Or Rob.*

That thought went straight to his dick and balls. Yeah, he wanted those fingers touching him, that mouth on his, and to find out where *else* Rob had freckles.

Good thing the shop bell rang, because if he thought about Rob much longer, he'd not be safe for work.

After he shoved the phone in his pocket, he greeted the customer—one of his regulars who came in to grade papers—poured her a simple cup of coffee, and settled in to wait for a reply from Rob.

If Rob had taken his advice about hiking, he might not have a great cell signal. Really depended on where in Settler's Cabin he was.

Nearly two hours later, his phone buzzed. He jumped in the process of trying out some coffee art on a cappuccino, but somehow, his leaf didn't look that sad. He slid the drink over to one of his more recent regulars—a freshman at Pitt—and she beamed at him.

"How do you learn to do that?"

"Would you believe, videos on the web?"

"Aren't you too old for the Internet?" She took the drink and gave him an innocent smile he didn't believe for one second.

"Hey, have respect for your elders!"

She laughed and went to claim a seat by the front window. Homework, probably. Or reading.

Brian dug his phone out. Yes, a text from Rob. He couldn't help grinning.

Can stop by any night. But does no work on Friday night mean you're free?

It did. He hadn't wanted to be presumptuous. Trust Rob to notice. He seemed to notice *everything*. Yeah, I've no plans for Friday night.

The reply came back almost immediately. Now you do.

He bit his lip and his jeans were back to feeling too snug. Shift ends at 6.

I'll be there, photos in hand.

Can't wait.

Waiting makes it better. ;)

Brian stared at the text. Did you just wink at me?

Me? Never.

You did just wink at me.

You're imagining things. Don't you have drinks to make?

The bell on the door clanked. Actually, I do. I gotta go.

See? ;)

Brian laughed and slid the phone into his pocket. Halfway through making the second drink for the couple that walked in, he realized he was smiling. Broadly. Enough that his cheeks hurt. And humming.

It wasn't a crush—it was downright *infatuation*. Yeah, he was too old for that, but he didn't give a fuck anymore.

He couldn't *wait* for Friday.

CHAPTER FOUR

THROUGHOUT THE DAY ON FRIDAY, ROB COULDN'T STOP checking his watch. Didn't help that he'd been stuck in meetings starting at eight in the morning. They ran pretty much straight through until four in the afternoon.

Thank goodness he'd asked Mallory, his assistant, to block out the time after that, or he was positive someone with a masochistic streak would've sent him a meeting request.

At least the morning meetings had been conference calls. He took them in his office and half listened while flipping through the photos he'd taken during his hike. That kept him from contemplating all the things he wanted to do to Brian that were entirely inappropriate for a first date.

Brian didn't seem the type to fuck ten minutes after meeting—or they would have. He still didn't have a sense of what Brian wanted or expected. A hookup? A relationship? Friends with benefits?

The sexual attraction was there, certainly.

Do you really want to date a workaholic like you? He

was better now, but the scars of overworking were still there. The regrets. The pain. Then again, dating would be better than living like a hermit, and it looked like *someone* needed to pull Brian out of that shop once in a while.

Might as well be him.

After he grabbed a quick lunch, the afternoon meetings with staff kept him engaged so his mind didn't wander far—just enough to worry that the day would never end.

But it did and as soon as the clock ticked over to five, Rob was out the door. He'd stripped off his suit jacket and tie, folded those into his backpack, and grabbed his bike. Didn't take too long to ride to his house, a rambling old Victorian he'd bought for a steal. The house had needed renovations back then, but it was sound and had great bones. A quick shower and a change into jeans and a t-shirt had him looking like a normal human being and not a CEO.

He chose to drive rather than bike—better not to arrive a sweaty mess, and he had no idea how late they'd be out. He was a touch early, but he didn't think Brian would mind.

Given the fucking huge grin that nearly split Brian's face in two—no, he didn't. At all. And there was part of the answer Rob sought.

This was more to Brian than a fling or a hookup.

That both relaxed him and warmed his heart. At this point in his life, he wanted more. Would have settled for less, but he'd had enough of casual hookups and random sex. He took his seat at the counter and laid his iPad down.

"Hey," Brian said. "Be with you in a few." He was steaming milk and there was a line of customers at the counter.

"Of course." Customers always came first—especially in a service business.

Brian worked as smoothly as normal, gliding through each drink and somehow managing to keep the orders in his head. It was more than Rob could manage—he had to write everything down. Desk littered with sticky notes.

Watching Brian work was a joy. There was something sensual in the way Brian held his hands, his body, and how he focused on each task. Brian clearly *loved* his work—that came out in every beautiful movement.

Rob couldn't help but wonder if that passion, attention, and focus extended to the bedroom. To be under those hands and eyes—he wanted that, desperately.

He ran a hand over his iPad cover. There were also the photos he both ached and feared to show Brian. He'd taken up photography as a hobby, sat through a few courses, read as much as he could—but he'd never shared this part of himself before.

It was private and *his*.

What would Brian think? Were his pictures any good? Was this just a way to humor him? After all, it was art—frivolous.

A bitter chuckle at himself. His father's words still haunted him, after how many years?

"Am I making you laugh already?" Brian had finished serving the last of the line of customers and was drying his hands. He hovered by the counter.

"I'm making myself laugh." He looked up at Brian. Of the two, Rob was certain he had a few inches on Brian, but he liked this—seeing that jawline and neck from below. The lights above the coffee bar framed his sandy hair perfectly. "I don't show off my photos."

Brian's posture tightened. He took a breath to speak, but whatever he'd meant to say was cut off by the damn door.

Rob was beginning to hate that bell.

For all the world, it looked like Brian had been about to say something important. Instead, he said, "Looks like my replacement's arrived."

All right, so he didn't *hate* the bell—now he could get Brian out of the shop, away from that brass noisemaker—and they could talk, uninterrupted.

Brian chatted with his replacement barista. "How's your grandmom?"

She twisted her face into something—unhappy yet resigned. "Not much better. It's hard, Bri."

Brian swallowed and there was conflict and pain in his expression. "Do you need—" He lowered his voice, but not enough that Rob didn't hear the next words. "Do you need tonight off?"

She rolled her eyes. "No. For goodness' sake, go on your date."

Date? Now that was good to hear, even if Brian did turn a beetlike shade of red.

The barista smiled at Rob. "Will you please take this man and get him the hell out of here before he turns into a *complete* pain in the ass?"

Rob rose and tucked his iPad under his arm. "It would be my pleasure." He crooked his finger. "You heard the woman."

Brian looked between the two of them. "But you two have never met! How can you already conspire against me?"

"Go." The barista pointed at the door. "Have fun."

Brian held up his hands. "I'm going, I'm going." He came out from behind the counter and ended up next to Rob, his face still flush and his fingers tapping nervously against his thighs.

"So, dinner?" They hadn't planned anything, but that seemed the logical choice, especially if this was a date.

"Sure. What—" Brian stopped and gave a bark of a laugh. "I don't know if I should ask this question, but what are you in the mood for?"

Rob chuckled, but didn't say *American*. Too on the nose. "You pick. I'm still finding my way around this neighborhood."

"Vietnamese? There's a place down the street."

He hooked his arm into Brian's. "Lead on."

Brian started at the contact, but they moved anyway, arm and arm out of the door. After a few steps down the street, Rob took pity and let go. Brian was so stiff, so trembly.

"I kind of liked that," Brian murmured.

"Oh?" Rob took his hand. "This is easier."

Warm flesh. Brian's grip was soft and body much more relaxed. He swallowed. "This really is a date, isn't it?"

"Are you surprised?"

Brian looked ahead, his brows furrowing as if he were *thinking* about the question. "Truthfully? No."

Still didn't make sense. But he had Brian's hand and they were on a date. He'd figure out what was behind those brown eyes eventually.

Another block and they were at the small restaurant. Didn't look like much from the outside, but the inside was warm and inviting. Red and brown hues to the decorations and the food smelled fantastic. They were shown to a small table for two.

After they ordered, Brian took a deep breath, put his folded hands on the table, and spoke. "So, how was the hike?"

Truly a first date, complete with an utterly adorable nervous partner. "It was lovely. So many trees budding or blooming. Tiny flowers. Ferns. Wait—" He flipped open the iPad, brought up the gallery, and handed it over.

Brian laid the tablet down and stared. Slowly, he flipped through each photograph, sometimes sliding back to the previous one. About halfway though, he focused on Rob. "These are incredible. You have a fantastic eye for light and composition."

That sounded like the praise of someone who *understood* photography. "Do you—are you a photographer?"

Happy lines from his smile lit Brian's face. "Believe it or not, I have a bachelor of fine arts, with a concentration in drawing, painting, printmaking, and photography."

Well, that explained that. Rob stared back. "Isn't an artist owning a coffee shop a little cliché?"

Brian laughed outright at that, and a nearby couple glanced their way. When he caught his breath, he answered. "Not really. Artists and writers hang out at coffee shops. You need to be out of your mind to run one." He flipped through more of the photographs. "Seriously, though. These are wonderful. You should make some prints and sell them."

"Sell... them?" Piddling, useless little things like that? Who'd be interested in a photo of fern heads in leaf litter?

A moment later, their food came.

Brian closed the iPad and set it to the side. They thanked their server and dug in. "Lots of people buy photographs. You won't make a ton of money, but..." He took a bite of his noodle dish.

He didn't need the money. Hadn't in a very long time.

He shifted in his seat and ripped basil into his pho. "I don't share my photos with anyone. It's... not something people want from me."

Brian lifted an eyebrow.

He supposed he needed to quantify that, somehow. "I was pushed very heavily by my parents to not have anything to do with the arts. We were barely scraping by growing up. Maths and science were seen as the way out of that. Art was... a luxury."

"So you don't want to be seen as indulging in something so trivial?" There was a hard edge to Brian's voice.

"No." He craved art, almost as much as companionship. "It's... complicated." He stirred the bean sprouts into the bowl. "I suppose... at some level, I don't want to dishonor my parent's memory. Even though—" He broke off. He'd hated the way they'd treated him. His drawings. His love of color. But this path was too damn painful, still.

Brian's mouth snapped shut. He struggled for a few moments, then spoke. "They're gone?"

God, he *hated* that phrase, as if his parents had taken a trip somewhere and would be back later. "They're dead. Dad had a heart attack several years back. My mother—" Grief welled up inside Rob. He should have been there for his mum, not halfway around the world, working too hard to answer his phone before his father had died. He shook his head. "Do you mind if we change the subject?"

"No, of course not. I'm sorry. I didn't mean to pry." Poor thing looked crestfallen.

He couldn't blame Brian, not after dropping that particular bomb. "You weren't. Point of a date is to get to know each other."

There was that flush again. "I do want to get to know you." He eyed the tablet. "You know, if you sent me the raw files, I could make up some prints. I have access to the equipment I need. You could see how you felt about having physical copies—for yourself."

He followed Brian's gaze. It was a good idea, actually. Something to force himself out of that particularly nasty mind-set. "Why don't you pick the ones you think would work best," he said. He didn't have the eye or the heart. All of his photos were both precious and horrible.

A faint but beautiful smile. "I can do that."

They settled in to eating their dinners, and an uncomfortable silence stretched between them. *Fuck.* He hadn't meant to kill the conversation entirely. He set down his spoon. "What about you? Still pursue the arts?"

Brian leaned back. "I used to. But, like everything else, it takes time. I do miss it, though. I loved to sketch with charcoals. Great for capturing the older industrial side of Pittsburgh."

"You like the urban industrial, too." Rob felt the past—his childhood—rise up and settle like a lump against his heart. "I grew up in an old coal town. Struggling. Some jobs in manufacturing." Not the easiest place to grow and thrive, especially when gay.

Brian nodded slowly. "So a place like Pittsburgh?"

"Except it never had a renaissance." Never had a chance. After he'd buried his mother, Rob hadn't been back, but he kept up with a few old acquaintances from time to time. The ones who still talked to him. "I'm not very good at changing the subject, am I?"

A pained smile from Brian. "Ask me some more questions?"

What do you want, Bri? But that wasn't something to say yet. "Since we're on the subject of family..."

That got him a much warmer expression. "Like I said, I

grew up in Bloomfield. My folks are still there. I have an older brother and a younger sister. And a metric ton of cousins and uncles and aunts."

"A big family." There was the longing, the need, the desire to be connected. He had *nothing*. "Only child," he added.

Brian shrugged lightly. "We're Italian."

He studied Brian, who looked, to his eyes—utterly American. "You never told me your last name."

Brian laughed. "You haven't either, you know." He took a bite of his dish.

Touché. "Ancroft. Robert Ancroft."

Brian repeated the name in his flat American accent. "You prefer Rob?"

"Over Robert? With friends, yes." And lovers. "Robert is—too formal."

Brian set down his fork. "Mine's Keppler."

"Like the astronomer?"

"Well, two *p*s, but yes."

Brian Keppler. Nice. Rob rolled it around in his head. "But Keppler isn't Italian."

A snort. "Yeah. It's German. I'm like an eighth German and the rest is Italian, but my branch of the family ended up with the German name." He reclaimed his fork and set to eating again. "It's a hell of a lot easier to spell than Nascimbeni, though."

A laugh bubbled up in Rob and broke through the painful knot in his chest. "That's true."

They settled into talking about Brian's family. His older brother had gone into the military and ended up a pilot in the air force. He flew commercially now. His sister was a biologist working in a research lab for one of the billion hospitals in Pittsburgh. They still all saw one another once a month.

"Family's important," Brian said.

Rob hid his wince. Time to change the subject again. "How'd you end up owning a coffee shop?"

"That's a long story," Brian said. He pushed his empty plate away. "Short form is that a friend opened one where Grounds N'at is now and I took a job as a barista there. He had horrible business sense, was pretty much a slacker, and when he realized it was damn hard work, he offered the whole thing to me for a song."

"That was a hell of a risk." Taking on a failing business and making it work was also quite an accomplishment.

Brian shrugged. "People liked the shop a lot. I mean, there's a ton of coffee places in Squirrel Hill, but we had regulars. I created the drink menu when I started and, well, it seemed a shame to close when all that was needed was some hard work."

So Brian the artist had become Brian the businessman. "And it's doing well now? Aside from the staffing issue?"

Brian's face twisted. "It's okay at the moment. But running a food service—it's never easy. You're always two steps away from disaster."

Hence the long hours. Sounded quite a bit like creating a startup, except for Rob, the days of constant work and worry were done. CirroBot could stand on its own now. "It's a lovely shop, Bri."

Brian dipped his head, his smile faint and embarrassment clear. "Thanks."

The server cleared their plates and brought the dessert menu.

From Brian's expression, there wasn't anything he saw there that appealed to him.

Nothing piqued Rob's interest, either. "I think I spied an ice cream place up on Forbes?"

"You did." There was a glint in Brian's eyes. "Shall we take a walk?"

"Could use one, yes." Walk off some dinner, get a treat, and maybe without this table between them, they could get a bit closer.

They paid and headed out. Brian didn't pull away when Rob took his hand. In fact, it was Brian who tangled their fingers together.

Rob let out a breath. "I wasn't sure how you felt." Especially after the whole family conversation.

A soft chuckle. "That makes two of us."

After all that flirting? He glanced at Brian. Had Rob somehow given off the wrong impression? "I'm very interested, Bri. I hope you'll give me a chance."

Another laugh—this one had the edge of nervousness. "I know. You're—" He swallowed. "I never thought you weren't interested."

Oh. So it was *Brian* who also didn't know what Brian wanted. He would have let go if Brian hadn't been holding his hand so tight. "Are you—"

"Yes." A quiet answer. "Yes, I am." There was almost a wonderment about those words.

Rob ran through all their interactions again. They did seem to be pointing in one particular direction—and if Rob was right—he needed to let Brian lead the way. Rob gave Brian's hand a gentle squeeze, and they stopped briefly at his car to drop off the iPad before continuing up the hill.

They reached the top of Murray Avenue where it intersected with Forbes and the ice cream parlor on the corner. Two cones later, they were walking hand in hand again. Now that the sun had fallen behind the horizon, the air had cooled. Still, they meandered down the business district, stopping to look in windows. This time, the quiet between them was cozy and warm. They were, for a time, on the same page—whatever page that was.

I like you, Bri. It had been a while since he'd even bothered aiming for a relationship. He didn't have family. Couldn't keep his own mother alive. The last guy he'd "dated" wanted only sex and cash. Work had been a blessing in a way—it kept people at a distance.

He'd hooked up once or twice since the fiasco with Greg. Stellar sex, which made him feel all the more lonely. Therapy had helped. And now?

Now he was walking down a street, holding Brian's hand and eating ice cream. So maybe he *was* ready for more. "Sometimes it's hard being what's left of your family."

Brian slowed. "And you're over here and not there."

Yes. A different country, but that didn't bother him. "I'd rather be here, to be honest. I miss England from time to time, but I built my life *here*." He paused. "And I'm a citizen now, so this *is* home." He waved at the street.

They stood by the window of a sweets shop and Brian faced him, his cone half eaten. "I wouldn't mind hearing that story sometime, if you want to share." Little blotches of melted ice cream slid down his fingers.

"Thank you." It was a kindness, both the offer and the realization that Rob might not want to share. "It's mostly boring, but—yes. I'll tell you sometime." Not tonight, because the walls of his past were too thin. Something about Brian seemed strangely fragile, too. He stared at the ice cream on Brian's fingers.

Brian must have noticed, because he stretched out the digits and looked. A sly smile curled his lips. "You *do* have a thing for cream, don't you?"

From melancholy to horny in no time flat. He drew in a breath. "I do, yes." He certainly wanted a taste of Brian.

Brian shivered. He tried to hide it, but Rob knew the dance well enough to see. He let his gaze move down Brian's body, and yes, that answer had made an impression. "Don't want you getting dirty."

"Oh," Brian said as he untangled his fingers from Rob's and switched the cone to the other hand. "I doubt that." He licked the drops of ice cream off his fingers.

Rob didn't bother to hide the tremor that ran through him, his intake of breath, or the hardening of his cock. Brian was very thorough sucking and licking and it didn't take that much imagination at all to think of that mouth and tongue on his shaft.

Brian finished the rest of his cone and crumpled the wrapper into his hand. "You're getting ice cream on yourself, too."

Rob looked at his own mostly eaten cone, and yes, chocolate had dripped onto his fingers. "Do you want to lick them clean, as well?"

Brian's brows shot up into his hairline and he inhaled. The answer was as plain as day on his face, though he didn't say a word.

Rob finished his cone, stepped in, and held out his hand.

The vein in Brian's neck pulsed out a fast beat and he seemed to stop breathing. But then he moved forward and his lips pressed against the chocolate on Rob's forefinger.

Rob gasped. Couldn't help it, not with Brian's tongue rasping against his skin and those warm lips sucking so gently. That touch radiated out and set every part of his skin on fire. Brian took his wrist and kissed and sucked all of the chocolate away, leaving Rob breathless, hard, and shaken.

He'd wanted the touch of those lips far too much, wanted more of Brian so badly.

"Better?" Brian's voice was shaky and thin.

"Yes." He cupped the back of Brian's neck and drew him into the kiss he needed more than air. Same warmth to Brian's lips, but now they were moving on Rob's. A faint taste of chocolate against Rob's tongue as he opened Brian's mouth and deepened the kiss.

Brian moaned softly, barely audible over the rapid rush of blood in Rob's head. Their bodies pressed together, their hard lengths brushing each other. Rob gripped Brian's waist and pulled him close.

God, this man. Soft and hard. Forceful, yet yielding as he surrendered to Rob—then demanded the same in return.

They broke apart slowly. Brian's eyes were wide and he licked his lips. "Chocolate."

"And cookie dough." Brian's ice cream flavor.

Brian laughed, but it was tight. Too tight. "There's something I should tell you."

A throb of cold leached through Rob. He loosened his hold, opening space between them. "Yes?"

"I've never done this before."

Rob's heart hammered in his chest. "Licked ice cream off of a guy's fingers?"

"Well, that, too." Golden eyelashes flicked up and Rob was staring into Brian's eyes. "I've never kissed a man before."

Oh. *Shit*. He didn't know what to say. Didn't help that his first instinct was to giggle, because there was *no way* that kiss was from a straight guy. He finally found some words. "But you're interested in me?"

"Oh, God, yes." It came out in a tumble, all strung together. "I just don't know what the hell I'm doing."

Standing on a sidewalk in public in Squirrel Hill. Rob slid his hands into Brian's. "You're not straight, are you?" He couldn't be. Closeted? Maybe.

"No I'm—" He swallowed and spoke through a tight voice. "I'm bi. Bisexual." Brian shook, and the deep lines were back in his brow. Tension upon tension. It wasn't nervousness—it was terror.

Everything clicked into place. All the hesitation, all the uncertainty.

Gay guys weren't always kind to bi guys. So many myths that led to cruel rejections. He'd seen that a few times. He knew that fear, too. Wondering if you'd made a mistake. Picked the wrong guy. Worried that heaven would quickly turn to hell and hate.

"Oh, Bri." Rob pulled him into a hug, his voice thick in his ears. "It's absolutely fine to be bi."

All the tension left Brian and for a moment, Rob was certain he was the only thing keeping Brian on his feet. Deep breaths that evened out. Brian found his strength and pulled back. "I don't live that far from here. Would you—" He bit his lip.

"I'll walk with you." He took Brian's hand at let him lead the way. He wouldn't spend the night, though. Not after that, no matter how hard he was or how much he wanted Brian.

From the heat of Brian's hand, the flush on his skin, and the moisture Rob spotted at the corner of Brian's eyes, he had a feeling Brian was too ripped apart inside to make any good judgment calls.

He wouldn't take advantage of that. He wanted more than a quick fuck—he wanted another date. Many, many other dates. He was *tired* of meaningless sex. Too old for that.

They walked around the block and back toward Murray Avenue on a street that ran parallel to Forbes. About halfway down the block, they came to a three-story house. "I live on the third floor," Brian said.

Very close to Grounds N'at. No wonder Brian could take so many shifts.

They stopped on the small covered porch and Brian paused by the door. "Do you want to come up?" Hope in Brian's voice and nerves everywhere else.

Again, Rob drew Brian close and kissed him, this time a tad more demanding. Wanting. Needy. They came together as before. No question as to their mutual desire. Brian was rock-hard. When Rob cupped his arse and ground against him, Brian made a little helpless sound in the back of his throat.

Lips sliding against lips and tongues fighting for purchase. Brian may have never kissed a guy before, but he had the whole process down pat.

God bless the women Brian had dated.

From the way Brian ran his hands down Rob's back, pressing fingers into muscle, when they did make it into bed, it would be hot and heavy and give them both bruises. Brian kissed like he wanted to climb Rob's body.

He wouldn't mind that at all. A hot, horny guy who'd never had cock, but came with years of experience? Sounded *exactly* like Rob's idea of fun.

Except tonight was not that night. He gently separated from Brian. "I want you very very badly." He stroked a thumb over Brian's cheek. "But I'm not going to come up tonight."

He steeled himself for Brian's disappointment, but his heart still flipped when it came. The furrowed brow, the way he pulled back. "Why?"

"I generally don't fuck on the first date." True, though he didn't *date* all that often. "I don't want this to be some kind of hookup. I want *more* than that—or at least the space for it to grow."

That smoothed out a great deal of those lines. Brian exhaled. "I'm *really* crappy with relationships." Brian leaned into Rob's touch. "But I want more than a hookup, too."

"Then it's settled." He kissed Brian again and lingered, loving the taste of his desperate need.

When they broke apart, Brian's breath was rough. "You're going to keep me up all night."

He liked that idea, too. Brian tossing and turning, jacking off to thoughts of him. He stepped close and whispered into Brian's ear, "After our next date, I'm going to find out what the rest of you tastes like."

"Fuck." It came out like a moan.

"Good night, Bri."

Brian swallowed. "That's easy for you to say."

"Not really." He took one of Brian's hands and pressed it against his hard shaft.

Another bob of Brian's Adam's apple. Fingers explored his length through denim and for a moment, he regretted not letting Brian take him upstairs.

Brian kissed his cheek. "Well now you can think about me, too."

Oh, they were going to have fun. "I will be." He stole another quick kiss. "Talk to you tomorrow?" He stepped back.

"You have my number." A quirky, sexy smile accompanied that.

He certainly did. Rob chuckled and waved, then headed back to his car before he changed his mind.

Given that his own head was spinning from Brian's admission, he had no doubt Brian's must be ready to fly off into the sky. Better to wait and do this *right* than to fuck the whole thing up.

He'd had enough of fucking things up to last a lifetime.

CHAPTER FIVE

Brian needed three shots in his cappuccino Saturday morning to keep his train of thought from slipping off the tracks and into how Rob tasted, the way he'd moved, the thickness of his cock, and just how hard Brian had come beating himself off.

As predicted, he'd spent a better part of the night with his brain wrapped around Rob and his hand wrapped around his dick.

He'd had the stamina of his youth last night, but that had faded into the early morning. His ass was *dragging*, and he'd no one to blame but himself.

Still, the morning had gone smoothly, despite the rainy weather. Customers were steady, but not overwhelming, and he'd finished the week's schedule ahead of time. As an added bonus, somehow he had next Sunday free. The *entire* day.

Granted, it wasn't yet noon, so who knew what the rest of the day would bring. Might have been cynical, but he never let his guard down against bad news. After all, the week he'd finally thought the shop was running *perfectly*, Sam Anderson had hired away Justin.

He didn't begrudge either Sam or Justin—the job was the perfect fit, and Justin had found Eli and converted that cold, standoffish man into someone full of joy and life. That had been a miracle to see—he'd followed the story of Eli's accident in the paper, back in the day, and had recognized Eli the first day he'd walked into the shop. Now he was a fixture—a married, happy one. He'd envied them both for the longest time.

Now his head was full of Rob. He'd been astounded, once he'd come down from the fire in his veins, that Rob hadn't rejected him.

It's absolutely fine to be bi.

That's not what he'd heard in college. Hearing those words from Rob had nearly shattered him to pieces right there in the middle of the street. So much he wanted to ask Rob. So much he wanted to *do* to him and with him.

The door opened with its usual clanging, and the postal carrier came in with a small stack of mail.

"Care for a cup?" Her hat and coat were splayed with water.

"I'd love one." She plopped the mail on the counter.

He poured his bold drip coffee into a medium cup, put a lid on, and handed it over. She liked it black and strong. "Stay dry."

"Funny man." She tipped the cup at him and headed out into the damp street.

He only had time to scan the pile before another swell of soaked customers poured into the shop, then it was a blur of lattes and mochas and macchiatos. Soy, skim, regular. Flavors. He moved and hummed and created them all. Even got some reasonable tips in the jar, too. Those would go to his baristas, later.

With customers taken care of, he took a closer look at the mail. Junk, a supply catalog for things he didn't need at the moment, and a bill from his coffee wholesaler. He opened that and scanned the invoice. Nothing he wasn't expecting—however, there was a second paper in the envelope. He read it and his stomach dropped.

He knew prices were bound to rise sooner or later. But this was more than he'd expected. *Shit.* He ran a quick calculation in his head. *Fuck.* He could absorb it for the time being, but man, that was going to make things tight. Especially with several baristas being due for raises—that he *would not* deny them.

Outside, the rain and wind picked up and Brian watched people scramble down the street holding on to their umbrellas. So much for his smooth day. He slipped the papers back in the envelope and took the mail into the back room.

He grabbed his laptop to send out an e-mail about the schedule and print a copy to post on the employee bulletin board. Some clicks and taps later and that was done. After he pinned the schedule up, he grabbed a mop and the "Slippery When Wet" sign—too many wet shoes on the wood floor. Didn't want anyone falling.

Couldn't afford it.

It took a few minutes to clean up the water and set the sign, but in that time, he already had an e-mail from Vance, one of his baristas. Brian's stomach lurched. *Problems come in threes*, wasn't that the adage?

Vance was a decent guy, but he'd been late to his shift one too many times the past few weeks and that had required a conversation. He'd *tried* to keep it light and *thought* they were okay, especially since Vance had sent in his preferred hours. Brian clicked open the e-mail.

> Hi Brian,
>
> I've been thinking about this for a couple of days now. I know I've been late a few times and yeah you're right that I shouldn't be. But I don't like being yelled at.

He hadn't yelled, had he? Brian chewed on his tongue, a chill creeping up his spine. Maybe he had raised his voice? Couldn't remember the details now.

> To be honest, working in the shop isn't fun anymore. Too tense and serious. I miss the old days. I think it would be better if I found a job more suited to me, so please take me off the schedule. I'm not going to be working at Grounds N'at again.
>
> Thanks,
> Vance

Brian stared at the screen. It was only after he chewed a piece of his nail off that he realized he'd been biting his thumb.

Holy shit. This wasn't good. Vance was a pretty laid-back guy. The doorbell rang. More customers. More wet shoes. Brian closed the laptop and tried to push the gnawing fear aside. Tried to stop his hands from trembling.

He managed to smile and joke and make the perfect drinks. But by the time he was done, he wanted to throw up.

Filling in Vance's shifts would have him at the shop twelve hours, four days a week. That free Sunday he'd been so happy about? Likely his last for a long, *long* time.

He sat down at the laptop and opened it. With shaking hands, he typed out an e-mail of his own, this one to Miranda.

Hey Mir,

I need you to be honest. Have I been hard to work with lately?

He didn't expect a reply, but one appeared maybe a minute later.

Honestly? Yeah, you have. You're tense and cranky most of the time.

Why? What happened?

That woman could read him like a book.

Vance quit. I didn't realize my mood was getting to everyone.

Well, fuck. I'm sorry, Bri. But yeah, your mood—at least with us—has been shit. We're working hard too. And we're sorry we're not Justin White.

Shit. Shit. Yeah, he had been beating that drum a bit hard.

Crap. I didn't realize how bad I was getting. I'll try to leave the worries at home.

You're never home. That's part of the problem.

Yeah, he knew that. But with a short staff, what else was he supposed to do? He didn't reply because he'd only come off as a defensive jerk. If Miranda saw a problem, then there was one.

If only she could work full- or even part-time. He'd make her a manager in a heartbeat. But what his employees needed came first. Except he'd been fucking *that* up royally.

Again the door clattered and a blast of chilled air whipped in.

"Wow!" The woman at the door paused to push it closed faster. "It's wicked out there."

He jumped at the voice. Anita, his most recent ex. She had quite the smile on her face, despite the weather. Thankfully, she left her umbrella in the little can by the door.

"Hey, Bri! You don't usually work this shift. What happened to the other guy?" She strode up to the counter, her dark curls swinging against her shoulders.

He couldn't even be mad. Never could with her. "He didn't work out."

"Ah, shit. Sorry, kiddo." Honest compassion there.

"You know how it goes," he said, then paused. "Probably better than most people."

Her gaze fell to her hands on the counter. "Yeah."

Oh. His heart sank straight to the floor when he followed her gaze, and there was the third thing, the big shiny rock on her hand. It had been months and *months* since they'd broken up. Still, it never failed to hit him in the gut when one of his ex-girlfriends got engaged.

He was the harbinger of happiness, but never for himself. "Hey," he said and he knew his voice was a mess, "Congratulations."

She was smiling again when he met her eyes, but there was pain and compassion there, too. "Thanks. Happened last week. He's a good guy."

"I'm sure he is, if he caught your eye." Because Anita? Beautiful woman. Good heart. Way smarter than he was and utterly hot in bed. His parents had adored her and hers had loved him. They'd worked so well in the beginning, but then it had fallen to pieces and they'd drifted apart.

Brian was standing in the main reason they were no longer together. He hadn't been able to let go of the shop and his lack of time had driven a wedge between them.

His fault, that. God only knew why Rob wanted to date him and why Brian had said yes. *This is not good.*

She stared at him the way she used to, back when he'd come to her, exhausted and tell her he didn't want to talk even though he desperately did. "Are you okay, Bri?"

He shrugged. "It's—been a little rough today."

"I can tell."

"You always could." He huffed a laugh. "What can I get you?"

She settled on a cinnamon-chocolate latte to go, one of his specials. "Something that warms the heart."

The process of making it was bittersweet and strange, and he didn't realize *why* until he reached for the whipped cream. He stared at the canister for a moment and memories of Rob's smile, his dimples, and the sweet taste of his kiss flooded back.

Not everything had been so terrible lately.

He held up the can. "Do you want?"

"Nah. No good with the lid. Just a dusting of those chocolate flakes you have back there."

Good. He'd rather share the whipped cream with Rob. When finished, he brought the drink over. "You know, I really am happy for you."

"I know. And someday, I'm going to be happy for *you*." She reached to pay but he waved her off. She only rolled her eyes and slapped down a five. "Take my money, Keppler."

He did and gave her change, which she tried to dump in the tip jar and he mock blocked her. They were both laughing by the end, much like old times. She wiped her eyes, and her humor slipped away. "Don't let this place eat you alive." She reached over and gave his hand a squeeze. "Please."

"I won't."

Her smile was the same one she'd always had when he lied. "I'll see you, kiddo." She headed to the door.

"Invite me to the wedding?"

She swung around, grinning. "Dude, how could I not? My mom still asks about you. She'd be horrified if I left you off the list."

He laughed at that, and gave her a wave. Then she was gone, back out into the storm. A deep twist in his heart a few minutes later left him breathless, not because of Anita, or Vance, or the conversation with Miranda.

He missed *Rob*. It was *Saturday* and he hadn't yet appeared. He wanted *that* voice, *those* freckles, *his* laugh. Not Anita's.

He pulled out his phone, but as he was composing a

text, the door blew open and a somewhat drenched, laughing Rob tumbled in.

"God, remind me to stick an umbrella in my car."

That beaming smile pushed every single thought from Brian's head. Rob was *here.* Brian's heart sang with joy.

You have it so bad for this man.

Rob slicked back his hair, but it fell into dark red curls against his forehead. "I spent three years in London, you'd think I'd have learned by now, but no."

More than one person eyed Rob and smiled. His damp t-shirt hugged his body in sinful ways.

"Need a towel?"

"Depends. Do you want me to drip on your lovely floor?"

Brian snorted, grabbed a towel from the back, and tossed it to Rob.

He snatched it out of the air. "I see the answer is no." It didn't take long for him to dry off his hair and face. He took a seat at the bar after setting the towel down on the stool. "Even my bum is wet. I swear, when I left, it was barely raining."

"Welcome to Pittsburgh. If you don't like the weather, wait five minutes." Brian shoved his laptop out of the way and lowered his voice. "It's good to see you."

"Likewise." His eyes had a green tint today, probably from his shirt. Or maybe the rain. Who knew?

Brian couldn't breathe, not with his heart so full in his chest and warmth settling into his core. It wouldn't take much to lean down and touch Rob's cheek or pull those smiling lips against his. Except they were in Grounds N'at and he was working.

He exhaled. "Want something warm to drink?"

"Wouldn't mind that at all." Rob glanced at the menu

board. “I don’t suppose you’d make me that dark orange coffee again?”

Any day. Every day. “Of course.” He even had some orange zest he could mix with the chocolate shavings. It took a few minutes, but Rob’s appreciative rumble when he set the drink down was worth the work.

He couldn’t help wonder if Rob sounded like that in bed and what the skin under that damp shirt tasted like. “I had a great time last night.” Despite the bumps in their conversations.

“So did I. Love to repeat it.”

A second date also promised more afterward. “Right now, I have all of next Sunday free.”

Rob sat up. “Do you?”

His eyes strayed to the laptop, but he nodded.

This time, the words were harder. “Are you sure?”

He lowered himself to the stool. “One of my baristas quit today.” His voice was a whisper. “It doesn’t affect Sunday’s schedule, but...”

Rob grunted and took a sip of his drink—and got whipped cream on the tip of his nose.

Without thinking, Brian reached out and swiped the cream off.

Rob caught his wrist. “Hey now, that’s mine.” He sucked the cream off, his mouth warm and slick, then let go. “Don’t you go stealing.”

Brian put both hands on the counter, mostly to keep from falling over. Had he not been sitting, he’d probably be on his knees.

Wicked mouth, wicked smile. As if that had been the most natural act in the world, Rob continued the conversation. “If you don’t mind me asking, why’d he leave?”

"I—" He'd been a dick. "I've been letting my stress show."

Rob raised the cup again, but didn't drink. "Then obviously you need a day off."

"But—"

"When was the last time you spent an entire day out of this shop? Let your employees run things without you?" Now he drank and Brian watched those lips touch ceramic. Rob raised an eyebrow.

"I don't remember." A month ago? No. Longer. Holy shit. No wonder he was losing it.

Rob set the cup down and it clinked against the saucer. "Look, even the boss needs a break. Trust me on that. Nothing will kill your business faster than running yourself into the ground."

That lit a different fire in his gut. "I know how to run my shop." It came out low and harsh.

Rob tented his hands, his smile gone, and said nothing at all.

The fear, anger, and worry flooded back in, drowning out the minuscule amount of joy he'd found. On some level, Rob was *right*. But taking time off wouldn't pay his bills or find him new baristas.

He raked his hands through his hair. "What do you want me to do?" That, too, came out harder than he'd intended.

A shrug. "Let me help you relax." Rob sipped his coffee around a very sly smile.

Of course customers chose that moment to walk in. Brian got up, his heart and head spinning, and made his way to the sink to wash his hands. By the time he was done, the group that had entered was ready to order.

Thank goodness the drinks were simple—three plain

coffees and three cookies to go. The floor under his feet didn't feel right. His head hurt. Everything ached.

He *did* need a day off. Sunday Miranda was working, and then Mark. Two of his best—they would keep the shop humming.

Once he was sure no customers needed him, he slid back onto the stool in front of Rob. "Okay. You win."

That earned him a smile. "So I've heard about this place —it's an abandoned steel mill and there's been a lot of work to preserve the site— Shit. I've forgotten the name."

"Carrie Furnace?" It was part of the old Homestead Steel Mill and a heritage site.

"Yes, that's it. Apparently, there are tours."

There were. There'd been some great events there—that Brian had missed due to work. The dagger edges of worry and fear vanished. "I've heard good things." It would be right up Rob's alley, given his skill with a camera. "You'll get some great shots."

"That's the idea." He peered over his shoulder. "Assuming the weather is better."

"I don't know—storm shots in old industry? Could be sexy." As was a drenched Rob. The rain had curled his hair into rings of red that Brian itched to run his hands through.

Rob finished his coffee. "I'm not keen on ruining my camera, though."

"Get some rain gear for it." He paused. "Maybe I can help you with that."

"Let's make a pact. You help me with photography and I'll help you stay sane." Rob held out his hand.

Brian grasped it and shook. "It's a date."

"Second one." The devil's grin went straight to Brian's balls.

"You"—he dropped his voice to a whisper—"meant what you said last night?"

"Every single word." Rob tilted his head. "Consider it part of keeping you sane."

Or driving him out of his mind. He shared a smile with Rob—then the door opened to a flood of customers.

For the rest of the afternoon, he served customers, chatted with regulars, and caught snatches of conversation with Rob, even showing him rain gear that would keep his camera safe. There were touches and glances. Laughter and warmth.

So much so that he shivered when Rob left for the evening and let a burst of cold air in. He still had another hour before close, and then all the cleaning.

The week loomed large. He fired off another e-mail to see if anyone could pick up Vance's shifts and Miranda claimed one. Sorry I can't do more.

So was he. But he'd make it through. He had Sunday to look forward to, and Rob's promise to help him relax. Those whispered words from Friday slithered through his brain and into his balls.

After our next date, I'm going to find out what the rest of you tastes like.

His second shiver had nothing to do with the chill in the shop. *Yes, please.*

Rob slipped off his headset and dropped it next to his laptop. One meeting down, too many to go. At least he had a half hour to get up, stretch, and grab a cup of coffee.

On his way to the kitchenette closest to his office, he rolled out his neck. Sitting for hours was killing him. He missed the days of tinkering in the lab. Long hours of functionality testing—which meant playing with actual robots.

Other engineers did that now, though he did roll up his sleeves and join them once in a while to keep his hand in. He tugged at his shirtsleeves. Wrong outfit for that, though. Business suits and hardware labs didn't mesh well, even when he left the jacket and tie behind.

The coffee machine in the kitchenette was a pod type. Pick your flavor and size. Mix and match. He grabbed something not flavored and stuck it in the machine. Wouldn't be as good as Brian's and wouldn't be served by that sandy-haired firebrand of a man.

God, how he wanted more than the little taste he'd had.

The coffee machine chugged and hissed and thudded its pod into some interior compartment. Rob grabbed his coffee and wandered over to the window to watch the traffic on Penn Avenue. Since Friday, every nerve in his body tingled at the thought of touching Brian. Unlike some of the gay men he knew, he never really had an issue with bisexual men enjoying woman. Women were people, too. Hell, back before he'd finally thrown up his hands and come out of the closet, he'd slept with some women. Pretty much cemented that it wasn't his thing, but he didn't begrudge men for whom it was.

But he understood the fear of rejection, of not being understood, of being used. Rob sipped his coffee, swallowed, and frowned at his reflection. He'd been there—especially when he'd made the mistake of not changing his clothes before going out or forgotten to take his watch off—the gold Rolex that signaled "one-of-us" to his business partners signaled something very different to the men he'd met at bars.

Brian hadn't even pried into his business. He was more interested in bikes and cameras and *him*.

Footsteps against carpeting. Rob didn't turn, but glanced past his reflection. "Hello, Todd."

"Hi, Mr. Ancroft, how are you?"

Rob closed his eyes briefly before turning around. "God, *please* call me Rob." Todd stood by the coffee machine clutching a rainbow mug as if it were a talisman. "Mr. Ancroft sounds like some pretentious git."

That loosened those shoulders and Todd huffed a laugh. "Sorry."

Rob waved the word away. "I have to thank you for recommending Grounds N'at." He frowned into his coffee. "Except for the part where I'm ruined for this stuff now."

Todd slipped his mug into the machine and set the contraption brewing. "Glad you enjoyed it. They brew a mean cup. Kind of does spoil you for everything else. Fazil and I hung out there all the time when we lived up the street."

"You've met the owner, then?"

"Brian? Yeah. Cool guy. Very creative. He'd come up with these seasonal drinks that no one else had... then everyone else had, if you know what I mean."

Rob took another sip, then pulled back. "I just *can't* with this stuff." He dumped the rest in the sink and tossed the paper cup.

Todd pulled his mug out of the machine. "How much time have you been spending there?"

Not enough. Rob swallowed that, but something must have shown, because Todd gave him the most *interesting* look, filled with a thousand questions. "I've spent some time talking with Brian."

Todd was verging on a grin, but he was smart enough to sip his coffee and not say anything.

"He's got an interest in photography and biking and—"

The smile broke through. "I'd hadn't realized how his interests ran."

Rob coughed. "Yes, well. Ruined office coffee for me. I suppose I'll have to fall back on my ancestral beverage." He opened a cabinet and rooted around for a box of tea that wasn't some berry-flavored dreck and found—of all things—English Breakfast. He brandished it.

Todd raised his mug. "Cheers."

Both of their phones chimed at the same time. *Shit.* "Is it ten already?" Rob ripped open the tea package and pulled out a sachet.

"Yup." Todd screwed up his face. "The Fortunlia call."

The bane of all their existences as of late. Rob found another paper cup and added hot water. "They can wait a minute for me to get my tea."

Todd smiled. "I don't have that luxury." He tipped his coffee to Rob, then hustled down the hall.

No—Todd didn't. There was the divide between him and the rest of CirroBot—it bothered him to this day. *Oh, suck it up. You're the fucking CEO.* He finished making his tea and headed back to his office.

He probably should mention his actual job title to Brian—but he wasn't quite ready yet.

That always changed things.

He closed his door, sat down, and put on the damnable headset. They were chatting on the call already.

"Hello, everyone, it's Robert. Let's get started, shall we?"

As the call dragged on, Rob drained his tea and stared out his window. Other voices were chatting about features and schedules, but all he could think about was the feel of Brian's lips and the way Brian had fingered his denim-covered shaft.

That memory merged with the wreck Brian had been on Saturday. Employees walking away were always hard to handle, even more so with a small company. Rob crossed his legs and stared at his foot while Fortunlia's line manager reiterated the feature he wanted *again*.

"We're working on it." That was Carter, his head of engineering. "We should be able to get it done by—"

Shit! Rob leapt for the unmute button. "The feature date proposals are listed on the road map."

Silence. *Good God.* "We've been over this before. You know our drop dates." Carter knew better than to say anything that deviated from the road map! Promising customers features that weren't done was asking for trouble.

"Of course," Fortunlia's manager said.

"Is there anything else, or are we finished for this week?" He knew he sounded annoyed—he shouldn't give that much away—but he was damn tired of coddling these people.

"No, I think that's all for now."

"Okay, then thanks, everyone." He waited until more than half the people on the call dropped off before hanging up.

At the rate this week was going, he was going to have quite a head of steam to blow off over the weekend as well. With Brian, who'd never been with a man, but certainly wanted to be. Rob slipped off the headset. He needed to be careful. No pressure. Nothing that Brian didn't want.

Honestly, spending the day with Brian would be its own reward. Photography, conversation, industrial ruins. If they didn't make it into bed, that would be fine, too.

Most of all, he missed companionship. He couldn't have that here at work, not sitting in this office. There was no one to go home to. No family to call. He missed that so much.

Sunday, he could slip off the CEO persona and be *Rob* with someone who didn't want him for his money. Who cared about *him*.

That was worth *everything*.

CHAPTER SIX

By Wednesday night, Brian was hallucinating about pillows while he made three mochas for a group of high school students who'd come in to work on their homework. He now knew viscerally what the expression *bone-tired* meant.

Still he managed a little coffee art on the top of the drinks.

He set the mochas out for the students—Dan, Jan, and Ev. "Here you go."

Each took their drinks to the table they'd commandeered. Good kids, all of them. They even managed to do their work when they spent an evening in the shop. They'd rotate through the different coffee shops in the neighborhood, but recently, they'd been hanging out at Grounds N'at more frequently.

"We like it here," Ev had said. "You accept us. Accept me." Ev had, earlier in the year, shakily explained to Brian that zie was gender fluid and preferred to be called *Ev* and had chosen different pronouns.

"All right," Brian had replied. "I can do that." And he had, endearing himself to the group.

Tonight he watched them with a lump in his throat. Back when he'd been their age, he'd barely heard the word *bisexual* in school. Part of him was envious of these kids; the other part said a little prayer of thanks to God for the change that allowed them to be who they were.

A little while later, Miranda came in for her shift. She inspected him as she walked past and around to the work side of the counter. "Dude, you gotta go home."

"That bad?"

"Truthfully, you look like ass." No malice in those words, just heaps of concern.

"I need to do the ordering," he said. "Couldn't concentrate hard enough earlier and keep the customers happy." He glanced out the windows. "Though I suppose I could take it home."

Miranda wrapped an apron around her waist and washed her hands. "Don't. Right now, that's the last thing you need to do."

True. He snagged the laptop from the back and plopped down at the counter.

"Something wrong with the ordering?" she asked. "You don't usually stress over it."

"Eh, the prices changed. Some of the items, too. I need to figure it out." The shop still had a decent amount in its rainy-day fund, but with the line between black and red becoming thinner and thinner, the sickening sense of dread in his gut grew every day. "I also need to write up a job posting. And post it." And hope they got even one decent candidate.

"Yeah, you need to get someone else in here."

"I know," he snapped. "I'm working on it. I interviewed someone on Tuesday."

She held up her hands. "Bri."

God, he was doing it again. He took a deep breath and let it out. "Sorry. I've been a bear lately."

Her mouth twisted into a grin before she turned away.

"What?" There was a bit of a whine in his voice, but that was better than anger.

She looked back. "You are *so* not a bear."

"What do you—" His brain caught up and he stuttered to a stop. Oh. *That* kind of bear. "I— Uh."

She snorted. "You should see your face."

One of the high schoolers—Dan—came up for a refill. "Just black, nothing fancy."

Miranda took the soiled cup and poured him a fresh one while Dan eyed him. "You do know what a bear is, right?"

Miranda snickered.

Oh for crying out loud. "Of course I do. Bears have been around longer than me." He paused. "And I'm not that old." Even if he did picture himself shaking his fist and telling the kids to get off his lawn.

Dan didn't flinch. "Does that mean you're into guys?"

Goose bumps spread over his arms. "Yeah. I am. Women, too." He shifted his gaze to the street again. "I suppose people in general."

Dan nodded. "Cool." He took his coffee. "She's right, though. You're not a bear." He returned to his friends.

"I know I'm not a bear," he muttered to no one in particular.

Miranda coughed something that sounded suspiciously like *twink*.

He huffed and woke his laptop up. If anything, he was a

fucking artist. He'd turned into a businessman along the way, but the art was still there, under that. Somewhere.

He chewed on his thumbnail. He had a DSLR. Ought to dust it off, charge up the battery, and take it with him to the Carrie Furnace site. Would be good to stretch those muscles again.

Right now? He had ordering to do.

A half hour later, while he was in the middle of typing up what he needed, the bell on the door rang. He ignored it. Miranda would take care of the customer and he *had* to get this ordering done.

A gold watch and shirt cuff slid into his peripheral vision and he looked up. *Rob.* A sly smile, those dancing eyes, and that smattering of freckles. Everything inside Brian somersaulted.

"Hi there," Rob said. "Come here often?"

Something that sounded like a giggle slipped out. Except Brian didn't giggle. "All the damn time."

"He really should go home," Miranda said.

Rob raised an eyebrow. "Should he?"

"He," Brian said, sitting up on the stool, "is trying to get some work done so he *can* go home."

"Mmm-hmm?" Rob rested his chin on his hand and poked at the laptop. "How much more do you have to do?"

"I—" He looked at the computer then back at Rob. "You're here on a weeknight."

Rob lowered his hand and looked around. "So I am."

He spied the high-school kids watching them and a different lump formed in his throat. "To see me?"

"There's no one else," Rob said. "I was sitting at home, bored out of my skull and I missed you. Texts aren't enough."

They'd been chatting back and forth throughout the day, when neither was busy. Little flurries of texts.

"How'd you know I'd be here?" Technically, his shift was over.

"Shop's open and it's not Sunday."

He was about to argue when Miranda laughed. "He's got a point."

Okay, he did. Brian rubbed his eyes. "Let me finish this mess, then I'm all yours."

Rob's smile was wicked and warm. "Good."

That single word zipped through him and woke him more than any jolt of caffeine. He stared at the figures on the screen and got back to work.

Fifteen minutes later, he closed the laptop. Orders were in, job was posted, and Rob was here—in a button-down dress shirt. No jacket, but the shirt was white and crisp and fine—the type that should have a silk tie to grace it. "You look nice."

Color touched Rob's cheeks and he rubbed his wrist—the one with the watch. "I should have changed."

Brian shrugged. "We're not a jeans-and-t-shirts-only establishment." Not with Sam and Eli working above his head. "We let people with full suits in, even."

Rob chuckled, but it was strained. Weird.

"What now?" Brian asked.

It was Miranda who answered. "He hasn't had dinner, you know."

"Oh?" Chin on hand, Rob looked like he could offer a contract for Brian's soul.

He'd probably sign it. "I had food."

"A cookie and an espresso isn't a meal, Bri."

"No, it's not." Rob rose, and crooked his finger, just like last time. "Time to go, Brian." Command in his voice and in the lines of his body. His smile promised so much more, if Brian followed.

His heart pounded in his chest. The things he wanted to do to that beckoning finger and the man behind it. "I—" He was on his feet before he realized, hands wrapped around the laptop. "Let me put this in back."

If he stared any longer, he might forget how to walk. He stowed the laptop in his safe before returning to the front. "Well, you have me." He left off the *Now what are you going to do with me?* part.

But that grin meant Rob had heard it. He pulled Brian close and kissed him. Just a brush of lips with a hint of what might come later.

It left Brian dizzy.

Rob kissed him in public, in his shop. In front of customers—and more than just the high schoolers—but he *didn't care*. He should have been full of angst and worry.

There was only giddy relief.

"Pizza?" Rob said. "It's quick and up the street."

Also on the way to Brian's apartment. "Perfect."

The high-school kids, the little snots, all gave him two-thumbs when he and Rob left. He waved at them before the door clanged closed.

"You have a fan club." Rob took his hand.

"They're good kids. I gave 'em a space to be themselves."

"You do that for a lot of people, I think." Quiet words. "Except yourself."

Maybe it was the warm spring night, or the sudden flipping of his heart, but he lifted Rob's hand and pressed his lips to Rob's knuckles. "You're giving me that."

No smile in response. Rob's expression was far deeper. "I'm so very glad I can." He gave Brian's hand a squeeze. "I didn't quite expect that when I first walked into your shop."

The last thing Brian had ever expected was to meet a boyfriend at work, mostly because he never expected to *have* a boyfriend. The pain and the joy twisted in him sharply, and he grunted.

Rob lifted an eyebrow.

"I—feel a bit—I don't know. Dumb? Childish? For waiting so long."

"Not the first man to catch your eye?" Curiosity there, not jealousy or anger.

"Oh God, no." Brian stroked the back of Rob's hand. "Just the first to make me want to do something about it."

Those lovely dimples formed, highlighting Rob's cheekbones. "Well, I do have a very important question to ask you."

Brian's heart skipped a beat. "Yeah?"

"Yeah. Mineo's or Napoli's?" He beamed.

Oh God, that *was* a choice. Some people were so die-hard about it, too. He was one of the few who loved both shops. Different styles, but both so good. "You have a preference?"

Rob shook his head. "Haven't been to either."

Well, they certainly needed to fix that. "Then Napoli's. I had Mineo's last week."

The entered the pizza place, ordered a few slices, and settled in at one of the tables. "I got the camera gear you suggested," Rob said. "And I think I want to take you up on your offer to make prints of a few of the nature photos."

Good, all around. "Send me a link to an album and I'll pick some out."

Rob didn't answer. He'd taken a bite of his slice and his eyes were closed. "Fuck, this is good."

Looked like someone got orgasmic from good pizza. "Do you like Italian, or just pizza?"

Rob pried open his eyes. "I like everything. But there's something about pizza. And lasagna."

"My dad makes the *best* lasagna." Brian picked up his slice and ate. He had no idea how his parents would react to him dating a guy.

"Your dad? Not your mum?"

"They both cook. Sometimes, Mom worked swing shifts, and Dad needed to feed us. Luckily, his mom was the keeper of the family recipes." Brian pulled pepperoni off his slice. "My mom makes killer wedding soup."

"God, I love that, too."

"I'll have to bring you to dinner sometime."

Rob froze and Brian couldn't put a finger on the expressions that crossed his face. "You'd do that?"

First he'd have to tell his parents he had a boyfriend. "Yeah. I mean, I have no idea how they're going to react to me being bi, but..." They were his family. "We're all close. I'm pretty sure they'll be fine with it." He hoped.

Rob didn't answer right away, so they ate in silence. When Rob finished, he slid the paper plate away. "I'm not used to family being supportive."

"Yours or..." He'd no idea about Rob's past relationships.

"Both." He got a distant look. "When I came out, it was rough. It was starting to get better, but..." He shook his head. "Too late now. The guys I've been with in the past were either estranged from their families or weren't interested in that kind of relationship." Rob rubbed at his wrist again.

That kind of relationship. Brian finished and nodded at the door. "Shall we?"

They tossed their plates and headed out. It wasn't dark,

but the day had chilled. Rob reached for Brian's hand. "Anyway, I hope everything works out with your parents."

"Me too." They walked up the street, getting closer to his apartment. *That kind of relationship* rolled around in his brain. With the women he'd dated, it'd always been serious, always the hope that dating would lead to more. "I've never dated casually."

"When I date, it's not casual." Rob said. "I wasn't always on the same page as my partners." Bitterness there.

They hit Darlington and walked the half block to Brian's apartment. "This is all new to me." The world had changed enough that there could be more than dating. He found Rob staring back.

"No," Rob said. "It's not."

That threw him. Then again... nothing felt different. He kept expecting some big shift in his brain, like a trumpet heralding that he was now queer. Not the normal giddy high of finding new partner. "Maybe you're right." They stood on his porch, still holding hands. "Was this date number two?"

Rob pulled him in, took his mouth, and Brian's legs wanted to crumple. The kiss put fire in his bones and an ache in his soul. Not aggressive or demanding, but those lips claimed him from the inside out. When Rob pulled back, his mouth curved into a smile, and his cock pressed against Brian's. "Yes."

Fucking alleluia! Brian shoved the key into the door and unlocked it. They didn't speak on the stairs, or when he unlocked the door at the top and stumbled into his apartment.

Brian's skin burned to be touched; his fingers ached to discover what lay beneath Rob's clothes. He'd never been so hard in his life.

The kiss Rob drew Brian into was needy and demanding and set his blood on fire. A tongue that teased along lips and teeth and claimed his mouth. Brian moaned, cupped Rob's ass, and pulled him close, his dick pressing against Rob's.

Hot, heavy, and everything he'd dreamed about for years.

In response, Rob tugged and pulled at Brian's hair until he gasped for air. God, he loved that. The ache, the surrender. A few of his ex-girlfriends had managed, but not with the strength Rob had.

"You taste so good," Rob murmured, hot words against flesh. He worked his mouth down Brian's neck, teeth scraping against his skin.

That was usually *his* line, but he didn't care at all. Rob rocked against him. Fuck, how were they still standing? And why did they have clothes on? He grabbed Rob's shirt and dragged him to the couch and they tumbled down onto the cushions. Rob slipped his hands under Brian's shirt and stroked his abs, making Brian twist and shiver. That and Rob's hot mouth against his collarbone had him about ready to explode. His balls had never ached this much from necking.

"God." Brian drew in a breath. "I want you so bad."

"I can tell." Rob skimmed a hand over Brian's dick and the pressure sent his pulse skyrocketing. He yanked Rob up by his shirt and kissed him hard and deep until it was Rob who whimpered underneath his lips.

Such a sweet sound. Brian kissed Rob's jaw, the stubble scraping his lips. Buttons were easy to open on Rob's shirt—thank God he wasn't wearing an undershirt.

Brian splayed a hand against Rob's chest, then sat back. Hair dusted Rob's ruddy shoulders and chest, with a thicker trail leading down into his dress slacks. His arousal was thick and unmistakable below his belt.

Freckles dotted his shoulders and his small pink nipples were hard buds. Rob's chest rose and fell with his rough breathing and met Brian's gaze, eyes blue in the cool light of the room.

Brian kissed Rob's shoulder and ran a hand over his stomach. He'd never wanted to explore a body so badly. Rob tasted of salt and his scent filled Brian's nostrils. Those hitches in Rob's breath sank straight into Brian's bones.

Rob scraped fingers across Brian's back, urging him closer and lower at the same time.

He knew that move, as well. He'd get there eventually. Brian shivered. No idea how good he'd be at giving head, but damn if he didn't want to try. However, there was so much of Rob between his mouth and his cock that Brian wanted to examine first.

The skin on Rob's chest was soft, but the muscle beneath delightfully hard. Brian cupped Rob's pec and flicked his thumb over the nipple.

Rob trembled. "Fuck." All moan.

"Like that?" Brian whispered over the other nipple. Before Rob could answer, he skimmed his tongue over the hard nub.

Rob tangled hands into his hair and hissed. "God, yes."

So, Rob was sensitive there. Given that he seemed to be urging Brian for more, Brian lavished his attention on one nipple, then the other, his fingers stroking and pinching when his mouth wasn't.

Rob moaned and cursed, his skin so hot under Brian's mouth and fingers. He loved every fucking second of it. The sounds, the way Rob rocked against him.

Should have tried this sooner—but then would he have

found Rob? Hard to tell. He drifted lower, licking over abs and nibbling at the trail of hair down Rob's torso.

Rob panted, his fingers caught in Brian's hair. "Sure you've never done this before?"

Brian flicked his tongue into Rob's bellybutton, and spoke against his skin. "Not with a guy." He settled between Rob's knees, kneeling on the floor. This was the point where he'd shuck a woman's jeans and panties and happily go down on her.

Rob let go of his head. "You don't have to do anything you don't want to." Soft words.

That, too, was often his line. He'd meant it and felt in his bones that Rob did. "I know." He *did* want to slide those dark gray pants off, find out if Rob was a boxer or briefs guy, and discover what his dick tasted like.

His own cock was straining at his jeans, balls aching, and every nerve vibrating with need for the man he knelt before. "If it's all the same to you..." He kissed Rob's stomach above his belt buckle, then undid it. "I really want to suck your cock."

Rob stroked his cheek and spoke in a voice that rumbled through Brian. "By all means, be my guest."

He undid the button and zipper, and peeled open Rob's pants. Briefs, from the looks of it, and black. The unmistakable bulge of an erect dick tented the cotton and curls of red hair peeked from under the waistband.

Brian's heart thrummed against his ribs. Good God, here he was at last. He mouthed Rob's shaft through the fabric and yanked his dress pants farther down.

A soft, unintelligible curse fell from Rob, all wrapped up in an accent far thicker than normal. Rob's hands twined in Brian's hair and his thighs quivered.

That hard-yet-malleable length felt so good beneath his

lips. Brian breathed in the scent of Rob's arousal and folded the briefs back until his shaft became free. They both inhaled at the same time. Heat rose from his toes to his head.

The carpet matched the drapes and God, every bit of Rob was gorgeous. He'd only ever glimpsed uncut dicks before, and now he had an up-close view. Perfect. Brian wrapped fingers around Rob's cock and stroked a few times, pulling soft moans from Rob.

When he looked up, Rob watched, eyes wide and lips wet. He rolled his hips in motion with Brian's strokes. "I wouldn't have known I'm the first," Rob said, his voice thick. "If you hadn't told me, I wouldn't have fucking known."

"Guess I'm doing something right." Brian shifted his gaze to Rob's dick and the clear fluid gathered at the tip.

"More than right," Rob murmured. His hands slid in Brian's hair. No pressure, but it was pretty clear what Rob wanted.

Since he wanted that too, he sucked the head of Rob's dick into his mouth. Bitter salt, but he knew his own taste well enough from experimenting. He hadn't expected the head to be so soft and silky. He loved the texture, the heat, and the noise Rob made. He ran his tongue over the top, around the crown, and pressed into the slit.

"Fuck, Bri." Tight words. Rob gripped his hair, pulling at his scalp.

He kept going, exploring how much he could take in at once, and running his tongue over veins and skin. Amazing heat, the way Rob's cock flexed and moved. So hot, so *right.* He licked at the shaft and stroked the head with his thumb.

Yeah, he could get *very* used to this. His whole body burned, his own dick aching with every lick and nibble he gave Rob's.

Rob thrust his hips, looking for more friction, and his groans and grunts were pure music.

Brian pulled down more fabric until Rob's balls were free. Those he cupped, feeling their weight. Didn't know if Rob liked it, but he enjoyed when his balls were played with, so he rolled Rob's in his hand and went back to sucking cock.

Rob's ass lifted off the couch and the pull on Brian's scalp was amazing. "Shit!" He fell back. "God... don't stop... please..."

Didn't want to. This was everything he'd thought it might be—intimate, sexy, fun. He pressed a hand against his own throbbing dick. Whipping it out would take too much time, but man did he want to beat off.

Rob's groans were deep, his hands tight in Brian's hair, urging a rhythm that matched the movement of his hips. Brian wrapped his hand round Rob shaft and gave himself over to sucking and licking and sliding his mouth up and down Rob's cock.

"Bri—" Rob's voice cracked and slurred. "I'm gonna come. You—might want to—"

Not a chance. He'd eaten women to orgasm, he'd do the same with Rob. Brian pressed his tongue against the underside of Rob's head and pumped his shaft faster.

"Oh, fuck—"

Rob's shaft thickened, then hot salt hit Brian's tongue. Rob's jizz was sharp and he seemed to come forever. Brian's moans mixed with Rob's and he swallowed as best he could, sucking and licking until Rob gripped his chin.

"Hey, hey, you can—" Little bit of pain in his voice.

He let Rob slip free from his mouth and sat back, gasping. His whole body shook with pride, exertion, and the desperate need to follow Rob into an orgasm. He'd never understood women who loved giving blowjobs, how it was such a turn-on.

He did now. Holy shit.

Rob gripped his shoulder "Come up here." Rough voice and he grappled at Brian's shirt.

He let himself be pulled into Rob's arms and Rob's mouth was on his, their lips and tongues fighting against each other.

It was Rob who broke the kiss. "I love tasting myself in you."

He bucked against Rob. "Loved tasting you."

Fingers on his cheek. "You have a bed in this place?"

He nodded, every part of him hot and cold at the same time.

"I think it's well past time we got out of our clothes and onto a mattress, don't you?"

"Yes." His voice shook. He swallowed, tasted Rob, and pushed himself to standing. Rob finished shucking off his shoes and pants. Even though Rob didn't know the way, Brian had the distinct feeling he was being led toward the bedroom. Especially when Rob pushed him up against the doorframe and pulled his t-shirt over his head.

"Enough of this." It landed somewhere in the room. Rob kissed him again, and the world tilted and spun. He barely felt the floor for the hum in his limbs.

He'd never been so high from foreplay. "Bed," he said, his voice as high as his brain.

"Jeans first, love." Somehow Rob unbuckled Brian's belt and undid the zipper and button all while kissing him hard enough to melt what was left of Brian's mind.

Love. Brian broke the kiss and gasped when Rob yanked his jeans and underwear off his waist.

"You're going to have to do the rest." Teeth scraped against his throat.

He was having a hard enough time standing. The thought of kicking off his shoes and jeans seemed monumental. But Rob held him up and he only tottered over once.

Laughter. "God, you're gone already, aren't you?"

"What?" Brian met Rob's smile.

Rob tugged him forward. "Bed. My turn to turn you inside out."

He already had, but before Brian could breathe, he was on the bed and in Rob's arms, every delicious inch of Rob's lean naked body pressed against his. He couldn't stop running his hands over Rob's back, his thighs, cupping his ass.

Unreal. A man—*this* man—in his bed. "You're here, right? This isn't some really vivid wet dream?"

Rob's huff of laughter shook the bed. "Oh, I'm here all right." He closed his hand around Brian's cock and stroked. "No dream at all."

Brian rolled his hips and pressed into Rob's hand. So fucking *good*. And man, Rob knew how to jack him off. He moaned into Rob's kiss, and pulled back. "You keep that up, I'm gonna come."

"Well, we can't have that." Teeth scraped his shoulder. "I haven't gotten started yet." Rob straddled his body and pressed him against the bed. "Told you I wanted to taste every inch."

He had, and *fuck*, he meant it, too. Started with a kiss to his lips, then down his neck and across his shoulders. After that, Rob took his hands and stretched them over his head, and didn't *that* ache his balls, the vulnerability.

He didn't know what to expect when Rob reached his

pits, but certainly not a teasing breath that tickled his sensitive flesh. He would have levitated off the bed if Rob hadn't been sitting on him. That touch, those teeth. Seemed like his skin was connected directly to his cock. Even after Rob had moved up his arm, the nips and licks only made him try to find friction and purchase for his dick.

But Rob sat on him in such a way that he got neither. He groaned in frustration.

Rob rocked back, his ass brushing Brian's cock. "Now that's a sound I love hearing." He released Brian's hands.

Mistake. Brian grabbed Rob's shoulders, pulled Rob down, and devoured his mouth. They rolled, hips rocking, nails scraping and digging against backs and sides, lips and tongues fighting for control.

"Someone likes things rough," Rob said between bites and thrusts.

He did, though right now? "Just want you. Any way I can have you."

A laugh. "And I want to take my sweet time. You'll have to deal."

Rob was hard again, and thrusting his dick against Brian's in a way that stole his breath as much as Rob's kisses did.

Rob found Brian's nipple and pinched and rubbed until Brian was nearly liquid beneath him. "Figured you liked that."

"Like everything." Especially the roll of their cocks together. Never experienced anything like that. Didn't know where he ended and Rob began. Pleasure coursed through him, heated his blood and stole his mind. He cupped Rob's ass and ground up against him, balls against balls.

Rob bit down on his shoulder and twisted his nipple

again.

Fire coursed through him. Sprinkles of pain on top of a mountain of unbelievable pleasure. He was so *so* close. "I can't—I'm gonna—"

Rob slipped a hand between them, and wrapped it around both their dicks—his shaft hard against Rob's. "You did promise me cream."

He was so turned on it actually hurt to laugh. "You... bastard." He took Rob's lips for a moment. "Rather come in your mouth than your hand."

Rob panted against his mouth. "I'd rather watch you come. Guess we'll see who wins."

Given how far gone Brian was, it wasn't much of a contest and not a fair one, not with Rob controlling the rhythm, nor when he pressed his thumb against Brian's crown.

Especially not when Rob looked down with that devil of a smile. "I want you all over me, Bri."

Brian bit his lip and fought against the heat and the light, but he was already there, pleasure sweeping over him in one intense rush. He arched against Rob and came hard, pumping out over his hand and dick—and that thought—his jizz slicking Rob's cock only made him come harder before his brain turned to jelly and his vision to blinding light. He heard Rob curse and dug fingers into Rob's arms, thrusting until pleasure turned to pain and his muscles gave out.

They panted against each other, limbs tangled together. Brian wasn't sure whose heart thumped so loudly in his ears.

The room smelled of sex and men, and Rob's neck tasted of salt. He planted kisses upon kisses, then slumped in Rob's arms.

Best he'd felt in months. "I kissed a boy and I liked it," Brian murmured.

Rob shook with laughter. "More than kissed." He held up his hand, fingers glistened with their combined fluids.

Brian couldn't help reaching for and sucking each finger, just like he'd done before. Except semen tasted *nothing* like ice cream.

Rob groaned. "You are far too filthy to be real."

"I'm real." He relaxed against the mattress, his body a mass of lethargy. "And I guess I really am bi."

Another laugh. "You are. You were." Rob sobered and stroked his cheek with his non-sticky hand. "Who you fuck isn't what defines your sexuality."

He knew that. Still, it was a relief to act on the truth. Unexpected tears pricked at the corners of his eyes. "It's hard to explain." Especially since he *still* didn't feel any different.

Wasn't he supposed to feel different?

"You don't have to." Rob said. His kiss was lazy and loving and exactly what Brian needed.

They separated and Brian glanced down. Two naked bodies, flush from sex and covered in spunk. Rob's lean legs were still tangled with his, his cock flaccid against red curls. "God, you're fucking beautiful."

Rob kissed his cheek. "So are you. Tall Americano, indeed."

He covered his eyes with his arm. "I'd like to think I'm more than a shot of espresso and a bunch of water. Americanos are so *easy*."

"You're delectable." Rob's lips were against his. "And you certainly do wake me up."

Brian slid his arm off his eyes and peered at Rob. "Why me?"

"Mmm. I could ask you the same question." Rob smoothed a hand over Brian's chest, raising goose bumps on his cooling skin. "Truth is, you're a handsome man. You responded to my flirting and you kiss like you were born to make love with your mouth... but most of all... I like you quite a bit. You're something of a kindred spirit, I think."

Not quite the answer he'd expected—though he hadn't known what to expect at all. "Kindred spirit?"

Rob stroked his cheek again. "You're a businessman and you care about your community. You're passionate about your art and you're a bit on the self-sacrificial side."

Oh. He rolled the words around in his brain. Yeah, all true, even the martyr type. "So not just a hot guy you wanted to fuck?"

Rob's smile was indulgent. "That, too. But I told you, I'm not in this just for the sex."

"Neither am I." Another thought rolled through his head. "This counts as sex, yes?" He thought it did.

"Frotting? Blowjobs? Absolutely." Rob kissed him on the nose. "Mind if I leave you for five seconds to get cleaned up?"

Not a bad idea. "Bathroom's over there." He waved in the vaguely correct direction. "I should do that, too. Except I'm not sure I can move."

Rob rose from the bed. "I'll take that as a compliment." He headed toward the bathroom. "Linens?"

"Little closet inside." Brian closed his eyes. He'd had sex with a man—with Rob. No fall of rainbow glitter. No feeling that he was a new and changed man. Only the realization that he had finally stopped hiding.

A few moments later, Rob knelt on the bed. "I brought a flannel and towel."

Flannel? He sat up and examined the offered items. Oh, washcloth. "Thanks." He took both and wiped himself off.

"Hamper?"

He waved off in the other direction and his head swam. "Fuck."

He heard the basket open and close, then the bed rocked. "Are you all right?" Rob's face was lined with concern.

"Yeah." He settled back on the mattress. "Tired as all hell, though."

"Good," Rob said. "You need the rest." He yanked at the covers. "Under you go."

Brian groaned but did as told, then shivered with joy when Rob slid in next to him. "Staying?"

"Planned to, unless it's a problem."

He pulled Rob close. "Never. Never ever ever." Because he was entirely done in by this man, even now. A definite connection had formed between them. He'd run with that as he had with every person he'd dated. Maybe this time, everything would work. *Please, please.*

The last thing he was aware of was a brush of Rob's lips against his forehead, then sleep dragged him down into darkness.

In the soft glow from the lights outside, Rob stroked Brian's hair and shifted carefully to not crowd him too much in slumber, though given how fast Brian had fallen asleep and how dead to the world he now was, Rob probably could have held him all night and not disturbed him. Still, Brian needed the rest, especially considering how he'd looked at the shop and given the quips from the other barista.

He'd also apparently needed to get laid, given his enthusiasm and energy. For a guy who'd never sucked dick before, Brian had been damn good at giving head. At everything else, too. Rob stretched his back and grunted. He'd probably have some bruises tomorrow.

As he watched Brian sleep, Rob spied the wear and tear of stress. Too many late nights, worries, and caffeine. He didn't know Brian's business, but he did know what overworking could do—what it had done to him.

Even now, Rob wanted to kiss Brian, taste him. Go down on him. Listen to those gasps and moans—see that moment of abandonment, when everything would be right in the world for Brian.

At least Brian would sleep. He glanced at the alarm clock on the other side of the bed. No idea when Brian needed to be up, but he could make a guess. Rob slipped from the bed and padded into the living room to get his phone. As an afterthought, he shut the lights off. When he slipped back into bed, Brian stirred.

"Leaving?" Sadness there and exhaustion.

"Not leaving." He cupped Brian's cheek. "Setting an alarm."

"Oh." Brian rolled toward him and pressed his lips against Rob's side.

Shivers up and down his body. No chance of getting it up again, but he wanted to wrap himself around Brian. Steal him away from the world.

He shouldn't be so caught up this soon. And yet... he stroked Brian's head. "Bri, what time do you get up?"

"Six thirty." Hot words against skin.

That would work for him as well—enough time to get

home, showered, and changed. Rob stared at the phone, then set the alarm to six fifteen. He had a feeling they might need a bit more time getting out of bed in the morning.

Brian slid an arm around Rob's waist. "Put that thing down and come back here."

He chuckled and set the phone down. "Whatever you want, Bri." He rolled into that warm embrace.

Brian buried his face into the crook of Rob's neck. "Promise?"

"Yes." Not the most brilliant vow to make—but it felt correct. He kissed the top of Brian's head. "I want to make the world right for you."

A sigh. "You have."

Rob closed his eyes. *Good.*

Rob stared out his window. The days had slinked along like mopey teenagers, sullen, dark, and annoying. Friday was closer to Sunday—but not there yet. He absently rubbed below his watchband—then froze. A nervous habit—and a reminder of a past he'd as soon forget.

A faint scar sliced across his skin from where he'd punched out a glass pane in his parents' house to unlock the back door. But he'd been far too late to save his mother. In the end, the paramedics had told him it was an accident and had dragged him to the hospital to stitch up the gash.

His mother had been covered with a sheet. No care in the world would bring her back. He couldn't save her. Not then. Not ever.

It had been far from an accident—they all knew that—but in the end, that's what everyone said. Accidental overdose.

When a meeting reminder popped up, he shifted in his chair and clicked the dialog box closed.

An uncomfortable thought chased through his mind. Was he trying to *save* Brian? He rubbed his forehead. Maybe.

Perhaps he should dial this back to a fling, a casual thing, not the serious relationship he craved—that Brian also wanted.

They'd woken to Rob's alarm on Thursday morning, completely tangled in each other. Brian had stared at Rob in wonder. "How'd you end up in my bed?"

"Shit, if you don't remember, I guess I'm a piss-poor lover."

A shit-eating grin from Brian. "Oh, I remember. And you're not that bad."

"Not that... ?" He'd pulled Brian in for a kiss and used those fifteen extra minutes to prove *just* how good a lover he was. Brian had come hard, gasping, crying out his name, and spilling himself into Rob's mouth.

Not bad, indeed.

Somehow, they'd both made it to work on time and had managed not to spend the entire day texting back and forth like love-smitten kids.

Another meeting reminder popped up. Zero minutes. Rob rolled his eyes and picked up his headset.

Smitten. That—was close to the truth. And potentially dangerous. He had a history of falling in love too easily and giving too much. Last time, that hadn't just broken his heart —it had nearly sunk CirroBot.

He clicked on the meeting link and let the software connect him. Already chatter in the background.

He'd made damn sure no one could ever take his

company again. Now it was only his heart and soul he had to worry about.

Brian didn't *need* to be saved—he needed to be loved. That? Rob could do with ease.

"Hello all," he said into the mic, "Are we ready to get started?"

The sooner this meeting was completed, the closer to Sunday he'd be.

CHAPTER SEVEN

Odd for Brian not to be in the coffee shop first thing Sunday morning. Stranger still to be standing out in front of his apartment waiting for Rob.

Usually he did the picking up, but Rob had insisted on driving. "I need to get to know the area. It sticks better if I'm behind the wheel."

Couldn't fault that. Pretty much the way he'd learned how to get anywhere in the North or South Hills.

He didn't expect Rob to pull up in a sleek silver Mercedes, though. He hadn't gotten a good look at the car the other night. Holy shit. Brian eyed the car. Newer model, too. He hurried to the passenger door, camera bag in hand.

"This is sweet." Leather seats. A dash that looked like something out of NASA. He closed the door and belted himself in. "I'm guessing this thing has GPS, so we won't need my phone."

His cheeks were flush, but Rob laughed. "Indeed it does, though I know the way."

Rob continued up Darlington, but rather than turn right

onto Shady Avenue to head down to the Parkway, like Brian had expected, he made a left, then a right to put them on Forbes. "You *do* know the way."

Rob grinned. "Well, I cheated a bit. Looked it up on a map before I left. Besides, I wanted to scope out a Turkish restaurant Todd Douglas said was at the corner of Forbes and Braddock."

"Oh God, that place is heavenly. Fazil dragged us there a few times."

"Perhaps lunch, after?"

"Please." Brian peered up through the sunroof of the car—all the bells and whistles. The weather had cleared up. Still the cool of spring, but rather than the gray of the past few days, the blue sky now sported white fluffy clouds above the budding green of the trees in Frick Park. "Looks like you won't need the rain gear after all."

"I brought it just in case." Rob flashed a grin. "Insurance against downpours."

He chuckled at that. "Like carrying an umbrella."

"Exactly." Rob paused. "Which probably explains why I always get rained on. I hate hauling those loathsome things."

"And here I thought you just liked to be *wet*."

Rob snorted and gestured to the cup holders. "Drink your coffee, Bri."

"You got me coffee?" He lifted the cup and saw the Grounds N'at logo. "You brought me my *own shop's* coffee?"

Rob arched his damned red eyebrows. "Pretty sure you'd have words if I'd brought you some other shop's brew."

He would have. Brian sipped, tasted the drink, and leveled a stare at Rob. "This is an Americano."

A grin was his reply.

Bastard. He stifled the giggle that wanted to come out. "What if I'd wanted cream?"

"Mister I'll-drink-this-wee-little-cup-of-coffee-that-will-cause-my-heart-to-go-a-mile-a-minute? Cream? Not in your *coffee*, anyway." His smile was *wicked*.

Heat to Brian's face… and elsewhere. Rob had him there. He preferred his coffee black *and* desperately wanted a replay of Wednesday night. Badly. "So what about you?" He picked up Rob's coffee, and sure enough, it was a smooth, milky blend with a hint of cinnamon. "Suave." He smacked his lips. "And creamy." He put the cup back.

"Bloody hell, now I have your spit in my coffee!" Mock anger.

"You've had more than my spit in your mouth." He'd nearly lost his mind when Rob had sucked him off Thursday morning. The benefit to that, and probably the sleep, was that he'd been mellow and calm the entire day. Managed to field several calls about positions and set up some interviews, too.

Rob's laugh sank into Brian's balls. Yeah, he wanted a repeat. More too, but he didn't know how to ask. Didn't know what Rob liked or didn't or— He bit his lip and stared out the window, idly fingering the leather handle of the door.

Quite an expensive car. A bit much for an engineer's salary. Despite having shared a bed and more than saliva, he didn't know that much about Rob's job.

They turned onto Braddock Avenue and headed down the hill. Rob shifted in his seat, the leather crinkling. "What kind of camera do you have?"

Brian pulled his focus from the window. "It's a Nikon D750. Got it a couple years ago because my dad had a ton of old Nikon lenses and it seemed a shame to junk them. Plus it's fun to play with vintage lenses." He picked up his coffee and sipped.

Rob nodded and turned down another road that curved toward the Carrie Furnace site. "Mine's a D4S. But I was starting from scratch."

Brian nearly choked on his coffee. "With a D4S? That's some scratch!"

Color crept up Rob's neck and he looked—sheepish. "It seemed like the best model."

"It's a fantastic camera. And you use it well," Brian said. "It's just... high-end. Professional-grade." Beyond what he could afford. "It's not a Hasselblad, so at least you didn't have to take out a mortgage for it."

They pulled into the parking lot for the Carrie Furnace site and Rob shut off the car. "I looked at those," Rob said. "But that would be like building a Michelin-starred restaurant to make a grilled cheese sandwich."

Brian snorted. "There *is* such a thing as gourmet grilled cheese."

Rob flashed a smile. "I know, but I'm not a gourmet kind of guy." He got out of the car.

Yes he was. Rob was 100 percent *gourmet*. Brian grabbed his bag, climbed out, and joined Rob at the trunk.

Rob slung a small camera bag over his shoulder. "Figure I'll need only the camera and some lenses."

"Ditto."

Once the car was locked up, they found the meeting point for the tour and waited with the other folks who'd come for the mid-morning time-slot. Brian couldn't help watching Rob examine the old industrial site. There was the artist's gleam and the churning gears. Rob unzipped his bag and pulled out the camera.

Surprisingly, he didn't use the screen, but looked through the viewfinder, obviously lining up shots, though his finger was nowhere near the shutter button. When he dropped the camera. He was smiling so broadly even his ears lifted. "This is fantastic!"

That joy was infectious. Brian patted Rob between the shoulder blades. "Kid in a candy store."

A laugh. "Only this kid has more than a few gray hairs."

True. "But they look good on you." He leaned in and dropped his voice. "Like a dollop of cream."

"You and cream," Rob murmured. His hand brushed Brian's but he didn't take it. Which was probably wise, given some of the looks they were attracting.

Pittsburgh had its good moments and a share of bad ones. Some people were more liberal than others. Still, it rankled. Brian straightened and casually stared back at an obviously offended lady.

She blushed and looked away.

"That'll happen often," Rob said.

"Don't care." Fear had kept him from being himself for too long.

Rob's voice took on weight. "Just... be aware. And careful."

"I don't look any different than I did five weeks ago." He didn't feel any different—other than being heels over head for Rob.

Rob lifted an eyebrow. "You do when you're with me."

Probably because he was so fucking infatuated. He examined the gravel at his feet and smiled. "Maybe."

A click of a shutter. Brian looked up. Rob flicked a dial on his camera, then held it out.

There on the screen was the evidence that proved Rob's point. The man in the photo looked smitten. Tinged cheeks, lidded eyes, and a smile that radiated happiness and desire. "Oh." Shit. He *did* look different.

"You're fucking adorable." Rob pinched his cheek.

"Hey!" Brian batted Rob's hand away and laughed.

The lady from before didn't look pleased, but just about everyone else was grinning, so whatever.

A moment later, the tour guide arrived. She gave a fairly normal introduction spiel that included dos and don'ts. "I see some of you are here to take pictures." She nodded at Brian and Rob. "No climbing on structures to get a better shot, please."

Rob put his hand over his heart. "Promise."

Satisfied by that, she finished by talking about the history of the site before taking them in.

As they walked onto the grounds, Brian took out his own camera. As they moved through the site, he listened to the tour guide with one ear and took plenty of interesting shots—hard not to find good composition. Old rusting structures. Weeds. Hulking buildings. Brick stacks. Blue sky.

More and more, he was drawn to Rob. The way he moved. How he held his head. The parting of his lips when he studied a piece of equipment. The sunlight in his hair, the light in his eyes, his goddamn heart-melting smile.

Brian took a few candid shots, then one of Rob giving him that look—the one that asked *what the fuck are you doing?* Rob held up his own camera, and they shot each other.

Brian hadn't laughed like this in ages, not since the early days with Anita.

He had it so bad for Rob. Part of him wondered if that was because Rob was a *guy*. His first. He walked on to study a Bessemer converter, a giant hulking crucible of steel. He didn't *think* so. Even if he hadn't been attracted to Rob, he was an interesting guy, certainly someone he'd want as a friend.

Over by the foot of a building, Rob crouched down to take a shot of a spring flower blooming against the rust.

Jesus, the man had an eye.

Rob took the photo and looked up and the delight there flipped Brian's heart over. Goose bumps rose on his arms.

No, there was more there than infatuation. And that was perfectly okay.

Everything about the Carrie Furnace site was brilliant, down to the sun that warmed Rob's back to Brian's occasional dumbfounded expressions. Those melted Rob's heart. This *was* a mutual romantic thing, not the wants and desires of a man who only wanted to fuck.

Then again, Brian had already invited Rob home to meet his parents.

A tiny sting there and fear. What if they didn't accept Brian? What if they hated Rob? He shook his head and searched for another interesting shot. What-ifs were deadly and he'd had enough of them in his life.

The tour was interesting, too. Little tidbits of history about the site. Built in the early nineteen-hundreds, it was one of the few remaining examples of pre–World War II iron-making tech. In a strange way, it reminded Rob of the village he'd grown up in, though they'd been a coal town and had nothing like this. Steel and iron had been farther north. Still there was something about this place that felt like home.

He walked around one of the brick stacks, looking for

the right shot when he spied Brian doing the same thing. Brian looked *alive*, eyes clear and his smile free of worry. Rob raised his camera, adjusted the focus and shutter speed, and held his finger over the button.

"Hey Bri!"

Predictably, that smile leveled on him, all sun and charm.

Snap. Snap snap snap. He captured the surprise, the laugh and the joy, and finally, the raised middle finger.

When he was done, he joined Brian. "Serves you right for all the shots you took of me."

"I have no clue what you're talking about."

"Bollocks."

He was entirely unprepared for Brian stepping in and kissing him hard. Desire from his head to his toes. He tightened the grip on his camera so he didn't drop the damn thing.

When Brian broke the kiss, he whispered "You're so fucking hot, that's why."

"You too." Rob breathed out the words, his pants too tight for public. Brian had taken to queer like a fish to water. Then again, he'd been that way all his life, so it made sense.

He'd acted similarly, until he'd gotten bloodied up on the street a few times. But the world had changed in twenty years. He prayed Brian never had to nurse physical wounds.

They all had mental ones, either from being out or in. Or both.

A whistle from the tour guide had them opening up a space. Rob glanced at his watch. Time was up.

They migrated back to the parking lot. After a final speech from the tour guide, she released them to their cars.

"You can stow your bag in the boot, if you'd like." Better

than at his feet in the front seat. He thumbed the fob and the hatch opened.

"Boot," Brian said, mimicking the vowel sound. "You know, I can teach you proper Yinzer if ya'd like."

Rob set his bag down and slipped his camera inside. "I'm not sure I can learn at my decrepit old age."

"How old are you, anyway?"

They'd not discussed that yet, had they? "Forty."

Brian snorted. "Not that old." He placed his bag and camera in the boot, too.

"Older than you, I'd say." Brian looked to be in his early to mid-thirties, though Rob had spied some lighter hairs on Brian's head that were decidedly *not* blond.

"Not by much," Brian replied. "I'm thirty-eight."

That was heartening. "So not robbing the cradle after all."

Brian's smile was wide. "Believe me, I certainly felt my age by Thursday afternoon."

Ah, yes. After they had tussled that morning and Rob finally had gotten his mouth on just about every piece of Brian. He pulled open the driver's door and looked over the top of the car. "That's what you get for being a little snot in bed." He climbed into the car.

Brian slid into the passenger's seat. "Well, I guess I know how to get you to suck me off again." There was that infuriatingly lovely smirk.

"Possibly." He turned the engine over and pulled out of the lot. "We should have something besides each other for lunch."

Brian stretched out his legs. "You did say Turkish earlier."

Indeed he had. They headed back up Braddock into Regent Square and found a spot near the restaurant.

"Let's grab our cameras and see what we got," Brian said. "All your lovely art shots."

Embarrassment rose. "I was just dabbling." He waved the suggestion away. "You're the one with the art background."

"But that's half the fun—scrolling through the roll right after. Could never do that with film." Brian stood by the boot and stuck out his lip in a mock pout. "Pleeease?"

"Oh, get off," Rob said, but he unlocked the boot, though every nerve twisted. He didn't know if he was exhilarated or frightened. What if Brian hated the photos? Then again, he knew some of them were good. Curiosity overrode common sense and he grabbed his camera. "Fine."

Damned if Brian didn't bounce on his toes and blurt out something like "Heee!"

He closed the boot. God, this man. He wanted to press him up against the car and take that grinning mouth until they both were moaning. "Were you like this with your girlfriends?"

The smile on Brian's face faltered. "Sometimes." He swallowed. "Too much?"

"No." Rob palmed his cheek. "I don't know why they ever let you go." He headed toward the restaurant.

A second later Brian caught up. "You mean that?"

He did. Before they entered the restaurant, he faced Brian. "You're quite a catch."

"Except for being a workaholic," Brian said.

Rob shrugged and pulled open the door. "But I understand that." Could work with it. He'd *been* there.

The greeter welcomed them and sat them at a table for two near the window; wasn't quite warm enough to be out on the patio yet. They set the cameras aside and perused the menu.

"Everything's good," Brian said, his gaze skimming over the lists of dishes.

"That's exactly what Todd said."

In the end, they ordered some appetizers and two main dishes—one lamb, one chicken—that they solemnly vowed to share with each other.

Rob resisted the urge to giggle like a schoolboy as they placed hands on hearts and lowered their voices to pompous proportions.

He'd never had this much fun with anyone.

Riding on that high, he grabbed his camera and handed it to Brian. "Here."

"Not going to look first?" Honest surprise.

"No—just don't tell me if they're horrible."

Brian took the camera and flicked the screen on. "They're not going to be horrible."

Brian wasn't the one sitting with a lump in his throat. *It's just a hobby*. Except it wasn't. It was art and he wasn't supposed to indulge in such things.

The smile slid from Brian and was replaced by a look of concentration and appraisal. He flipped through several photos—Rob could tell from the flash of the screen and Brian's eyebrows knitting. After a few more, Brian's whole body relaxed "Now, see..." He turned the camera so the screen faced Rob. "This is stunning."

It was a photo of the main building, the sun catching on a few remaining slivers of glass, and pigeons rising above it. The colors and light blended about perfectly. If he hadn't known it was his own work, he'd have agreed wholeheartedly with Brian. He met Brian's gaze. "Maybe."

Brian raised an eyebrow. "Who has an art degree?"

Rob laughed. Bastard. "Okay."

Brian flipped through a few more, but then their food came, so he set the camera aside.

About halfway through devouring their appetizers, Brian shot him another of those pointed looks. "I told you, you have a good eye. The photos are fine."

There was a hardness to that, as if Brian needed to shove that thought into Rob's head—which he did. Rob set down his fork. "My parents didn't consider art worth my time when I was a child, even when they were assignments for school. Upper-crust stuff."

Brian's fork hovered in the air before he too set it down. "My parents went out of their way to make sure we had grounding in art. But you know, we went to church every Sunday. Singing, music, all those paintings and statues—art was tangled into everything in my life."

Ah, yes. "You're Catholic."

"Well, nominally."

"I was raised Presbyterian and taught the value of good, hard work." Since that was what put food on their table.

Brian sat back. "So how is it that *I'm* the workaholic and you're dragging *me* out to have fun?"

Rob laughed. "Well, I did get over a great amount of my youth." He sobered and his gaze fell on the cameras. "Just not all of it."

Brian didn't look away. "Rob, it's my professional opinion that you're an artist." He picked up his fork. "So suck it up."

How strange those were the words that brought mist to his eyes. He shook his head, but a smile pulled his lips wide. "Brian Keppler, if you keep saying things like that"—his breath hitched—"I'm going to fall in love with you."

Brian blinked a few times—then took his own shuddering breath. "I'll keep working on that, then."

"Please." More than anything, he wanted to teeter over that edge into the joy of love.

CHAPTER EIGHT

Brian's head spun. Rob fall for *him*? He was the one trying hard not to make this whole dating thing into more than it was.

They'd been in bed, what, once? Then again, he and Anita had pretty much fallen into bed on the first date. Granted, they also hadn't lasted.

But that relationship had been serious and sexy right from the get-go.

He stole a piece of lamb kebab off Rob's plate. "When we're done here, we can take a better look at all these photos." He wanted to check out his own and take a better look at Rob's.

Photography was something he could encourage, a way he could give back to Rob for the joy he'd brought into Brian's life. The shit with the shop ate at him hard. Rob was a bright spot in his otherwise too-tense life.

Rob glanced out the window. "Seems a waste to stay inside on such a nice day, though."

That was true. "You said you bike?"

Rob's smile could almost be called lustful. "I do." He

snagged a piece of Brian's chicken. "Any trails you want to try?"

"Try?" Brian leaned back in his chair. "I've biked them *all.*"

That got him an eyeroll. "Next thing you'll tell me is that you're part of Bike Pittsburgh."

He had to bite the inside of his cheek to keep from laughing. Must not have kept the expression off his face, though.

"Fucking hell," Rob muttered.

"Well, I'm a member, but a lot less active because of the shop." He leaned forward. "Biking's a passion."

Silence for a while. Rob seemed to be chewing on a lot more than just the lunch. He took a sip of water, then spoke. "You gave up quite a bit for your shop."

A stab of pain. "Yeah." Free time. Part of his sanity. Relationships. Money. "But it's been worth it."

Rob nodded, but without that sense of agreement. "So, where would you recommend for an afternoon ride?"

Brian mused. Rob lived in Bloomfield. He was also the one driving and they had camera equipment to deal with. "Why don't you drop me off at my apartment and I'll bike to your house. From there, we can take the Heritage Trail. If you want, we can bike to Homestead or for a challenge, we could ride over and catch the Montour Run Trail.

The light in Rob's smile sent little shivers down into Brian's core.

"I'm game." Rob looked down as his plate. "Though if we're going to bike, I should stop stuffing my gullet."

"Same here." Brian flagged down the waiter and asked for to-go containers and the check.

When those came, Rob lifted the folder with the bill before Brian could get his fingers near it. "Hey!"

"My treat." His voice was firm, as was the gaze he leveled at Brian.

He'd also paid for their entry into the Carrie Furnaces site. "I pick up dinner."

Rob's expression didn't waver.

"I'm serious."

A crack in that hard line, then it crumpled into a soft smile. "All right."

Victory. He didn't mind being wined and dined, but he didn't want Rob paying for everything, even if the card Rob pulled out was as gold as his watch.

He divided up the leftovers into two boxes, Rob signed the check, and they headed out to the car. A few minutes later, they were back in Squirrel Hill and in front of Brian's apartment.

"Are you one of those Lycra shorts-wearing bikers?" A good part of Brian hoped the answer was yes.

As if Rob could hear the thoughts rolling through Brian's head, he raised a brow. "I have been. I could be if you're wearing something similar."

He preferred the padded and wicking clothes for longer rides. "You just want to check out my ass."

"I've seen your arse. It's quite lovely, as is your front. But you know what they say about fair play, Bri."

"I'll be at your place in a half-hour or so. You can see how I'm dressed then." He unbelted and grabbed his food. "I guess I need your address."

"I guess you do." Rob grabbed his phone and typed something in. A moment later, Brian's buzzed in his back pocket. "There."

"Trunk?"

"Boot." Rob pressed a button and the latch popped. "I'll teach you proper English yet."

"Eh, we won the war." He grinned and closed the door on a huff from Rob. He grabbed his camera bag from the *trunk* before closing it.

After a wave, Rob drove off and Brian climbed the stairs to his apartment. It wasn't until after he'd stowed the leftovers and his camera gear that he took out his phone and read the address Rob had texted him.

He slapped a hand over his mouth to keep the horrified laughter in. Oh, this address he knew well. Same street as his parents' house, but a couple blocks away. Rob now owned the house of his former babysitter.

Welcome to the neighborhood, indeed.

Brian changed into his biking gear, grabbed his helmet, stuffed a change of clothes into his backpack, got his bike, and headed down to the street. He made sure his repair kit was in his bike bag, and headed out.

The direct route, the path he'd have taken driving, was more dangerous on a bike, so he took one with wider shoulders until he got to the bike lanes in Bloomfield, then turned onto Rob's street. He zoomed around a parklet and down the street until he came to the house that used to belong to Mrs. Kaminski, the babysitter for *all* of the Keppler kids.

The old Victorian house had changed. Rather than the drab beige and brown, the house was now dark blue, with teal and white accents. Decorative scrollwork had been added.

Shit, the place looked good. High-class. *Gourmet.* He walked the bike onto the porch. At least Rob had kept the stained-glass window transoms—though a clear pane had been added in front, probably to protect the older glass.

He rang the bell.

Moments later, Rob opened the door, his trim body encased in dark biking pants and a bright yellow and white top that clung to his chest like a second skin. Rob looked Brian up and down. "Nice."

That smile knocked Brian off his feet every time.

"Should I come in or—"

"Why don't we save the tour until after, if you don't mind? We'll have more time to... linger." Rob's gaze raked over Brian's body again.

Yeah, that was true. "Plan." He handed his backpack to Rob. "Mind stowing this for me?"

"Not at all." Rob vanished for a moment, then rolled his bike out the door before locking it behind him.

As they headed down the stairs to the street, Brian spoke. "I already know my way around this house."

Rob's eyebrows hit his hair. "You do?"

A tingle of delight in surprising Rob. "Yeah. My folks live on the other side of the parklet"—he gestured down the street—"and the lady who lived here was the aunt of my mom's best friend, so she'd babysit us sometimes." He climbed onto his bike.

"When you said you grew up in Bloomfield, I didn't think you meant *right here*." Rob pointed at his feet and mounted his bike.

"Well, more down there than here, though we roamed all over. Bloomfield isn't *that* big a neighborhood."

Rob looked back at the house. "I kind of gutted it." A hint of nervousness in his voice. "Hope I didn't kill any of your childhood memories." He strapped his helmet on.

"I doubt it. Was very seventies inside. Figured anyone who bought it would do that. Outside looks great."

"Thanks. Though it was more like very sixties."

He chuckled. "I'll give you that." Mrs. Kaminski had been stuck in an era. "Ready to go?"

"Lead on."

Brian pushed off and led Rob through Bloomfield and down into the city until they got to the bike and walking trail that ran along the river. Nice day to be out, which meant for a good portion of the ride they rode single file, and took care not to startle the walkers and runners. The trail widened up at Point State Park, and Rob moved next to him.

"I never get over that." He nodded at the fountain.

It was pretty impressive. A 150-foot plume of water shooting straight into the sky. Brian slowed. "Wanna stop for a bit?"

Rob nodded and they did. "Do they pull the water from the river?" He tipped his head back and shielded his eyes from the sun.

"Nope. There's a fourth river underneath."

"Really?" Rob lowered his hand. "You're not taking the piss are you?"

Ah, there was a true Britishism. Brian gave him his best cheesy smile. "Look it up sometime. There's a glacial aquifer."

From that dubious expression, he had no doubt Rob would. It was a wonder he didn't whip his phone out right there.

Rob shifted on his bike seat and took off his helmet. "I've read they do fireworks down here on your holiday." He fiddled with the straps.

"You mean the one where we celebrate kicking British ass?"

Rob's reply was dry, but came with a smile. "That would be the one."

"Yeah, they do. It's a madhouse, but worth seeing at least once." He looked out over the river. "We should come down for them." He spoke softly. A chance, to suggest an event like that months in the future.

The sound of Rob's bike moving closer. Fingers cupped his neck. "I'd like that."

He turned and met Rob's kiss. It was fairly chaste as kisses went—lingering, but not devouring. Still, it put more desire and heat into his body than any of the others had.

They were truly dating. Not a one-night stand. Not a trial thing—no. Long-term. Into the future.

In his bones, he felt that potential. A joining of histories. In the taste on his lips, the way Rob smiled at him, the lift of his red hair in the wind and the trace of freckles across Rob's nose.

He couldn't breathe for what that *meant*. This wasn't what he'd anticipated when Rob had walked into his shop, but here he was, falling and falling and falling.

"What's the matter?" Rob brushed a thumb over his cheek.

"Nothing. Just... heavy thoughts." So many.

Something in Rob's expression shifted. "Good ones?"

"Yeah." He breathed the word out.

Rob's smile warmed Brian's soul. He nodded at the trail. "Shall we keep going then?" Rob strapped his helmet back on.

"Yes." For as long as this path took them together. He wanted to ride forever.

They pushed off and continued down the trail.

CHAPTER NINE

Rob had biked often while he lived in Chicago, but less so during the CirroBot transition to Pittsburgh. Felt good to be back in the saddle on a long ride. Couldn't beat the company, either. More and more, he found himself relaxing around Brian, his presence a joy and a balm.

Though, knowing Brian had played in the house Rob owned was a bit unsettling. Hell, he was practically neighbors with Brian's *parents*.

At least he had renovated the place to within an inch of its life. Except for the layout and the lovely woodwork, nothing of its former "glory" remained. That would make taking Brian upstairs later much easier on his mind. Having sex with him in his former *babysitter's* house was odd, indeed.

He'd put his stamp on the place, though. Intended to put down roots. Even claimed belongings from storage. He had a *home* again.

Rob watched Brian's back as they biked along the Monongahela River and his heart did a little tumble in his chest that had nothing to do with exertion. Maybe someone to share it with, in time.

That exchange at the fountain, the look in Brian's eye—fear and wonder—they echoed in Rob's head. They'd been serious from the get-go, but there was a difference between dating because the person was fun, the sex was great and *hoping* something might come of it—and *realizing* something might come of it. Wanting that.

A voice in the back of his head reminded Rob he'd been serious about someone before. He didn't often think about that fucker anymore. They'd started out in similar circumstances—a chance meeting, an instant connection. Great sex, some common interests, but in the end, Greg had been after one thing—and Brian didn't want that from Rob.

What Brian wanted from Rob *was* Rob. Perfect. Almost too perfect.

Brian sat up on his bike and glanced back, teeth flashing as he spoke. "Gonna take the bridge."

Rob pulled up in tandem, since there wasn't anyone else on this part of the trail. "The Hot Metal Bridge?" This part of the trail he knew fairly well. He'd used the Hot Metal to go to the South Side Works and into the South Side proper often enough.

A nod. "Figured we could head to the Waterfront and keep going or turn around, depending on how we feel."

He'd gone to the Waterfront once or twice to see a movie. Big shopping complex. "Sounds reasonable. Especially since we don't have to fight that hellish traffic on the roads."

Brian smiled. "Thank God for bike trails."

They returned to single file when they came up to some runners and headed over the incredibly sturdy bridge. The trail opened up again, and he scooted up next to Brian. "What's the story behind that bridge anyway?"

"Oh, it carried hot metal."

That made no sense. "What?"

Brian slowed to a stop. When Rob settled next to him, Brian waved toward the South Side Works on one side of the river and an office park on the other. "This was all part of the J&L Steel Mill. They literally had cars on tracks that hauled hot steel from one side of the river to the other."

Rob stared at the bridge. "You're shitting me."

"Nope. When we get back, I can show you photos on the Internet."

He put a hand on his hip and tried to picture that. It explained why the bridge was so massively over-constructed on one side. "There's a lot of history here, for such a young place."

He grinned. "You probably have dinnerware older than this country."

Rob huffed a laugh. "No." The humor fled. "Growing up, all our industrial history was laced with pain when the mines closed." Much like his past in England. He fiddled with his brake lines, pushing them back and forth. "There's still quite a lot of pride here for that past." He gazed at the office buildings. "And so much for the present and future."

Brian studied him. "Losing the mills was awful for the city, but a bunch of good heads got together and laid the seed for what Pittsburgh is today." He shifted his bike around. "I almost left. I'm glad I stayed."

"I wouldn't have met you."

Brian furrowed his brows. "Probably not." He clasped Rob on the shoulder, leaned over, and kissed him—just a quick touch of lips. "But I'm here. You're here." The next kiss was longer and deeper.

Brian could *kiss*. Passionately, sweetly, as demanding as fuck. All three at once. Every time those lips met his, Rob's world tilted.

Brian broke away. "Shall we keep going?"

"The ride? Or... ?"

Brian's eyes danced and he took Rob's soul with another touch of his lips. "The ride," he said. "At least for now."

That would be a bit more interesting, given how hard he'd become. "Then let's go."

At least he wasn't the only one sporting a bulge. Brian pushed off and began pedaling. Rob followed. He didn't need to, the trail being what it was, but he enjoyed not having to lead for a change. Too much of that in his daily life.

Besides, couldn't beat the view of Brian's back and arse.

They rode down a long stretch of trail and past a waterpark before they reached the Waterfront complex.

And *complex* it was. Buildings and cars and bits of old industrial equipment. He recognized pieces from their tour of the Carrie Furnace site. "How much of this area were mills?"

Brian sat back on his bike, coasting along. "Pretty much all of it. If it was flat, it was a mill or rail lines or both. Kind of amazing to look at old photos. So much has changed, but some things haven't at all."

That described Rob's life to a *T*. But Brian was changing that life, with every minute and hour, and smile.

Rob's cheeks hurt from grinning. He put his head down and followed Brian.

Brian led Rob down the trail until they reached a break that led into the shopping area. There, they slowed, dismounted and walked their bikes into the little village-like part. The tidy and faux environment of The Waterfront was at odds with the rest of Homestead. Brian had never quite gotten used to it.

"Oh look," Rob deadpanned. "A Starbucks."

Brian raised an eyebrow. "Don't even think it."

Rob grinned back. "Oh, come on. Don't you ever go in and order for the hell of it?"

"Do you have any idea what would happen if I were caught by one of my customers?" He'd never ever hear the end of it. Bad enough someone once saw him drinking coffee at Eat n' Park, even if it *was* with a slice of pie.

"Hmm." Rob eyed the shop. "A chewing-out?"

"Yup." He led them around to the back of the shop. In a tiny garden, benches circled a concrete water fountain. "I mean, hats off to them for making fancy coffees common. Wouldn't have my shop if they hadn't turned the whole country into junkies, but..."

"Not going to sleep with the competition, as it were?"

Brian laughed and took Rob's hand. "Exactly. I'd much rather sleep with you." Those cheeks. That smile. His head whirled.

Rob laced his fingers with Brian's. "You're lovely, you know."

"My former girlfriends would disagree." Well, maybe not. But they'd all called him a thoughtless asshole at some point, which wasn't entirely incorrect.

They parked their bikes next to one of the benches. "You've mentioned them before," Rob said. "To be honest, I'm not sure why you haven't been snatched up by some woman. Or man."

"You mean married?"

Rob nodded.

Brian sighed, a knot forming in his gut. He sat. "Mostly, the shop. Sometimes we realized we weren't compatible and broke it off early, but the ends of my long-term relationships come back to the shop." He pulled out his water bottle from its holder and sipped. "Married to Grounds N'at." That's what Anita had said.

Rob lowered himself next to Brian. "Ever get close?"

A flash of pain and he flinched. "Yeah. Anita. She was —" He let out a breath. "Smart. Talented. Sexy." The pain lingered, along with the loss. They'd had something.

Rob squeezed his thigh and it was a comfort. "What happened?"

He chewed on that question, turning events over in his mind. The good times, the fights. The way he dismissed her when he was too busy. He'd never put all the thoughts about their breakup together before. "I let her go." He couldn't quite keep the sadness out of his voice.

Another squeeze from Rob. His expression was open and sympathetic.

He continued. "Justin had moved upstairs to Sam's and the shop had this huge hole in the schedule and I—" He sat back, choking on the rest of the words. He'd been upset then. Worried. Sleepless and working all hours. No time for Anita at all. The shop was more important—which said something about him. "We started fighting about the time I spent at Grounds N'at. My hours. Everything."

Grounds N'at still hadn't recovered from Justin leaving —the chaos in the shop spoke to that, as did his hours. People quitting. *Shit.* "Anita has her own career—she's a patent lawyer. It's nine-to-five. Orderly." Like Rob's.

The horror of *that* sank into his flesh like teeth. He didn't want to lose Rob. What if he did? *Shit shit shit.*

Rob wore his concern intently, leaning forward, his lips parted, brows knitted together. "You loved her."

"Yeah." He had, but not enough. "She's engaged now."

Rob's shoulder's dropped and sadness pushed the curve of his mouth down. "Must have hurt to find out."

"Yes and no. I'm happy for her. She's a damn fine person and deserves joy." In the end, he'd made his choice. "The shop eats a lot of my time—as you've seen. That's not the kind of partner she wanted for the long run. I can't blame her for that."

Part of him had wanted to be that man for Anita—but he couldn't let Grounds N'at go and that's what it would have taken. The shop was his *life*. He'd put everything he had into it.

Rob took his hand. "You deserve joy, too, you know."

Such a simple statement, spoken in that soft, sweet voice. It hit Brian like a gunshot through his gut and he blinked a few times against the sting. When was the last time he'd been *happy*?

Right now. In the moments he'd shared with Rob, joy infused him.

When he looked over, Rob's smile was tinged with sadness. "You work so hard, do so much. You need to remember yourself sometimes, even when you're the one running the show."

The words were like water quenching his parched soul. "Will you help?" He wanted the delight Rob brought. Craved it. He could merely sit next to Rob, and he'd have everything he needed.

"Any way I can." Rob tightened his grip on Brian's hand.

"Things are rough now." He spoke around the lump in his throat.

Rob's chuckle was low. "Then I'll make sure to drag you away whenever I can."

Perfect. "I can be stubborn and pigheaded."

"No." Rob mimicked surprise. "You? Never!"

Laughter bubbled up and he let it out. He smoothed a thumb over Rob's knuckles. "What about you? You said you were a workaholic, too."

"I am." Rob stretched out his legs. "And my job *is* demanding, but I've had to let go of my iron grip here and there." He chuckled. "Right now, I'm trying to take my own advice." He nodded at their bikes. "You can help me, as well."

That might keep them both sane. "Now that you've heard my tale of woe—why the hell are you single?"

Rob snorted. "Similar reasons. Often worked long hours. Then I was moving from one town to another." His expression turned inward and distant. "After the debacle of my last relationship, I decided to take some time off from dating. Or fucking. Or whatever the hell we were doing." Bitter, bitter words.

"I sense a story there." Tension reigned in Rob, from the cords of muscles in his arms to the way his knee bounced. Brian stroked his hand.

"Not really." Rob shifted on the bench. "He was young and hot and great in bed, but not interested in me outside of it, which made sense considering my age."

"You're not old." There was a bit of silver in the red at Rob's temples, but he'd seen Rob naked. Prime of his life.

A sly smile and a dark chuckle. "To him I was and he was correct to think so." He shook his head. "I was a right idiot with that one."

There was more, given the way Rob pushed his sports watch around his wrist and stared at the bubbling fountain.

Brian knew better than to push. He'd learned that lesson from his siblings, from Anita, and from himself. More would come in time.

"There's something I should tell you." Rob met his gaze and there was trepidation in his eyes. "I'm not an engineer at CirroBot."

Wait, what? Brian blew out a breath. "You don't work there?" Why lie about *that*?

"No—I do. But I'm not an engineer. Not anymore."

He couldn't quite wrap his head around what Rob was trying to say. "Not... anymore?"

"I used to be. Our first products? I designed them. Built the prototypes, all that, but—" He licked his lips and exhaled. "Bri, I founded CirroBot. It's mine. I'm the CEO."

"You founded CirroBot?" Suddenly, all those hints pointing to Rob being well-off slotted into place. "Oh! I guess that makes sense."

That beautiful little furrow formed above his nose. "*What* makes sense?"

"You bought, gutted, and renovated a house. You own a Mercedes, a Rolex, and an expensive camera." He shrugged. "That takes money."

"It does. *Especially* that renovation. The stories I could tell there..." Rob leaned back against the bench. "But money is the other reason my last—whatever the hell it was—didn't work."

A younger man dating an older, wealthy guy. "He wanted your money."

Rob's smile was thin. "He demanded my money, or he'd let everyone know I was banging a nineteen-year-old."

Nineteen? Holy shit. "Wow, you weren't kidding about *young*." Half the kids he interviewed weren't much older.

Rob's cheeks reddened and he pulled away from Brian. "Yeah, I know what it looks like. I'd claim a midlife crisis, but that wasn't it at all. He looked a hell of a lot older and I thought—" He shook his head. "Well, doesn't matter what I thought."

Brian reclaimed Rob's hand. "It does, though. What you thought matters."

A bitter laugh. "I *liked* him. He was an amateur standup comedian and getting a degree in literary studies. Saw his act and he was fabulous, so I hung around to talk to him afterward and we hit it off really well." He paused. "One thing led to another pretty damn fast and we were seeing each other regularly. After a couple dates, I thought there was something other than a good fuck there."

"He didn't feel the same way?"

"Well, he was interested in more than sex, but it wasn't *me*. I was—as he put it—a cock to ride for a meal ticket. Nothing more."

Beneath Rob's dismissive huff and the thousand-yard stare, there was a layer of pain that took Brian's breath away. "That's... horrible!" To be used like that.

Rob's expression cracked and a bit of that hurt leaked out in the downward pull of his mouth. "He made good on his threat. Told everyone he could find in my social circle that I'd been fucking him." Rob swallowed. "People knew I was gay, which closed doors with some folks—business is a *strange* field when you rise to the top—but I didn't much care." He pulled his hand from Brian's grasp and ran both of them through his hair. "However, a gay man at my age sleeping with someone barely legal isn't looked nearly as kindly upon as a straight man doing the same thing."

"So a businessman banging a woman still in college—"

"Gets a slap on the back and an 'atta boy!' But I got *children* pulled away from me at parties. As if a nineteen-year-old with a goatee and tattoos looks anything like a child." A bite to those words. "I'm not a fucking monster."

"I'm guessing no one said anything outright."

"Oh hell, no. Just murmuring, whispers, and disapproving looks." Rob thumped back against the bench. "It took a woman to point out the hypocrisy of the whole thing when one of the other men in our little business circle had an affair with a woman nearly the same age as his nineteen-year-old daughter. You should have seen the handshakes and winks he got, right up until his wife found out. She ripped everyone a new hole at a Christmas party. Well, except for me."

Rob pulled out his water bottle and took a long drink. "She pointed out that I had the decency not to be married when I started fucking a college coed." He spat the words out and took another draw of water.

So, not a good ending at all. "Is that why you moved the company to Pittsburgh?" A fresh start and less aggravation.

"God, no. The pool of talent is why we moved here. The stuff they're doing in the Robotics Institute at Carnegie Mellon. The hospitals. The other schools in the area. Plus, a reasonable cost of living. Made economic sense."

"And you're not the only gay CEO in town."

A laugh. "True. There's a few of us queer folk running around, not just your friend Sam."

Brian took Rob's hand again and entwined his fingers. "So *that's* why you were adamant you wanted more than just a one-night stand."

Rob's featured softened. "Yeah. I don't particularly want to be just a cock again."

"You're not." Brian looked down at his feet for a moment when heat touched his cheeks. "What we've done has been fantastic, but you're so much more than that." He waved at the bikes to punctuate his point. "Your photographs are stunning. And... everything else you do."

"You—" Rob reached over and stroked his cheek with the back of his hand. "Haven't even discovered everything else yet."

No, he hadn't. "But I will."

Rob answered with a grin and a quick kiss.

"I'm also not in it for the money." He'd stand on his own two feet.

That earned him a longer, deeper kiss that sent his pulse as high as biking uphill did.

"Oh, I figured that out pretty fast," Rob said. "You're serious about Grounds N'at and hard work. You treat people fairly. None of the signs of someone looking for a sugar daddy."

Brian couldn't conceive of that. He needed to be working. Even when his focus had been art, he'd had a million projects going at once, plus teaching drawing as a volunteer for a youth program. "I didn't even like my folks paying for things when I was in college."

"They still insisted?"

He laughed and nodded. "Still do. I keep telling them to spend my inheritance. We all do."

Rob rubbed his wrist, the happiness leaking away. "Sounds so different from what I grew up with."

"What did you grow up with?"

"I—" Rob's whole body stiffened and he exhaled. "I'm not sure I'm ready to talk about that yet."

An honest answer. It pained Brian that Rob wasn't, but

at the same time he was grateful for the truth. "It's all right. I won't ask again."

Rob caught his hand and gave it a squeeze. "No, *do* ask again. I want to share it with someone. Just not right now."

Well, sitting by a fountain behind a Starbucks in bike shorts and tight colorful tops probably *wasn't* the best time for deep conversations. From Rob's pained look, the answer wasn't good. "Should we hit the trail again?"

Rob nodded and glanced at his watch. "We could go a little longer, then head back. I made a reservation at the Church Brew Works for seven."

Sounded ideal. "Then let's go."

CHAPTER TEN

DROPLETS OF WATER FELL FROM ROB'S HAIR ONTO HIS neck. He and Brian climbed back up into Bloomfield, and by the time they reached Rob's house, they were hot, sweaty, and tired.

The whole ride had been glorious. The conversations and watching Brian's lovely form. Those powerful legs and broad back. He wanted a taste of Brian so badly he was half hard most of the ride home.

They reached his house and dismounted. Brian followed him onto the porch. "Leave the bike out here, or..."

"Best to bring it inside. Never had that much problem in this neighborhood, but out of sight, out of temptation."

A nod. "My folks insisted we put things away for the same reason."

He had Brian lean his bike against the wall by the front door, next to his. Later, he'd put his back in the garage.

A glance at his watch told him the time. "We have more than two hours until we need to leave for the pub."

A cocky-ass smile. "Oh good." Brian stalked forward, his bulge quite clear in his shorts.

Oh, he'd caught a live one when he'd picked up Brian. He'd known that, but nothing cemented it more than the way Brian pulled Rob forward—no holds barred—and took his mouth. Rob fought with Brian for dominance, lips and teeth nipping, tongues tangling, but lost when Brian's very clever fingers stroked Rob's very hard cock through his bike shorts. Even with the extra padding, it was torture.

Damn, the man could kiss when he wanted to. Wholly, passionately, in ways that melted Rob's bones and tightened his balls. Took his breath and made him pray that this time a relationship would work.

Brian was so much more than someone to fuck—everything about this day had proven that. At the moment, though, he didn't mind Brian's hands on him. At all.

Rob broke the kiss, but that didn't stop Brian. He shifted his mouth to Rob's neck and grabbed Rob's arse, pulling them together. Cock against cock, with only fabric separating them.

"Can't get enough of you," Brian murmured against his skin.

"Same." Rob tangled his hands into Brian's hair.

He wanted sweet moments. The laughter and the enjoyment of sharing each other's days. But these? The hot and heavy ones? He craved those right now. "We should move this into another room."

Brian opened space between them. "I'd say show me the way, but I know the layout of this house, unless you moved the master bedroom."

Rob chuckled. "No. I did steal that tiny room next to the master bath, though." He slid his hands to Brian's shoulders and stole a quick kiss. "Come up and I'll show you what I've done."

Brian's fiery desire was there, especially in the way he

slid his hand over Rob's arse again—someone had a fixation —but he nodded. "Expand the bathroom?"

"Mmm-hmm. Added a closet, as well." Room for his suits, plus a few playthings and his porn collection—that needed to be kept from prying eyes when he hosted the required dinner parties. He grabbed Brian's wandering hand and pulled him toward the stairs.

When they reached the top, Brian stared at the hardwood floor. "Did you put down wood? This was carpet."

"No. All of this was under that hideous olive thing." He'd also had the gold and green wallpaper stripped from the hall and had it repainted a tasteful, if slightly on-the-nose lavender.

Brian's ardor had abated. He walked like a cat into the master bedroom, all tiptoes and careful movements. "Well, shit. You've done a lot."

Rob wrapped his arms around Brian and kissed the nape of his neck. "Mostly I paid people. But yes. I pretty much redid the whole house." Especially the bedroom. There'd been carpet here, too. Tan shag that should have been ripped out in the '80s. The previous owner may have been lovely, but she hadn't had very good taste. There'd been wallpaper. Golden flowers. And she'd painted over the dark wood moldings.

A travesty. He'd paid quite a bit to have that undone.

"It's like a whole new house." Brian headed for the bath.

"Or a proper old one." He kept a hand on Brian's back as they moved, letting it slide down to brush against Brian's arse. After all, that was only fair.

As if he'd sensed Rob's thought, Brian spun and kissed him. Rob's back hit the wall and Brian's mouth was on his again.

God, that body. The tight biking gear seemed to accentuate Brian's powerful arms and shoulders and his trim frame. Rob slid his hands down Brian's back.

The bulge that contained his thick cock ground against Rob's dick. "Maybe the bathroom can wait." Brian scraped teeth over Rob's jaw.

"Slate shower built for two." He tilted his head to give Brian more access to his neck while curling his fingers tight into Brian's locks.

"So what you're saying..." Brian found the edge of Rob's shirt and yanked it up. "...is we should get naked and wet?"

Over his head went his shirt and landed somewhere near the bed. "Get clean, then dirty."

Brian lips hovered near his. "I like how you think." His mouth closed on Rob's as Brian slid his hands up Rob's chest and teased his nipples.

Legs turned to jelly, but it didn't matter since he was pressed against the wall by Brian's unrelentingly hard body. He moaned into Brian's mouth.

Everything was bright and sharp. The contrast between the dark wood and light walls, the tang of Brian's flesh, the blond of his hair framing his brown eyes. The room smelled of their sweat. "This isn't the bathroom," he whispered between kisses.

"You're not naked yet." Brian stepped back, his fingers tucking into Rob's waistband.

"Neither are you."

Brian didn't answer. He yanked Rob forward and into his arms. Next thing he knew, he was being carried into the bathroom. Quite a feat, given he had a few inches on Brian.

It took his breath away. Little sparks went off at the back of his head and an ache in his heart had taken up residency. He tried to etch their laughter, their smiles, and kisses into his memory as Brian spun him around and around.

These were moments he wanted always. Better than photographs, more powerful than *anything*.

Brian set him down on the tile floor of the bathroom. "This *is* nice."

He'd kept the old claw-foot tub to soak in, but it wasn't practical for everyday use. The shower, however, was—and more. Large and slate, it had a rainfall showerhead and side jets.

While Brian eyed it appreciatively, Rob moved behind him and grasped the bottom of Brian's shirt and returned the favor. That piece of clothing landed somewhere outside the bathroom. He had Brian's biking shorts down to his knees a moment later.

Lovely, hard cock. He reached around and stroked Brian's shaft.

Brian caught himself on the glass wall of the shower. "Unfair."

"Completely fair." He kissed Brian's back and stared into his faint reflection in the glass. Someday, he'd fuck Brian like this, hands planted against the shower wall, legs spread wide. Not today, though. "If you take off the rest of your clothes, maybe we can get in and have fun."

Brian's hips rocked in time to Rob's strokes. "Having fun right here." He looked over his shoulder. "Lose the shorts and we'll talk."

Cocky bastard. Rob slipped a finger between those round, tight cheeks, and let it brush Brian's hole—then stepped back to pull off the rest of his clothes.

Brian's whole body shook and he turned, eyes a bit wider.

That's right, Bri. This is a bit different, isn't it? Rob stroked himself. "Not into arse play?"

Brian's gaze focused on Rob's cock. He licked his lips. "I've never—bottomed. If that's what you're asking."

Not unexpected. "But you've topped?"

"Well—I've been dating women, after all."

"Some straight guys like to be pegged. Or fingered, I'm told." He shrugged "I'm not expecting you to bottom. I told you—whatever you're comfortable with. I was just curious."

Brian relaxed, though Rob knew that look—the curiosity—the interest. Brian's gaze flicked up to meet Rob's. "Right now, what I want is you in that shower of yours."

Rob closed the distance between them, and pulled Brian into a kiss. He teased those lips open and bit the lower one—gently. Little gasps so close to moans from Brian. He let the lip slip from his teeth. "What I want is your cock in my hand inside my lovely shower. But *someone's* still not completely undressed." Rob teased Brian's dick and balls long enough for Brian to bite his own lip—then let him go.

He walked into the shower and turned on the water.

There was the sound of shoes hitting tile. Rob turned after setting the water temperature and got a very nice view of Brian's arse.

A moment later, Brian joined him in the shower. "We ought to make some attempt at getting clean." He walked under the showerhead and water sluiced over his shoulders and down his back. "Biking is sweaty work."

It had been, even though the trails had been flat for the most part. Still, miles of riding.

Rob grabbed the body wash and poured some onto his palm. "There's fun to be had in getting clean." He beckoned Brian out of the stream and ran his hands over Brian's shoulders and down his abs. Suds and rock-hard quivering flesh. Brian's breath hitched as Rob worked lower. Down his legs, up over his arse and back. He ended by washing Brian's balls and dick. Good excuse to fondle and stroke until Brian yanked him into a kiss that burned Rob to his toes.

"My turn." His voice was as rough as his kiss.

True to Brian's words, he grabbed the body wash and worked over Rob's body, though he started at the back and massaged Rob's arse long enough to turn Rob's legs to jelly. God, he loved being touched there. Didn't mind being fucked, either.

Brian might not be into anal, but he certainly knew his way around that part of the body. Rob moaned into every stroke, grope, and even the slick finger Brian ran over his hole. If Rob had to guess, Brian was a bona fide ass-man. Did that hold true for Brian's taste in women as well?

After pressing a kiss to Rob's rinsed globes, Brian worked down each leg, then back up, paying close attention to Rob's upper thighs. When Brian brushed his taint, lightning shot through his veins and he groaned.

"I see what you mean about this being fun." All laughter there.

"Cocky sonofabitch," Rob muttered.

Brian rose. "Am I?" He pooled more wash into his hands, and slid them over Rob's shoulders.

"Yeah." Rob fought with the desire to pull Brian forward, washing be damned—but then Brian closed his finger around Rob's nipples and he lost the ability to think for the lights sparking in his vision and the heat rushing through his nerves.

Rob's whimper wasn't absorbed by the sound of the water. Neither was Brian's deep chuckle. Hands slid over

Rob's abs then wrapped around his dick. Slow strokes. Brian rolled his balls and Rob gasped and thrust into Brian's hand.

"Think we're clean enough?" Words whispered into Rob's ear.

"Fuck, yes." He grabbed Brian's neck and arms and pulled him into a deep kiss. The water ran cooler now, but he didn't care—he was on fire for Brian.

Steamy, sexy Brian. He chuckled.

"What?"

"Hot and full of steam."

Brian rolled his eyes. "I still think I'm more interesting than a watered-down espresso."

"Ah, but the finest of coffees have all those"—he licked Brian's clavicle—"notes. Blueberry and florals and all that." He took another nibble. "And you taste so damn good."

Brian kissed Rob's shoulder. "Flattery will get you *everywhere.*"

Indeed. It had gotten him one hell of a blond in his arms.

Everything was wet and slick and wonderful. Rob chased water down Brian's neck and rolled those delightfully sensitive nipples between his fingers.

Brian's fingers scraped up Rob's back, leaving lines of fire and delight. His teeth brushed Rob's neck. "Fuck Rob, I really want to—" He pressed his forehead into Rob's shoulder and moaned.

Not one of pleasure, though. Frustration. They were both so hard.

He relented on the nipples and tipped Brian's head up so he could see his face. "Really want to what?"

Brian's expression was full-on nervous. More so than Rob had seen before.

Brian licked the water from his lips. "I want to fuck you. I mean—"

Ah. "So?"

"How do you even ask that?" Brian trembled ever so slightly. "Is it too presumptuous? I mean, I guess guys have to have a way to... ask. But... I know not every guy bottoms or even wants to and how do you..."

He was rambling and it was fucking adorable. Rob pressed a finger against his lips. "So, Mr. I-Top-Women, ever do anal with any of your girlfriends?"

Brian nodded, his eyes wide.

Bingo. Definitely a thing for asses, then. Rob skimmed his thumb along those lips and let his hand drop. "How did you ask them?"

The tension leaked out of Brian and he laughed. Water cascaded down his arms and torso. "Well, I ask if they'd ever done it, and if they liked it."

"And if they hadn't?"

"Ask her if she wanted to try."

"So." He took Brian's head in his hands and kissed him, deepening it until Brian opened to him and wrapped his hands around Rob. They thrust against each other, dicks sliding together. When Rob broke the kiss, he stroked Brian's cheek. "Yes, I've bottomed. And yes, I like it." Not as much as he enjoyed topping, but he'd take whatever Brian offered.

Brian swallowed. "I—uh—didn't bring anything."

He patted that lovely blushing cheek. "I'm a gay man, Bri. I have all the condoms and lube we need."

A shiver ran through that lovely body and Brian pulled Rob closer, massaging his arse. Rob's turn to shudder. He nipped at Brian's shoulder and Brian spoke hot in his ear. "Why the hell are we still in the bathroom?"

Good question. He reached around and turned off the water, but it was Brian who pulled him from the shower. They didn't even bother with towels—too busy running hands over flesh and mouths over lips. Brian's warm hand closed on Rob's cock and stroked him slowly and evenly until Rob couldn't breathe without moaning.

"I want to be inside you." Brian spoke against his neck.

Rob scraped his nails across Brian's thighs, and thrust into his hand. "Bedroom's behind you."

Brian found his mouth, and Rob's legs—his whole body —trembled. This was new, this needy, demanding side of Brian. The one who plunged his tongue into Rob and stroked and fondled him until he could barely stand. He spoke between Brian's ferocious kisses. "Need—to be—on the bed. Now."

Brian rumbled something that might have been a laugh, but was far too primal. He pulled Rob toward the door, then turned him to face the bedroom. "Then you better get on it." He punctuated the command with a slap to Rob's backside that made him flinch, gasp, and move forward, his balls tight and cock aching.

Fucking hell. This was going to be fun.

Blood pulsed in Brian's ears and he stroked his cock as he watched Rob swagger out of the bathroom, one cheek of that perfect freckled ass reddening from the smack Brian had given him.

God, he'd never wanted someone this badly. Wanted to bury himself in Rob, be one with him. He followed Rob, heart and head spinning. The man was a wicked drug. Couldn't get enough.

Rob opened his nightstand and pulled out a bottle and a box—condoms and lube—and tossed them on the bed. He turned, his smile delicious. "How do you want me?"

Every way he could possibly have him. "On your hands and knees." That had been the easiest way to start with his girlfriends, and there was a zing through his veins at the thought of Rob moaning face-first into the mattress.

Rob climbed onto the bed with ease, but then he'd done this before—Brian hadn't. Well he had, but... "Fuck." He snatched up the bottle and the box and joined Rob on the bed.

"For someone so desperate, you think too much," Rob said. He shimmied his hips.

God, the man was beautiful. Long limbs, powerful thighs, that amazing ass. Brian slapped the other cheek and Rob jerked forward. "Like that?" He smoothed his hand over flesh, soaking up the heat from Rob's skin.

Rob exhaled, his voice laced with need. "Would prefer a different kind of slapping, if you don't mind."

"Is this where I get to call you a cheeky bastard?" He sat up and drew his hands down the length of Rob's back. He pressed his cock against Rob's crack, delighting in the shiver that ran through Rob.

"Fucking colonials. All talk, no action."

He grasped Rob's hips and pulled him tighter. "Remember who won the war."

A grunt. "And you've been kissing our arses ever since. You should try it."

That would be something, but he wasn't sure he wanted to eat ass. "Maybe someday." He drew back and parted Rob's cheeks and there was his hole. Same. Different. He stroked Rob's taint to his balls.

Rob pitched forward and went down on one arm. "Damn it, Bri!"

Now that was better. Rob panting and squirming. His. He fondled Rob's sac for a bit before putting a condom on and grabbing the lube. He slicked his fingers and circled them all around the outside of Rob's entrance.

Rob muttered curses against his arm, his body trembling with every stroke. "Fucking tease."

"Yep." Girlfriends had told him that, too. He loved seeing them on edge. Wanted Rob there, begging and cursing. "Should have warned you."

Another laugh. "Oh, I knew *that* the day we met."

"Did you?" Brian breached Rob with his finger. Hot, tight heat. Feeling Rob clench around his digit only tightened his balls and hardened his cock.

"Uh—" A moan. "Yeah. Did."

He pushed in deeper. "You going to be able to take me?" He pulled out and pressed his finger in again.

Rob pushed back on his hands and laughed. "Just you wait." Brian heard the smile around those words.

"Don't think I can." He slid his finger out and lubed up his dick.

Rob's hip was warm and tense beneath his hand as he lined up and pressed forward. Rob opened to him and he slid into his tight heat. They both moaned—deep and long. That sight, his cock half buried in Rob, lit every nerve in Brian's body. He dug his fingers into Rob's hips, pulled back, and rocked forward, harder this time.

Rob went down on his other arm. "Fuck—"

He couldn't tell if that was pain or pleasure in Rob's voice. He backed out a bit. "Am I—? Are you—?"

Rob thrust back, taking Brian's dick nearly to the balls.

He could barely breathe for the pleasure that raced through him.

He must have moaned or gasped or something, given Rob's devilish chuckle.

Oh, was *that* how it was going to be? Brian braced himself, gripped Rob's slim body, pulled out, and slammed back into him hard. Then a second time.

Rob's fingers curled into the sheets. "God, yes!"

Good. So fucking good. He pounded into Rob, watching his cock vanish into that stretched hole, feeling every gasp and moan and wiggle Rob made.

He should have done this ages ago. Only if he *had*, he might not be here with Rob—and there wasn't anyone else he wanted, not by a long shot. No woman, no man.

Just the cursing British ginger taking every inch of his cock. His balls ached, but he fought against the need to spill. He wanted this to last.

Rob matched him move for move, moan for moan, his skin flushed red and covered with the sheen of sweat. Brian pulled Rob's hips to his and stopped moving. Only their combined shudders rocked them.

"Don't," Rob said, his voice hoarse and thick, "don't you dare stop."

Brian shifted and pressed in as deeply as he could, driving Rob's shoulders into the mattress. "I want you to feel all of me."

"Fuck, Bri—" It was almost a whimper. He squirmed. "Please, I need—you."

"Good." Brian reached around and found Rob's cock. He stroked it until it was rock-hard and Rob was babbling something unintelligible. Then he moved again, fucking Rob with long, slow strokes. But it was almost impossible to jack Rob off at the same time.

How *did* guys do that?

He gripped Rob again and thrust in deep. The sight of Rob's red hair and freckled back writhing in pleasure, the trace of his spine, the cleft leading to where Brian's cock slid deep inside Rob. It was almost too much to take in.

He wanted to taste Rob's sweat, kiss that sweet expanse of his back. He drove forward and pressed his lips against Rob's spine.

"Bri—" A breathy sound, musical and full and whispered reverently. "You feel so fucking good."

"Love this." Brian kissed Rob's heated skin again, shaking both their bodies with his thrusts. "Me in you."

A chuckle, then a moan.

Closer, he needed to be closer. Brian gathered Rob into his arms and pulled him up and against him, and fucked him hard and deep.

Rob grunted with each stroke, his breathing harsher and louder than before. He rolled his head back onto Brian's shoulder. "Oh fuck, don't stop!" Hands gripped Brian's ass, urging him on.

No qualms about giving Rob everything he had, hard and fast. He found Rob's tight nipples and fingered them. "Like that?" He sucked Rob's earlobe into his mouth then held it between his lips.

Whimpers and gasps were all that came from Rob. He turned his head, and the lobe slipped from Brian.

Eyes nearly all pupil and a wide-open mouth.

Didn't take Brian much to claim it for his own. His tongue and his cock plunging into Rob. Couldn't tell whose moans were louder, whose body shook and trembled more. The world narrowed down to the scent and the sound of Rob, their bodies moving together, their rhythm, the way they fit perfectly.

Heaven. Rob around him, whispering his name into his mouth. Rob's hands urging Brian on. Intoxicating. Lightning in his veins. He drove harder and deeper into Rob.

He was so close. Rob, too, judging by the tightness of his body. He stroked Rob's cock. A moment later, Rob's fingers closed around his, helping, encouraging.

"Please," Rob begged. "Please, please. Please. Nearly—"

They worked Rob's cock together. Brian's mind spun in circles, tighter and tighter, his balls aching with Rob's every gasp and shudder. Hot and perfect. He rammed into Rob and the mattress bounced and creaked, adding to the pounding.

Rob stiffened in Brian's arms, his whole body one tense cord and Brian could barely move inside him.

"Oh God, Bri..." Rob's free hand scraped against Brian's thigh, then he shattered, uttering a long, horse moan. His cock thickened, pulsing as ribbons of semen shot onto the comforter.

Holy fuck! Brian's heart rate shot through the roof. Seeing Rob come—feeling him come—*making* Rob come—Brian pressed his mouth to Rob's back and took Rob over and over until the heat and the light overtook him. He cried out and buried himself deep inside Rob and came. The sweeping roll of his orgasm seemed to go on and on. He kissed Rob's spine, clutched at his chest and wished for all the world they could stay in this moment forever.

Together. One.

Brian couldn't say how much time passed before his mind made sense of light and sound again.

Rob's breathing was still harsh. "Damn." The word was joyful and came with a laugh. "I envy your former girlfriends."

Brian's breath caught in something that was halfway between a croak and a cough. "I should—" He slid out of Rob.

A little moan of disappointment. Brian echoed it.

Rob turned and lowered himself to the bed, lying on his side, all ruddy and shining. Especially his wide smile.

Brian sat back on his heels. "I ruined your bedspread." Dark wet marks highlighted where Rob had come—and how much. He should lose the condom, but he wasn't sure he could stand. His head spun like a top.

Or was that his heart?

"Technically," Rob said, sounding a hell of a lot closer to normal than Brian felt, "I ruined my bedspread. You merely helped."

"Merely?" He stroked Rob's hip, enjoying the softness of the skin and the hardness of the muscle beneath. "If merely is what you think of *that*, I need to fuck you harder next time."

Rob shivered. "More than merely." His voice was soft. "But feel free, next time."

Rob really was a masterpiece. And inexplicably his. Brian patted that thigh.

Unfortunately, his dick was softening, and the condom threatened to add to the wet spots. Brian groaned and crawled to the end of the bed. "I'll be right back.

He found tissues in the bathroom, tossed the condom, and washed his hands. His reflection in the mirror startled him. Same post-sex look. Except he'd just fucked *Rob*—as if he'd had any idea of how to do that in the first place.

He shook his head at himself and flicked off the bathroom light. He joined Rob on the bed. "All kidding aside, that was fine?"

Rob rose, took Brian's face in his hands and kissed him

on the nose. "You're fucking adorable. You pound me hard enough to shake the foundations of my house, until I can't remember my name, and make me spurt across my bed, and you ask if it was *okay*?"

"Uh—" He squirmed. Okay, maybe he was overthinking things. "Anything I could do better?"

Rob stroked his cheeks, fingers oddly cool. "Honestly? Only way you could have improved that was if you'd stuck a cock ring on me to keep me from coming so fast and pounded me all night long."

Shit. The images that brought up. He licked his lips. "I — Wait. You have a cock ring?"

Rob didn't answer, just pulled him into a toe curling kiss. When they broke apart, Brian had to gulp to catch his breath and slow his heart. "One problem… I'd come too fast, too."

Rob's devilish dimples formed. "Oh, Bri. I have more than *one* cock ring."

He must have been making quite a face, because Rob's laughter was deep and long. Then he pulled Brian down onto the bed and kissed him. Again and again and again.

CHAPTER ELEVEN

While Rob ached slightly from being fucked, the pain was a pleasant appetizer to dinner. After another quick —and separate—round of showers, he drove Brian to Church Brew Works for dinner. Reasonable brewpub with excellent food located in a decommissioned Catholic Church, complete with the fermenters where the altar would have been.

"I love this place." Brian slid into the seat. "Though my parents still haven't been here."

This place was so close to his house. If they hadn't biked all over creation, he'd have suggested biking here. "Why ever not?"

"It's too sacrilegious for them. They came to Mass at this church sometimes." Brian looked around. "But I'm glad they saved the building. They've done preservation work, too. Maintaining the stained glass and all that."

"So I've read." When he'd first looked for houses, his real estate agent had taken him here and given him a small history lesson about the area. "I could see how eating and drinking in a place you used to pray might be uncomfortable. Especially if you're still practicing."

"Which they are." Brian closed his menu.

Before Rob could continue the conversation, the waiter came and took their beer and food orders.

The ache in Rob's arse when he shifted on the wooden chair only made his lips twitch. Brian certainly could fuck the way Rob liked it—hard and demanding. He didn't bottom often, but he'd repeat that in heartbeat with Brian. And yes, with a cock ring on, too. If he were to be on the receiving end, he preferred the pounding to last a while.

Brian's cheeks were tinged with red again. Rob extended his hand across the table, and after a moment's hesitation, Brian placed his own hand in Rob's grip. "Something the matter?"

Brian's blush deepened. "I still have to tell my folks I'm dating a guy."

Ah. An ache—like an old wound reacting to a coming storm—flared in Rob's chest. "You said it would be fine before... are you sure?"

"I think? But I don't know." Quiet words. "I mean, they've never reacted badly to anything LGBTQ. Didn't freak out when same-sex marriage became legal or anything like that. They've met Justin and Eli—knew I went to their wedding." He shrugged. "But—"

"You're their son."

"Yeah." Soft, nervous words.

Their beers came, thank goodness. This topic brought too many old memories close to the surface. Shouting. Tears. Slammed doors. He took a long sip of his beer.

Brian fingered his glass. "Every month we have a family dinner—my parents and brother and sister. It's next Sunday." He lifted his beer and drank.

"And you plan to tell them?"

Brian nodded. "I don't want to hide it. Don't want to hide *you*."

A different ache in his chest. Warmer. It stung in a way that brought moisture to his eyes. "I—thank you." He took a breath. "I know family is complicated. If you need to..."

"No." A single strong word. "Look—I hid this part of myself for so long. I'm *done*." This time it was Brian who reached out.

Rob slipped his hand into Brian's. "Why now? Why me?"

Brian ran a finger around the top of his glass. "Been asking myself that, too. Maybe because I'm thirty-eight and the world has changed and I don't give a fuck what anyone else thinks." He met Rob's gaze. "You walked into my shop and brought the freaking sun with you. I've been blinded since."

Now that was a line and a half. He couldn't help laughing. "Get off."

A squeeze of his hand. Brian's smile was as warm as it was serious. "I'm not joking."

His heart tumbled around in his chest at that. "Good." The word was too thick in his mouth, but it made Brian beam and blush again.

Like always, he'd fallen fast. Usually that meant he'd smack up against the ground at some point, but he intended to enjoy this particular fall for as long as it lasted.

He hoped the ground never showed up.

Their food came and they spent the rest of dinner stealing bits from each other's plates, laughing, and talking about where they wanted to bike next.

Rob set down his fork and pushed his empty plate away. "Someday I want to bike the Great Allegheny Passage."

"Just the Passage, or all the way to DC?" Brian finished his beer and set the empty glass down.

"At least to Cumberland, Maryland. I'd love to do the whole thing, too, but that's a long haul." He'd need at least a couple of days to make the trip to Maryland. "There are places catering to bikers along the way."

An absent nod from Brian. "There was an article in the paper awhile back from a reporter who did the ride to DC." Brian frowned. "I wish the shop were in a good enough place to do something like that."

Rob bit his tongue to keep from grilling Brian about work. The few times he had, Brian had shut those conversations down. It had been such a perfect day so far, no need to ruin it. "Maybe someday you can."

A wan smile. "Maybe." A peek of tongue from his pink lips. "I'd love to go with you."

Oh, the trouble they'd undoubtedly get in together. And the *nights*. He shifted again and wondered if Brian was the least bit interested in bottoming. He wouldn't mind sinking into that body sometime. He glanced at one of the saints in the stained-glass window and laughed.

"What?"

"I confess, I'm having impure thoughts."

That brought out Brian's big grin. "Me too."

"Well, let's go do something about that, shall we?" He caught the attention of their waiter and asked for the check.

A couple of minutes later, they were out the door and heading for his car. A few minutes after that, he pulled into his narrow driveway and around the back of the house. By the time they got into the living room, Rob's hands were tangled in Brian's hair and his mouth was on those devilish lips. He pushed Brian up against the wall and took his time claiming his mouth, his chin, and his neck.

Lovely little gasps and moans. Brian's hips rocked, his dick hard against Rob's thigh. "We should—"

He slid a hand over Brian's chest and fondled his nipple through his thin t-shirt. The rest of the sentence was lost in a breathy moan. He kissed Brian again and let his lips hover over Brian's. "We should what?"

Such wide eyes, so full of want and need. God, how he loved turning Brian on, then inside out. His queer-as-fuck barista, his Americano.

"Bed." Brian pressed his hand against Rob's bulge, sending waves of heat through his limbs. "Now."

He leaned in, thrusting against Brian. "Eager, aren't you?" He grazed his lips over the stubble on Brian's neck, then bit at the flesh there. "We have all night."

A soft moan. "Now who's the tease?"

Oh, sweet Brian. Rob took both of Brian's hands and stretched them up before pinning them against the wall. "Seeing you is a tease." He pressed close, cock to cock. "Your voice, your body, that mind." He sucked on Brian's lip.

The groans were deeper now. "Glad I'm more than a cock to you."

He was. "So much more." Their bodies meshed so well. "Though I adore every inch of your dick."

That got him a laugh. "You can have it again, any way you want. Mouth, hand, ass." Even though Brian's arms were still pressed above him, he leaned his head forward to catch Rob's lip. "Anything."

Having Brian buried in him had been quite the experience. Rob thrust hard against his trembling body. "Perhaps you're right about taking this to bed." He let Brian go and stepped back. "After you." He gestured to the stairs.

Brian licked his lips. "You just want to stare at my ass."

"There's a lot of things I want to do to your arse, but we'll start with staring."

Brian's eyes widened—but he headed for the stairs. Rob followed, and yes, it was a fine view, those cheeks in tight denim, the seam running down between the crack. Naked was even better. He cupped one cheek and let his fingers drift between Brian's legs.

Brian damn well nearly tripped. He grabbed the railing and stopped. "Shit, I can't think when you do that!"

Rob stopped one step below and kept fondling Brian's taint through the denim. "Can't help it when you wear such tight clothes."

"Oh, so it's the *clothes* that are the fault, hmm?" He looked over his shoulder, a grin showing his teeth. "Not your wandering hands or overactive libido?"

Rob slapped him playfully on the butt. "Up you go." Brian resumed climbing the steps. "Your libido is just as active." And his hands as wandering.

"My parents told me never to play on the stairs." They made it to the top, and Brian pulled Rob into a kiss, his hand working at the button of Rob's jeans.

Rob couldn't help but flinch. It had nothing to do with Brian and everything to do with his parents. There been very little fun to be had, on the stairs or otherwise. "You're lucky they cared." Hopefully, they would still care after the following Sunday.

A pause in Brian's movements. Brian cupped Rob's face with one hand. "Don't mean to hurt you."

"You aren't." He kissed Brian, then whispered against his lips. "Keep going."

A grin there, and Brian took Rob's mouth, parted his lips, and unzipped his jeans.

God, the wicked things Brian did to Rob's cock once

he'd gotten his hand down Rob's pants. He nearly forgot his own name when Brian slid to his knees and sucked down his cock right there at the top of the stairs.

Hot, eager mouth. A tongue that darted and teased. Those brown eyes looking up at him. Rob slid his hand over Brian's hair. "Such a good cocksucker."

Brian visibly trembled and moaned at that, and doubled his efforts.

"Like hearing that? Cocksucker?" He stroked a finger over Brian's forehead.

He pulled up, but kept jerking Rob off. "Yeah, I do." Soft words. "It's hot and reminds me of who I am."

"You're my bisexual barista who loves sucking dick as much as eating pussy."

Another visible shiver. "Yeah. I— Yeah." Brian's eyes were large and his face flushed. He swallowed. "I'm your lover."

Yes, he certainly was. Rob cupped his chin. Someone also seemed to like a bit of power games, which was *fine* with Rob. "Mmm, you are. And you fucking love my cock, right?"

Brian nodded.

"Then you better put your mouth back to work and show me how good you are." He tightened his grip.

And if that didn't encourage Brian. He closed that hot mouth around Rob's shaft and licked and sucked as if his life depended on getting Rob off. Rob threaded his hand through Brian's hair and rocked his hips. "Fuck, yes. Just like that."

Brian's deep moan vibrated through Rob. With each stroke, Rob sank a bit deeper into Brian's throat.

"That's right. Take it all." He doubted Brian would—deep throating took practice. Hell, his own gag reflex got to him on occasion. But he sure enjoyed Brian's attempts to swallow every inch. Seeing his cock slide in and out of Brian's mouth, watching Brian's eyes glisten at the corners when he looked up for approval—burned his blood and tightened his balls.

Except Brian was making his legs shake, which made standing tricky, especially with the stairs so close.

He pulled Brian off his dick and slipped his thumb between those pouting lips. "Bedroom. I want you naked and kneeling at the foot of my bed." He let Brian go.

Not even a word. Brian rose and headed into the room, pulling his shirt off as he went. By the time Rob followed, Brian's shoes were off and his pants were around his ankles. He stripped everything else, and knelt exactly as Rob had ordered, right at the foot of the bed. His whole chest was flush and his dick hard. Beautiful. Brian on his knees. For him.

More than anything, Rob wanted to pull Brian up, press him down onto the mattress, and fuck him until they both came. He knew Brian wasn't ready. He might never want that—which was fine. So many other options, after all.

He shed his own clothes and sat down on the bed. "Tell me what you want, Bri."

A swallow and a shiver. "I want you to come down my throat." His gaze met Rob's, and there was such determination there. "I want to be the best you've *ever* had."

Rob's chest tightened. He'd had some mind-blowing encounters in his life. Sex that made him soar and sore, but nothing had prepared him for the amount of emotion Brian wrung from him every time he opened his hot American mouth.

That had nothing to do with Brian's ability to swallow dick. He stroked his cheek. "You're pretty damn fine."

A self-depreciating chuckle. "Considering I don't know what I'm doing?"

He ran his thumb over Brian's lips, then pressed it between them. Soft and warm, Brian's mouth was a delight. "You know what you're doing." He fucked that mouth with his thumb until Brian squirmed on his knees. "You only need more practice."

He slipped his thumb from Brian's mouth and Brian chased after the digit.

"If you're so eager—" He sat forward and pressed the tip of his cock between Brian's open lips.

They both moaned. Brian's mouth felt so fucking *good.* Couldn't fault Brian's cock-sucking skills, not the way he bobbed, sucked, and licked until it was all Rob could do to grip the comforter and thrust in time. "Fucking hell, you're a natural."

A groan. Brian drew back. "You taste good." He licked the tip, delving his tongue into the slit, then mouthed down Rob's shaft to the base.

Yeah. Natural, indeed. Even exploring, Brian hit all of Rob's spots. Heat pooled in his spine and his balls tightened. It took all Rob's self-control not to pull Brian's head up and feed his cock back into his mouth.

Tentatively, gently, Brian nuzzled Rob's balls, then kissed his sac.

Rob held his breath as lightning shot through his veins, tingling down his arms to his fingers. He stroked Brian's hair. "Suck my balls."

A flash of those brown eyes, then Brian took in a nut.

Rob shuddered and gasped, both from the warmth and the pressure. He leaned back as Brian shifted from one sac to the other, rolling them in that fucking amazing mouth of his.

Too much. Too hot. Rob lifted Brian's head by his chin, the skin of his sac cooling in the air of the room. Brian's lips were curved into a cocky-ass smile, and his hand moved between his legs. "Liked that?"

That was obvious. Rob smoothed his thumb over Brian's chin. "So did you."

"Love making you moan." Brian shifted, giving Rob a nice view of him jerking off. "Hottest fucking thing in the world."

"Then why don't you finish the job?"

That was all the encouragement Brian needed. He swallowed Rob so fast that Rob gave Brian one of those moans he loved.

"Fuck," Rob murmured. He took Brian's head in his hands and slowed his efforts a bit—including holding him still when Brian swallowed as much as he could. A whimper and a shudder, and Rob let him draw back. "I like fucking you deep, Bri. Think you can handle it?"

In answer, Brian went down on him, father down than before. Not all the way, but damn if the man didn't have control over his gag reflex after all. Rob closed his eyes. "Yeah, like that."

Brian did exactly that again and again and again, until Rob was clutching Brian's head and moaning each time Brian swallowed him. On the last time, he'd taken Rob practically to the root, his mouth stretched so wide around Rob's shaft.

Rob's balls were so fucking tight and his blood *burned*. One more like that and he'd empty himself down Brian's slick throat. "Gonna come."

Another fucking chuckle. Brian licked and sucked the head. He met Rob's gaze with eyes that defined smoldering, then slowly—very slowly—took every inch of Rob's cock into his mouth.

Hottest thing Rob had ever seen or felt. His vision hazed and he moaned as every bit of tension released and he spilled his balls down Brian's throat.

Even after he'd finished, Rob shuddered and gasped, because Brian hadn't stopped. No, he'd just swallowed every drop and kept going. Every nerve in Rob fired and his moan turned into something close to a sob. "God, Bri, stop. Please."

Brian eased off him and sat back, his expression halfway between concerned and a smirking mess. "How's that?"

Little bratty fucking—Rob hauled him up and kissed him, tasting his own salt and musk. They ended up tangled on the bed, Brian moaning beneath Rob, his very hard cock thrusting against Rob's thigh.

"That was exquisite." Rob traced his fingers over Brian's face. "You taste so good with my seed on your lips."

Brian shivered beneath him, but said nothing. Something close to worry crossed his brow.

Rob smoothed it out. "What's wrong?"

Silence for a bit. "What's it like? Being fucked?"

Ah. Curiosity, not worry. "In the arse?"

Brian nodded. "I've never done anything..." He trailed off for a second, then focused on Rob. "But you liked it."

"I did. I do." Rob rolled over on his side and ran his hand down Brian's chest. "I would think it's different for every man." He pinched Brian's nipple between his fingers and relished the catch of breath. "Just like everything else is." He let go. "Some men don't like anal at all. Some love it."

"You?" Definitely curiosity there.

He huffed. "My *yes* is those jizz stains somewhere up

above your head." He waved up at where he'd come earlier. "For me, it generally depends on the partner. It has to be someone I trust."

That made Brian's eyes go wide.

Rob kissed his nose again. "I love it when you act all innocent."

A laugh and a sheepish grin. "This all still feels new. And... perfectly normal."

"As well it should."

Brian propped himself up on his arm. "I want to try."

A zip of pleasure ran through Rob, but he was too spent to get it up a third time, at least for a while. "Why don't we see if you even like having your hole played with?"

A flush and a nod.

"And I can return the favor for that rather lovely blowjob."

"Oh good." Brian flopped down on the bed and put his hands behind his head. "'Cause you taste good with my come on your lips, too."

Fucking hell. Not an innocent bone in Brian's body. Rob wrapped his hand around Brian's shaft and stroked a few times—long enough to make Brian's eyelid's flutter shut and a groan part his lips.

He patted Brian's thigh. "Scoot yourself up to the pillows, and I'll get the lube."

A shudder ran through Brian. "Okay."

Rob slipped off the bed and retrieved the bottle from the nightstand.

This would be interesting. Looking down at Brian, he could certainly envision Brian in the throes of orgasm, his dick rocking in and out of Brian's body. Maybe they would get there. And if not? Well, Brian made a damned good top, no doubt about that.

Brian shivered when Rob climbed back in bed. He'd loved making Rob come, both by blowing him and fucking him. He'd enjoyed Rob's mouth around his dick and frotting had been mind-blowing.

Every way he and Rob had gotten off had been hotter than hell. In some way, that reminded him of Anita. They'd never failed in bed.

But he'd never had anything inside his ass, not even his own finger. He'd thought about it enough, especially after watching porn, but had been too chicken to try.

This could be a disaster.

Rob must have sensed how nervous he was because he set the lube aside, laid down next to Brian, and drew him into a deep kiss. He smoothed a hand over Brian's chest, stopping to tease his nipple.

Even when Brian moaned into Rob's mouth, he didn't stop—kissing or pinching. God, his balls ached for release. He thrust against Rob's thigh.

He'd been hard since the drive back from dinner and there still wasn't a part of Rob that Brian didn't want to lick and suck.

Rob must have felt the same way, because he broke the kiss, slid his mouth down Brian's body, and licked at his abused nipple before trailing lower.

"Could spend ages here," Rob whispered before licking and sucking at his abs and stomach.

"Or you could move lower." He fingered one of Rob's curls.

A dark chuckle. Rob kissed Brian's bellybutton, then shifted downward. Warm breath on his cock. "Bend your legs."

Brian did and Rob settled between his thighs.

Hot fingers stroked the tender flesh there. "I rather like this view." Rob followed his fingers with his tongue.

Electricity through Brian's veins, followed by goose bumps. "Fuck." He closed his eyes.

That's when Rob swallowed the tip of his cock.

Brian arched against the mattress from the sheer pleasure rippling through his nerves, firing them off like Christmas lights. He gasped and moaned and twisted on the bed. When he finally could see again, he got the most awesome view of Rob taking him entirely in one go.

God, that mouth. He found Rob's head and curled fingers into his soft strands. Rob cupped his balls and played with them until Brian couldn't see or think straight. "Gonna come if you keep doing that."

Rob backed off. "Can't have that yet." He kissed the tip and drew his tongue down the shaft, but rather than mouth his balls, like Brian expected him to, Rob pressed his lips to Brian's taint.

Fuck. Brian gasped and pushed his head back against the pillow. He was so sensitive there. Couple of girlfriends had figured that out during blowjobs, but they'd just stroked him—not mouthed him.

"Thought so," Rob muttered. Then he hummed and went back to licking and sucking.

Cock. Taint. Balls. Thighs. Not enough to make him come, but enough to bring him right to the edge over and over. He couldn't think to put syllables together to curse.

A faint click caught his attention, but only until Rob closed his mouth around his dick. Cool, slick fingers pressed against his taint—and before Brian registered what that meant, Rob touched his hole. Pressed against it. Circled it.

Fuck. Heat straight to the back of his brain and down

into his balls. What came out of his mouth was something between a whimper and a moan.

Rob's chuckled vibrated his cock until he pulled off. But those fingers stroking over his hole never stopped. "How's that?"

"Good," he croaked. So fucking good. He wanted to claw his way off the bed, but couldn't get his limbs to work. "Oh God, Rob."

"Mmm. Nice." Rob's voice was deep. "I'm going to slide my finger in. Relax and push back. Tell me if you want me to stop."

"Okay." He breathed out and shivered when the lube bottle snapped again. Every bit of him shook with need and lust and—

Rob kissed his thigh, and pressed his finger against Brian's hole—and in.

Air left Brian's lungs. Didn't hurt, not at all, but the intensity scrambled his brain and stole his thoughts.

Rob fucked him slowly, and Brian squirmed against the tingling that ran up his spine and the intimacy of Rob's breath on his thigh.

Rob moved *inside* him and it felt... good. Filling. He exhaled and closed his eyes.

"How's that?" Rob's words were as gentle as his fucking.

"It's... different." Lethargy in his voice. "But good." Getting better, actually. He shifted his hips and spread his legs wider.

Rob chuckled. "Let's see if we can do better than good."

Next time Rob pressed in, it was harder. Little daggers of pleasure arced up Brian's spine and his breath caught. Rob repeated the thrust and soon was plunging in and out with quick, sharp thrusts.

Brian's toes curled. Holy shit. "That's—better."

"Hmm."

Wasn't sure what the hell Rob did, but every fucking nerve in Brian's body fired with lust. His balls tightened and the top of his head must have cracked off because it felt like his brain exploded. He clutched and the sheets and groaned. "Oh, fuck!"

Whatever Rob had done, he did again, with the same results. "Good fuck or bad fuck?"

"Good!" He practically cried out the word. "Just—don't stop. Please—please don't stop." He rocked his hips in time with Rob's thrusts.

Shit. If it felt like this with one finger, he'd never survive Rob fucking him with his cock. He twisted the bedspread in his hands. Why why why hadn't he tried this ages ago? He groaned and gasped.

"Shit, Bri. You're so fucking tight." Rob kissed his thigh. "Can't wait to have my dick inside you."

"You could—you could—" He wanted that so badly, the need for Rob sudden and intense. To be fucked like he'd fucked Rob.

"Not tonight," Rob said. "I'm more than a little spent." He mouthed Brian's balls. "I think you're going to enjoy this anyway."

He could barely see for the sparks of gold and white hazing his vision every time Rob thrust his finger in. His balls fucking ached, which didn't make sense, since Rob hadn't even touched his cock and he'd gone soft, despite his blood being on fire.

"I'm going to add a finger." Rob slipped out completely.

The loss was almost painful. Brian exhaled and, even to his ears, it sounded suspiciously like a whimper.

A little puff of warm breath on his balls. "Don't you worry. I'm not leaving you empty for long." There was the sound of the lube bottle snapping, the cool slick liquid on his skin and around his hole, and then the pressure of Rob entering him.

Brian arched against the mattress, Rob's fingers plunging in deep and rough. A little pain, but so much pleasure. Stretched and fucked and claimed. "Oh, God." Thin, breathy words. The pleasure ripped through him and built in his balls.

"So, better than good yet?" Deep, dry amusement in Rob's voice. His thrusts picked up speed and hit that spot in Brian that shot lights into his skull with every damn stroke.

"Yes!" The answer came out as a squeak. So fucking good, he couldn't put words together. "Shit, I should have—Rob—please—" He wanted to come so badly, but his hands were still clenching the bedspread and if he let go, he might hit the ceiling. Or shatter into pieces. He wasn't sure what all was holding him together.

"Fuck, you're beautiful," Rob murmured.

When Rob's mouth closed on Brian's cock, he nearly lost everything—his mind, his body, his soul. Might as well have gotten out a Sharpie and scrawled "Property of Rob" across him. Somehow he managed to let go of the bedspread and tangle his hands into Rob's hair.

Rob swallowed his cock, running his talented tongue over the shaft, pressing everywhere. All the while, he slammed his fingers in and out of Brian's ass.

Heaven and hell mixed together. Heat and flames and pleasure. His whole body shook as if he'd been plugged into a wall socket. When Rob took him to the root and drove his fingers in, Brian couldn't climb any higher.

"Rob—" It was the only warning he managed before he was coming and coming, the flames consuming and shaking him. Felt like forever, the trembling and shattering, the blinding light.

He'd never had an orgasm spent him so completely. An eternity later, he managed to see and think again.

Rob was humming contentedly, his head resting against Brian's thighs, his fingers moving slowly inside Brian.

What came out of Brian's throat when he tried to speak was nothing more than a wheeze and a croak. God, Rob's fingers *still* felt good. How was that possible? He closed his eyes and his heart tumbled around in his chest.

Rob kissed his thigh. "I'm going to assume you liked that."

Loved it. Every moment. He struggled to prop himself up and peered down at Rob. "I've never come like that in my life."

Lovely eyes, almost green in the light that filtered through the windows. "That's only your first time." Rob finally slid free from Brian.

He shuddered, both from the loss and from Rob's words. "Please tell me it won't be my last."

Rob's grin was full of teeth as he crawled up Brian's body and kissed him. "If I have my way, that will be very far from the last time you come with me inside you."

His moan was swallowed by Rob's mouth. A sharp spike of desire ran down his spine, followed by a single thought: *I love this man.*

Terrifying that. Utterly. Always the beginning of the end for him.

He didn't want to lose Rob, but he had no idea how to keep a relationship going. They all left him in the end—he drove them away. The shop ate his life.

Rob broke the kiss and smiled. "I'll be right back."

He licked his lips, tasting his own jizz, and nodded.

Water in the bathroom—Rob washing his hands. Brian lowered himself back to the mattress and stared at the ceiling, thoughts chasing thoughts chasing pleasure and hope.

Rob understood the pressure Brian was under, maybe more than anyone he'd dated. Rob had built his own company, after all. Maybe the shop wouldn't come between them. Maybe this could work.

Was it too soon to be in love? How'd that work with men, anyway? He only knew himself—and he was as odd as they came.

When Rob returned, they both slipped under the covers. Brian curled up into Rob's strong embrace. "You're quiet." Soft words against his forehead. Then a kiss.

Brian nuzzled Rob's neck. Tell the truth? Probably the best idea. "I'm a little overwhelmed."

"From the sex?" Warm fingers stroked his back.

"From everything."

A chuckle. "Everything? Well, I know the waiter from dinner was cute, but..."

He tickled Rob's ribs and they moved against each other, their laughter filling the room. "I'm trying to be serious here."

"Oh, love." Rob brushed the hair from his eyes. "I know."

"Love," Brian repeated.

Rob kissed him. "Is that a problem?"

"No." Not really. "But my track record isn't good."

"Neither is mine."

Great. Brian closed his eyes. "So we can fuck this up together."

Another laugh. "Or make it work."

He kissed Rob's shoulder. "Let's try that."

Rob's answer was to pull him closer. Warmth, the smell of salt and sex and Rob. Everything Brian wanted. He teetered over the pit, peered into the unknown, and sent up a silent prayer to the universe. *Please. Just this once, let it work. Please.*

CHAPTER TWELVE

Brian was beginning to hate mornings, at least when he'd spent the night with Rob. Waking up meant ending their time together rather than starting a new day. Rob showered and they dressed, moving easily around each other, but an air of sadness cast a shadow over the morning.

Plenty of time for Rob to drive him back to Squirrel Hill, where he'd clean himself up and change before heading to Grounds N'at. That left one issue, though.

"What are we going to do about my bike? Didn't see a rack on that Mercedes of yours." He sat on Rob's bed.

Rob stood at a floor-length mirror, tying his tie. "I have one, but no—it's not on right now." He tightened the knot and smoothed the silk out. "I can bring it to you sometime this week, if you're free in the evening?" He turned and faced Brian.

Fuck, businesswear looked damn good on Rob's long, lean figure. A simple tan suit and white shirt, paired with a dark red tie that brought out the color of Rob's hair.

Brian's balls tightened. Those were the kind of clothes that deserved to be peeled off Rob at the end of a day.

"Wednesday." The word was thick in his mouth. "I'm off Wednesday evening."

Rob's smile was knowing. So was his walk as he closed the distance. "Like what you see?"

No time to answer, because Rob's mouth was on his, so he put the emphatic *yes* into his kiss and pressed his palm against Rob's dick and balls.

Rob broke the kiss with a chuckle. "So I should wear the suit Wednesday night?"

"Please." Brian took Rob's tie and pulled him down for another kiss. But after a few moments he relented.

Rob's grin slipped. "We should head out."

"Yeah." Brian rose and grabbed his backpack.

Driving across town didn't take long, not this early in the morning. Soon—too soon—they pulled up in front of Brian's place. He unbelted and fiddled with one of the straps on his bag. "That was the best day I've had in a long time." He met Rob's gaze. "Thank you."

"My pleasure." Low murmured words. "And very much the same for me, by the way. You're—" A little color touched his cheeks and he laughed. "Fucking lovely. I couldn't ask for a better man."

That flipped his brain in about seventeen different directions. Rob probably could find a better guy, but he wasn't about to tell him that. "I—" He really was falling in love. *Shit.* "There's never been anyone like you."

Rob pulled him over and kissed him, then spoke against his lips. "We could spend hours like this." He sat back. "Wednesday?"

"Yes." God yes. "I'll text. Call."

A grin. "You'd better."

Nothing else to do but get out, so he did, shut the door, and stood on the sidewalk. Rob's grin was all dimples and freckles and sunshine. He donned his sunglasses—same ones he'd worn that first day—and pulled away.

That absence left Brian bereft but giddy. He had a boyfriend. A hot, sexy one who—dare he even think it?—loved him back. Pretty heady stuff that churned his brain and the blood in his veins as he climbed the stairs to his apartment, showered, and changed.

He'd fucked Rob. Good and hard. Then Rob had turned him into ash with his fingers and his mouth. They'd biked. They'd talked. Taken photos at the Carrie Furnace—so many events packed into one day.

He wanted more, so much more. Hours, days, weeks. If it weren't for the shop—

He clutched the edge of his sink. His shop. For the first time since he'd opened it, it almost wasn't the most important thing in his life.

Rob. Just as it had that first day, his name rang in Brian's head. Rob Rob Rob *Rob*.

He was in trouble. Dating Rob felt like an *affair*.

A glance at his watch told him he should head out. He needed to be at the shop about a half hour before opening to prep for the day.

The walk usually cleared his mind, but today his brain only churned more and more. The scent of Rob's shower gel, the feel of Rob's fingers inside him, the sound of Rob's groan when he came.

Opening the shop was done by rote memory because his heart and head weren't at work yet—those were tangled up in the sheets on Rob's bed.

Shit, he needed to get it together. He had a series of interviews starting at noon and his first customers would walk in soon. Five minutes before eight, he unlocked the door and fired up an espresso for himself.

Eight on the nose, Sam Anderson strolled through the door. Brian put down his cup and donned his professional face. "Hey, Sam. Your regular?"

"I'm nothing, if not predictable." Sam stood by the register.

A large cappuccino with 2 percent. Brian started in on Sam's order. Halfway through, it suddenly occurred to him that Sam must know Rob and he nearly dropped the frothing pitcher. He finished Sam's drink and handed it over.

A curious expression on Sam. "How's it going?"

"Good." The answer was automatic and not quite the truth. "Actually, great in some ways. In others..." He shrugged. "Replacing Justin's been hard."

"I'd say I'm sorry, but..." Sam tipped the cup to Brian.

He couldn't help the laugh. "I know. Honestly, Justin was wasting his talent here. I knew he'd move on." He leaned back against the counter. "And then the whole Eli thing..."

Sam rolled his eyes. "Those two."

As if speaking an incantation, the door clattered open and both Eli and Justin entered. Sam visibly bit back his smirk. "Thanks, Brian."

"No problem."

Sam exchanged a few quiet words with his employees and headed out.

"Morning," Justin said. "Don't suppose you'll let me back there...?"

Eli tapped his cane on the floor. "You're lucky he lets you pay."

"He's right." Brian crossed his arms. "So what'll it be?" While he would love Justin behind the counter, having him there only would remind Brian of the loss.

"Same as the boss-man today. Except two shots."

He didn't even have to ask Eli for his drink—he nearly always got an Americano with room for cream. If he didn't, he let Brian know.

Eli was a creature of habit—except when he wasn't—but he signaled his change.

He got started on their drinks. Pouring hot water into Eli's Americano only reminded Brian of Rob and his breath caught. Rob inside him. He inside Rob. The way they fit together—in and out of bed. Took all his concentration to finish the damned order.

At least Justin hadn't ordered whip. He handed over the drinks.

"Rough night?" That from Eli as he presented his credit card.

The card tumbled out of Brian's grasp and onto the floor. "Shit." He picked it up and ran the transaction. God, he needed to get his head on straight. "No." If you didn't count the sex.

"Must have been a *good* night then." Justin sipped his drink, but Brian saw the smile.

"Dude."

This time, Justin's smirk was visible, as was Eli's grin. Thankfully, they didn't rib him anymore. After they left, the shop filled with customers and he had no time to think about anything until Miranda came in at eleven thirty.

Even then, he spent a good fifteen minutes catching up on dishes and wiping down tables before his first interviewee arrived. Impressions worked both ways—he wanted a clean shop. He scanned the notes on his laptop to get a sense of the first person he'd be talking to. Beth, a college student at Carlow majoring in political science.

She'd done a couple months at a Starbucks between high school and college. Could be promising.

He snapped the laptop shut and leaned against the counter. They finally weren't swamped and he and Miranda could talk a bit.

"Hey, how's your grandmother?"

Miranda's normally cheerful disposition faltered. "Not as good. She's… forgetting stuff. Not all the time, but—"

"Enough?"

"Yeah." She dusted her hands on her apron. "I need to talk to her doctor."

Family was rough. His grandparents were still ticking, but one of his great uncles had developed dementia, bad enough that they'd had to put him into a home. "Hey, I'm sorry."

A pained smile. "I'm just grateful you keep me on for a few shifts here and there. Helps keep me sane."

That worked both ways. "Anytime. You're one of my best."

Miranda laughed, then sobered. "Thanks." She turned away to wash the milk pitcher, but then faced Brian again. "You need to tell the others they're good, too."

Brian ran a hand through his hair and cringed. "I know." The shop bell rang and a nervous young woman stepped in. "Speaking of which…"

"Good luck," she murmured. "To both of you."

Yeah. Four interviews. Four very different people. They all needed a little luck.

Three hours later, he shook the hand of the last of the candidates—a man close to his own age and already working two other jobs—and watched him leave the shop.

Couldn't tell if luck had been with *anyone* today. None of the candidates had been awful, but he didn't connect with any of them, either. He let out a breath and headed back around the counter to type his thoughts into his laptop.

He wouldn't find another Justin, yet he kept hoping. "Shit," he muttered under his breath.

Miranda leaned up against the counter next to him. "Oh, come on, Bri, they weren't that bad."

They hadn't been. "I just don't feel like any of them meshed."

She frowned, but it was thoughtful. "I could tell."

"But I still need to hire *someone*." More than one someone. Three, ideally, but with rising costs, two would be more manageable until he figured out how to balance the budget. Probably needed to rejigger the menu.

Miranda bumped his shoulder. "Who'd you like the best?"

Good question. "Lamont. Smart and driven. Never worked in a coffee shop, though." He couldn't hit the ground running like Beth could with her experience. The third candidate, Nick, had been a bust—to young and too flighty. And the fourth? He felt for Rich, but working around his schedule would be a nightmare.

On the other hand, he worked around Miranda's and was damn lucky to have her.

"People can be trained, you know." She looked up when more customers poured into the shop, and headed to the register.

Yeah, they could. He closed the laptop and washed his hands, then helped Miranda with the orders.

Three decent candidates. None perfect. Three slots he could fill. Hire them all? At least on a provisionary basis. Especially if Rich would be like Miranda and very part time —that wouldn't break the budget, would it?

Well, he'd think about it, anyway.

CHAPTER THIRTEEN

By the end of Rob's morning meeting on Wednesday, he was ready to get the hell out of the office. It wasn't yet noon.

He stood and stretched, grabbed his mug, and headed to the kitchen to make tea. The office coffee still tasted wretched even though it was supposed to be near–coffee shop quality, according to the supplier.

Perhaps "near" meant the Dumpster out back. He swallowed his own snort and pulled out a teabag, soaked it in hot water, and stuck it in the microwave for another thirty seconds. The water from the instantaneous hot water tap was *never* hot enough.

He should just bring in an electric kettle.

Once the microwave beeped, he headed to the nearest window to peer out at the world. At least today was calmer and he'd see Brian tonight.

Both Monday and Tuesday had been awash with in-house customer meetings, including wine-and-dines. He and Brian had texted during the day here and there, and spoken on the phone in the evening, but nothing erased the ache to be near him.

He'd downloaded all of his photographs from their Carrie Furnace adventure and longed to show the rest to Brian. He'd even picked out a half-dozen to see if Brian thought them worth printing.

Footsteps behind him in the kitchen. Rob turned to find Todd stuffing a pod into the coffee machine. He wandered back over. "Is it me, or is that stuff awful?"

A smile played around his lips. "It's not awful. Not Grounds N'at, but it's not bad."

Rob huffed. "So it's *me*." He drank his tea.

The machine chugged and spurted. "This *is* pretty mechanical," Todd said. "I'm guessing you get personal service from Brian."

Rob nearly choked on his tea. *Cream in his coffee.*

Todd turned beet red in an instant. "Oh my God, I didn't mean—" His eyes widened and the color that had risen drained just as quickly. "I'm so sorry sir, I didn't mean —" Horror stripped the words away.

Laughter poured out of Rob. He set his cup down on the counter because he was shaking too hard to hold it and waved Todd's fears down. When he could breathe again, he spoke. "No, it's perfectly all right." He swallowed the giddy giggle.

Personal service. Oh yes. In *spades*.

Todd was still white as a sheet.

"Oh good God, it's fine," Rob said. He leaned against the counter. "I know you didn't mean it the way it came out. But—" He shrugged, his own face hot and sore from grinning. "There's some amount of truth there."

The blush came back to Todd, but so did his smile. He

took his cup from the coffee machine and sipped. "So it's working out?"

That caught Rob off-guard. Then again, who *else* did he have to talk to? At least Todd had *some* connection to Brian. "Remarkably so."

An absent nod, as if putting a few things together. "That's good." He paused. "Can I say that I'm very happy to finally be working at a place where my relationship isn't a thing of horror?"

Rob leaned against the counter. "I take it your previous company wasn't as liberal?"

"On paper, it was. But..."

Rob grunted. "Well, I do have skin in the game. I promise we'll practice what we preach."

Todd's blush had faded, embarrassment shifting to gratitude.

That was heartwarming. He'd known from the start that employees, not the owner, made a company in the long run. "I'm glad the coffee's not bad for everyone. I'd hate to think we were giving folks swill."

Todd lowered his cup. "This is far better than a lot of places."

He had a feeling Todd wasn't just talking about the coffee. A second later, both of their phones buzzed.

"Meeting." Same word, spoken at the same time. Rob chuckled and gestured to Todd to take the lead. They were heading for the same place—a status meeting from the hardware team.

Thankfully, it was short and productive. The latest prototype was moving along well, and the software gurus, like Todd, were itching to get their hands on it.

By the time Rob returned to his desk, his earlier crankiness had vanished. He still desperately wanted to see Brian, but he could balance that with the good of the day, his job, and his company. Brian would be there tonight and so would he—in a nice, expensive business suit. If that whet Brian's whistle, he was more than happy to use that to his advantage.

He pulled out his phone and texted Brian. Still on for this evening?

Rather than a reply text, the phone rang. Brian calling. *That* was unusual. He answered. "Hi there."

"Hey," Brian's voice, soft and resigned. "Figured it would be easier to call."

A rock formed in Rob's stomach. "You have to work tonight."

"I—yeah." Sadness and frustration. "Mark called in sick. Down with a hideous cold."

"Which is exactly what you want in the food service industry."

Brian laughed. "Sneezing and coughing all over your customers and their drinks is *so* in style." His voice quieted. "I'm sorry."

He clicked his tongue. "Happens. So you're off at eight, then?"

"And I work opening tomorrow."

Of course he did. That was a pretty regular thing. As was working all twelve hours the shop was open. Wasn't tenable in the long run. "I still need to bring you your bike."

A long pause. "If you bring the bike tonight, do you think you could... stay? I really want to see you and I feel like shit about—"

"Yes." Spend the night with Brian? Any night. Every night, if that wouldn't fuck both their sleep schedules. Couldn't get enough of the man in his arms.

An exhale. "Thank you."

"Bri." He kept his voice soft, despite his closed office door. "Life happens. You can thank me after I make you come tonight."

That earned him a groan. "Unfair."

He chuckled. "I'll be in my suit."

"Completely unfair." Rob's voice was quiet, but gritty. "I'm around customers, you know."

"Mmm." Yeah, that could be problematic, couldn't it? Heat pooled in his belly and he pressed a palm against his hardening dick. "Sorry."

"Liar." Brian laughed and a bell rang in the background. "I gotta go. Pick me up at eight thirty?"

"Yes, of course."

"Can't wait. See you then."

They both said good-bye and hung up.

Well, change of plans, but not entirely. A night of Brian next to him in bed? He'd take those when he could.

Rob lingered in the office until six, folded his suit jacket, stuffed it into his backpack, and rode his bike home. After a shower and a quick bite to eat, he got Brian's bike mounted onto his car, then packed a few things before standing in his closet and contemplating suits.

He could put back on the one he'd been wearing. Dark blue. Professional enough. Or perhaps gray or black.

Which one would appeal to Brian the most? Turn him on? Make him hard? He didn't know. Brian had loved his tan suit—perhaps that? Didn't feel quite right, either.

Power games or fashion? Both. Brian was an artist and appreciated aesthetics. If he wanted something more than that, Rob was happy to oblige. He pulled out a suit he'd have worn to a board meeting—dark brown and perfectly tailored. A nod to his tan suit but more appropriate for the time of day. He paired it with a crisp white shirt. After a moment of thought, he pulled out his black-and-gold-striped tie, far too aware of the Pittsburgh connection with *that* choice.

Brian had been born here. He'd appreciate the thought, no doubt.

He was a minute late by the car's clock when he stopped in front of Grounds N'at. Brian's smile was a brilliant and welcome sight when he opened the passenger door and slid in.

"Hey." He swallowed. "Shit, you look good."

Couldn't help his own smile. "Glad you like it." Took a bit to get to Brian's place—his street was relentlessly one-way, and often parked up. "I don't suppose you have a driveway..."

"Actually..." Brian pointed at the narrow alley between his building and the next. "There's spots in back. No one uses them, though."

Probably because driving between the brick walls was like threading a needle. But Rob managed.

No fooling around on the stairs—not with Brian holding a bike in his hands, but once they were up in the apartment and the bike safely stowed, Brian stepped back.

Rob had never seen that hungry a look from Brian before.

"That's better than the other suit." He took a step forward and his gaze met Rob's.

Power games, indeed. A shiver ran through Rob, followed by heat that sank into his balls. From the looks of things, it wasn't *Brian* who'd be on his knees tonight.

He'd happily play it that way, too. "It's my boardroom suit."

"Wheeling and dealing?" No more distance between them. Brian slid his fingers under the lapel and pressed his thumbs against the fabric.

Handles, should Brian want to push or pull.

Rob's heart ticked faster. "Something like that." It came out as a whisper. Brian's lips were too close to his to speak any louder.

"A goddamn CEO." Brian pulled Rob to him, their bodies touching. His lips brushed Rob's. "What the hell are you doing with me?"

He stroked Brian's arms, enjoying the rock hard muscle beneath. "Whatever you want me to do with you."

A chuckle. "I don't even know where to start." Brian nibbled Rob's bottom lip, sinking heat into Rob's bones. "A suit like this on a man like you should be peeled off one piece at a time."

Desire and anticipation had Rob harder than sin. Brian had barely touched him. "You're right. You're much more than a simple Americano." He caught the dance of Brian's eyes. "Though you *are* blazing hot."

Brian took his mouth and stole his breath and moans. He didn't let go of Rob's suit, even as he pushed Rob up against the nearest wall, his thigh hard against Rob's dick.

"So many options." Brian scraped his teeth over Rob's throat. "Bend you over the couch? Make you kneel? Take each piece of clothing off you, then fuck you in my bed?"

Warmth flooded through Rob. He cupped Brian's arse and rocked against his thigh. "What, only *one* option? Where's the fun in that?"

Brian's breath caught and his fingers twitched against

Rob's chest. "You want it all tonight." He smoothed out the lapels, gliding his hands down Rob's torso.

"I've been sitting in an office for three days thinking of good coffee, my fingers fucking your arse, and the taste of your cock. Of *course* I want it all."

Brian's smile turned wicked. "Ever knelt in that suit of yours?"

"This one? Never. Not for anyone. Not that kind of suit." Truth. Rob had never considered giving a blowjob in one of his bespoke suits. Now he *craved* sinking to the floor.

Brian clasped his tie. "I want your mouth around my cock."

"Do you?" He wanted to hear the order. Needed Brian to say it. Their gazes met and the air felt electric.

"Get on your knees. Now."

Not much room between the wall and Brian, but he dropped, sliding his hands to Brian's hips and pressed his mouth to the denim covered bulge in Brian's tight jeans.

"Shit!" Brian tangled his hands in Rob's hair. "You're gonna make me come before I fuck you."

He let up and nuzzled Brian's thigh. "Guess I should have brought one of my cock rings, hmm?"

The grip in his hair tightened. "Guess you better unzip my jeans."

Oh, he could do that and more. Didn't take long for Rob to free Brian's hard dick from those jeans. He stroked the length and licked the head.

Brian moaned. "God, you look—you feel—" Wide brown eyes peered down at him.

Who had whom? Not that it mattered—Rob had what he wanted. He closed his mouth around Brian's cock and savored the taste of salt. Silky and hard. Perfection.

A groan and Brian thrust deep. Rob opened his throat

and closed his eyes, enjoying the headiness of losing control and gaining every bit of it. Brian fucked him—no doubt about that. His head was held tight, the pain in his scalp a glorious thing. But he'd brought Brian to this moment, too, with his looks, words, and desire.

Obviously, Brian had fucked like this before. He knew how to slide in deep and when to let Rob breathe. They found a rhythm of groans and thrusts, pain and pleasure that slipped Rob from the world and into delight. Was a wonder he didn't shoot his own load looking up at the rapture on Brian's face.

"So fucking good." Brian's words were raspy and low. He pulled out and stroked himself. "Lick the tip."

Rob did, lavishing Brian's cockhead with every bit of his attention.

"Wonder what your business buddies would think if they saw you now?"

Rob kissed Brian's dick. "Some of them would be horrified. Others might pull up a chair and watch." He looked up at Brian. "People are complex."

"They are." Brian reached down and hauled Rob to his feet. Once more, his back hit the wall and Brian took his mouth.

Brilliant. His body was on fire, his dick hard, and balls aching. "Fuck me, Bri." He muttered between kisses. "Take this suit off me, strip me bare, then fuck me until I come." He was done with being a CEO for the day. Much better to be Brian Keppler's lover.

Brian swung him off the wall. "Bedroom."

Halfway across the living room, Brian grabbed him by the tie, kissed him, then pushed his suit jacket off. At the doorway to the bedroom, Brian unknotted his tie and pulled it free from his shirt. A few buttons were ripped off in

Brian's effort to lick and nip at Rob's collarbone, but that's what tailors were for. Both of their shirts hit the hardwood before they reached the foot of the bed. Brian backed him against the mattress and pushed him over.

A breathless landing plus enough time to watch Brian shed his shoes, socks, and jeans. Then he hovered over Rob.

"You know, it's more exciting now that I know what it feels like." He undid Rob's belt.

He couldn't help run his fingers through Brian's hair and over those impressive shoulders. Fuck, the man was mouthwatering. And *his*. "You mean being fucked in the arse?"

Brian licked his lips, unbuttoned, and unzipped the suit pants. "Yeah."

"That was only my fingers."

Brian looked up, his smile crinkling the skin around his eyes. "I know. Must be something else with a cock."

"It is." He kicked his shoes off and helped Brian slide his pants off his legs. Didn't quite expect Brian to kneel and peel off his socks, too. "When you're ready for that, let me know."

"I will." Brian slid his hands up and down Rob's thighs, the warmth and friction lighting his veins. He couldn't stifle the moan when Brian settled between his thighs and gripped his cock. "But not tonight."

The quip Rob had on the tip of his tongue turned into a deep groan when Brian slid his mouth over the head of Rob's cock.

This was what, his third blowjob? Fourth? How the hell was he so talented? "Jesus." Rob threaded his hands into Brian's hair. "That's so fucking good."

He pulled off and stroked Rob. "Apparently I have an oral fixation." Shiny wet lips on that smile.

"More than happy for that." Rob exhaled. "Your mouth is a wonder of nature."

A laugh, but rather than go down on him, Brian let go and stood. "Up the bed with you."

Yeah, he'd take a nice good fucking in lieu of a blowjob. Rob scrambled up the bed and lay down against the pillows, hands behind his head. "How do you want me?"

"Same answer as before. Every way I can get you." Brian grabbed a condom and lube from a drawer in the nightstand and leaned down to kiss Rob.

Warm lips that tasted vaguely of salt. Rob ate that up, enough that Brian groaned and pulled back. "Someone else has a magic mouth." He climbed onto the bed and sat on Rob's legs. "I want to see you tonight."

"Good old-fashioned vanilla missionary." He grinned up at Brian. "I can work with that." More than work. He loved watching his partner during sex, whether topping or bottoming. Something about being able to see and kiss and feel their breath.

Rob freed Brian's legs from under his body, pulled them up and pushed them apart. Rob bent his knees and drew his feet in. The better to meet Brian's thrusts later.

"I was going to say something like 'there's nothing vanilla about the way I plan to fuck you tonight'." Brian opened the bottle of lube and poured some onto his hands. "But you know, real vanilla is rare and expensive." He gripped Rob's shaft and stroked it.

The coolness of the slick took Rob's breath until Brian's hand and his strong touch had him hot and moaning again. Not surprising that Brian knew how to jack off with precision. Rob gasped and twisted against the sheets. Brian provided enough pleasure to keep Rob groaning and hot, but not enough to let his balls spill. The bastard.

"God, Bri."

A chuckle. Brian's voice was smooth, almost conversational, except for its deep tone. "Vanilla comes from the seed pod of an orchid. Hard to grow, hard to get." Brian stopped fisting Rob's cock, but only to rip open the condom wrapper.

The sound sent a shiver down Rob's spine, as did Brian's wicked smile when he rolled the condom over his own cock.

This wouldn't be gentle. The need and heat that radiated from Brian told Rob that.

"So, maybe I will fuck you in a vanilla manner, tonight." More lube, this time slicking his hole. Brian gripped his thighs and lifted him. "You're rare and hard, and entirely mine."

He couldn't even reply when Brian pressed in. Felt too fucking good, being stretched and filled and taken. Sharp, hard thrusts. His gasps mixing with Brian's moan. The way Brian closed his eyes when he fitted himself inside Rob was exquisite to see.

When Brian exhaled he opened his eyes, he smiled. "I could do this to you every night." He thrust in deeper, hitting Rob just right.

"Wouldn't mind that," Rob murmured. He found Brian's shoulders and grasped them, pulling him closer.

Mouths met. Tongues. Brian pulled at Rob's legs and arse and thrust in deep and hard, over and over until Rob's chest and lungs hurt from gasping and groaning and trying to catch air between the kisses and the intensity of the fucking.

"You want vanilla? Really?" A bit of anger there.

"I want you." Rob scraped his fingers over Rob's biceps. "You."

"Americano?" Deep staccato thrusts that drove thoughts, words, and breath from Rob.

"There's—room—for—cream."

Brian froze, buried inside Rob, and quaked. Not an orgasm, though. Laughter. Throaty, joyful, laughter that shook both of them.

"Oh fuck," Brian whispered. He pressed a kiss to Rob's lips. Then another. "Oh God, Rob." Slowly, he moved again. Gently, but with the same purpose that flared in his expression. A singular desire.

This man could *love*, not just fuck. Smooth, slow strokes that sent fire up Rob's spine. Rob pressed his head back against the pillow and moaned Brian's name. "Please."

"Like that?" He rocked into Rob and his hand closed around Rob's cock. "Feels like you do."

"Fucking love it. You feel so good." Words whispered against lips. "Love—love—"

Brian's mouth met his.

"Love you."

Couldn't tell who said it. It was in his mind and heart and soul. He'd tried pushing the emotions back—he *knew* it was too soon—but here and now, he meant it. Everywhere else, too. In the shop. At work. "Bri." He was close, between Brian's thrusts, his hand stroking, and those words in the air between them. "Please."

Brian's eyes were dark and his lips moist and plump. Sweat licked at his forehead and they rocked against each other, that perfect friction building and building. "Love everything about you," Brian whispered. "Even your fucking coffee puns."

A hiccupped laugh and then a moan. "You started it."

Brian's thrusts picked up speed. "Gonna finish it, too."

"Please." Please. *Please.* Rob slid his hand to join Brian's around his cock. He wanted to come before Brian did, wanted to be fucked through his orgasm, wanted to cry and moan until his throat hurt and his body sang. He was so... close...

A toothy grin above him. "Want it so bad, don't you?" Brian drilled him and there was no stopping the roll of pain and pleasure that stripped Rob from the world. His balls tightened, vision hazed and he tumbled off the cliff into unending bliss.

Warm semen coated his hand. Seconds or minutes later, Brian arched above him, pounded him hard enough to rock his bones, and shuddered out his own pleasure until they came to rest together, breathing hard into each other, their heartbeats blending and merging and breaking apart.

Brian moved first, his hand stroking Rob's hair. He kissed Rob's neck and whispered, "Say it again."

"Room for cream?"

Brian moaned and pressed his forehead into Rob's shoulder. "You *ass*." He laughed, and tears pricked at the corners of his eyes, like the one's Rob felt at his.

"I love you."

A happy sigh. "Yeah, that."

"Too soon?"

"No." Brian propped himself up and pulled out of Rob. "I'm a hopeless romantic."

"Good." He tugged at Brian's hair.

"What's good? The romantic part or the hopeless part?"

That made Rob chuckle. He kissed those sweet lips. "The romantic part. You're far from hopeless."

Brian snorted. "Just wait, you'll see." He levered himself up. "I'll be right back."

Rob relaxed into the pillows, the afterglow warm and fuzzy on the edge of his senses. He should get up and clean himself off, but the bed was warm and soft and his body hummed. He closed his eyes.

The mattress rocked. "Falling asleep on me?" Something warm and wet touched his chest.

Rob cracked open an eye. "No."

Brian leaned over him, wiping away semen with a wet flannel. "Liar." Light laughter in that word.

He shrugged. "Maybe a little. It's been a long week." He held out his hand. Brian handed him the cloth and Rob wiped off his hands.

"It's only Wednesday." Brian trailed his fingers over his thighs.

"Don't remind me."

When Rob handed the flannel back, Brian pitched it into a laundry basket on the other side of the room. Perfect shot.

They slid under the covers together. "Trouble at work?" Brian caressed Rob's forehead and pushed back his hair.

"No. Customer visits. Lots of meetings. Always being on." Rob ran his hand over Brian's shoulder. "What do you do to get arms like this?"

A huff of laughter. "You like built guys? Thought I was a twink."

"You are a twink and big-muscle guys don't do anything for me, but this—" He rolled fingers over Brian's bicep and Brian flexed. "This makes me want to devour you whole." He kissed Brian's shoulder. "I like arms."

"Pushups and pull-ups," he said. "I sometimes bike over to Frick Park. They have one of those fitness trails."

"Don't stop on my account," Rob murmured against his skin.

Brian pulled him closer. "I won't." He pressed lips to Rob's neck. "I like the sound of you devouring me whole."

"Mmm. My lovely vanilla Americano." Everything was so fucking perfect. Brian's arms around him. The afterglow of sex. How relaxed they both were. Every night should be like this.

"With room for cream."

"And love," Rob said.

"That too." Brian kissed him. "Lots of love."

It was about damn time. Love was a fragile, wonderful thing. Rob pressed his forehead to Brian's shoulder and prayed his heart wouldn't shatter again.

CHAPTER FOURTEEN

THE NEXT COUPLE OF DAYS AT GROUNDS N'AT WENT BY smoother and faster than they had in months. So far so good with the new baristas Brian had hired. Training was going well. A steady flow of customers came and bought drinks, cookies, and brownies. Pastries were delivered on time. The books were balanced and, though the numbers were very tight, he was in the black. Sam and his crew filtered in and out with regularity.

Brian kept waiting for the other shoe to drop. Sure, he was still working ridiculous hours and was exhausted all the time, but it couldn't be *this* easy, could it?

In a fit of desperation or need for something *different* in his caffeine routine, Brian switched from shots of espresso to Americanos with a pump of vanilla. No cream though. Not yet.

God, how he wanted Rob. His presence. His laughter. Everything. He'd had this kind of high with Anita, except with Rob it felt deeper. Needier. More urgent. He didn't know why.

Because you're fucking in love with him, you idiot.

Yeah, that. *Too soon?* Rob's voice in his head. No, this was normal for him, the connection that stole his heart. He shoved away what *also* usually happened.

It helped that Rob was on the other end of his phone, either by voice or text, to keep him sane.

On Friday, Rob had sauntered in just before eight, waited, and chatted while Brian closed up the shop. They walked to Brian's, matching strides. That night had been bliss and light. He'd cooked a quick meal for them and discussed Rob's photos. After that, they'd tumbled into bed, hot and heavy for each other. He'd gone down on Rob, loving the taste of him, the way he took control and the deliciously dirty things he murmured in his British accent. They'd spent themselves twice that night before sleeping, and once again in the morning, horny as teenagers.

Admittedly, he'd not had a lot of sex back then. He doubted his muscles would have protested as much at eighteen, but he'd take the pain that came with age and experience. No awkwardness, no fumbling—even though he still wasn't sure what he was doing much of the time.

He hadn't asked Rob to fuck him yet and Rob hadn't pressured at all, content with anything Brian was willing to do. Frotting. Blowjobs. Mutual masturbation. Letting Brian top him.

Rob was pleasure incarnate, his long body both pliable and domineering.

Brian wanted more than a quick overnight if he were going to bottom. He was nervous as fuck about the prospect, even after the amazing orgasm Rob had given him. Figured the extra time would help. Maybe.

Wouldn't happen this weekend, though. He'd worked all Saturday training Lamont. Today was the monthly Sunday dinner with his parents and siblings.

He still had no clue how to tell any of them about Rob, especially his folks. *Hey. No, I didn't go to church on Easter. I'm not really going anymore. Oh, by the way, I'm dating a guy.* Fraught with peril, even if his parents had always been open-minded. They were still very Catholic in the end.

Today felt like a promise, though. Golden and full of sunlight with fluffy white clouds in the sky. The trees were leafing out, and all around spring had settled in and bloomed. He'd spent the morning working on editing Rob's photos. Man, if he'd had half Rob's untrained eye, he could've made a living as a professional photographer. Just about every shot from their trip to the Carrie Furnace was well-composed, on point, and stunning. There were little hiccups with the lighting and cropping, but he could teach Rob how to avoid those.

With a little post-processing, no one would ever know anyway.

Shit, he couldn't wait to show Rob the shots. Utterly professional pieces. They deserved to be framed, sold, and enjoyed like the works of art they were.

He still couldn't get over what Rob had said about his parents and their lack of support for the arts. Maybe because Brian had grown up in Pittsburgh, art and music had been encouraged right along with everything else, despite his parent's blue-collar background.

It helped that the Carnegie Art Museum was attached to the Natural History Museum, which was attached to the Carnegie Library. That had been a one-stop shop of brain-filling enjoyment when he'd been a kid.

When the clock ticked to one, he grabbed his helmet, backpack, and bike and headed out the door. After a quick stop at the coffee shop to see how Mark was getting on with

Rich, and to grab an Americano to drink, he rode down to his folks' place.

Weird to think that Rob was only a few blocks away in Mrs. Kaminski's house. He circled the parklet, fighting the urge to show up on Rob's doorstep. There was still time before he needed to be at his parents'. But no, not with the way he and Rob melded so quickly whenever they were together. They'd fall into conversation or tumble into bed if he stopped there first, and he'd never make it to dinner.

He needed to open up to his parents and siblings. Over the summer, there'd be family events he'd want to bring Rob to. He simply couldn't hide this. He didn't *want* to.

He headed down the street in the other direction and hopped off his bike when he got to the house he'd grown up in. Only his parents' car was parked out front. As was usual, he was the first of his siblings to show. After chaining his bike to the porch, he walked in.

Smelled like home. A zip of spices, some kind of lemon cleaner, and a trace of his mom's perfume. "Hey, I'm here," he called.

"In the kitchen." His mother's strong voice echoed through the front room. He dropped his helmet and bag on the couch and headed through the dining room to the large kitchen at the back of the house—the reason his mother had chosen this place way back when—or so she'd said.

Cooking was his mother's vocation and his father's art. No one left the Keppler house hungry, ever. Often they left with extra food.

Family Sundays were usually Italian, but his mom had branched out in his youth, cooking just about everything under the sun and trading recipes with neighbors. Scouring cookbooks for new and interesting dishes.

His mom, her long silver-and-blond hair pulled back

into a ponytail, was pouring sauce into a large baking dish when he entered the room.

Brian bounded over and gave her a kiss on the cheek. The pan was full of wide noodles with ricotta peeking out at the edges. *Fuck yes, lasagna!*

His dad was probably putting the noodle maker away. While lasagna was Dad's meal, since he'd retired, his parents cooked together. "Meat or spinach?"

"Spinach." She pecked him on the cheek in return. "Zoe has decided to be vegetarian again."

Zoe had been vegetarian in high school, but quit while in college, due to the wacky schedule every student had. "Well, it *is* a healthy choice." He'd even cut back on meat.

Her mother chuckled. "Those were her exact words."

His brother, Len, would give Zoe *some* flack, but he loved spinach lasagna more than regular, so there'd be peace.

Food always brought them together.

"Dad in the basement?"

As if the question had summoning powers, the stairs from the basement creaked and his father appeared through the door. He brandished two wine bottles. "No meat in these!" He set the bottles down, and clapped Brian on the back. "Great to see you."

His father looked good, which was a relief. He'd had a bout of bronchitis the previous month that had left him looking far older than Brian wanted to think about. The telltale signs that the years were rolling by were there, though. His father's hair was thinner and not the near-black it had been. Both his parents had more lines on their faces than Brian wanted to acknowledge.

But right now, both were healthy and happy. Even

though he had his issues with God, he sent up a silent *thank-you* anyway.

Couldn't hurt.

His father sat down at the kitchen table. "How's life treating you?"

There was the flutter of nervousness. *I met a guy dad. I think I'm in love.* Was that even something he could say? "Oh, the usual ups and downs. Shop's been busy and I've been there a lot. Lost some baristas. Replacing them has been hard, but I just hired three new people, so hopefully things will ease up." He grabbed a chair and joined his father at the table. "Life's good, otherwise." Really good. Robert Ancroft good. Heat touched his cheeks.

Shit, this was going to be hard.

The blush must not have been visible, since his father didn't react. "Good help's hard to get. Hope the new folks work out for you."

"Me too." He leaned against the table. "I can't keep working the hours I've been working. I've been... short with people. That doesn't help."

"Don't beat yourself up, hon." His mother slid the pan into the oven. "You're human."

Couldn't help the smile. That was a common refrain, one he'd heard throughout his childhood. "I know."

His mom dusted her hands together. "Now that dinner is in the oven..."

She didn't have to say more than that. Both he and his father rose and headed toward the sink. His mom would wash, he'd dry and his dad would put everything away.

Helping with the dishes now meant he could beach his overstuffed ass on the couch after dinner while his brother and sister took care of clearing the table. They'd grouse about how *unfair* that was, but it wasn't his fault he was the clever one.

"How was the ride down?" His mother filled the basin. "I always worry about you and that bike of yours. Too many accidents in the news."

"The ride was beautiful. This spring's been good for biking. Did a bunch of trail riding the other weekend." He paused. "And I stick to the quieter streets and the bike lanes, Mom."

"Don't hassle him, Alice. Exercise is good for stress."

She rolled her eyes and threw the utensils that couldn't go into the dishwasher into the sink. "I don't hassle."

Brian laughed. "Hey, I worry about the cars, too." He took a wooden spoon from his mom, dried it, and twirled it in his hands before turning it over to his dad.

"Hmm." His mother eyed him and handed over a large plate to dry. "Who's the woman?"

He nearly dropped the thing. "What?"

"You have that glow about you, hon. The one you get when you've started seeing someone. So, who is she?"

He dried the plate carefully, his hands shaky and his face red hot.

"Um." This was *so* not the way he intended to come out to his parents. Holy shit. He handed the plate over to his dad and braced himself against the kitchen counter for support, heart ramming against his ribs. Both his mom and his dad had confused expressions. "It's... he. A guy. I'm dating a guy."

His parents looked at him, and then at each other.

"You're gay?" his mom said.

Good God, his legs were shaking. "No... I'm bi. Bisexual. I... like women and men."

"Well, that explains it." His dad walked over to the cabinet and put the plate away.

"So, then who's the guy?" His mom washed a mixing bowl, then held it out to him.

Brian stood still, gripping the counter, staring at the water dripping off the bowl. This was *not* how he expected his parents to react. Or not react. Slowly, he reached out and took the bowl. "You... what explains what?"

"Oh." A touch of color blushed his mother's cheeks. "When you were younger, we thought you might be gay and kept expecting you to come out, but you never did. Then you started dating women... and..." She shrugged.

"We figured we were wrong," his dad said. "But I guess we weren't entirely off base, huh?"

Wait, *what*? "You thought I was *gay*?"

"You collected a lot of photos of that young actor from *My So-Called Life*, dear."

Oh God, yeah. He had. He coughed. "Well, okay." He handed his father the bowl and took a pile of damp utensils from his mom.

"And all those men's health magazines," his father added.

That too. Lithe and muscular male bodies. He also had pored over the ads for guys clothing. "I was... confused as a teen."

"Sounds like you weren't at all." His dad pulled out a drawer and put the mixing bowl with the others.

His mom bumped his shoulder with hers. "So what's his *name*?"

"Rob. Robert. But he likes Rob." He was babbling. His parents were *okay* with this? They... kinda knew?

The world tilted, righted itself, then tilted again. He

steadied himself against the counter and took a breath. "You don't mind?"

Another exchange of glances and his Dad cleared his throat. "You remember Joe, from the factory?"

One of Dad's best work buddies. There were three of them, his dad, Joe, and Darren.

Oh. *Oh.* "Wait, are you about to tell me that Joe and Darren ...?"

His dad shrugged. "Yeah. Found out a couple years ago. They're getting married this summer, now that they can."

Well, shit. "This is weird."

"Bri." His mom washed her hands, dried them, then pulled him into a hug. "Did you think we'd disown you? Hate you? Never!"

"You're our son, Brian." His dad's voice was uncomfortably thick. "We'll always love you."

He relaxed into his mom's embrace. "I didn't know *what* to think. I mean—" He drew back. "You guys still go to church and everything."

A snort from his father. "There's God and Jesus and the Mass. There's the church and the people... and then there's the *hierarchy*." He waved a hand. "Those bishops should be plucking logs from their eyes rather than pointing fingers."

Wow. His heart thudded in his chest. "So, if I brought him to dinner?"

"You'd better," his mom said. "You should have brought him tonight."

"I still have to tell Len and Zoe," he said. "I want to make sure everyone's okay before..."

Back at the sink, his mom washed a pot and handed it over. "They'll be thrilled." She huffed a laugh. "Well, Zoe might feel outnumbered in the guy department, but she'll come around."

Zoe *loved* meeting his girlfriends. Grew up with too many boys, she said. He dried the pot and handed it over.

His mom bumped him again. "So what's Rob do? How'd you meet?"

A warmth settled over him. They *really* were okay with this. Holy shit. "You realize I'm going to have to repeat all of this at dinner, right?"

His father laughed. "Can't stop your mom."

No, he couldn't. While they finished up with the dishes, he filled his parents in on Rob and about the time his mom stopped grilling him, the front door banged open.

"Hey! Two for one!" his brother called. That was followed by a yelp. "Hey!"

"I'm my own person." Zoe's voice echoed through the air.

They thumped into the kitchen. "Didn't have to smack me." Len rubbed his arm.

"Sister's prerogative."

After that, it was hugs and chats and noise and wonder. Brian was so light-headed and relieved that he wasn't sure his feet were touching the floor.

When the oven timer beeped, their mom shooed Brian and his father from the kitchen. "Go pour the wine."

She had Zoe and Len make a salad.

Ten minutes later, they were sitting around the table, staring at the lasagna their mom set down.

"It's like you know me," Len said.

"I gave birth to you." His mom sat back. "Let's say grace."

They did, and while he repeated the words by rote, everything his dad said flooded back. Joe and Darren. His criticism of those running the church. The acceptance that he was dating a guy.

He couldn't help the giggle when they finished.

"What's your problem today?" That from Zoe. "You've been in the wine already?"

"No," he said. "I—uh—" He caught his mom's eye.

"Brian has some news."

Both his siblings stared at him.

Geez. *Thanks, Mom.* Brian swallowed and heat rose to his face. "I have a boyfriend."

They stared at him harder.

"I'm bisexual. I met a guy. His name's Rob and he's kind of—" That giddy laugh escaped again. "—Amazing."

Zoe leaned back in her chair. "Wow."

His brother, however, nodded. "Makes sense."

"Wait, what?" Zoe whipped her head to stare at Len.

Len snorted. "Oh, come on. You ever go into his room when we were growing up?"

Brian rubbed a hand over his face. Maybe the posters on the wall had been a giveaway. All the actors and actresses he'd found hot. "So this is news to *no one*, huh?"

"It is to me," Zoe said, her face pink. "I kinda wanted to be the queer in the family, but you beat me to it."

Oh. All of the attention shifted off of him. "Um... sorry?"

Zoe's smile was sincere and joyous. "Hey, saved me having a heart attack figuring out how to tell Mom and Dad."

"You know, we're both sitting at the table..." His mom handed the salad to his dad and picked up a knife to cut into the lasagna.

She blushed harder. "I'm gay. Well, lesbian, but... yeah."

He took the salad from his dad and fought the urge to burst out into a laughing fit. Man, he'd have a story to tell

Rob tonight. After putting salad into his bowl, he handed it off to Len.

"Knew that, too," Len said. "I've been in your room as well." After taking his share, he passed it to Zoe.

"Doesn't matter what any of you are," their father said, gravel in his voice. "You're our kids and we love you. End of story."

"Not completely," his mom said. "Are you seeing anyone, Zoe?

She rolled her eyes. "Mom!"

Len laughed.

Unexpected tears pricked in Brian's eyes. His family loved him. Accepted him. One another. Nothing, and everything, had changed.

His dad always said there wasn't anything more important than family. He held out his plate and his mom placed a nice large slice of lasagna on it. "Eat up," she said.

Zoe talked a little about her girlfriend. Len, as usual, had no one in his life. "Kinda hard when work takes you to different cities all the damn time." He shrugged and smiled, a picture of contentment. He loved flying, so Brian wasn't surprised. "Maybe someday."

Over dinner and wine and brownies for dessert, he spilled his guts, answering the questions about how he'd met Rob, what he did, and how serious things were.

After the last question, Brian bit his lip. "I don't know. Maybe pretty serious? He's..."

"...Dreeeeaaaamy?" his sister said.

He threw a napkin at her. "He's British." He paused. "And a redhead."

"Oh God," his brother said. "No wonder you're glowing."

"I am not!"

Len clapped him on the shoulder. “Sorry to say, but you look happier than you have in years. Probably could read by you in a dark room.”

He couldn’t argue with that. At all.

By the end of the night, he was more than a little stuffed, had a whole container full of leftover lasagna and brownies, and really didn’t want to climb the hill back home on his bike in the dark. Thank God Len offered to drive him.

“Got a rack on the back of the SUV, and everything.”

Hugs all around. He pulled his sister close. “If you ever need to talk...”

She mock-punched him in the stomach. “Works both ways, you know.”

Yeah, he probably should call more often.

Detangling from their childhood home always took time, but eventually, he and Len got his bike on the SUV and were on their way. The silence between them was broken by Len.

“I’m really happy for you. Seriously.” A quick glance. “My brother. Dating a high-powered CEO.”

“I don’t know about high-powered...”

“Dude, I read the business news. I know who Robert Ancroft is.”

Weird, really, weird to hear Rob’s name from his brother’s lips. “I *don’t* read the business news. I think he likes that about me.”

Len laughed. “Probably because you treat him like a normal guy.”

Rob, normal? Rob was the hot guy he wanted to pull into bed. The one he couldn’t get enough of. The one he’d had on his knees.

He kept that to himself—some things you didn’t share

with your sibs. He shrugged. "I'm just grateful Mom and Dad and you guys are okay with it."

"Bri, you're *you*. Of course we're okay."

"Not all families are." He studied his hands. "I get the feeling Rob's weren't."

Len was quiet for a while. "You're my little brother. I'll always have your back."

They pulled up in front of his apartment. "You have my back 'cause I'm always one step ahead of you."

Len punched him in the arm, then pulled him into a hug. "You're a jackass."

"Love you, too, Len."

He got out, grabbed his bike, and headed up into his apartment. Once everything was put away, he changed into a pair of gray sweats and flopped down on his bed.

Almost eleven—dinners at his parents seemed to go on forever and yet fly by too fast. He sent a quick text to Rob. You still awake?

A minute later, his phone rang. "Yes, of course I am."

Hearing Rob's voice warmed his blood. "Hey."

"Hey yourself. How'd it go with your family."

He couldn't help the laugh. "Unbelievably well. They knew."

"That you were dating me?" Incredulousness in his voice.

Brian slid a hand over his bare stomach. "No, that I was bi." He paused. "Well, not exactly that I was bi..." He filled Rob in on the conversation he'd had with his parents.

A laugh. "Good lord, that must have been something."

"It gets better. So Mom basically set me up to spill my guts at the dinner table to my siblings... and after I did, my sister quips that *she* wanted to be the queer of the family."

Silence, then a huff of laughter. "And no one set anything on fire?"

"Nah. Everything was cool. Though my mom was ticked that my sister's been dating for six months and hasn't brought a girlfriend over yet."

Another exhale. "Jesus." Rob's voice was heavy with emotion. "Your family sounds amazing."

Mist in his eyes and gravel in his throat. "They are. I want you to meet them."

Whispered words from the other end. "I'd like that."

"You're one of the best things that ever happened to me. I want to share you with the world."

"You're fucking fearless," Rob said. "And I love you."

Those words were lightning in his heart. "Love you, too." He did. God, he did.

They talked until far too late and after many yawns on both their parts, finally said good night. Brian slipped under his covers, set his alarm, and turned off the light.

His family. The shop. Rob. Everything was going to be okay.

CHAPTER FIFTEEN

For Brian, the following week flew by. Maybe getting everything out in the open with his family helped, or perhaps because the scheduling at the shop had fallen into a decent rhythm and his twelve-hour shifts had fallen off. Oh, he was there most days, but between the new hires, Mark, and Miranda picking up a few more hours, he'd had time off. Most of it was on weekdays, so he hadn't seen Rob as often as they both wanted, but they managed.

They'd found time Wednesday evening to look at the work he'd done on the photos Rob had sent him. He'd had proofs made up of eight photographs, the best of the best.

"These—" Rob's hands shook when he held the proofs. "These can't be mine."

"You'd think you'd remember taking them." Brian rested his chin on his hand and grinned at Rob.

A huff that might have been a laugh or a groan. "I do. But..." He shuffled through the proofs and set them down on Brian's kitchen table. "These are pieces of art."

"Yes." Brian lowered his hand. "They're *your* art."

A little furrow grew between Rob's brow. Like his

hands, his whole body shook ever so slightly. A few blinks. "I don't know how to thank you." Rob met Brian's gaze. "You have no idea what that means to me."

He had some idea. Wanted more, but Rob was coy with his past, especially when it came to his family. "I'm sorry your parents weren't supportive."

Rob sat back. "Oh, they were in their way. Not for this." He waved at the photographs. "They pushed me into the sciences. Maths. Engineering. Neither of them batted an eye when I took shit apart. They only had disdain for"—he waved at the table again—"frivolous things."

"Art isn't frivolous." That came out stronger than he'd intended.

A small smile from Rob. "I know. Believe me. I don't share the opinions they held."

Curiosity overrode common sense. "What happened?"

Rob tapped a finger on one of the photos and for a moment, Brian thought he'd punt the question again. "They were never happy I left home. In their minds, I should have stayed and gotten a job there. Lived with them, especially since I wasn't going to be marrying and having kids. They had the whole 'Fine you're gay, but please don't fuck men' thing down pat."

Brian flinched.

Rob waved the reaction away. "There are reasons I came to the States, as conservative as this country sometimes is—there are places here where it's *not*."

"And now, there are more places."

Rob nodded. "Anyway, we had a falling-out partly because I refused *not* to be gay, but I was here and they were there, so I didn't think much of it." He paused. "Then my father had a massive heart attack and died."

"Shit." He couldn't imagine losing his dad, even now. "How old were you?"

Rob looked down at his hands. "Twenty-nine. I was living in California."

Brian stared at him. Rob looked up and his eyes were dry.

"I flew back and everything was in shambles. The house. My mother. The town. Everything." He sighed. "I felt like such an arse for leaving them. Everyone looked at me as if I was the biggest tosser. I'd abandoned my parents, after all."

Brian and his siblings had all stayed in Pittsburgh, though Len flew all kinds of routes. Their parents had made it clear, though, that they were fine with any of them moving. "You have to live your own life at some point," Brian said, echoing his father's words.

Rob nodded. "But at the time, I agreed with everyone. It was grief and shock. I quit my job in the States, shoved everything in storage, and moved in with my mom. I had enough saved up that I could afford it for a time. By then, I had a green card, so coming and going was easier."

"You obviously came back to the States."

"Eventually." Rob rubbed at his wrist. "First, I managed to find a job in the area, despite the economy. But whenever I was out of the house, Mum was despondent, so I quit that pretty quickly. I tried to get her help..."

He pushed back and stood in one rapid motion, turning away from Brian. "And I was becoming pretty depressed myself. No job, no friends, money dwindling. Not a single one of my father's mates cared enough to stop in for a chat with my mother—we were all alone."

"Rob..."

He turned and his expression was grim. "I couldn't take

it. I told Mum I was going to Leeds for the weekend. I needed to get away. Figured I'd find some clubs, maybe a fuck, who knows. I... had the best weekend I'd had in a long time. Hooked up. Danced. Slept." He tugged at his hair. "When I returned... I knew something wasn't right, because my key didn't fit into the lock."

Brian couldn't quite wrap his head around that. "She had the locks changed while you were gone?"

A single nod. "I went 'round to the kitchen door—she usually spent her days in there, drinking tea and reading. And she was there, except she was slumped over the table."

Oh Jesus. Brian's blood ran cold.

Rob rubbed his wrist. "I punched out the windowpane. Sliced myself up bad getting the door open. Then I dragged Mum out of her chair and called nine-nine-nine—but she was cold, Bri." Rob's voice broke.

Brian climbed to his feet, closed the distance between them, and pulled him into an embrace.

Rob shook and wrapped his arms around Brian. "I've had no one to tell this to." He took a breath. "She was cold and dead. A teacup sat next to her, and her pills, the one she took every day. Apparently, she'd taken a week's worth in one sitting."

Brian felt Rob's hollow laugh and he pulled back. "She killed herself. I'd abandoned her, just like my dad had, and she killed herself because of it."

Brian rubbed Rob's arms. "You didn't leave her, you came back. You didn't abandon her!"

Rob kissed his forehead. "You're sweet. And correct. She'd planned it from the beginning, right after my father died. I threw a spanner in by rushing home and not leaving her." He traced a finger down Brian's face. "I know that in my head, but my heart's never quite caught up." He pulled away and strode to the window. "Now I'm an orphan."

Brian shivered and followed. It wasn't cold, especially on the third floor now that the weather had warmed. He wrapped his arms around Rob and kissed his neck. "You're not alone."

Rob took Brian's hand and lifted it, placing it on his chest—over his heart. "No. I'm not. Thank you for that."

They stood like that for some time, breathing each other, holding their bodies together as cars drove past on Darlington. Brian was the first to move, to rotate Rob away from the window. "Come to bed with me."

A faint smile. "Thought you'd never ask."

They stripped without word and slid under the covers, flesh to flesh. Rob's skin was cool and soft, but his muscles so tense beneath. Brian kissed him and pulled him close. "I have off Saturday."

"Do you?" Whispered words.

"Thought maybe you'd like to go hiking up in McConnells Mill."

A sigh and Rob relaxed, molding his long body against Brian's. "That sounds lovely." He cupped Brian's face in his hands. "Should I bring my camera?"

"Of course. There's an old mill and a covered bridge and trials and..." Brian nestled against his shoulder and breathed in Rob's scent. "Always bring your camera. You're an artist, aren't you?"

Rob's laugh was closer to a sob. "I guess I am."

Brian listened to Rob's pulse beat steadily, in counterpoint to the ragged nature of his breathing. After a time, that evened out and Rob shifted his legs, then his body, then his mouth, and every inch of Brian flared. "You don't have to—"

"Shh." Rob kissed him, his lips sliding sweetly against Brian's. Not demanding, but it melted every bit of Brian anyway. Their bodies moved and slid, creating delicious friction, cocks rubbing together, so much like their first night.

Intimate, heady, perfect. Senses ignited, skin tingled. Brian's moans were caught and returned by Rob. Hands moved and touched and pinched and caressed. He whispered Rob's name against his freckled skin, veins on fire as their bodies rocked toward bliss. Murmurs of promises and love.

In the end, he broke first, a cascade of sparks firing along his spine and he spilled against Rob, slicking the skin between them. His lungs ached for air as he cried out his release.

Rob joined him, coming hard a moment later, hot against his stomach. They both continued thrusting and moving until the pleasure was too much to handle. Brian bit Rob's shoulder to stifle a moan. "Can't..."

Rob was all breath and shudder. He curled his fingers into Brian's hair, his mouth brushing Brian's cheek.

When they stilled, Rob murmured against his neck. "You're a wonder. Thank you for tonight. For all of the nights. For everything."

The world swam in lazy circles around Brian. Would that they could stay wrapped like this. Two bodies, two souls tangled together. "I haven't done anything. You walked into my life and swept me off my feet."

"Did I now?" That beautiful smile.

He brushed one red curl from Rob's forehead. "Blew in off the street, all sunlight and charm."

Rob pecked him on the nose. "Hopeless romantic."

He pulled Rob in for a much longer kiss, plying his

mouth open with lips and tongue until Rob's breathlessness returned, then relented. "Or something."

"Fucking hell." Rob squirmed against him. "You keep that up..."

Brian rolled until he straddled Rob. He wasn't hard and neither was Rob. They were both a wonderful sticky mess. "I could, if you want."

"Mmm." Rob closed his eyes. "Want to. Don't know if I have the energy."

That was fine, as well. "Let me get a towel, then."

He rose, grabbed what they needed to clean up and sank back under the covers with Rob. "I should thank you. For giving me part of myself."

"Didn't though." Rob's words were filled with sleep. "You always had this."

"Freeing it, then."

A chuckle. "Didn't do that, either."

Brian propped himself up on his arm and laughed. "I'm trying to complement you here."

Rob cracked open one eye and smiled. "I know. But you took the steps to grab me. I merely walked into your life."

"Well, then thank you for that."

Rob reached up and pulled Brian down. "It's been my pleasure."

Their lips met. It had been Brian's pleasure, too. And his sanity. He'd never been more at ease with himself than when he was with Rob.

For the first time in a very long while, he felt whole.

An entire day with Brian away from the city was a dream come true for Rob. Carrie Furnace had been nice, but so close to home. Biking hadn't removed them from the city, either. While McConnells Mill was only an hour away, being here felt like they'd left everything behind—their jobs, the city, the stress.

Brian had been right about bringing his camera. The mill and the covered bridge made for stunning shots, especially against the newly green trees and the swollen stream that fed the sluice damn. The air was heavy with cool moisture and the fresh scent of warm earth. They both spent a good half hour snapping shots in and around the mill before heading out on their hike.

He twined his fingers with Brian's. "Do you come up here often?"

Brian kicked a stone down the path. "Not so much anymore, with the shop and all, but when we were younger, my folks would take us up here and let us burn off steam by hiking and running our brains out. Or take us down to Moraine State Park, rent some canoes, and let us exhaust ourselves." He looked up at the trees. "I always loved the water and the trails and... everything."

A man after his own heart. He gave Brian's hand a squeeze. "I can see why." He paused. "There are places like this in Britain, especially north and west. But we never traveled much. There were always places to walk. Fields outside town." He looked around. "Nothing like this, though. This is... spectacular." So green. So many trees! To think, he'd balked at first when the board had proposed moving CirroBot to this area. He'd have missed so much if they hadn't convinced him.

Brian rolled his shoulders and took a deep breath. "I should do this more often."

Yes, he should. Rob could see the stress peeling off of Brian in layers. He walked taller and smiled wider. There was an actual spring in his step and color on those amazing cheeks. "Well, I do love to hike. And bike. I'm guessing there must be somewhere around here to do that, too?"

Brian nodded. "Moraine. Can also swim there, though if you want to do that, we might as well go up to Erie for the weekend. It's not the ocean, but the beaches are nice."

That was a good sign—Brian thinking about an entire weekend away. Those new hires of his must be working out. "I'd love a beach getaway."

Such light in Brian's laugh. "We'll do it, then. Whenever I can get the time."

Hopefully soon.

They fell into a comfortable silence and walked through the woods. A few times, Rob pulled Brian to a stop so he could photograph some wildflowers and once to capture a chittering squirrel scolding them from a tree.

Utterly delightful. The best day.

A horrible electronic buzzing cut through the bird songs and the rustle of leaves. Brian jumped and pulled his hand from Rob's. "Fuck." He whipped his phone from his back pocket and stared at the screen. In that instant, all the tension returned to Brian.

No. Goddamn it. Rob's heart ticked up a beat.

Brian answered. "Hey, Mark. What's up?" A pause. "No, I'm"—Brian looked around, his eyes wide and wild—"out of town."

Bloody fucking *hell*. Rob curled his hands into fists.

"Did you call Miranda?" This time the pause was longer and Brian's face fell. He pushed his hand through his hair. "Shit. Everyone? And Beth can't stay?" He kicked at the ground. "I forgot she has a class tonight."

Brian met Rob's gaze and his face was so damn pale.

"I— Uh." He glanced at his watch. "I can't make it by

then." Panic in his voice. "No, no, if you're that sick, you can't come in. I'll figure something out." He swallowed. "Thanks for the call."

Brian held out the phone again and just stared at it, skin white, eyes wide, breath coming too fast. Rob touched his shoulder. "Hey, hey."

Trembling muscles beneath Rob's hand. "Mark can't make his shift. Sounded horrible. Says he's been throwing up all night. He passed out around dawn and just woke up." Brian looked away from the phone, but didn't focus on anything. "Beth's shift ends in thirty minutes." A whisper of words.

There was no way they could be back at Grounds N'at in that time. None. Even if they ran back to the car, that would probably take a good twenty minutes. Then an hour's drive.

Brian sank down to his knees, as if his legs could no longer hold him. Given how much his hands shook, that might have been the case. Rob crouched next to him and took his hand. "Bri—breathe."

"Can't." Brian said. "Beth can't close the store. Doesn't have a key. Can't set the alarm. God, I shouldn't have..." He trailed off, a touch of color blossoming.

Shouldn't have left the city with Rob. Never gone hiking. A bitter taste in Rob's throat. Oh, he knew this was a fluke. You couldn't predict illness. But a voice—his business sense—wondered if Brian hadn't been cutting things so close to the edge with personnel—would this have happened? Hard to say. Right now, he had to be a boyfriend, not a fucking CEO. "It's okay."

"It's not," Brian snapped. He pulled his hand from Rob's.

Like a punch to the stomach. He gritted his teeth and

said nothing. Brian was upset, but God, he *hated* when people—boyfriends especially—did that. He was trying to *help*.

After a moment, Brian met his gaze. "Sorry—that was unfair."

Rob nodded. "I know you're upset. But let's take a moment and figure this out."

"There's nothing to figure out. I'm *screwed*, Rob."

Maybe he was, but he was also in a full-blown panic. "Who has a key to your shop? Knows how to set the alarm?"

A flicker of sanity in those panicked eyes. "Miranda, Mark, me, and..." He took a breath. "Justin."

"Justin White?"

Brian nodded. "When Justin left, I had him give the key and the code to Sam, since they were right above me. In case of an emergency. But I think Justin still has the key."

"Well, I think this counts." Sure as hell did in his book.

Brian was already pulling up his contacts. A moment later, he held the phone to his ear. "Justin? It's Brian. I know this is really odd, but I need to ask you a big favor." A pause. "Okay, so Mark has the next shift at the shop, but he's down with a stomach thing and I'm up at McConnells Mill and —" He stopped and blushed. "Yeah, with Rob." Brian blinked. "No I just need you to—" He pulled the phone away and looked at it ruefully. "He wants me to put him on speaker."

That was odd. Rob shifted on his feet, ankles protesting from the long stint of crouching.

Brian tapped something on the screen. "Okay."

"I wanted a witness," Justin said, his voice tinny over the phone. "Because I know Brian's not going to listen to me."

"I just need you to close the shop. I'll reopen it when I get back there."

The resentment drove ice down Rob's spine. He tried not to frown at the leaf-strewn trail. Of *course* Brian would rush back.

"Yeah, and that's why I wanted to be on speaker. I'm going to work Mark's shift for you. You stay up there and *enjoy* yourself. You hardly ever get a day off."

"I can't ask you to do that!" Brian's voice pitched higher.

Justin was eminently reasonable. "You're not. I'm *offering*. Look, it's Saturday. Eli and I have nothing planned and I was going to go biking anyway. I always liked working the shop, and this is a *small* thing, Bri."

Brian exhaled and looked up at Rob. "What do you think?"

Oh, that was a fucking loaded question. He cleared his throat. "I'd love to spend the rest of the day with you. You know I would."

Brian's face hardened.

"But I also know you need to do whatever makes you comfortable." Which, in all likelihood, was to rush back to the shop. That place was his first love, indeed. Not like Brian hadn't warned him.

"Brian, stay up there." That from Justin. "I know I left you in a lurch when I went to work for Sam. Let me do this, as a friend."

A sigh. Brian ran a hand through his hair. "Okay. But man, I really owe you one now." Brian's decision was probably influenced more by Justin than Rob, which hurt, but he'd take that if it meant they could have the rest of their day together.

A laugh. "Don't worry about it, dude. This will scratch

that itch for the barista experience." A pause. "Now you two have fun."

"All right. Thanks, Just."

They hung up and Brian rested the phone and his other hand on his thighs and looked like he'd just run a marathon. Rob rose on aching shins and knees and shook his legs out. He held out a hand. "Can't be comfortable kneeling there."

Brian started and looked up. "Yeah, it's not." He took the offered hand and Rob pulled him up. "I still can't believe Justin's going to work the shop."

"He seems like quite a nice man."

A nod. "Best barista I ever had." He glanced at the phone again and tucked it into his back pocket. "I wish I could find another like him. Or Miranda could expand her hours. Or Mark. Something."

All that tension, back in Brian's body. Rob resisted the urge to scream at the universe. It wasn't fair—not to Brian. "The new people seem to be working out."

They started down the path again. "Oh, they are. But it'll take a while before any of them are ready to... well... be a manager."

"Are you the only one at that level, then?" No one else? That seemed a recipe for burnout.

Brian kicked a stone down the path. "Pretty much. I trust Mark and Miranda to close and open, but they can't work the hours I'd need for that position."

And the new hires would take time to earn Brian's trust. "Still, grooming one of them for that wouldn't hurt."

Another stone flew down the path. "Can we *not* talk about this?" A clip to those words and a furrowed brow. "Let's just... enjoy the walk." That last bit was spoken through practically gritted teeth.

A lump formed in Rob's throat. So much for *that*. They

did continue, but Rob's mind wasn't on the scenery or the shots he could take or *anything*.

He had made a *suggestion*. A mild one. His cheeks burned and he glanced at Brian.

Eyes downcast, Brian's mouth was a thin line. Hands clenched at his side, knuckles white. Rob slowed to a stop.

A moment later, Brian did, too, and met Rob's gaze. "I—I'm sorry. I can't stop worrying."

"I know." He tried to keep the resignation from his voice, but Brian flinched, so *that* was an utter failure. Like this trip.

"I'm trying, Rob."

Brian wasn't, but on a certain level, Rob understood. He sighed, swung his camera out of the way, and pulled Brian into a hug. His stiff body melted a fraction. "The shop will be fine."

"Justin shouldn't be working there."

Unspoken words hung around them.

"He wants the best for you." Rob stroked Brian's back. "So do I. You *do* need a break once in a while."

Brian pulled away. "I don't have that luxury. This isn't a nine-to-five gig." He swallowed and looked up. "You knew that when you started dating me."

Rob nodded. He had and had accepted it. Only it was hard watching someone you love work himself to death. For a moment, an image of his father flashed before his eyes. He turned away and studied the trail. "Do you want to go back?"

Silence but for the forest and the birds and the distant murmur of water.

He swung to face Brian. "Do you want to go back?" This time, he enunciated each word with force. He hadn't intended to let his frustration show. But damn it, if Brian kept this up, he, too, would have a heart attack at fifty-one. Then where would Rob be? Sitting despondent at a kitchen table as well?

Brian's face drained of blood and his hands uncurled. "I —yeah. I do. I need to."

Yep. There was the stab to his heart. "All right." He headed back the way they came. After a moment, Brian caught up, his posture heavy and worried.

He was being unfair to Brian—the shop was his, after all. And once upon a time, he'd felt the same way about CirroBot. Until Greg blackmailed him. Until he'd looked in the mirror and seen his father. Until he'd collapsed from the pressure. He took a breath. "I worry about you."

Brian said nothing, but did raise his head.

"The stress isn't good, Bri."

A grunt. "Yeah, but you telling me what to do doesn't help that at all."

This... was a spat. A fight. Rob almost laughed. The realization chipped away some of Rob's anger. "I wasn't trying to tell you what to do. Just... talk it through." He reached out and took Brian's hand. "It's your business, Bri."

"Yeah, it is." He rolled his shoulders and sighed. "I know I should let Justin do the shift, but—I can't let go of the guilt."

That was an issue. Especially when it meant that Rob was the source—his pulling Brian away. "You can't be there twenty-four/seven."

"I have to be." Soft words.

Rob let it go. The silence fell between them on the walk back and it lingered when they climbed into his car. There was nothing he could say or do.

Just hold on and hope that Brian would get the shop together before the stress destroyed him. Or them.

CHAPTER SIXTEEN

Brian watched the trees whiz past on I-79 as Rob drove back to Pittsburgh. He swallowed against the burning in his stomach. Justin was going to kill him.

Worse, Rob had gone silent. No smile. No quips. Not even music on the radio—only the sound of the tires on the road and his breathing, some of which fell into heavy sighs.

Yeah, he'd fucked up. Both with the shop and with Rob. He shouldn't have gone so far from town—but he'd wanted Rob to see a part of his childhood. And now he was reneging on the whole day when Justin was perfectly content to slum it back in Grounds N'at for a few hours. He glanced over. "I'm sorry." Whispered words. He doubted they'd bridge the gap that had formed between them.

Rob glanced his way—a quick meeting of eyes before he focused on the road.

"I know you are." He slid his hands on the wheel. "And I understand how you feel."

"You're still mad." That much was obvious. He'd had spats like this with Anita.

A furrowed brow. "Not mad. Disappointed." He looked

over again, and there was a good heaping of sadness in the lift of Brian's eyebrows. "I'd been looking forward to spending time with you. Seeing you relaxed."

Instead of the tense and tired mess he normally was. Brian scrubbed his face. He loved Grounds N'at. But every so often, a voice inside asked if it was worth it.

He didn't know the answer anymore.

Regardless, he had a responsibility to his employees and customers. That was the pact he'd made when he'd opened. Be a good neighbor, locally and globally. That meant paying people well and sourcing the right coffee, teas, and pastries, and keeping the place open.

As much as he loved spending time with Rob, the shop had to come first. "It's a bump. Things will get better."

A small smile. Rob reached over, took his hand, and squeezed it gently. No words, but there didn't need to be.

Brian exhaled. They could get through this. Somehow, he could balance the shop and Rob. He leaned back against the seat and let the warmth of Rob's hand untangle the knots in his heart until they got too close to Pittsburgh for Rob to drive one-handed.

When they reached the Squirrel Hill exit, Rob finally spoke, his voice soft. "Do you want me to drop you off at the shop or at your flat?"

He had his hiking boots on and jeans and a t-shirt under a light jacket. He didn't *need* to go to his place—except for dropping off his camera. On the other hand, a few extra minutes to clean up wouldn't hurt the situation. "My place."

Rob nodded. They exited the Parkway and drove up Murray—past Grounds N'at, which seemed to be in one piece.

What did you expect? It to blow up while you were gone?

Doubt gnawed in his stomach. Maybe they should have kept hiking. Too late to change his mind.

A few turns to put them the right direction for Brian's street, and Rob pulled up against the curb. "Give me a call later?" Same soft voice, but tension lurked in Rob's shoulders.

Shit. Heart in his throat, Brian nodded. "Not going to stop by the shop?"

Rob's hollow laugh cracked Brian's heart. "No. I need to be home for a while, I think." He cupped Brian's face. "I'm not mad." Not the brilliant smile Rob usually wore, but a smile nonetheless.

"Just disappointed."

Rob stroked his cheek and his smile fell away. "Love isn't always easy."

No. It wasn't. He leaned against Rob's hand. "I'll call."

That little grin returned, thank God. "Go, before you give yourself a coronary."

Brian nodded. He got out, grabbed his stuff from the trunk, and watched Rob drive away. The lump in his throat didn't fade at all.

He stashed his stuff in his apartment, changed his shoes, and jogged down to the shop. When he opened the door, Justin's exasperated look lodged another rock, this one into his stomach.

"Dude, you didn't." Justin shook the fringe of hair from his eyes. "You seriously *didn't*."

Man, he'd had enough of being berated for doing the right thing. He slipped behind the counter and into the back room. Predictably, Justin followed, standing at the door. Brian rounded on him. "Did you expect me to enjoy myself while you were here working for nothing? You're not even my employee."

"No, I'm your *friend*. Doing you a *favor*. And yeah, I kinda did expect you to enjoy your day off with your boyfriend." Justin slowly untied his apron. "But I guess I was wrong."

"Justin—" Brian leaned against his desk. "I'm fucking grateful you bailed me out, but the whole thing ate at me. I *couldn't* enjoy myself. Not when I should have been here in the first place."

Justin set the apron down on the counter. "You can't be here twenty-four/seven. That's not good for you, for your health, or anything."

Nearly Rob's exact words. He couldn't argue with them. Even now, his body twitched from the stress and the sadness. The lump in his gut wouldn't leave and he hated the disappointment that had been carved into Rob. "It's my shop."

Justin scratched the back of his neck. "I know. I get it. Just— Don't let it eat you alive."

Easier said than done.

The bell on the door rang, and they both stiffened. "I guess I should go." Justin backed out of the doorway and headed out into the shop.

Brian followed and made for the sink. "Thanks for everything, Justin."

A flash of a smile, then Justin was ringing the bell on the door. Brian stepped up to the counter to take the next order.

Some of the anxiety melted away when he got into the swing and the rhythm of working the shop. But the ache in his gut remained, as did the vision of Rob's frown burned into his mind.

He managed to be his smiling and mostly friendly self for the rest of the day. After the last customer had left and he'd locked the door, he took out his phone and stared at the screen. He wanted to call Rob. Dreaded calling Rob. But Miranda opened Sunday morning, and he owed Rob his time—any time he could give him, especially after today.

He dialed. "Hey."

"I was wondering if you'd call." Amusement in those words. That untangled the knot in Brian's spine.

He headed back to the counter and sat down on Rob's favorite stool. "Just locked the door a moment ago. Still need to clean things down, but I wanted to see if I could come over tonight."

"There isn't a time of day when I don't want to see you, Bri."

Now he understood that whole heart skipping a beat thing.

Rob continued, his voice silky as dark chocolate syrup. "Shall I come pick you up, then?"

"Yeah." It came out breathless. He rubbed his leg, well aware at the developing tightness of his pants. "I should be finished in about a half hour."

"I'll be there."

They hung up and once more, Brian stared at the phone. He may have disappointed Rob today—but that seemed to be a memory now. Good.

All he had to do was never do that again.

Twenty-five minutes later, Grounds N'at was spotless and the cash drawer was balanced down to the penny. Brian set the alarm and locked the door. Somewhat early for Rob to drive by, but the night wasn't that cold and he needed to breathe air that didn't smell like brewing coffee.

That scent clung to his clothes and—not for the first time—he wondered how *any* of his partners put up with it.

Rob's silver car slid up to the curb and he rolled down the passenger window. "Hey honey, looking for a good time?" A flat twang to that—not at all a British accent, but an impressive impersonation of an American one.

He sauntered up to the car and bent down to peer in. "Isn't that supposed to be my line?"

Rob laughed and spoke in his lovely British voice. "Well, given that neither of us is paying..." He waved to the passenger seat.

Brian opened the door and flopped into the car. "Look, I'm—"

Rob held up his hand and the words died in Brian's throat. A crooked finger and a beckoning gesture had Brian inching closer. When he was in reach, Rob wrapped his warm hand around the back of Brian's neck and pulled him the rest of the way to his mouth.

God. Rob kissed better than any person he knew. Sparks and heat ran from Brian's head to his toes and straight into his cock. He moaned and Rob pulled back. "None of that," he said.

Brian swallowed. "Thank you."

Rob's smile was back, bright and stunning. It lit up the car. "Put your belt on, and we can go."

"Should get a few things from my apartment." Especially if he were spending the night. "Assuming..."

Rob chuckled. "Yes, do assume. I intend to make up for lost time." He pulled the car away from the curb.

After that sentence, it took Brian all of three minutes to run up the stairs, shove shit into a backpack, and run back down to Rob's car. God, his heart. His cock. He didn't know which ached more—or why Rob simply picking him up was such a fucking turn-on. Not like they hadn't had sex before.

But they'd never *fought* before today, if that was even a fight. He wasn't sure about anything anymore.

Rob wasn't mad, and that's what mattered. He was playful and hot and demanding and Brian wanted to fall to his knees for that. Had the situation been reversed, he'd still be carrying around a giant grudge on his back.

He slid into the car and tried to hide his cringe. The shop had been his focus for so long, he had trouble thinking beyond it, even when it came to Rob. Shop first, everything else second.

Was that fair?

Rob tousled his hair. "You're still tense."

"Long day." It came out as a croak.

"Hmm. I may have an idea that might help."

Anything that involved Rob would help. Wall-banging dirty sex, or watching a movie and eating popcorn on his couch. Didn't matter. "Dare I ask?"

They headed down to Bloomfield. "Let it be a surprise."

Goose bumps rose and he leaned back against leather. "Okay."

When they got into the house, Rob's smile became a sly thing that put fire in Brian's blood. He nodded up the stairs. "Bedroom."

Yeah, he was hard now. Well, harder. He climbed up, Rob following behind, while his cock and lungs fought to see which one could ache more.

The room was dimly lit and a faint trace of something woodsy and clean filtered through the air. Rob's body wash? He paused inside the doorway and let his backpack slide from his shoulder. Being here felt good, like the hike had before his phone had rung.

Rob slid an arm around him and pulled him back against his long body and hard bulge. A kiss to the neck. "Better?"

"Being here is always good." In Rob's arms, when the shop was closed, he had no worries in the world.

A chuckle. Rob took his backpack and set it on a chair near a reading lamp and picked up a large beach towel. "So one of the other hobbies I picked up over the years was massage."

Oh. *Oh*. Brian saw the little bottles on the far nightstand and his whole body flamed. "Really?"

"Mmm-hmm. I figured you could use one. Work out your stress." The corner of his mouth ticked up and he spread the towel over one side of the bed. "Clear your mind for a little while."

Rob's hands on his body? Shit, that would put one thing into his brain. He exhaled. "I'm game."

There was that deep chuckle again. "I can tell."

Yeah, his erection was pretty damn noticeable. Brian shrugged, a touch of heat on his cheeks. "Guilty."

"What you should be is naked and lying on my bed." Rob pulled off his own shirt.

If that wasn't encouragement. He stripped his clothes and crawled onto the bed. Rob had him lay face first on the towel and arranged his limbs and neck so he was comfortable.

Rob shed the rest of his clothes down to his briefs. "I should buy a table at some point." He picked up a bottle of oil. "But this will do for tonight."

"It's fine. I—" He groaned when Rob's slick hands glided over his shoulders and he started working the muscles there. "Oh God." Pleasure and pain as Rob found every single knot.

"Be a good man. Relax and enjoy."

So, so easy to do. Brian closed his eyes and tried not to groan or squirm too much as Rob warmed his back and worked each muscle group in turn. While it was utterly sensual to have Rob touching him, it also felt good in a way that wasn't sexual.

Shit, he'd been tense. Parts of his back, both upper and lower, had enough knots in them to keep Rob busy for months.

Heat and movement and strong fingers. The scent of oil. Rob's breath against his skin. Brian shivered.

"Cold?" Rob murmured.

"No." The word came out languid, akin to his jelly limbs and deep breaths. There was only one part of his body that hadn't *quite* gotten the message to relax. "That feels great."

He already knew what Rob's slick hand around his cock was like. He rocked his hips.

A chuckle and Rob slid his hands to Brian's ass. "Probably not had your glutes worked on before." He kneaded Brian's ass cheeks.

No, he hadn't and his moan was all kinds of confused. So, so good to have Rob's fingers work out the tension in those muscles, but God, he was so turned on by Rob rubbing and pulling his slick hands over his ass.

His body melted as his cock hardened. "Unfair."

"Oh, I don't think so. There are *so* many ways I can turn you into a quivering and moaning wreck." Rob kissed the small of Brian's back. "This is just one of them."

He could only whimper and rock against the bed.

The entire time, Rob didn't stray near his hole. No, the bastard seemingly touched every part of his ass *but* his crack —then worked lower, to his legs.

A different kind of pleasure there, one that was pure relief until Rob hit his calves. They hurt like fire. He lifted his head from the pillow. "Oh fuck!" He twitched his leg away. "Jesus."

"I think your calf muscle is one giant knot." Rob pulled Brian's leg back down and rubbed his calf again—lightly this time. "Let's work on your foot, then see if I can get those muscles to loosen up."

The foot massage nearly had him drooling into the pillow. Tingles all the way in his skull when Rob pressed in on a particularly stubborn knot.

"Feels so good up to my head."

"It's all connected." Rob worked his way up Brian's leg, this time lightly touching the calf. Felt better.

"Like that," he murmured. "Is good."

"Going to work a little deeper. Yelp if it hurts." Laughter in his words.

Brian snorted, then gasped when Rob pressed harder. Still not as bad as before.

After the legs, Brian was close to passing out and even his dick had relaxed—until Rob ran those warm hands over his ass again, then up his back. This time, the touch was anything but therapeutic. Brian shifted and bit his lip. "This is good, too." It came out as a whisper.

"Mmm-hmm." Rob pinched his ass. "Turn over."

Brian did, and there was Rob, standing over him, bare chested, bare legged, his shaft hard under the thin fabric of his underwear. A flush ran up his neck and his grin was toothy and wicked.

"Fuck, you're beautiful."

Rob traced a finger down the center of Brian's chest. "So are you." He poured more oil on his hands and leaned over, palms gliding across Brian's shoulders. "Especially your arms."

He worked down one, fingers making Brian gasp as he hit every sore muscle group. Brian repeated with the other. More oil and his palms slid over Brian's torso.

"Your chest is grand, too." Fingers pressed into pecs and skimmed over nipples, sending conflicting signals again. *Relax*, his body said. *Fuck me*, his mind and cock screamed. He groaned and met Rob's gaze.

The devil had dimples.

Rob's slick hands slipped to Brian's abs, and he gave up all hope of trying to remain still. He rocked his hips.

"Want something?" Rob's voice was rough and deep. He worked closer and closer to Brian's cock.

"Yeah. Touch me." He was dying under those hands. Hot blood pounded in his head. All he wanted was Rob's hand around his shaft.

"I am touching you." Laughter and dancing fingers over his stomach and up his side.

He gasped and moaned and caught Rob's hands. "On my cock."

Rob straightened and reached for the bottle of oil. "I want to hear you say it, Bri." There was a gleam in Rob's eye.

He shivered and arched his back. "I want your hand around my dick." He took a breath. "Hell, I want your mouth on my balls. I want you naked and on top of me. I want—" His breath caught.

He wanted Rob inside him. Not just his fingers, either.

A twitch to Rob's smile. "Let's start with that lovely cock of yours, and see what happens from there?"

Brian exhaled and bent his legs so Rob could kneel between

them. Finally, Rob's warm, talented hand wrapped around Brian's dick and stroked. Tight. Firm. Silky smooth from the oil. Brian rolled his head against the pillow and moaned.

He lifted his hips and thrust into Rob's fist. "I like this massage."

A laugh. "I fully intend to give you a happy ending." He pressed his thumb against the head of Brian's dick and slid it over the slit.

Brian could only groan and work his hips faster. The closer he got to bliss, the more Rob loosened his hand.

"I'm not ready for cream from my Americano yet."

Brian choked on a laugh. "Really? *Really?*"

Rob let go of Brian's shaft and climbed over him until his lips were inches away. "You fucking love it."

That was the worst part. He did. The stupid puns. The coffee jokes. The cream. Everything. "Love you."

Rob devoured his mouth, his tongue opening Brian's lips, stroking, tasting every inch. Brian melted into the mattress, his blood thick in his veins and his head and body on fire for Rob. Their lips touched, and brushes of arms and legs—so close—so far. When Rob relented, Brian had to catch his breath.

When he did, he stared up at Rob. "Touch me."

A small smile. "Where?"

Nerves tingled and pinpricks danced up the back of his skull. "My ass. My hole."

A barely audible chuckle. "Why?"

Oh, Brian knew Rob understood, that he wanted to hear the words. Intimate desires and unspoken needs finally spoken out loud. Hot. *Sexy*. He'd never been on this side of the game before. "I want you to fuck me," he whispered, "with your cock."

"You sure?" Gentle words. "Not every guy needs a dick in his arse."

He stroked Rob's strong arms. "I *want* your dick in my ass. The other night was—" Utterly amazing. "I can't even describe it."

Rob stole a kiss. "I need to wash the oil off my hands. Doesn't play well with condoms."

That's why he hadn't gone down Brian's crack. "Part of your plan all along?"

A laugh. "No." He climbed off the bed. "But I like leaving my options open." His smile was pure delight, as was the way his chest had reddened. He vanished into the bathroom.

Brian slid one leg out and wrapped his hand around his dick. Little shocks of ice and heat danced up and down his limbs. Rob's fingers in his hole had felt so good pounding and stretching him. But this... the unknown was nerve-wracking.

Rob returned to the bed and pulled off his underwear, freeing his dick and balls.

Fuck. He'd had Rob in his mouth, knew his girth. He met Rob's gaze and hoped he didn't look as nervous as he felt.

Rob fetched a different bottle from his nightstand and a foil wrapper. "On your hands and knees, Brian."

He shifted and did as Rob ordered, his heart ramming against his ribs. He shivered and burned and his exhale was one long shudder.

Rob fingered his balls. "Relax."

Every vein blazed at Rob's touch. "Hard to do when you're driving me crazy."

A snort. "Just you wait."

Cool liquid ran down his crack and he gasped when Rob circled his hole.

God, yeah. *That.* Sparks up his back. He let his head drop.

"There you go," Rob said.

He pressed a finger in and Brian couldn't help the whimper. Felt natural—normal—to rock back.

"You do love this, don't you?" Rob fucked him with his finger, gently at first, then harder until Brian had the towel under him—and maybe the comforter under that—clenched in his hands.

He couldn't answer, only moan in rhythm to Rob's thrusts. Felt so good each time Rob hit his prostate. He lowered himself to his forearms.

Far too soon, Rob pulled his finger out. Foil crinkled and there was another snap of the lube bottle. The bed rocked slightly.

Oh God. This was happening.

A press of lips against the small of his back. "Just like with my finger, relax and push."

Then the thick tip of Rob's cock settled against his hole and pressed in. Brian gasped as Rob stretched and opened him—no pain, not really—but an immense feeling of fullness. Like before, he couldn't wrap his head around the sensation. Trembling, he pressed his forehead against the mattress.

Rob slid a hand over Brian's back. "Breathe, Bri."

"I am." Came out like dust. "Feels—feels—" He lifted his head and rocked back slightly. Yup. Rob was inside him. Holy hell. Every nerve in his body sang. "Good."

"Feels fucking *amazing*." Rob gripped Brian's hips and pulled out a fraction before thrusting deeper.

Air caught in Brian's lungs. Then again when Rob

plunged in deeper still. Then he was sliding in and out and Brian couldn't breathe without moaning.

Finger-fucking had been intense. Now he was losing his mind over and over again. He rocked in time with Rob, their bodies finding the perfect rhythm.

Each stroke drove fire into his brain and sparks against his vision. "Rob... God... I can't..." Couldn't take much more of this. Didn't realize he was capable of being driven this high, way past the point where he should have been shouting and coming. So fast, so intense. But when he stroked himself, he wasn't even hard.

"You feel so damn good." Rob's words were slurred with passion and need. "Fuck, Bri—" He thrust in harder.

Hearing Rob out of his mind drove a red-hot spike of desire straight through Brian. He'd done that. Turned Rob inside out. His cock thickened in his hand. "Like fucking me?"

Rob slowed his thrusts. "You have no idea." A murmur of words.

Brian rocked back, wanting more of that sweet rhythm, of Rob sending sparks up his spine. "Been there, done you."

Rob's next thrust knocked him down against the mattress and stole all his breath. "Don't get cocky with me." Command there. "Certainly not when mine's in *your* arse." Rob picked up speed. "Remember, I've done this before." Rob's words brushed like silk against Brian's overheated skin.

He hadn't. Not like this. Couldn't even moan, only gasp and curse.

Rob pulled him up, then drove into him, deep and hard until there was only pleasure and light and heat and moans. His. So loud, echoing in the room.

"Yeah, that's it." Rob said, his voice hot in Brian's ear. "You fucking love my cock, don't you?"

God, he did. He couldn't even think to form words, only gasps of breath.

Rob wrapped a hand around his dick. "This familiar?"

Exactly how he'd fucked Rob. He rolled his head against Rob's shoulder and caught a glimpse of the freckles across Rob's nose before he had to close his eyes against the blinding light in his head, the crackle of fire in his blood and the unending pleasure that Rob rammed into him over and over.

His orgasm hit so fast, so unexpected that he shouted against the intensity of it, pumping his cock in Rob's fist, his entire body shuddering against Rob's. Gold fireworks stole what was left of his vision and heat burned through him.

He'd die from this. Too much pleasure shifting toward agony.

Rob's own cry was as loud and he plowed into Brian deep and hard until Brian thought his brain would explode from ecstasy and pain.

Eventually they both slowed, folded, and collapsed onto the bed, Rob heavy, but not uncomfortable, on top of him.

He'd never come like that, not to the edge of agony. Never had the entire world vanished. His whole body ached in glorious ways and his brain didn't want to form words.

Rob kissed his back between the shoulder blades, his warm lips electrifying Brian's over-sensitive skin. "I'll be right back."

He groaned when Rob pulled out. Every bone felt like liquid. Probably because he was still on fire, despite the fading glow of his orgasm. A puddle of Brian.

The bed shifted and Rob stroked his back. "You still with me?"

Brian lifted his head. Freckles, those same dimples, and a lovely smile. "I think?" Brian rolled onto his side to see Rob better. "Please tell me you'll do that again."

His chuckle was almost musical. "Whenever you like."

Anytime. All the time. "That was something else."

The dimples deepened when Rob flashed his brilliant grin. "Glad you enjoyed it."

Way more than he'd expected. "It—I need—" Still couldn't put emotions into words. The towel under him bore exactly how much pleasure Rob had driven from him. "Is it always like that?"

"I don't know," he murmured, then leaned in to take Brian's mouth. After a kiss that had Brian moaning, Rob spoke, lips to lips. "I guess we'll have to find out."

A scatter of heat ran through his body. He shouldn't be turned on—and yet he was. But his body couldn't catch up quite as fast. The hiking, the stress, and the massage exacted their toll. Lethargy had him closing his eyes. "Not tonight."

A laugh. "You look about ready to melt, and while I would love to fuck you again, I'm not far behind you in the exhausted department."

He snickered. "Old man."

"Mmm-hmm. An old man who made you beg and scream and come all over my nice towel."

Yeah, he had. "Probably should shower." If he could stand. "The oil..."

Rob slipped off the bed and stood. "I'll give you a hand."

He held out one. Brian curled his fingers in Rob's and Rob pulled him off the bed and into his arms. They moved with the same sense of non-urgency toward the bathroom, touching and kissing—not to tease—but to taste. To exist—be with each other.

God, he loved this man. Loved that the world vanished, that his body sang, that his heart and soul ached as much as his well-fucked body.

Even the shower was a study in exploration, their hands and tongues finding those places to stroke, to touch, and finally, to clean all over again.

Part of him wanted his cock to rise, for his libido to be that of a teen again, but there'd been too much pleasure heaped on the stress of the day. Even Rob only managed to get semi-hard.

But Rob's eyes, his smile, those were exhilarating and quickened Brian's pulse. They dried each other off and headed back to bed. Rob tossed the towel into his hamper and slid under the covers next to Brian. "Please tell me you have tomorrow off."

And there was the shop again, inching between them like a jealous lover. "I can't," he whispered. "But Miranda works opening shift."

"So I have you all morning?" In the dim light of the room, Rob traced his fingers over Brian's cheeks.

"Don't have to be in until two."

Rob's lips were on his, opening him and just as quickly, the shop was gone. Fingers danced against his skin, driving heat into his blood and sapping the last bit of energy he had. When Rob relented, there was a huff of warm breath against his cheek. "I can fill those hours quite nicely for you."

Fill more than the hours, Brian bet. "Can't wait." In the quiet of Rob's room, Brian kissed Rob's shoulder and closed his eyes. If every night could be like this, his life would be complete.

CHAPTER SEVENTEEN

Rob paced in his living room. Since the day of their interrupted hike two weeks earlier, everything between him and Brian had eased out. Yes, Brian spent an inordinate amount of time at his shop, filling in far too many shifts. That hadn't changed. But when he was with Rob—he was entirely *with* Rob. Bike rides, working on their photographs. Dinners. Shopping. Geocaching. Whatever they did together, Brian was wholly there.

That had been the silver lining to the uncomfortable episode. They'd always been so matched in bed—now they moved with the same grace and passion outside of the bedroom.

He checked the wall clock. It was almost exactly five minutes later than it had been the last time he'd looked—and still about an hour before Brian would arrive at his place.

They were going to the Keppler family dinner, where Rob would meet not just Brian's parents—but his brother and sister, too.

Rob had walked into hostile board meetings when

earnings were down, and ruled the room. He'd stood in front of jaded venture capitalists and given cases for why they should hand him hundreds of thousands of dollars and gotten the cash he needed.

Never in his life had he been the nervous wreck he was right now. He wouldn't be facing business men and women —but Brian's *family.*

His own had been tiny and dysfunctional and now dead and buried. All his previous relationships had either been short or meaningless.

How was he supposed to act? What was he supposed to say? He was forty years old, not some bumbling teen.

He didn't even *have* siblings. What did he say to them?

When the doorbell rang, he nearly jumped out of his skin. A glance at the clock told him it was far too early for Brian to have arrived.

Except when he opened the door, that's who stood on his doorstep. "Hey."

No bike helmet. No bike. Just a backpack slung over one shoulder. "Hi." He opened the door wider. "You're early."

Brian's grin was sheepish. He strode through the door. "Yeah. I decided to take the bus rather than bike." He stowed the bag near the stairs. "It's warm and I didn't want to be a sweaty mess."

Rob liked when Brian was a sweaty mess, especially when he made him that way. There were no showers quite like the ones with Brian. "Pity."

Brian chuckled and leaned in for a kiss. "Well, I am early."

That was just invitation enough to deepen the kiss until Brian squirmed. Lovely. But as much as he wanted Brian, perhaps right before meeting his parents was not the time to fuck. He broke the kiss. "I'll save the cream for dessert."

Red flushed Brian's cheeks. "No appetizer?"

For someone only two years younger, there were times when Brian exhausted him. He took a taste of those lips again. "I'll make it up to you."

A fake pout, then a smile. "I brought your prints."

That made Rob's heart tumble in an entirely different manner and he pulled Brian toward the living room. "Really?"

Brian resisted long enough to grab his backpack and extract two pieces of heavy cardboard. They sat down on the sofa. "Need to get them matted and framed, but I thought maybe you might want to sign them first."

Sign them? That twisted something in his brain and his eyes misted. "You're joking."

"No." Brian got one of his very serious looks. "Not at all. You're the artist."

Why did that put the fear of God into him? A moment later, Brian pulled out a set of eight glossy photographs from between the sleeve and Rob's breath caught.

He knew the top image. He'd taken it up at McConnells Mill—part of the water wheel, the stream, and the spring trees in the background. Seeing it as a print—the fucking thing looked professional. Like a puzzle or a photo from a magazine or a work of art. So much better than the proofs had been.

He couldn't speak.

A small, sympathetic smile on Brian, one that was quickly slipping toward amused.

Bastard. He knew.

The next was from the Carrie Furnace. A wild pansy blooming in the ruins of industry. Rust and steel and nature.

Again, he knew he'd snapped the shot, could even smell the air and feel the excitement in his body, but the image took on a life of its own.

The other six photos were the same way. Stunning. Unbelievable that he'd captured those moments, even though he knew in his bones that he had.

He leaned back against the couch, his hands shaky. "These are… lovely."

Brian took the photos from him and set them on the coffee table. "They are." He took Rob's hands. "They're yours."

No one could take that from him, either. Not his dead father and mother. Not a blackmailing lover. Not his job. Not even Brian, who'd helped him reach this point. He took a breath. "I don't have a pen." Didn't even know what type would be best.

But lovely Brian did, of course. He reached into his backpack and pulled out a pen, every motion an act of saying *I love you*.

Rob swallowed, uncapped the pen, and signed on the bottom edge, where he'd seen such signatures on photographs before, and his heart just about beat out of his chest. When he was done with the photographs, he recapped the pen, placed it on the table, and leaned back. He could barely see through the mist in his eyes.

Silently and reverently, Brian collected the photographs and put them back into their sleeve. "I'll get them framed for you."

That was too much. He crooked his finger and beckoned Brian closer and of course he came. Rob pulled him the rest of the way, brushing his lips against Brian's. "Thank you," he whispered into Brian's ear and held him tight, until the enormity of the emotions in his chest settled down.

Brian stroked his hair. "You're welcome." A murmur of sound.

How long they sat there holding each other, Rob didn't know, but when his clock gently chimed the hour, he loosened his hold on Brian. "Did you plan to completely shatter me before we went to your parents?"

Brian opened space between them, his whole being a mix of amusement and contriteness. Entirely adorable. If they hadn't had to walk several blocks in a few minutes, Rob would have pulled him off the couch and straight upstairs.

Brian scratched the back of his head. "I knew you'd be nervous and wanted to make you feel better. I guess I screwed up."

"Not at all." It had worked. He wasn't as worried about Brian's family, not when his heart was full of heat and light. He kissed Brian, a gentle sip of his lips, and rose.

Brian glanced at his watch and stood. "Yeah, I guess we should go." His smile was broad. "You ready for this?"

Rob couldn't help the laugh. "At forty? Absolutely not."

They went anyway. Despite it having rained for the better part of Saturday, the clouds had lifted enough for sun to dry the pavement. A breeze had blown much of the humidity away and the fresh air cleared Rob's head and put his emotions back together.

Soon, they were in front of a house smaller than his—more of a row house than his Victorian. Before he could even prepare himself, Brian caught his hand and pulled him up on to the porch and through the front door.

"I'm home!" Brian called out.

The reply came from where Rob guessed the kitchen might be. "We're back here."

Still holding Rob's hand, Brian led him through the house into the kitchen and holy hell, he was staring at Brian's parents while holding Brian's hand. His throat tightened completely.

Boardrooms were *very* different from boyfriend's parents' kitchens. Smelled a damn sight better in here, but oh, the scrutiny was even more intense.

"Mom, Dad, this is Rob." Brian gave his hand a squeeze, then let go.

"Hello. Very nice to meet you." Somehow, he sounded normal, despite the constriction in his chest. He held out his hand to Brian's father.

No hesitation at all. A firm shake. "Tony," he said. "And this is Alice, Brian's mother."

He would have known that if he'd seen her anywhere. Same eyes. Same smile. But rather than shake his hand, she drew him into an enormous hug. "You're as handsome as Brian said."

And wasn't Brian a pretty shade of red when his mum let Rob go, though given the warmth on his cheeks, he probably wasn't far behind.

"Yes, well." His laugh came out as more of a squeak. "He can exaggerate."

She patted his arm. "Not this time."

"Mom!" Yes, Brian was horrified and it was perfect, so much so that his cheeks hurt from smiling.

Fucking lucky man. His parents were gems. "Something smells fantastic," he murmured and peeked over at the stove.

That redirected everyone.

"Homemade ravioli," Tony said. "Beef and cheese. The cheese ones are for Zoe though, so I hope you like beef."

Rob bit his tongue to keep *there isn't a meat I don't like* from popping out. "Beef is absolutely fine." He paused. "Did you make them? Brian said you both cook?"

Indeed, both beamed and launched into how they'd made the pasta and the filling and worked in the kitchen together. It was heartwarming and beautiful. Halfway through, he slipped an arm around Brian's waist. A hitch of breathing from Brian but a minute later, he relaxed into Rob.

This was exactly how family should be and *everything* he'd never had.

The lump in his chest returned with vengeance and it must have shown, because Brian's mom took a step forward. "Is there something wrong?" Same concern he'd seen on Brian countless times.

He tried to smile around the pain. "Nothing at all. This is wonderful. I've been here"—He glanced at his watch—"ten minutes?" He met Alice's stare. "I never had this."

Another hug from her, this one bigger and warmer. "You're welcome anytime."

"They mean that, too," Brian said.

Of course they did. They were the people who'd born and raised Brian and apparently the apple didn't fall that far.

"So," Tony said, "Brian says you're a CEO?"

He couldn't quite resist rolling his eyes. He gave Brian a rather poignant look.

He held up his hands. "Hey, you are."

"It's true. I am. Please don't hold it against me."

Brian's parents laughed at that.

He was proud of his work and how far he'd gotten, but so many people had misconceptions about CEOs. Or perhaps he was different. He didn't know.

Brian caught his hand again. "He's also a photographer."

Once again, a burning face. "I dabble."

"You do more than that."

"Bri—" Even he heard the exasperation in his voice. Oh God, they *sounded* like a couple. The knowing look that passed between Brian's parents. A moment later Rob huffed a laugh. "Your son has been trying to convince me I have talent."

"Tons of it."

"And I've been resisting him."

Tony snorted. "Good luck. He's like his mother."

Brian poked Rob in the side. "I get to have a professional opinion." He went in for a full tickle.

Rob caught his hand before he could truly embarrass them. "Yes, yes. BFA. I remember."

Another amused look from Brian's parents. Thankfully, the front door banged open, and a woman's voice cried out, in practically the same manner Brian had, "I'm here!"

"That's Zoe," Brian said, then shouted, "We're in the kitchen!"

"Well of course you're in the—" A woman with short black hair and a few piercings on her ear walked through the door and stopped dead in her tracks. "Oh, *wow*. You must be the boyfriend."

"That would be me, yes." He couldn't help the smile. "You must be the sister."

She had Brian's blush, but recovered quickly. "Last time I checked, yeah." Her smile was like everyone's in this family—warm and inviting.

He would have introduced himself, but the front door sounded again. Once more, a call came, and this time both Brian and Zoe answered.

Rob turned to Brian's parents. "Does this happen *every* time?"

"Pretty much, yes." Alice said. She dusted her fingers on her apron, then untied it.

"I hear a voice I don't know." That from the man who walked into the kitchen.

Holy hell, the genes in this family. Brian's brother was taller, but had the same all-American looks. Darker hair and he wore the uniform of a commercial airline pilot. He lacked Brian's warm brown eyes and amazing arms, though.

His gaze was stern. "So, *you're* the guy dating my little brother?" He crossed his arms and stared hard at Rob.

Fuck. Brian had said everyone was onboard with this. He resisted the urge to step back, and glanced at Brian.

Brian lifted a brow and snorted. "He's fucking with you. This is Len, my overprotective *elder* brother." He entwined his warm fingers with Rob's. "And yes, this is my boyfriend, Rob."

Len cracked a smile that tore away the mask and held out his hand. "Good to meet you."

His shake, like Tony's was firm and friendly. "Likewise." He managed the word, but his heart was beating a bit fast.

As if Brian knew, he bumped his hip and gave his hand a squeeze. "You just get in, Len?"

Len's shoulders dropped. "Yeah. Should have been back around eleven, but there was a large weather system in the plains causing all sorts of delays and reroutings. I'm just glad I'm home in time for dinner."

Maybe it was the fleeting feeling that Len didn't like him, but he wanted to make some sort of connection. "Sympathies," he said. "I used to fly a lot." Too much. Thank goodness there was less of that now.

"Chicago, right? Not a bad hop, but the timing's always a crapshoot."

Rob nodded.

Tony cleared his throat. "Len, would you mind fetching some wine from the cellar?"

A large smile. "Never in a million years. Red or white?"

Tony gestured to Rob. "Guest's pick."

"Red would be the most appropriate, yes?"

Len nodded and cracked a grin that was almost as brilliant as Brian's. "Good choice."

He said that to *Brian*—which meant it wasn't about Rob's wine selection. His cheeks couldn't get hotter.

No wonder Brian was fast on his feet with the quips. Growing up in a family like this? You'd have to keep your brain and tongue sharp.

As Len vanished down into the basement, Brian's mom spoke. "Zoe, why don't you and Brian make a salad. Rob can help your dad set the table."

Now that was odd, but nice to be thrown into the family like that. Tony gestured to the living room, and Rob followed. "She wants us to use the good plates."

"Not on account of me, surely." Still, he took the white china plates Tony pulled from the cabinet and handed to him. He laid them down in the appropriate spots.

Tony snorted. "Of course for you. Who else?"

Rob swallowed and took two wineglasses from Tony. Cut crystal. "I'm—" He shrugged and held up a glass. "Not *this* fancy."

Tony eyed him, very much in the same manner Len had. "You're a CEO."

"I am, but... this isn't business." He wouldn't feel so helpless if it were. Silverware followed. Actual silver, with a slight tarnish to its glint.

"So, is tonight more or less important than business?"

Oh yes, he was being tested, but there was only one answer to that question. "Far *far* more important." The words scraped against a tight throat.

Tony nodded. "Hence..." He gestured at the table and the expensive setting.

Rob straightened. "I understand." He clamped down on the rest of his thoughts.

"But?" Cloth napkins. Tony was pulling out fucking cloth napkins and napkin rings.

"I'm a kid from a coal town, under it all. I'm not—" He stopped and laughter took him, enough that he grabbed the back of the nearest chair for support.

He was standing in the house of a kid from a steel town. Brian's house, in Pittsburgh. "I suppose," Rob said, "this is where you tell me to stop being a pillock."

"Does that mean dumbass?" Tony's smile took all the edge off that.

Rob chuckled. "Exactly."

"Who's being a dumbass?" Brian carried a salad into the room and set it on the table.

"Me," Rob admitted.

"You're balking at the china, aren't you?" Brian's smile was a mile wide. So was Zoe's.

And the crystal. He shrugged, which was as close to admission as he was willing to give.

"Mom and Dad break out all the stops for..." Zoe paused. "Well, you're the first *boy*friend, but you know."

"I could get out the slide projector," Tony said.

"No!" Zoe and Brian spoke at the same time, horror on their faces.

Rob leaned against the chair and laughed. "Now that's true family hazing."

"They usually leave that for Christmas." Len strode in, carrying two wine bottles. "So beware."

"Noted." Assuming they made it that far. Goose bumps on his arms. He met Len's smile with one of his own.

Finally, Alice came in with the ravioli and sauce and placed those on the table and they all shuffled around to their seats—Rob's was predictably next to Brian's. Grace was said—the Catholic version he barely knew—then the wine poured and food shared.

"So." Len passed the salad to Rob. "How's the shop?"

Everyone saw the screwed-up face Brian tried not to make. "It's... busy." He piled some greens into his salad bowl. "Scheduling's been complex."

Not really. Brian took all the unworked shifts. Rob chewed on his tongue and took the offered salad.

"You're not working those awful hours, are you?" That from Alice.

Brian dropped his shoulders. "Like I said, it's complex."

Nothing that hiring a few additional people wouldn't solve. Rob didn't know coffee, but he knew staffing. He handed the salad to Zoe.

"Do you two actually get to see each other?" Her eyes were the same shade as Brian's.

The worry Rob felt lay in her gaze. That fear resided in each of them, including Tony. Brian stared at his plate, his scowl stony. Rob slid a hand on Brian's leg and gave the tense muscles a squeeze. "Of course we see each other. We make time." *He* made time, but the rope of tension beneath his hand loosened. "I understand the pressure of owning your own business."

Brian lifted his head. "It sucks sometimes." He covered Rob's hand with his own. "But it's getting better. The new hires are working out and summer's coming. It's always easier to schedule when everyone's out of school."

The concern in his family faded and the rest of the food was passed around.

Len talked a bit about his flights and some of the crazier things that had happened. "Had one passenger get rip-roaring drunk in first class and nearly start a fistfight with his neighbor. Except his neighbor was an air marshal, so that ended quickly and in handcuffs." He shook his head. "But we had to make an emergency landing because of the idiot."

Zoe recounted a win at her lab—one of her experiments had completed successfully and the data had been quite good. Rob understood some of the terminology, but other bits flew over his head—not exactly his field even if some of his robots were for the medical industry—but he understood the excitement of good data.

"So you'll be able to build off of that?"

She nodded. "Oh yeah. Might even be able to get a grant to continue the research."

Alice coughed. "And are we ever going to hear any more about this girlfriend of yours?"

A very quiet chuckle from Brian and Zoe got a sheepish look. "Um. Her name's Jyoti. She's from India. I didn't know if..." She trailed off.

Fearful of the racial differences? Rob studied Brian's family. Both Alice and Tony sat back, but it was Alice who spoke. "Would you like to bring her to dinner sometime?"

Zoe nodded. "She's vegetarian, too."

Len nodded absently and dabbed his ravioli in sauce. The smile on his face was mirrored on Brian's.

"I'm sure we can manage," Alice said, almost bemused.

Zoe exhaled and relaxed. "Thanks, Mom."

Tony shook his head. "You'd think after all these years,

you kids would realize we're gonna love you no matter what."

"Well, I do," Len said. He popped a ravioli into his mouth. He met Rob's glance and his smile deepened.

Now there was a story he wanted to hear. He'd have to ask Brian later.

"I do have a question," he said to both Alice and Tony, "if you don't mind something a bit personal?"

They looked at each other and then at him. Both expressions were inviting, and Alice nodded.

"Brian said you were both still Catholic." They'd said grace. There were pieces of religious art in the house, plus some palm branches tucked behind a crucifix. "How does that work? I mean..."

"How can we be fine with a bisexual son and a lesbian daughter?" Tony watched him over his wineglass.

Rob swallowed and nodded.

Alice swirled her wine, a movement that reminded Rob so much of Brian. "God is love. Mankind isn't always. I'd rather err on the side of love."

"I wish more people erred on that side."

A huff from Brian. "Trouble is, loving your neighbor is *hard.*"

So very true. Rob had seen that play out in his hometown.

Silence reigned until Zoe started the next round of conversation. She threw a question to Rob and it hit him right in the head. "What about you, Rob? How's your life?"

His life? "It's grand." He not so secretively grabbed Brian's hand under the table and grinned at him. Even playing second fiddle to the coffee shop, being with Brian was a wonderful thing. But he had the sense that they wanted more about him and what he did.

Rob set down his fork. "We've been developing some new robotic medical devices at work. They're still in prototype, but everything looks promising." He stopped and huffed a laugh. "I could go on at length, but I might begin to sound like a salesman if I do."

"What about your photography?" That was from Tony.

Brian squeezed his hand. Hell, he wasn't going to win this one. Might as well be honest. "I never considered it more than a hobby, but I love it. Capturing slices of the world other people miss. Looking at things from a different perspective." He paused. "My parents were never keen on the arts—not for me anyway. So it's also a rebellion, I suppose."

"He's really good. I should have brought the prints." Brian patted his hand, then resumed eating his meal.

"Oh God, no. You would have embarrassed me more than I already am." He reached for his wine.

"Welcome to the family," Len said. He raised his wineglass.

A wave of wonderment spun through Rob and he was left frozen for a moment. Carefully, he grabbed the glass and matched Lenny's toast.

No words, though. Couldn't push them out of his throat. He took a sip of wine, and the conversation moved on to Tony's gardening exploits and the sheer number of tomato seedlings he had under grow-lights in the basement.

Len's words echoed in his head. *Family?* Maybe. He *wanted* that, dearly. Wanted a life with Brian—but one that didn't involve Brian exhausted every waking hour of the day, or on pins and needles that something would go wrong with the shop.

He enjoyed this, though. Sitting at the table with *a* family, one that accepted him for who he was. That had been a far cry from his own parents, even after he'd become successful. Didn't help that he'd been fucking some random bloke while his mother was swallowing pills.

Rob set down his wine. Shit. Why did he have to think about that *now*? The ravioli felt like lead in his stomach.

Brian rubbed his shoulder. "Hey..."

The past was over and done. He tried a smile. "No worries."

That didn't wipe away the concern written all over Brian.

"Honey?"

He knew instinctively that Alice addressed him. He met her gaze and felt his muscles unknot. "I didn't have the best relationship with my parents." He looked around the table. "This is so very nice and I don't want to spoil it with my past."

Tony nodded, as if he understood. "You're welcome anytime. Brian says you live in the neighborhood?"

"In Mrs. Kaminski's house," Brian said.

Zoe clanked her fork against her plate. "No shit! I hope you at least changed the carpeting."

He couldn't help the laugh. They all knew that house. "I more or less gutted it."

"It looks fantastic," Brian said.

That was a safe topic to dwell on—the here and now. Rob detailed the renovations, the oddities he'd found, and a few of the items left behind—a lamp, a vase, and a painting—with notes from Mrs. Kaminski's children. They wanted something of their mother to remain in the house. "I haven't figured out where I'll put them, but I will." He'd work them into his life, in honor of the former owner.

"You didn't tell me that," Brian murmured.

"Well, there's still more of me to discover."

"*That* sounds like a challenge." Len said.

Goodness, how he loved that blush of Brian's. Still, Rob peered at Len. No malice, but there was *something* there. He just couldn't put his finger on it. "Life's a challenge."

"Ain't that the truth," Tony said. He seemed to consider his wineglass and his words, but shrugged. "I hope you have room for dessert."

He did. Barely, but yes. Especially when it turned out to be homemade tiramisu. By the end of the meal, Rob was stuffed to the gills. The worry he'd had over spending the evening with Rob's family had melted away.

They all pitched in to clean up the meal. His job was simple—take the vegetable cuttings out to the composter in the back, drop them in, and throw some leaves on top.

He did as told, reset the lid, and marveled for a moment at the garden beds tucked into the small backyard. He should think about starting a garden. He glanced at the composter. And learning how to make his own dirt.

When he returned to the house, he wasn't surprised to find Len standing on the back porch. "Nice night," he said.

Rob nodded. "And a nice garden." He dangled the little bucket he'd carried the vegetable bits in. "Wonder where they got that contraption from?"

"The composter? It was free when they signed up for a composting class. I'm sure they can give you the info." Len rubbed his chin and watched Rob.

Slightly unnerving. "Is there something wrong?"

"No." Len dropped his hands. "I'm just hoping you'll be able to pry Brian away from that shop of his sometimes."

Rob couldn't help the bark of a laugh. "Likewise."

That brought out Len's smile.

"I do understand where Brian's coming from, though."

A nod. "I read the business news."

So he knew Rob's public image. Here he was, the hotshot CEO, with a little waste pail in his hand. "It's mostly true."

Len shifted and leaned against one of the porch roof supports. "I don't doubt it."

They eyed each other, and it struck Rob that Len was just as wary—and worried. "I'm not here to break Brian's heart."

Len's turn to laugh. It was long, but not nearly as musical as Brian's. "No, no. *That* I get. The most likely person to break Brian *is* Brian." He sobered. "I guess I wanted to tell you not to give up on him."

This was a very odd conversation. "I never imagined the brother of any guy I dated would tell me to *keep* dating him. Expected the opposite, in fact."

That smile was so familiar. Len looked out into the garden. "I love my bro, and I wasn't surprised when he came out—he's been pretty obvious and *oblivious* as to how obvious most of his life. He's brought home two other people before you and I have no doubt he loved them."

There was a *but* there.

Len pushed himself off the wooden pillar. "But he's never looked at *anyone* the way he looks at you."

Oh. Rob tightened his grip on the little pail, lest he drop the damn thing.

"I—" He didn't know what to say.

"Thing is—I'm more worried about you than him. Like I said, I love my bro, but he can be an incredible dumbass."

Like the other weekend up at McConnells Mill. Rob nodded. "Yeah, I know."

Len clapped him on the shoulder and nodded toward the door. "Good. Then you're one step ahead."

They walked back into the house and into the warmth of the rest of the family.

Brian held Rob's hand as they strolled back to Rob's house. A true stroll—they were too stuffed to manage anything faster—and they each had a bag of leftovers as well.

"I don't think I've eaten that much in ages," Rob murmured. "Your parents are wonderful."

"So are you." He was giddy with relief. Everyone had got along and Rob had taken the... outspokenness of his family in stride and genuinely enjoyed himself.

Rob's smile crinkled his eyes. "I'm just a bloke from a coal town."

"Dating a guy from a steel town. Your point?" He grinned.

Rob laughed but his smile slipped. "Not too many years ago, we couldn't do this." He squeezed Brian's hand. "At least not as we are now."

No. Brian studied the parklet they crossed to reach the other half of Rob's—and his parents'—street. "I'm not sure I would have flirted with you, even five years ago."

Rob seemed to chew on that. "Your brother said he's known forever."

Brian kicked at a stone and laughed. "Len's damn observant. I tried to play it cool with posters of my favorite bands and movies. Making sure I had women as well as men, but... I guess it was pretty obvious." He paused. "But five years ago, I still believed guys could be either gay or straight, at least outwardly. They'd only be accepted..." He trailed off.

Rob squeezed his hand. "There are still fuckers out there who think that. But it's getting better."

"I hope."

Another squeeze. "Me too." Rob's voice was warm.

When they reached Rob's, they parted long enough to go into the house and for Rob to store their leftovers in the fridge, then Brian drew Rob into his arms. "I'm not going to run off with some woman."

Rob's chuff was pure amusement. "Oh, I know that." He brushed his lips against Brian's. "You're a give-your-heart-to-one-person type of guy."

Heat down his spine. "Got my number."

A sinful grin. "I sure did." He stole another kiss and gestured at the couch. "Shall we be more comfortable?"

Good idea. Once there, Rob was in his arms and Rob's mouth was on his. Not demanding, though. These were gentle kisses. Tastes. Touches.

He ran his fingers through Rob's hair and pressed lips against his cheeks and neck. While his blood heated, he had no need to run straight up to the bedroom. After a while, they ended up snuggled together, his head on Rob's chest.

Rob stroked his hair. "What did your brother mean when he said he knew your parents would always love you?"

Brian ran his hand down Rob's leg, the denim warm against his fingers. "Len got into a lot of trouble as a teen."

"Don't we all?"

"Kind of. His involved juvenile court."

Rob shifted and Brian looked up into his face. "Really? He doesn't seem the type."

Brian shrugged. "Dad always said he was too smart for his own good. Got bored. Acted out. Fell in with the wrong crowd." He remembered those days, the worry. The yelling and the crying. Len sitting on the floor of his room, tears in his eyes. *Don't you dare fuck up like I did, Bri.* "He spent some time in a detention center, ended up getting a lot of counseling, and as soon as he graduated from high school, he signed up for the navy."

A nod. "Structure. Rules."

"Something like that. My parents weren't lenient or anything—I don't know. There's stuff Len doesn't talk about. When he came back from his tours, he was way more serious in some ways, way less in others. Still himself, though."

"Older?" Rob ran a finger over his cheek.

That, too. Brian had been in high school when Len left and nearly out of college when Len returned. He'd missed Len something awful in those days, but he, too, had grown up. "He'd become a pilot in the navy and loved it. I think it appealed to his wild side." He slid his head down to rest it in Rob's lap. "Less now, with commercial flights. He says it's like driving a bus, but he wouldn't give it up for the world."

"No girlfriend?"

Brian blinked. "No." There'd never been any that he'd known of. Or boyfriends. "I don't know if he's dated at all. He's never talked about it."

Rob stroked his hair. "That's interesting."

He rolled that around in his head. "I— Maybe I should ask him about that sometime." Len kept things close to his chest. Out of all of them, he was the most reserved, despite the wild side.

Brian closed his eyes and breathed in the mingled scents of Rob's house, Rob, and the traces of his parents' place that still clung to Rob's clothing. "The only bad thing about dinners like that is all I want to do is sleep."

Rob's chuckle rocked their bodies. "Same." He caressed Brian's shoulder. "Do you want to stay here or go upstairs?"

"Bed sounds wonderful, if you don't mind me disappointing you."

Rob snorted, and leaned over to kiss him on the head. "Being with you is never a disappointment. Nor is sleeping next to you, or waking up to your smile."

His throat tightened and he pushed himself off Rob's lap.

"I adore sex with you," Rob said. "But I also adore *you.* Not every night needs to end in orgasms." He climbed to his feet.

Brian rose. "Well, that's good." He wanted to be more than just a bed partner. "Though, I *like* the orgasms."

Rob took his hand and drew him toward the stairs. "There's always tomorrow morning."

Yes, there was. With any luck, there'd be truckloads of tomorrow mornings in their future.

CHAPTER EIGHTEEN

Brian let the cell phone fall to his chest and blinked at the ceiling of his apartment. He was ready to bike down to the Allegheny River and heave his phone into the water, just as soon as he crawled out of bed and could see straight.

Miranda, who had a shift this morning, couldn't make it. Her grandmom had been taken to the hospital overnight and Miranda was still there. God, Brian understood. Family was the most important thing.

But he'd also worked every day for the past three days and not the usual six-hour shifts—literally the entire day—all twelve-plus hours. Just him, even during the busiest times. Everyone was either sick or out of town or in the middle of some fucking crisis. A perfect storm of shit descending on the shop. Seemed like it had been that way since his last day off—the day he'd taken Rob to his parents a week ago. Two weeks ago? He wasn't even sure what day it was. Phone read Wednesday.

Today was *supposed* to have been his morning off.

Time to stop moping and haul his sorry ass into the

shower. He had about twenty minutes to make it to the shop and get it opened. Ideally, he should've been there by now, but nothing recently had been *ideal*.

After the world's fastest shower, he headed down to Grounds N'at. Didn't even bother shaving—he could get away with a day's worth of scruff. Somehow, he managed to get the store ready and unlocked right before eight. He quickly downed three shots of espresso.

A watery Americano wouldn't cut it today.

Fuck, he was *tired*. Bone-weary. Not enough sleep, too much caffeine, and too many hours on his feet. He'd had no time to figure out what he needed to cut from the menu now that prices were up—and the comfortable cushion of cash he'd set aside dwindled each week.

Sales were down, too.

On top of everything else, he missed Rob horribly. They'd texted and talked on the phone, and Rob had stopped in a few days earlier, but they hadn't spent any quality time together since they'd had dinner with his folks. The shop had been *nuts*, between scheduling conflicts and trying to finish Lamont's and Rich's training so they could work on their own.

Beth was up to speed, which was good, but he didn't feel comfortable about handing her a key to the store yet—he'd done that too soon with Ethan, and look where that had gotten them. Of course losing Vance had also driven him to this point, too.

Regardless, either Mark, Miranda, or he had to open and close the shop.

Right now? It was mostly him. Fitting punishment for his fuckups, but it meant he had hardly any time for Rob.

Sometimes, Rob would pick him up and spend the night, but lately he hadn't had the energy for anything other than falling asleep. Even mornings weren't great—everything hurt and he always wanted five more minutes of sleep before he had to slog into the shop and start the day again.

The worst part was watching Rob's smiles go from honest to pained. He'd seen that with Anita, too, when the shop had swallowed him whole.

Seeing Rob hurt was a kick to the ribs. Especially when he hadn't any fucking clue what to do to fix it. He'd tried everything.

The shop bell rang and he resisted scrubbing his face with his clean hands.

Eli and Justin, thank goodness. He could be less bright and chipper for them. He got started on Eli's drink. Justin ordered something different every time.

Both men wore frowns. Justin tipped his head. "I thought you had off this morning?"

"Miranda's grandmom's in the hospital."

Justin's face fell more. "Shit."

"Yeah, so here I am."

Justin opened his mouth to speak, but shook his head instead.

Brian finished Eli's Americano, and turned back. "Know what you want?"

Justin peered at the board, then shrugged. "I'm going to be dull and mimic my husband today."

"I am *hardly* dull," Eli said. "And you know it." He hooked his cane over his arm and stirred creamer into his takeaway cup.

There was Justin's grin, the one that won over every single customer Grounds N'at had ever had. "Yes, dear."

Eli raised an eyebrow, put the lid on his cup, and drew an imaginary tick mark on an imaginary board.

Justin smiled and grabbed a lid while Eli paid. When Brian handed Eli his change, Eli dropped the whole lot into the tip jar. "Take care of yourself, Brian."

It felt like an order. "I am."

Same raised eyebrow, but no tick on any board. He saluted Brian with his cup, then they were both out the door and heading to the office upstairs.

Yeah, maybe he wasn't. But he was stuck. Nothing to do but ride the situation out until things calmed down.

Hopefully he wouldn't lose Rob in the process. He pulled out his phone. Rob would be at his desk by now, so he texted the same message he'd sent every day as of late.

Thinking about you. Miss you.

There wasn't a reply right away. Rob often had a morning meeting—and Brian had customers walking in the door. He shoved his phone back into his pocket.

Even after he waded through the morning rush and checked again, Rob still hadn't replied.

Brian cringed. That, too, had happened with Anita when their interactions had dwindled to short text messages.

A pain in his chest and a keening in his heart at the thought of Rob breaking things off. Crushing and visceral. He gripped the counter's edge until the blasted bell on the door rang, and he pushed the turmoil in his soul away, pasted on a smile, and brewed coffee.

Somewhere around eleven, his phone finally buzzed.

So sorry. Long in-person meeting! I miss you too. More than I can say.

Like a lifted weight from his chest.

How's your morning been?

Brian stared at that text, then typed the truth. Hard. Miranda's at the hospital w/ her grandmom. So I'm working all day.

The reply was almost instantaneous. Shit. She ok?

Don't know.

You ok?

He huffed a laugh. *Yeah. Tired.*

I can imagine. This is day four, isn't it?

Of working full days. Yup. Of course Rob would know. He knew Brian's schedule better than Brian at this point.

Yeah. And another tomorrow.

Wow. I'm sorry, love. I know it's rough.

It was killing him, if he wanted to be honest with himself, which of course, he didn't want to be.

I'll be fine.

He wanted to crawl under the counter and cry. He loved the shop, but right at the moment, he hated every single bean and porcelain cup.

A longer pause.

I'm here for you, Bri.

Shaking fingers. *I know.*

But for how much longer, since Brian couldn't be there for Rob?

Let me know when you're free again, and I'll take off work. Do whatever you want to do.

Sleep. He wanted to sleep and stop having anxiety claw its way through his gut and throat every day. He wanted to stop shaking when the mail came.

I'll let you know.

Love you, Bri.

Love you, too.

And he did, so much. Brian tucked away his phone and scrubbed his face, then got to cleaning dishes and wiping down the counter and tables before the lunch hour rush began.

Around one thirty, Miranda came in. She didn't look heartbroken, which was good, but she looked as tired as he felt. "Hey, how's your grandma?"

She sat down at the counter. When Brian gestured to the espresso machine, she shook her head. "I'm too wired." She paused. "Grandmom's alive and... okay." She twisted her lips.

Not good. "What happened?"

"She fell. Lost her balance. Broke her arm, and bruised up her hip real bad." Miranda cradled her head in her hands. "But the pain meds aren't good for her. She's more disoriented than ever and—" She broke off. "I don't know what's gonna happen."

"If there's anything I can do—"

She waved the words away. "Shit Bri, you've kept me on. That's above and beyond. I'm your most irregular employee ever."

"You're also my best." Utterly and completely true. If she could work more hours, that would solve a ton of issues.

She smiled, but it was pained, as if she understood his thoughts. "Doesn't help if I'm not here."

Yeah. "It's fine. We're going through a bump, that's all."

Her smile dropped away. "Bri, this is worse than before, and you need a break." She tipped her head. "Everyone can see you're at your limit."

He started to reply, but the shop door opened and several people trickled in. Miranda waved him away.

After washing his hands, he took their orders and started in on the drinks. None were that complex and his mood had lightened enough that the smile didn't feel forced this time. Nor the friendly banter. When they took their seats over by the window he turned back to Miranda.

"I'm just tired."

"And stressed."

"That, too." He shrugged. "Nothing I can do. Maybe over the summer I can hire a few more people. But we have our hands full training Rich and Lamont."

She nodded, and eyed him. "When was the last time you saw Rob?"

God. It was like she *knew* him. Then again, they'd worked together for how long? He rubbed the back of his neck. "About a week ago?"

"Quality time?"

She was either asking about conversation or sex, but it didn't matter. "More like me passing out in his arms."

A grunt and she pulled out her phone. "You're working Saturday night, right?"

That was the current schedule. "Yup. Mark in the morning, with Rich, and me in the evening with Lamont."

"Switch with me, since you're taking mine today." Miranda looked up.

He stared back. "Seriously?" She didn't do Saturday evenings, especially on holiday weekends.

"Yup. I owe you one, and you need a day off."

"But your grandmom..."

She winced. "Well, here's the thing. Even if she's out of the hospital, which she should be, she's going to be in rehab for a while. I'm still gonna need to go see her, but she won't be home."

So Miranda had flexibility. "I—don't know what to say." Fortune from misfortune.

"Say, 'Yes Miranda, I'll switch shifts with you so I can go spend an entire day with my handsome British boyfriend.'"

God the heat in his face. He coughed. "I'll switch shifts."

"Good man." She glanced at her phone again. "I gotta head out."

"Mir, I'm incredibly grateful..."

"Remember that when I start pestering you for more hours."

"You pester me for more hours, and I'll come over and mow your lawn and wash your car in gratitude."

She laughed and rose. "I'm going to remember you said that, Keppler!"

So would he, and if she did ask for more hours, he'd do exactly as he said. Holy fuck, that would solve so much.

He gave Miranda a wave then grabbed a cookie to tide him over. He needed to get food of some kind, but another cluster of customers came in when Miranda left, so he put that out of his mind.

"Hey," he said to the woman who sidled up to the counter, "What can I get you?"

After this batch of slinging coffee, he'd text Rob the good news.

Rob's phone buzzed in the middle of his weekly leadership meeting. Normally, he'd glance at it, just to make sure it wasn't an emergency, then ignore it. This time, two words jumped out at him: Off and Saturday.

The room vanished and he must have vocalized *something*, because Carter stopped in midsentence. "Something wrong?"

Rob looked up and *everyone* in the room was staring at him. Shit. He must have the reddest face if the heat and embarrassment creeping up his back were anything to go by. "No. Some unexpected news. Not company related." He clicked the phone off and shoved it into his jacket pocket. "Please go on."

He was laser-focused the rest of the meeting, even with that text burning through his blood.

Brian had Saturday off. All of it. A freaking miracle, especially given this was a holiday weekend. Memorial Day. The unofficial start to summer. And the beast had released Brian from its claws for a day.

When Rob got back to his office, he put his phone on his desk and slipped off his suit jacket. He shouldn't be so harsh about the shop. It was a good place. But it was fucking killing Brian, no doubt about that. Every time he tried to pry from Brian what was going on so he could help, Brian shut him down. Didn't want to talk about it. Got snippy and angry.

I know how to run my shop.

Yes, he did. Something wasn't working, though. He stared at both the phone and his computer. He should look into the business of running a coffee shop. If nothing else, he could figure out how to help more subtly.

In the meantime... He snatched up his phone and leaned back in his desk chair.

Out of my meeting. Of course I want to spend the day with you!

No answer right away. Probably customers. Rob set the phone down, woke his computer, and dug into his e-mail.

A few minutes later his buzzing phone startled him.

Great! I work Friday night. Pick me up?

Always. He'd expected that. Planned for it. Dinner, too?

The way I haven't been eating? Yes, please.

That he'd noticed. In the past few weeks, Brian had lost weight. Rob saw it and felt it when he held Brian in his arms. It wasn't bad—but it wasn't good, either.

We'll go anywhere you want.

Even Burgatory??

He'd even brave the Waterfront on the Friday night before a holiday weekend. That counts as anywhere, yes? I'll swing by at 8:30.

I can't fucking wait. I need a break from here.

Now that was good to hear. Can't wait either.

Ooof. After school rush. Talk later!

Rob glanced at the clock. Just after three. That made sense. Well, he merely had to make it through the rest of today, Thursday, and Friday.

If he could give Brian one day of happiness, that would be worth all the pain.

CHAPTER NINETEEN

SATURDAY MORNING, ROB WOKE TO SUNSHINE AND THE ruckus of grackles perched in the tree next to his house. He blinked at Brian sleeping next to him.

So last night *hadn't* been a dream. Sure felt like one.

He'd picked Brian up and driven him to Burgatory as promised. They'd feasted on outrageously good hamburgers, mounds of fries, and milkshakes—Brian's laced with rum.

Seeing Brian smile and laugh had been like a fucking drug—turned him inside out with happiness. They'd spent the evening discussing photography, biking, hiking, and art. Plans for the future. No mention of work *anywhere*. By the time they'd gotten home, they'd fallen into bed. A little fooling around, but they'd both been so exhausted that sleep came quickly. Brian was running on nothing, and after Rob's long week, he needed the rest, too.

Waking next to Brian was heaven. He'd missed his warm presence and amazing smile in his life so damn much. Even now, his soul ached. How long until the next time he woke up next to Brian? These days were so rare. Life could be perilously short. All those *we shoulds* could become *why didn't wes* so fast.

He pushed that aside. Brian was here, now and that's what mattered.

Rob took a long breath and listened to the cacophony of the birds. No idea what the time was, but he'd let Brian sleep himself out. After that, the day could be whatever Brian wished for. He closed his eyes, but as much as he wanted to drift back into slumber, his body had other needs.

Well, damn.

Careful not to disturb Brian—though the man slept like the dead—he flipped over and grabbed his watch. Seven-fifteen.

Way too early to wake Brian.

Rob slipped out of the bed and headed for the bathroom to take care of the reasons he couldn't fall back to sleep. When he emerged, Brian stretched his limbs out and blinked at him through mostly lidded eyes. "Is it morning?

The sunlight should have given that away. "For some definition... it's still early, though. Sleep if you need to."

Brian pressed his face into the pillow and groaned. "Need about a hundred more years," came the muffled reply.

Rob chuckled and crawled back into his side of the bed. "Take what you want."

Once he was in arm's reach, Brian grabbed him and snuggled against his chest. "Want you." His limbs were heavy and loose. "Inside me."

A dance of electricity cascaded over Rob's skin and he pushed a lock of hair out of Brian's eyes. "You're half asleep." Though, there was something to be said for making love to a needy, sleepy partner.

"Am not." And if to prove the point, he licked Rob's nipple.

Lightning to his brain and balls. Rob arched against Brian. "Fuck."

"Yes, please." Brian pressed a series of kisses down the center of Rob's chest.

Rob pulled him up, took his mouth in a rough kiss, and rolled him onto his back. When Brian moaned and squirmed beneath him, he relented. "I guess you *are* awake." He ground against Brian.

Sleep still clung to Brian, but his cheeks were flushed and his dick hard against Rob's. "Told you."

So he had. Rob stole another kiss before reaching over to the nightstand. Didn't take long to put a condom and lube on, nor to press against Brian's entrance.

When Rob slid into him, Brian relaxed and rolled his head back. "Oh God, yeah."

Hot, tight, and yet so pliant. He hadn't expected Brian to love bottoming so much. Then again, it was the one time Brian could let go. Those beautiful brown eyes, so warm and needy, Brian urged Rob on with whispers and murmurs and groans from kiss-swollen lips.

Rob pushed deep and withdrew slowly, before rocking in again. Didn't take too many strokes before they found a rhythm that left them both gasping and breathless.

God, he could do this every day. Make love to Brian. Watch his flushed cheeks and neck grow redder, feel Brian's nails bite into his back and arse. Listen to his gasps and moans. Sweat and sex mixed with the slight floral scent of clean sheets. "Like this?"

Brian pulled him down until they were lip to lip. "Love this." He paused, and there was moisture rimming Brian's eyes. "Love you."

Oh, Bri. Rob kissed him because he couldn't speak through a tight throat. He answered with his body, moving inside Brian slow and soft until Brian's kisses turned into bites. He quickened the rhythm until he plowed into Brian hard and fast and they both grappled with each other.

Brian shook under his thrusts, his grip on Rob's arms almost painful. "More." He spit the word through gritted teeth. "Don't want to think—want—only you."

Take Brian out of his mind? That was a challenge he would accept. He pulled out. "On your hands and knees."

Brian groaned, but complied.

"Trust me." He pressed his hand just below Brian's neck. "Shoulders on the mattress."

A whimper this time.

Rob stroked himself. Such a lovely sight—Brian squirming, arse in the air. With his free hand, he traced fingers over Brian's arse cheeks, then slapped each hard.

Brian yelped, then moaned. "Fuck!"

"That's the idea." He added a bit more lube before thrusting inside Brian.

Brian panted and melted against the bed. "God..."

He gripped Brian's hips and picked up speed. "Like that?"

"Yeah. God, Rob..." Brian moaned the words. "So good."

For him too. He had an inkling about what got Brian off. Same reason Rob liked bottoming sometimes—and why he liked blindfolds and rope.

Rob gathered Brian's wrists together, pulled them to the small of his back, and held them there.

A hitch in Brian's breathing and another whimper.

He slowed his strokes, letting Brian flex and shudder under him. "This okay?"

An exhale and a whisper. "Yeah. It's—yeah." A little hint of wonder there.

"Good." He pushed in deep. "Right now, you have one job." He leaned down as close to Brian's head as he could manage. "Take my cock and love every single second of it."

Another groan, but he saw Brian's smile and that was what he needed. Rob straightened then drove furiously into Brian, over and over until they were both swearing and moaning. Brian begged for more and more and more,

Fuck, Brian was hot and tight and *perfect.* Those moans of "please" and "yes" and "Rob" were music playing along Rob's every nerve. Each stroke rocked them both and Rob's blood burned with need. He closed his eyes and focused on the way Brian clenched around him, the timbre of breath and the pitch of his cries. Skin and muscle flexing beneath him. Wrists shifting as Brian clenched and unclenched his hands in Rob's grip.

He was so close to heaven, but he pushed back against the crashing tide. Before he could reach his free hand under to beat Brian off... Brian shuddered and tensed all around him.

"Oh fuck... Rob..." All the warning he had before Brian was yelling and coming and tighter than he'd ever been before. No hope of holding off his own orgasm. Rob rammed into Brian, riding the wave of pleasure until he was blinded by light behind his eyes. He pumped his hips, buried himself in Brian, and spilled every last bit of himself. They both collapsed onto the mattress.

Somewhere along the line, he'd let go of Brian's wrists. Good. He couldn't think through the spinning of his head to do much more than press kisses to Brian's back.

After ages, or a few minutes, Brian sighed happily. "Shit, that was good."

Rob managed a chuckle—and pulled out of Brian. The condom could wait a bit. "Took me by surprise."

"I've never—" He stopped and huffed a laugh. "Well, I haven't been fucked that much—but I've never come without anything touching my dick."

That could be pretty spectacular when it happened. "We can try replicating the process, if you'd like."

Brian laughed and rotated to face Rob, all limbs, flushed skin, and smile. "You're *such* an engineer."

"Guilty." He propped himself up and leaned over to kiss Brian. "Anything I can do to make you happy."

Brian's smile fell away. "Being with you." He sank against the pillow. "Just let me be with you."

Rob stole another kiss. "I can do that, for as long as you want." He'd hold fast to Brian as much as he could—even if the shop tore Brian apart. At some point, it would get better.

It had to.

"Let me take care of this." He stripped off the condom and rolled out of bed. By the time he came back, Brian's eyes were closed and his limbs loose. Rob chuckled and pulled the covers up.

Brian stirred and cracked a lid. "Sorry. I'm..."

Easy enough to plant a kiss that shut Brian up. "It's not even eight yet. Sleep in. You deserve it."

"Mmm."

And that was all Brian managed before sleep caught him. Rob found a pair of gray sweatpants, donned them, and left Brian to sleep off sex and too many workdays.

He grabbed his personal laptop from his office before heading downstairs. There *had* to be a way he could help Brian with the shop, or at least prod him in the right direction.

Brian was killing himself. Rob tasted it in Brian's

desperate need for oblivion and felt it in the thinness of his body. Nothing about the situation was tenable. Rob could hold on to Brian forever, but in the end they'd both go down if the issues at Grounds N'at weren't solved.

Rob didn't know the first thing about running a coffee shop, but the Internet *must*. It was only a matter of finding the information.

He dug out some of the beans he'd bought from Brian, ground them up, set his coffee brewing, and opened his laptop.

Time to start searching for answers.

Awareness flitted back to Brian bit by bit. He didn't want to give up the wonderful softness of the bed he was in or the pleasant sleepy buzz in his body, even though the day tugged at him and the slight scent of brewed coffee tickled his nostrils.

Rob's house. Rob's bed. Always a refuge from the world.

He was sore in every right way. Achy and stretched—inside and out. He reached out his legs and his arms to their fullest, luxuriating in the huge bed, opened his eyes, and sat up.

God, it was almost ten in the morning. He'd managed to sleep another two hours after Rob had fucked him into blissful oblivion.

Rob wasn't in the room, but that wasn't a surprise. He wasn't overworked and underslept. The shop. God... Brian scrubbed a hand over his face and tried to quell the rising panic in his throat. Relax, *relax*!

He wasn't at the shop because he didn't *need* to be at the shop today. Mark was there. Then Miranda. Everything would be fine. They would have called if there'd been an issue.

Call... *fuck*! Was his cell even in the room?

Fear rammed a spike through his chest and he scrambled off the bed to hunt for his clothes. His jeans were in a crumpled heap at the foot of the bed... and yes. There was his phone.

No messages. No missed calls.

He sat down on the bed, too aware of how hard his heart beat. His hands shook.

Holy shit.

Good thing Rob was downstairs. That little stint would have earned him a frown and a creased brow—and he'd have to watch the weight of worry press down on Rob. Again.

Like it had onto Anita.

He owed Rob for putting up with him. Not giving up. But damn, he didn't need to push it by acting like this. Once he could breathe again, he found his overnight bag, hopped in the shower, and threw on a fresh pair of jeans and a t-shirt.

When he made it to the kitchen, he poured himself a cup of coffee and headed out onto the back porch. Rob's hair glinted copper in the sunlight and he sipped coffee while tapping away on his computer.

Brian let the screen door close behind him with a not-so-subtle bang. That was something that hadn't changed about the house in all those years. "Are you working?"

Rob's cheeks tinged and he closed his laptop. "God, no. Just piddling around on the Internet." He leaned back in his chair. "Feeling better?"

Brian took a seat across the table. "Yeah. I haven't slept like that in weeks." Not since the last time he'd spent more than a few fleeting hours in bed with Rob. "Kind of feels like I haven't seen you in ages."

Rob's smile was soft. "You haven't. Not really."

Couldn't help the cringe. "I know. The shop..." They'd fucked a few times, quick tumbles in bed. Nothing quality. Not doing this... sitting and talking.

Rob waved his hand, then glanced at his laptop. "I just wish there were some way I could help you. Lift the burden."

Not a chance, there. For one, Rob had no clue. For another, Brian didn't need help—he needed things to stop being shitty. He sipped his coffee. "I'll be fine."

He heard the argument in Rob's inhale. Saw it in the furrow of Rob's brow.

"Bri, you're not fine now." Rob's shoulders dropped. "You're not eating. You're not sleeping..."

"You're not my mother." It came out snappish and whiplike. Brian set down his mug and looked away.

A sigh. "I'm not. Though, I bet your mother would say the same thing, for the same reason." A clink of Rob's mug against the metal patio table. "I'm worried about you."

She *would* say the same, and yes, for the same reason. Brian folded his hands and leaned his elbows on his thighs. "I'm—" But he wasn't fine.

Brian looked up to find Rob watching him, that long face made even longer and thinner by the intensity of worry.

Rob shifted in his chair. "I told you, I can be a workaholic, too. I'm familiar with the effects." Dry words.

"Ever burn out?"

Rob shifted his gaze to the yard. "Yes."

One simple word. So much weight.

"It wasn't pleasant. So much went wrong leading up to

it—the whole thing with my parents and never getting over that, my relationships, CirroBot nearly going under." He gave a short laugh. "A flood of personal and professional misfortune."

Brian knew that feeling. "What happened?"

Rob pursed his lips and met his stare. "I collapsed at work. They hauled me to the hospital and pumped me full of electrolytes. I'd, quite literally, run myself into the ground." He mimed someone falling over with his hand.

"I'm not that bad."

Rob gave him a look that could only be described as dubious. "What's that Pittsburgh word for when someone's being a jackass?"

He scooped up his coffee and answered. "Jagoff."

"Ah, yes." Rob crossed both arms. "Stop being a jagoff, Brian."

Nothing to do but drink his coffee. At a certain level, Rob was right. He sighed and stretched out his neck. "I'm not trying to be, you know."

Rob's expression softened. "I know," he murmured. "But I see you, Bri. Maybe better than you do."

God, he'd heard that before—not those words—but those thoughts. That he wasn't taking care of himself, that he was close to burning out.

He hadn't before. He didn't plan to now. "Can we change the subject?"

Rob reclaimed his coffee mug and nodded. He didn't look happy about it, but he didn't say another word.

The silence was almost as bad, because it let his brain turn over all that Rob had said, and realize how right he was. He shook it off and peered out into the yard. There were more plants out there, now. And some fencing. "Are you growing a garden?"

A slow nod. Rob leaned back. "Your father had extra tomato and pepper plants. He left them and a note on my front porch a couple weeks ago."

That was odd. "Dad usually has just enough..."

Rob's beautiful smile finally appeared. "I gathered that when the garden soil, and the wooden frames showed up a couple days later, along with a note to call him when I had a chance to start planting."

Heat to his face. "Oh my God. I'm so sorry!"

But Rob grinned. "No, it's fine. I wanted a garden." He swallowed some coffee and for an instant, there was such loss and pain. "And it was nice to have someone... do that for me. A neighbor. An elder."

A father. The unspoken word hung in the air. "My folks really like you."

"So I've gathered." He gestured out into the yard. "Took the better part of three evenings." There was a flush on Rob's cheeks again. "And your mom dropped off pasta the other day."

Wow. "Sounds like they've adopted you."

Rob nodded. "I don't quite know what to make of that, to be honest. I mean, we've only been dating... how long have we been dating?"

"You walked into my shop in mid-March."

Rob nodded. "And it's Memorial Day Weekend."

Right. So, a little under three months. Not long at all, but they'd both been pretty clear about how serious they'd wanted this to be.

As Brian watched Rob finish his coffee, he couldn't actually contemplate a time *without* Rob. Felt like he'd always been here—would always be here. "Too fast?"

So many times they'd asked that question of each other.

Rob shook his head, as always. "No." He shrugged.

"Well, maybe the parental adoption thing, but I appreciate that more than you might imagine."

From what Rob had explained, Brian could understand that. He studied the garden again, then the sky, with its white clouds and sunshine. "Wish I'd brought my bike."

Rob grunted. "There's always our feet." He stretched out his legs.

A walk would work, too. "I could really go for some pancakes." There had to be a breakfast place somewhere in Bloomfield now. He eyed Rob's laptop. He wasn't as familiar with the area as he used to be. A lot had changed since he was a teen.

Rob must have put two and two together, because he chuckled. "I could make you pancakes, then we could go for a walk that didn't involve satiating your stomach." He patted the closed laptop. "No searching necessary."

"Except I kind of wanted chocolate chip pancakes."

Rob rolled his eyes. "Do you think me some kind of heathen that doesn't have chocolate chips?"

"I—wait—heathens don't have chocolate chips?"

There was the smile Brian so craved, full of teeth and dimples. Rob stood. "Come with me." He grabbed his laptop and headed into the kitchen.

No choice but to follow. When Brian entered, the laptop was on the kitchen table and Rob was brandishing a bag of semisweet morsels. "I have these. Or if you want something more wicked, I have Dutch chocolate sprinkles."

"Dutch chocolate...?"

Rob put the bag down on the counter, pulled out a box from the pantry, and handed it to Brian. A label in Dutch and a picture of toast with... chocolate jimmies on top. "What evil magic is this?"

Rob's laughter filled the room. "From the people who

gave us stroopwafels for tea, chocolate sprinkles for your breakfast toast." He paused. "Or pancakes."

"Neither the Dutch nor you have ever lead me astray." He handed the box back. "These, please."

Rob put the bag of chips away and pulled out eggs, flour, and a bunch of other ingredients. "This is pretty much a one-person job. Have a seat."

"You're making them from scratch?"

Rob waved away the question. "Let me play. Your job today is to relax."

"But—you're working for me. Not exactly relaxing for you."

Rob peered over his shoulder. "I enjoy cooking, so it is. I don't get to do anything for you very often."

Mostly because there hadn't been any time, lately. Brian looked down at the floor.

"Brian, be a good man, and let your boyfriend take care of you for a day."

He snorted. Rob was right—he did need to relax. "All right. Pamper me then."

A smile that warmed the room. "I plan to."

True to that promise, he did. The pancakes were excellent—even better than the best place in town—and after they cleaned up the cooking mess and Rob grabbed a shower, they headed out for a leisurely stroll around Bloomfield. So much had changed due to the influx of people working for Google and the other tech companies popping up around the city, plus expansion of the nearby hospitals.

Not so much a working-class neighborhood anymore. Which was both good and bad. He was glad his folks owned their house—they wouldn't be priced out of an apartment due to gentrification. But it was also nice to see new stores and shops and run-down houses being renovated, just as Rob had done.

Mixed emotions, there.

The more they walked, the more he unwound. While out, Rob stopped in a couple of shops and picked up a few things. "I thought I might cook dinner. It's a lovely day for grilling." Fresh vegetables for a salad.

Brian wasn't about to argue with that, especially not when Rob said there were steaks in the fridge. "You planned this, didn't you?"

That sly smile. "Perhaps."

When they got back and everything was put away, they ended up on the living room couch.

Despite being in Mrs. Kaminski's old living room, everything here spoke of Rob—including Rob twining his fingers in Brian's hair and nibbling and licking his way down Brian's neck.

He pulled Rob closer, cupping his ass. He lifted his chin to give Rob more skin to kiss. "We should do this more often."

A scrape of teeth. "Would love to." Rob stroked Brian's face. "Whenever you want. Whenever you can."

There was the shop again. Always the shop. "I'm trying."

A little frown. Rob ran a thumb over Brian's lips and he couldn't help but open his mouth and suck it in.

Whatever Rob had intended to say devolved into a groan.

That was a sound Brian loved. So was the hard kiss that followed. "If you keep this up," Rob said, "I'm going to fuck you on the couch. Then I won't be able to do anything to you tonight. I'm an old man, remember?" He palmed Brian's dick.

Brian thrust against Rob. "So am I."

With Rob, it didn't matter. Orgasm or not. Brian needed and wanted to be with Rob. If only the shop didn't eat him alive every day.

Rob kissed him and relented. "Maybe we should watch a movie instead of me driving you wild."

"I have no problems with you driving me wild." Brian stroked Rob's thigh. "But you're right about later tonight."

Another huff and Rob leaned against the back of the couch. "Alas. We should have met in our twenties."

Life would have been very different then. A little flutter of fear and shame—left over from those years—flicked through him. "I wouldn't have gone near you." He'd lusted after so many guys in college. Never touched one. The straight ones weren't interested. "Gay guys didn't trust bi guys back then."

Rob rolled his eyes, but he also looked contrite. "A lot of them still don't." From the angles of his face and the pursing of his lips, Rob was remembering some of his own past. "I never felt that way." He met Brian's gaze. "And I'd like to think, had we met, we'd been friends at the very least."

Maybe. Maybe not. He'd shied away from any guy he felt a sexual pull toward. Safer that way. But Rob was... Rob. He leaned in and kissed him. "I'm glad we met now, though."

This time, they explored each other's mouths and necks leisurely. Tasting, kissing, murmuring things that made no sense. Rob was warm and solid and real, but all the hours he'd worked started to catch up with Brian, leaving him heavy in Rob's arms.

"Nap time?"

He'd slept enough. "No."

"Movie time, then?" Rob stroked his head.

That would work. "Just don't let me sleep or I won't tonight."

"I have to let you sleep tonight?" Wicked, wicked words that send a bolt of lust to Brian's balls.

"Didn't you just claim to be an old man?"

Rob didn't say a word, just stole another kiss.

Warmth spread through Brian and he laughed. "All right. What movie?"

"I was thinking something particularly queer, like *Lawrence of Arabia*."

From the expression on Rob's face, he wasn't kidding. "I —is it?"

Rob frowned. "Have you *never* watched it?"

Heat flooded straight to his cheeks. "Um—well, no."

"Oh, good God." Rob stood and headed for his shelf of movies. "That settles it, then." Took him all of a minute to pop the disk into the player and return, remote in hand.

"At least you're not tossing me out." It was a classic, sure, but there were lots of movies he hadn't seen.

Rob plopped down next to him. "I'll only toss you out if you haven't seen *Casablanca*." The bright-ass smile gave away his joking.

"*That* I have seen." When Rob opened his arms, Brian was more than happy to settle against his chest.

"I think you'll enjoy this," Rob murmured against his forehead. He started the movie and his warmth seeped into Brian's bones

In the end, Rob was right. The movie was gripping. Long, but that didn't seem to matter. And yes, surprisingly queer. "How the hell did they manage that?"

A gentle shrug from Rob. "We've always been here." He picked up the remote and turned the movie off. "Pulps and movies, even with the not-so-great endings, they were places we could find ourselves, even for a while."

Brian chewed on that. "I never really see myself anywhere."

"Mmm, and it had an effect, yes?" Sadness in Rob's voice.

"Of course." Still did in a way, though he was fed up—and old enough—not to care.

Rob pressed a kiss to his temple. "Steak?"

As if on cue, Brian's stomach rumbled and he laughed. "Guess there's your answer."

While Rob grilled, Brian meandered out into the small garden and took a closer look at his father's handiwork. Peppers and tomatoes in their little cages. Parsley. Basil. None of these plants were leftovers. This was a gift to Rob... one *never* offered to any other person he'd brought home. He stared up at the fence that circled Rob's yard. He'd played out here as a child. Even buried a few Matchbox cars in the earth for safekeeping. Treasures. He wondered if Rob had found them, or if Mrs. Kaminski had years ago.

The day was as warm as his heart. Life was *extraordinarily* strange.

Footfalls behind him and arms circling his waist. Rob's breath played along his neck. "You're thinking again."

He'd never grow tired of the little shivers that spun down his body when Rob held him. "Smoke from my ears?"

A chuckle. "Something like that."

"Ever since I met you, I keep thinking I should feel like a new person, a different person, because I've changed who I am."

"Have you? Changed?" Honest curiosity there, tinged with confusion.

That was the thing. He hadn't. "No."

"Didn't think so." Rob loosened his grip. "So what's on your mind?"

"Just... that. Here—right here—I'm more myself than I've ever been."

A kiss on the back of his neck. "You've been staring at the tomatoes too long, love."

He chuckled and turned around in Rob's arms. "I'm serious."

Rob nodded. "I know. Honestly, today you look better than you have in weeks."

He wasn't at the shop. Outside of his panic this morning, he wasn't even stressed about the shop. How long had it been since that were true? Tomorrow, he'd go back to work and none of the problems he'd escaped today would be solved. "I wish—" He shook his head. "Never mind." He couldn't have this moment forever, but at least he had it for today.

Rob stepped back and took his hand. Sympathy there, and love. How the latter had happened, Brian couldn't fathom. "Come have dinner."

He followed Rob onto the porch.

They ate and drank and laughed. Later, they took another walk, admiring the neighborhood and counting the rabbits in yards.

That night, Rob drew him upstairs, laid him down with kisses and touches and mutual moans, and made love to him until he couldn't breathe or speak or think.

As he drifted off to sleep, he clung hard to the day, desperate to etch every moment into his mind and heart. This was the life he wanted... craved. Needed more than air.

In the end though, sleep dragged him down into darkness and his thoughts slipped away.

CHAPTER TWENTY

Rob stood at the window near the kitchen at CirroBot and nursed his cup of tea. He had a break between meetings, so he'd taken the time to walk and stretch. Sitting too much. *Thinking* too much.

He should go for a ride tonight. Would do him some good and maybe clear his head. If only he could entice Brian out, too. Rob sighed, sipped his tea, and contemplated switching back to the office coffee.

He hadn't been to Grounds N'at for more than two weeks—not to drink coffee or *talk* with Brian. He'd picked Brian up a few times and they'd fucked and slept and murmured a half-dozen words between them, but that had been it.

Not enough—not for his soul, not for a relationship. That fucking shop was eating the life out of Brian, slowly but surely. Any attempt he'd made to talk about the issues had been met with snappish disdain.

While Rob knew the aggravation of being second-guessed, at some point Brian needed to grow the hell up, realize he needed help, and not treat every overture of support as if Rob were trying to school him in business.

Anger didn't become Brian, at all.

Worst of all, he *missed* the man he was supposedly dating. Ached for the laughing Brian, who talked photography and biked, and even watched old movies with him. Rob hadn't seen *that* Brian since their Saturday together over Memorial Day weekend.

Hell, even Brian's mum had called Rob, asking after her son. Apparently, he'd missed their family dinner due to work. Talk about *awkward* conversations. He didn't want to dump on Brian's family about Brian.

"I know they're understaffed," he'd murmured back. "And he's been working nonstop since Miranda's grandmother came home."

"I thought he'd hired a few people?"

So had he. "I guess they're not trained up yet? I don't know." Brian still hadn't given any of his newer employees a key or the code to the store.

Silence for a bit on the other end. "It'll get better," she said.

He nearly laughed, but it would've come out dark and bitter. Brian kept saying that too, and so far it had only gotten worse. "I hope so."

They'd ended the conversation after a short discussion about his garden and when Rob had hung up, the hole in his heart had only ripped open wider.

He couldn't keep doing this. He'd told Brian he'd hold on—but he'd also told him from the beginning that he wanted to be more than a cock.

All he was right now was someone for Brian to fuck or be fucked by. Stress relief. A way to get off.

Rob finished his tea and crumpled the paper cup in his

hand. Something had to change. They had to talk, work this out.

For the hell of it, he made one of the office coffees and lugged that back to his desk. Bitter as all hell. No cream. Fit his mood perfectly.

He pulled out his cell phone and chanced a text to Brian.

> Hey, thinking about you. Don't suppose you have any time off coming up?

No reply—which meant Brian was probably busy. He slid the phone on his desk and pulled up his e-mail and calendar.

A nudge on a request from one of their larger customers, Agella, for an in-person meeting, which meant flying to California. He'd put off scheduling it, mostly because he and Brian had talked about some long-distance biking over the summer.

He snorted and glanced at his phone. Summer was here. Rob rubbed the scar on his wrist and swallowed against the sudden pain in his throat.

Dreams upon dreams. He couldn't hold up his business for Brian, not when he was merely an afterthought nowadays. He shot an e-mail back, more or less stating he was free whenever they were. He wouldn't—couldn't—let his life revolve around Brian anymore.

He loved Brian, but he'd been an idiot for love and sex before. CirroBot deserved better from him. Time to get serious about both parts of his life.

He sat forward and sorted through his e-mails. His contact at Agella sent back a set of possible dates. Rob chose mid-July—a month from now—to fly out for a weeklong meeting. He sent the details to Mallory to finalize and plan.

A month gave him enough time to figure out what the hell was going to happen with him and Brian and—

His phone buzzed.

Hey, sorry. We've been slammed. Lots of kids now that school's out.

Brian should hire some of them, but Rob wasn't even going to suggest it, lest he get his head bitten off.

No full days, but Mark is closing tomorrow and Saturday.

That was something, at least. Do you want me to swing by Saturday?

God yes. I miss you so much.

Rob's spine and chest ached and it took a moment to catch his breath. As do I.

BTW, I'm training Beth on closing. Gonna start rotating her in.

Oh thank God. About bloody time. That's good!

Thought you'd want to know.

Brian's way of saying he was trying to improve things. Rob leaned back in his chair. Maybe he was worrying about the relationship for naught. Seemed Brian was getting his shit together.

Thank you, I do, yes.

So I'll see you Saturday?

Oh yes. Just like old times.

Hopefully, it would be. Rob put down his phone and eyed his cold coffee. In the end, he drank it. Bitter penance for doubting Brian.

On Saturday, he could get a decent cup of brew.

So far everything that could have possibly gone wrong for Brian on a lazy Saturday morning had. First, upon opening, he'd found an entire gallon of milk had been left out overnight. He'd let Beth run through the closing procedure and when she'd finished—everything had *looked* fine, but he hadn't checked behind the counter—and there the milk was, all nice and warm on a shelf and not in the fridge.

He dumped the whole thing down the drain. He had enough, but what a waste. It also meant Beth needed more training on closing procedures, which left him holding too many shifts. Again. Still.

The order of brownies that should have arrived from the local organic bakery *didn't*, so now there was a nice hole in the pastry display. His most popular item, too. Then Lamont had called in sick, leaving him the sole person manning the shop.

To add even more *excitement*, Jan, Ev, and Dan had been goofing off and had managed to topple their drinks all over their table and the floor—and onto the college professor next to them, the one who always came in to grade papers.

The professor was a gentleman and only mildly admonished them. His jacket had taken a beating—but not any of his paperwork or books, so he was fine.

Ev hadn't been quite as lucky—Ev's sketchbook was now a soggy mess and zie looked about ready to cry.

Hadn't helped that Brian had snapped at them, his voice echoing through the shop. "Goddamn it! Don't you three have something better to do?"

He'd regretted that outburst immediately. Several customers left and all three kids looked crestfallen.

He'd cleaned the mess up, with their help. "I didn't mean to yell like that. I'm sorry."

They'd mumbled some words, Ev had tucked the notebook in a plastic bag, and they'd all slinked out of the shop, leaving the place uncomfortably silent in their wake.

The professor had packed up not too long after.

Fucking hell. Alienating his customer base. What a way to start the weekend. He rubbed his temple.

Of course, it was also the day to work on payroll, the ordering, and the schedule. God, he didn't want to look at any of that.

Even the thought of Rob coming in didn't quell his frustration—or fear. He should cancel—too much work to do. If Lamont were here, he could concentrate on the ordering. But flying solo—he had only bits and moments to figure out how to make all the numbers he needed to match to, well, match.

As soon as Rob arrived, he'd expect Brian's attention. A coffee. Chitchat. Everything he didn't have *time* for.

Brian closed his eyes for a second to keep the tears of frustration in, then went back to washing mugs.

His skin itched for Rob's touch. The way he made Brian's worries vanish—at least for a time. He missed their talks and rides and—*everything*. Lately when they saw each other, they more or less fucked and slept.

The sex was okay, but didn't have the passion it once had. That was his fault—too exhausted and drained for anything but getting off—and *that* was unfair to Rob.

Here he was *resenting* the thought of Rob's presence. Brian took a deep breath and finished up. Yeah, jagoff was the right word.

The shop door rang and another flow of customers—ones that hadn't seen his unprofessional outburst—walked in.

He did need the night off. Needed to see Rob. He pasted on a smile and served the group of women the best coffee he could, even if he were slowly coming to hate every damn roasted bean in his own damn shop.

They settled into a table near the window.

Good.

He slipped into the back room to get his laptop. Best get as much of the administrative stuff taken care of before Rob walked in. Scheduling was the easiest—though his own number of shifts were hellish and left him with very little free time. No issues with payroll. He started in on the ordering.

Good God. He barely knew what to get anymore. Everything had increased in price and some of his—and his customer's—favorite items were no longer available. Didn't help that the past several orders had been all kinds of screwed up, which had forced him over budget on stupid shit like paper cups in sizes he barely used.

In between customers, he did a quick double-check of his inventory. He knew what he needed—figuring out what to order was a different matter.

Plus he still had to call the bakery and bitch about the lack of brownies.

The bell on the door rang—and Rob walked in.

Brian hid his cringe and checked his watch. It was nearly twelve thirty, which meant an hour and a half of entertaining Rob while he tried to figure out the ordering.

Rob's smile vanished and he took a seat. "Now's not a good time, I take it?" Apprehension in his voice and concern etched into his face.

"It's been a rough day. And I still have the ordering." He waved at the laptop and all his notes.

"I can take a trot around the neighborhood. Come back closer to two." Such sincerity. The need to help. That had always been there.

Brian rolled his shoulders to loosen them. "I don't want to throw you out..." He looked up at the board. "Want anything?"

A frown, but that smoothed out. "Whatever is the easiest for you."

"Drip coffee," Brian said. "But you deserve better than that."

Rob chuckled. "Do I? I want to make your life easier and yet—" He waved at the counter.

In reality, Rob wasn't helping. "I don't mind." A lie, but he *shouldn't* mind.

Rob—his boyfriend—was here to see him. Spend time with him.

He turned and started working on a cappuccino. Easy enough, but not so plain that he felt like he was stiffing Rob. Even if he never asked Rob to pay.

Once the drink was finished, he slid it over and sank onto the stool next to his laptop. "Let me try to get this hellish stuff done."

Rob took a sip of his coffee and closed his eyes. "So much better than office coffee."

He had to laugh at that. "I sure hope so."

Rob's grin was wide and warmed Brian's soul. "What's the problem with the orders anyway? Don't you have a set inventory?"

Like a shock of ice water thrown on him. "Of course I do. I'm not an idiot." He gritted his teeth and turned away. "Problem is, they keep changing what's available."

"Mmm." Rob sounded noncommittal. When Brian looked back, Rob's expression was neutral. Businesslike. As if he knew *anything* about this shop or what went on behind the counter.

Brian slapped his hands down on the paperwork and slid it over. "Want to do it for me, Mr. CEO?" Because he was done with the little hints that he didn't know how to run his business.

Rob blinked a few times and set down his mug. "Bri..."

"Seriously." He shoved the laptop in his direction, too.

"Brian." This time it was a bit louder and laced with concern. "What are you doing?"

He caught a breath, then another. "Trying to run my shop." His heart hammered too fast in his chest.

"I know that." Soft words. Silence between them while Rob studied him. "Do you really want my help? Sometimes outsiders see what insiders can't." Another pause. "Or I can go walk around the block for a while."

He didn't want Rob to leave. He didn't want Rob to stay. Everything was tangled in his head and ripping apart like tissue paper.

"I don't know." That was the truth.

Rob fingered his cup. "I've been doing some reading..."

Oh God. Anita had done that, too. "Let me guess. Some articles off the Internet on how to start your own coffee shop." Couldn't help the scorn that dripped off the words. Didn't want to.

Rob's cheeks flushed.

Bingo. "It's all shit, you know. If running a place like this were easy, everyone would be doing it."

Rob straightened, his face darkening. "You're not the only coffee shop in Squirrel Hill, you know."

No. There were at least a half-dozen. Several on Murray alone. "Why don't you go to one of them, then?"

Rob drew back, his brows creasing, but didn't say a word.

God, his head hurt so bad. Lightning flickered in his vision. Brian pulled out a piece of paper from his stack. "This," he said, shoving it under Rob's hands, "is what I normally order." He scrawled a number on his notebook. "This is my budget." Lastly, he pushed the laptop over. "And here's the ordering pages for my vendors. Enjoy." He got up and walked into the back room.

Once out of the sight of customers, he placed his hands on the edge of the counter that ran along the back wall, leaned over, and tried to catch his breath. Almost impossible with the way his heart was beating.

Fuck. What *was* he doing? Rob was right to ask that. Nausea forced bile into his throat. His shop was going to hell and he'd just handed over ordering to a man who knew *nothing* about Grounds N'at or what it needed.

A voice in the back of his mind whispered, *He's just trying to help.*

He didn't *need* Rob's help. He'd never dream of telling

Rob how to run his high-tech company—why did Rob have to stick his nose into Brian's business?

Granted, he'd shoved it under Rob's nose a moment ago.

Brian rubbed his face. God this day was... horrible. He needed a do-over, but life didn't give you those.

The bell on the door rang and Brian sighed. Back to it. Serve customers and figure out how to tell Rob to mind his own business—literally.

When he returned to the shop proper, a mother and her young son stood by the counter and Rob was peering at Brian's computer while wearing knitted brows and lips pressed into a very thin line.

Shit. He slid a smile over his apprehension and took the woman's order. A mint mocha for her and milk and a cookie for her son. Easy enough. He made her coffee—even indulging in some art on top. A carton of milk, a straw, and a chocolate chip cookie later, they'd taken up residence at the table Ev, Jan, and Dan had vacated earlier.

Once his customers were settled, Brian turned his attention back to Rob. "Don't tell me you're actually ordering things." He kept his voice low, but couldn't keep the sharp corners from the words.

Rob met his stare and there was heat there. In his voice, too, despite the soft volume. "No. But I am beginning to understand why this place is falling apart."

Anger seethed into Brian and he pulled the laptop away from Rob. "It's not falling apart," he snapped. "You don't know shit."

An ugly snort followed. "Really? How many hours have you worked this week, Bri?"

Too many. He glared at Rob.

"Why the hell are you ordering from those vendors?

Everything's twice as expensive as it ought to be. You can do better on the pricing. There's some sites—"

"Shut it." He ground the words out.

Rob blanched.

God. There were too many people in the shop for this. He sank down on the stool in front of Rob. "I don't want to hear about the sites you've found. Or any other so-called wisdom you've gleaned from the Internet. I've seen it before, usually from my exes."

Even less color in Rob. His lips were curled into a deep frown.

"Yeah, there are cheaper places, but I'm not a penny-pinching asshole and my customers deserve *quality* goods sourced from *ethical* companies. How about you, Rob? You buy cheap for those robots of yours? Little components lovingly made by children in forced labor?"

The horror that rose in Rob was almost gratifying to watch. His voice was a whisper. "I'm trying to help you, Bri."

He glanced at the screen of his laptop and there was one of the cheap-ass, crappy-supplier web pages open. "I don't need your help." His heart tried to pound its way out of his chest. How could Rob even *think* this was help?

"Brian..." There was a whine to the edge of Rob's voice, as if Brian were being the unreasonable one.

"You know what I *need*, Rob? For you to shut the fuck up and get the hell out of my shop."

Rob froze, his eyes wide. He swallowed, Adam's apple bobbing. "All right." Quiet, clipped words. He stood, pulled out his wallet, and threw down two twenties. "For the coffees." Then he turned and walked out, the shop bell ringing as the door shut behind him.

Brian exhaled and stared at the money. A cool

numbness washed over him, blotting out the crackling in the back of his head and the ache in his chest. He picked up the bills and stuffed it into the tip jar.

At least now he'd have time to do the ordering properly. He gathered up his paperwork and laptop and ignored the shaking in his hands and the tears pricking at the corner of his eyes.

It wasn't even two yet.

Rob was gone.

Rob marched up Murray Avenue toward his car and tried to swallow the burning lump of anger lodged in his throat. Implying that he used child slave labor to fuel CirroBot? Fucking *hell* if he'd put up with that kind of shit from anyone, let alone someone who professed to *love* him.

That obviously had been a lie.

The rock in his throat grew and the burning moved into his eyes. What a way to end a relationship.

He'd been trying to lend a hand, not tell Brian how to run his damned business. Even ethically sourced, there ought to have been less expensive vendors.

Rob pulled out his cell phone.

No texts. Not that he expected any—Brian had made his wishes extraordinarily clear. Rob's heart squeezed in his chest, tight enough that he couldn't breathe. He'd looked forward to this evening for *days*. Time with the man he loved. An afternoon together. Dinner. Maybe heading into Frick Park for a long walk. It was June and beautiful. Warm nights. They could watch fireflies in the grass.

He'd strung lights up on his back porch. Had giddy little

visions of sitting outside, Brian in his arms, and enjoying the time together.

Gone. All of it. Ground to dust, much like the coffee in Brian's shop.

His whole body shook and he sank into the driver's seat, his gut burning, hands trembling.

Brian had told him to get out. To leave him alone. There'd been finality there.

This was not a spat—it was the end of the line. He'd thrown down money to pay for all those free cups of coffee.

The photos—his photos—were a loss. He crumpled those thoughts up. They were shit anyway. Just Brian being *nice* to him. Probably because he was a decent fuck in bed. Wasn't that what Greg had said before he'd blackmailed him? *You're a good fuck, but it's not like I love you.*

One inhale, then another. Breathe. He had to breathe. Once he was home, he could fall apart. Let the anger and the sadness take him down, then the grief and rage. His emotions always came like that—had even after Greg, and God knows he'd been glad to be rid of him.

Brian—

A sob nearly broke through his tight control.

No. Fucking *no.* Not here. Rob clenched his phone in his hand and brought up Brian's contact information and blocked him.

After that conversation, he didn't want to hear from the fucker again. Let him burn in hell. Hopefully that damn shop would crumple down around his shitty little head. There'd be no future with Brian. All the hopes and dreams, Rob would set those on fire and burn them into ash.

He tossed the phone on the passenger seat and pressed the ignition button. Clinging hard to the power of his anger, he pulled out and drove up the street, and out of Brian's life.

Halfway to his house, the stinging in his eyes set in. He blinked it away. By the time he pulled in front of his home, his jaw hurt from clenching it. Brian should have been with him. They should have been walking in together. Making plans for the evening. Kissing, touching, laughing.

Instead, he walked in alone, the house echoing with his harsh breaths. Practically every room had Brian etched into it. Here they'd watched movies. In the kitchen, he'd made pancakes.

Rob set his keys, wallet, and phone down on the counter.

Out on the porch, they'd talked and drank and smiled. He stepped out into the yard and took the short steps required to reach the garden Brian's father had given to him. Helped him plant.

Oh God. How would he explain that to Brian's parents? Would they even speak to him again? *Hey, your son was a giant arsehole to me and threw me out of that shop that's going to eventually kill him.*

"Fuck." He whispered the word to the earth.

He hadn't exactly been a saint during their snitty conversation, but he certainly hadn't deserved to be treated with such venom and unceremoniously thrown out like that. As stressed and tired as Brian was, there wasn't any excuse for his behavior.

It was the kind of argument that should have had them both huffy, then apologetic, then talking, but it had swung so wildly out of proportion, so fast... there was no fixing it.

To imply that Rob was unethical? Brian didn't know what went into Rob's business, for goodness' sake. Had never even asked. Didn't care.

He stared at the blossoms on the tomato plants and winced.

Maybe he shouldn't have mentioned other vendors or looking up information on running coffee shops. Brian got twitchy whenever Rob had made suggestions in the past. At some level, Brian was right—Rob didn't know the first thing about coffee—but he knew *business* and it was plain to see that Brian was struggling.

Physically, mentally, and judging from the little bit he'd seen, financially, Grounds N'at was crumbling.

Why couldn't he let Rob be a sounding board? The only time that had happened had been up at McConnells Mill, when Brian had no other option—and after Rob had helped solve that crisis, Brian had run back to his precious baby *anyway*.

Oh, he understood putting heart and soul into a business. He'd done that with CirroBot, but there was more to life than work. He'd tried to show Brian that—thought he had.

But no, Brian loved that shop more than anything else, including Rob. In all likelihood, Brian would go down with the sinking ship and all the stress, and end up like Rob's father—dead too soon.

"Bri," he said to the plants, "I'm sorry I couldn't help you."

Couldn't hold on, as Len had asked. Couldn't be the love Brian needed to keep him from destroying himself.

Finally he let the tears slip, and knelt next to his garden as they fell silently onto the earth.

He was a failure as a friend *and* as a boyfriend, just as he'd been a failure as a son.

CHAPTER TWENTY-ONE

Brian made it through Sunday by sheer force of will, a half-dozen shots of espresso, and by hanging on to every last shred of anger he had. His shop was *not* falling apart, and he'd prove it.

Except by Monday afternoon, when the bills came in, there was an inkling of truth lurking in the envelopes.

He wasn't running in the black anymore. He had enough in the rainy day fund to cover it, but between costs going up, the new employees, and less customers, the shop was slipping away.

He closed the laptop and eyed the tables beyond the counter. There were less people here than he'd expect on a sunny June day. Even the newly placed outside tables were empty.

Lamont was working closing with him. Except there wasn't much to do. Brian pulled out his phone, almost out of habit, expecting to see a text from Rob—but no. Not after telling Rob to go the fuck away. Still, he'd half expected Rob to reach out. Then again, he hadn't contacted Rob, either.

A deep ache rose in his chest. He'd fucked that up perfectly. No dimples, no red hair, no sweet smile and lovely laugh. Bike rides were out. Hiking. Photography—

Fuck! He'd never had Rob's signed prints framed. His heart sank. By now, it was somewhere in his shoes. It hadn't beaten in his cold chest for days.

He shoved his phone back into his pocket. Still should get those prints framed. The shop could ship them to Rob when they were done. He'd promised Rob—

Love. He'd promised love.

Prickling up his arms. He rubbed it away.

Finally, the shop door rang, heralding the entrance of Eli and Justin. "Coffee break?"

Justin's smile was as bright as always, though the fuchsia ends to his hair were brighter. "You bet."

Eli's grin was more restrained and it fell away the longer he looked at Brian.

So Brian turned to Lamont. "I take the orders, you make them?"

Lamont nodded. "I need the practice."

That he did. Great on the register, not so good putting together anything more complicated than an Americano. Getting better. Slowly.

A large Americano was exactly what Eli ordered. Justin ordered a medium cafe mocha. Lamont's brows furrowed at that, but he started both orders.

Justin leaned against the counter. "How's life?"

He hoped his shrug covered the wince. "It's going."

Eli still had that penetrating and thoughtful frown and Justin's gaze flickered over Brian and then the shop itself.

Lamont placed Eli's drink down. "I left room for cream."

That teased a grin from Eli. "Good memory. Thank you!"

Lamont smiled in return and went back to Justin's drink. One pump of chocolate, then another and another and ...

"That's too many." Shit. "You're going to have to start over."

It must have come out too harsh, because Lamont jumped and set the cup down. "You said five."

"For a large. He ordered a *medium.* You're holding a damn medium cup." How hard was that to figure out?

Crestfallen didn't even begin to describe the way Lamont looked. Brian sighed. "I'll make it."

Justin murmured something to Eli. A moment later, he was behind the counter and hauling Brian toward the back room. "Hey, Lamont," Justin said. "Finish that one up. I like extra chocolate."

Once they passed through the doorway, Brian shook himself free from Justin—who stood between him and the doorway to the shop. "What the fuck are you doing?"

"I could ask you the same thing." Justin gestured behind him. "What the hell was *that*?"

"That—" He peered around Justin. "He's still learning."

"And you call that training?"

"Yeah, I do." Brian sucked in a breath. "He keeps getting the orders wrong."

Justin stared at him and Brian recognized horror under the anger.

This was not what he needed today. "I don't have time for this."

He tried to push past Justin, but despite his advantage of height, he ran straight into Justin's hand. "The Brian who trained me was infinitely patient and helpful, not a snappish oaf."

Ouch. He stepped back. "I'm not—" Except he *had* been rough on Lamont. Unkind. He swallowed. "You hardly needed training."

Justin's eyebrows rose into his fuchsia hairline. "You have a piss-poor memory."

Did he? He glanced behind Justin. Eli was chatting with Lamont and they were both laughing.

His heart dipped. None of this felt right.

"I had the exact same issue with the chocolate syrup." Justin spoke softly. "Always wanted to put more in. You had me remake 'em... but you were kind about it. Told me I would get it eventually. Did that with everything I screwed up—which I did a lot of in those first few weeks."

Thinking about it now, he remembered. Brian chewed on his tongue. "You're saying I was a dick out there."

Justin nodded. "Yeah, you were. And if you keep being one, you'll lose him. He's a good guy."

Lose him. Good guy. Brian caught himself on the counter. Too late for one person.

"Bri?" Justin was at his elbow, gripping his arm. "Are you feeling okay?"

No. Not with his heart cracking open again. "I..." God, he hadn't even said it out loud. That would make it real. "I broke up with Rob."

"Oh shit." It came out as an exhale. Justin let go. "You *didn't*."

"He was—" Trying to help. In all the wrong ways, but still. "It didn't work out."

"The shop?"

Brian cringed and nodded.

"Well, shit." Justin pushed his hair away from his eyes and looked quite a bit older and wiser. "That explains some things." He shook his head. "Look, I know you're stressed and I know you're heartbroken. But you *can't* take it out on your workers."

"I know."

"Yeah, you do and yet—" He nodded behind him.

Brian rubbed his forehead. "Point."

"Have you called him?" Soft words.

Rob. "No. I'm not going to."

"Bri... sometimes we say stuff we don't mean. It's stress or fear or whatever the hell." He fiddled with his wedding ring. "Trust me."

"I'm *not* calling him." This time he succeeded in moving past Justin, but he quelled his anger once out in the shop.

When Lamont glanced over, he had the look of someone who'd been yelled at one too many times.

Brian winced. Justin was right—he used to be a better manager. He'd fucked up. Time to suck it up and fix his mistakes.

Justin followed him out of the back, silently took his coffee, and he and Eli nodded their good-byes. Once they were out of the shop, Brian took a breath and turned to Lamont. "I owe you an apology."

Lamont tipped his head in surprise and wariness.

Ouch, but he deserved that appraisal. "I should never have snapped at you like that. Or any of the times I have."

"Well, I can't say I appreciated it. I'm still new here, Brian."

"I know." He ran a hand through his hair. "Or I should. I've been—"

"Stressed?" Lamont grabbed a rag and started cleaning the frothing wand.

"Doesn't mean I should be taking it out on anyone else." He picked up his laptop and the paid bills. "Won't happen again."

"Good." Lamont met his gaze, his dark eyes as penetrating as Eli's. "Because I like it here. It would be a shame to have to move on."

Brian swallowed at the underlying threat. Fuck up again and Lamont would walk—and while he might not have command of making all the drinks—customers liked him. Hell, Brian liked him. The drinks would come in time.

Justin was proof of that.

He headed into the back to stow the laptop and reached for his phone to text—

Fuck. He was not texting Rob. It took all his energy not to let out a sob. Rob didn't trust Brian to run his own shop. No matter how much Brian wanted to reach out, he'd made up his mind.

He straightened and watched Lamont. At this point, Brian wasn't sure he trusted *himself* to run his shop anymore, but without Rob in his life... Grounds N'at was all he had.

For the first time since he opened the place, that thought crumpled his heart and soul.

You're the one who tossed him out.

That was starting to feel like the greatest mistake of his life.

"THIS MEETING WITH AGELLA IS EXTREMELY important, Robert," Christopher Zaccardi said.

Rob resisted the urge to throw off his headset. Fucking board of directors. They'd all been on his case, lately. Chris wasn't usually a dick, but when he got nervous, his asshole nature came out. Rob tapped the unmute button. "I'm well aware of that, Chris. I've been doing this job for a while."

Silence on the other end, then a sigh. "It did take you some time to schedule your visit."

He winced at that, glad this was a phone conference and not video chat or an in-person meeting. He had. Perhaps too long. Putting personal ahead of business.

But since Brian wouldn't do the same ...

"I was still settling into Pittsburgh," he said, "but you're correct. This is an important visit. I let Agella pick the best time for them."

That seemed to mollify Chris. "Well, if they chose the timing, July is fine."

Rob rubbed his forehead. "What aren't you guys telling me?" He remained majority owner of CirroBot, but barely. He'd handed much of the power over to the BoD. Seemed like a good idea at the time. Until they started keeping him out of the loop.

"What do you mean?" More nervousness from Chris, and Rob nearly succumbed to the need to violently abuse his headset.

"You're not the only board member who's called me this week." Rob leaned back in his chair. "What are you guys doing with my company?"

"It's not entirely yours." There was a bit of a bite in Chris's response. "We're not doing anything."

"Yet."

A chuckle. "You did bring us on to help you."

He had. Some days—like today—he regretted it. The tension of not being in control, the frustration, the need to be in the driver's seat.

Pain stabbed through his heart and he exhaled against it.

Brian. This was *exactly* what Brian must have felt—must feel. Except it would take a lot longer to run CirroBot down.

Wouldn't take much to sink a tiny coffee shop.

"Robert?"

"Sorry. I was... thinking. It's not easy to give up control."

Another huff of laughter. "Don't I know it." A pause. "It's all forward thinking at this point. But every deal, every breakthrough—they're important."

There were two paths—well, three—for a company like CirroBot. The first—folding—he wouldn't contemplate. They'd come too far for that. Which meant there were two options: Be bought by someone larger or go IPO and get listed on a stock market. They *could* remain private—and had in a volatile market—but sooner or later, all those private shares would start burning a hole in everyone's pocket.

They were doing really fucking well at the moment.

In his heart, Rob was a technologist. Oh, he performed the role of CEO well enough, but he still ached for the hardware bench. Occasionally dreamed in code. Which is why he had a CFO and a board of directors to handle his blind spots—like what to do with the company now. How to grow it.

"You know I'll do my best to get Agella on board." Rob toyed with the cord of his headset. "I wasn't stalling on the meeting. I... needed to handle some personal things." Now they were handled, for the worst, but there it was.

A grunt from Chris. "Pleasure before business?"

"No." He studied his laptop. "My father dropped dead

when he was fifty-one. Some things have to come before business because that can't be all there is." If only he could have explained that to Brian.

A creaking over the line—Chris shifting in his seat. The man had a wife. Kids. Spent quite a bit of time away from them. "Understood." He cleared his throat. "Have they sent you an agenda yet?"

A very loose one. He sent it over and strategized with Chris until they were both satisfied with how Rob would approach Agella, then said their good-byes and hung up.

Rob lifted the headset off and placed it on his desk, his thoughts whirling around the future of CirroBot—and what could have been with Brian.

He rubbed a finger over his lips. He'd screwed up. In his effort to help, he'd barged in with no knowledge whatsoever. The owner in him understood how much that hurt, but the lover? Goddamn, he had just wanted to make things better for Brian.

For his effort, he'd gotten cursed at and tossed out of Brian's life. There wasn't anything *other* than business for Brian.

He spent the rest of the workday pulling his thoughts away from his failed relationship and squarely back on his company. Meetings, some demo, scheduling, and more meetings. By the time he biked home—still in his suit despite the heat—he was exhausted.

He changed into shorts and a t-shirt and went outside to his little garden. The least he could do was take care of it, after all the effort of Brian's father. A few weeds had crept in and he pulled those. Blossoms and a few tiny green tomatoes and peppers on the bushes.

Sitting in the grass in the sun kept his body warm—but

not his soul. This task, as enjoyable as it was, reminded him of Brian.

He ought to figure out what a garden like this cost to build and slip an envelope in the Kepplers' door, though Tony would likely stuff the envelope back, along with some choice words.

Did they know? Rob finished tidying up the garden, stopped inside for a second to wash his hands and grab a beer, then plopped down on the large lounge chair on his back porch. He kicked off his beat-up boat shoes.

The pain, the ache, the need for Brian lingered all around, in the scent of the earth and in the taste of his beer. The faint whisper of wind chimes from a few houses down.

There, itching through him, was the desire to reach out. Maybe Brian was sorry—but would that change anything? Rob took a draw on the bottle, leaned into the padding of the chair, and studied his toes. They'd end up circling around to the shop eventually, and it was pretty obvious where Rob ranked in Brian's life when it came to Grounds N'at.

Brian had warned him, too. All of his relationships fell to that place.

Rob wiggled his left big toe and sighed. Would he give up CirroBot for Brian? That was a legitimate question.

Yes.

If it meant keeping Brian, then yes. But the answer—and the question—wasn't fair. After all, he'd made changes at CirroBot so he *could* have more free time, even before he'd met Brian. He could quit tomorrow, and not have to worry about a paycheck for a very, very long time.

There was a great deal of privilege in that.

Besides, he never asked Brian to give up the shop. But

watching Brian grow stressed and sick and unhappy—and knowing he wasn't important to Brian—that was too much.

Maybe asking Brian for more time together wasn't fair. He didn't know.

He closed his eyes. Didn't matter at this point. He was used to living with the ghosts of others. He'd get through this, too.

CHAPTER TWENTY-TWO

Since the day he tossed Rob out of Grounds N'at, Brian found it harder and harder to paste on a smile and add that happy lilt to his voice during the workday.

And all he was doing lately *was* working. He wiped a table free of crumbs and checked the state of the half-and-half pitcher.

He'd had two shifts off since he'd told Rob to get the hell out, and every hour in Grounds N'at was like walking barefoot on broken glass. Less and less people frequented the shop and he couldn't blame his customers for not wanting to be served by the world's grumpiest barista.

He rubbed his forehead.

Even the folks from Sam's company weren't coming down as often, and when they did... They all knew, from the looks and frowns and glances.

When Fazil came in, he had the same long, worried look that Eli usually wore, sans the penetrating gaze. Fazil studied the counter after ordering and stood in silence while Brian made his mint latte.

He finally spoke when he paid. "You know, I've been

there." He contemplated the top of his drink then looked up.

"I remember," Brian said. Fazil had returned from a business trip a wreck of a man—partly due to reuniting, then breaking up with, his old high-school boyfriend. Brian had been worried about him. *Everyone* had been. "But it worked out for you." Todd had moved to Pittsburgh and a few months later, they'd eloped and bought a house.

Fazil studied Brian. "Todd took a big chance."

"Somehow, I don't think Rob's going to take that kind of chance."

"Maybe he's not the one who needs to."

That punched Brian hard in the chest. He wavered and reached out for the counter to steady himself.

Fazil nodded and dropped a dollar into the tip jar. "See you later, Bri."

Harder and harder to catch air. Brian scooted sideways from the register and sank down on the stool. The bell on the door rang when Fazil left, adding to the whirling in Brian's mind. His cellphone burned in his pocket.

Maybe... maybe Fazil and Justin were right. He pulled his phone out and stared at the screen. Worth a try.

He called Rob—and it went straight to voice mail. "Hey, it's me. I—just wanted to talk. I hope—I hope you get this." Brian ended the call.

The shop had only two customers in it, and for once he was glad for the small numbers. He wasn't sure he could stand. Numb didn't even begin to describe how his legs felt. So he sat and stared and tried to get his breathing back to normal.

Eventually, he got up and puttered around the shop, cleaning things, taking stock, and checking his phone every five minutes for a reply.

Nothing. He tried a text. Nothing.

Tingling from his toes to the back of his head. Had Rob *blocked* him? He lowered himself onto the stool again. Had to admit it was a distinct possibility, especially after what he'd said.

Shit.

By the time Beth came in for her shift, Brian was sipping water in an effort to quell the rising nausea. His heart wouldn't slow down, and he hadn't even had that much caffeine today.

In her expression was everything he feared. He must look *awful,* which meant customers saw the same. "That bad?" he murmured.

She frowned, but it was sympathetic. "You look like you haven't slept in days." After she tied on her apron, she washed her hands.

The truth from Beth's lips. He *hadn't* slept... not well, at least. "It's been quiet today." The shop, his phone. Everything but his brain and heart.

Beth took stock of the shop. "You know, I can handle the rest of the day and closing if you want to head home." She paused. "You've been here every day for a week and I know it's been rough."

He'd worked longer than a week straight. But he wasn't about to correct her, or look to see how long it had been since he'd had a day off. Beth knew how to close and how to set the alarm, the whole thing. They'd finished her training, but he hadn't let her close solo yet. He ran a hand through his hair. At some point, he *had* to have faith in his new people. "Yeah, okay."

She stood taller. "Really?"

He nodded. "You're right, it's not been a good week for

me. I could use the time off... and I trust you." He met her gaze. "I do."

Her smile brought out her dimples, and seeing those was a bittersweet thing. Reminded him too much of Rob. But it was also gratifying to see her happy to be working in the shop.

That hammered home *another* truth. "I should apologize for the way I've been recently. I've been..." He struggled for a delicate word, but gave up. "I've been an asshole. It's not fair to you or anyone."

Even if he couldn't turn the shop around, he didn't need to make anyone else's life miserable.

She twisted her hands in her apron. "That means a lot, Brian. You *have* been hard to work with sometimes." She glanced around the shop. "Everyone's noticed."

He winced, but it was the truth. He hadn't seen Dan, Ev, or Jan in ages. Or some of the other regulars. "Gonna try to fix that."

She nodded and stepped forward to grip him on the shoulder, a warm, friendly touch. "Start by going home and relaxing. The shop will be fine, I promise."

He had to trust her. *Had* to. Didn't have anyone else and he wasn't functioning. Too exhausted. Too strung-out. He ditched his apron, gave her a wave, and walked out the door.

He was greeted by a warm, partly cloudy day. Perfect for biking, hiking, or grilling. He wouldn't be doing any of those, least of all with Rob.

Brian trudged up Murray to Darlington, body aching the entire way, and climbed the stairs into his warm and stuffy apartment. Throwing open all the windows helped, as did changing into shorts. He left off the t-shirt.

Though his stomach whined at him to eat something,

the thought of food roiled. Nothing in the fridge looked palatable and his cabinets were empty, but for soup.

Too warm for that.

Delivery meant pizza but none of the good places delivered, so he might as well throw on a shirt and go out for something healthier. Greener. He'd been consuming a whole bunch of crap lately. Except dining out would remind him he was alone and why.

He flopped on his bed and stared at the ceiling, fingers and toes tingling and twitchy. Now that he was home, he couldn't relax, not when his head hurt and his heart felt too heavy to be lodged in his rib-cage.

He'd never hurt this bad from a breakup. Usually there was heartache, but also an underlying sense of relief, of freedom. A chance to do his own thing. Focus on the shop. Photography. Whatever.

Now? Only the hollow depths of anguish and a deep sense that he'd done something horrible and irreversible.

He'd fucked up. This time, he'd completely fucked up.

Still no response on his phone. He checked the time—midafternoon—and called again. Once more, he got voice mail immediately.

That... wasn't good. He slid the phone onto his nightstand. Usually it rang a couple of times, even when Rob had it muted. A creeping sensation gnawed up his body and he covered his eyes. More and more likely Rob had blocked him. No reply would come. Rob didn't want to hear from him at all.

He sat up slowly and studied his bedroom. He'd lived on the sparse side since starting Grounds N'at, first out of necessity, later practicality. The shop ate a decent amount of time even when it ran smoothly. Besides, other than photo editing, he preferred activities that kept him out of the house and enjoying life.

Right now? Life was shit. Work was shit. Brian closed his eyes and tried to slow the pace of his heart.

When he and Anita had broken up, he'd spent his next day off in the Laurel Highlands, hiking. Now he couldn't muster the energy to walk a couple of blocks to get a damn meal.

When his phone rang, he nearly jumped out of his skin. Rob?

He snatched it up, but no, it was Len. Brian steeled himself—Len always knew when he was upset, just from his voice. Still, he went for chipper and upbeat when he answered. "Hey, bro, how are you?"

A pause on the other end let Brian know he'd blown *that* performance. "I'm fine. On layover in Atlanta. Figured I'd call and catch up." Another pause, then the inevitable question. "What's wrong?"

Everything. He sighed and ran a hand through his hair. "I—uh. It's the shop. And Rob and—" His voice caught in his throat.

A shuffle of something on the line. He imagined Len leaning forward like he did in person. "Shit, Bri. Did you break up with him?"

"Yeah," he whispered. He had. That moment—Rob's slapping down forty dollars and walking out—the paleness of his skin and his haunted look—it was now etched in Brian's memory. Tears pricked at the corners of his eyes.

A sigh from Len. "Please tell me it wasn't because he's a guy."

Brian stopped breathing for a second because he couldn't believe what Len had said. "No. Why would you —?" Anger sparked in his chest. "Did you think I was *lying* about being bi?" That was the *last* thing he expected from his brother.

A sharp laugh. "God, no. Like I said, I've known for years. But you did step out for Rob. Didn't know if this was you getting cold feet... or because of the shop."

Everything with Rob had felt natural. Right. Except *this*. "The shop." Brian swallowed. Never any other reason. All his relationships fell to Grounds N'at—and his pride. "Shop's been bad. I'm in the red and there are less customers. Higher prices on supplies..."

A grunt. "And you're working more hours?"

He nodded, though Len couldn't see that. "I know that bothered Rob. I've been there most days." Too many days. Not enough free time together.

Then, Saturday had happened.

Len spoke soft words, tinged with a loving overlay of *you dope*. "Of *course* it bothered him. It's hard watching someone you love work themselves into the ground."

"I'm not—" He barely got the words out.

"Brian." Sharpness to Len's voice.

Okay, yes, he was grinding himself down to nothing. He saw that in the mirror every morning. Defeated, he spoke again. "I know. He wanted to help me."

"And you got snotty and vicious at his suggestions? Like you did with Anita?"

Brian cringed. In the end Anita had walked out on him. *I can't compete with this mistress.* She'd waved her hand to encompass the shop and left.

He doubted Rob would have walked away. Too much of the problem solver. He'd have stayed until they'd figured something out.

Another sigh from his brother. "Shit. I really hoped he'd be different for you."

Brian's heart and lungs tightened and he had to push the words out. "He is."

Silence from Len. Only the faint sound of his breath told Brian he was listening.

"He *is* different," Brian said. From Anita, from any of his other lovers—as few and far between as they'd been.

"What do you mean?"

"I screwed up, Len. With Rob. I didn't want—" His arm shook. Hell, his entire body shook. "God, I was so angry. It'd been a horrible day and he started talking about the shit he'd seen on the 'net and—I snapped. Now he's gone." He'd never felt like half of his *life* was missing after Anita had walked out. He'd been upset, sure, but... God. Rob and him. He couldn't imagine life *without* Rob.

Everything he wanted and needed for the future was tied to what he and Rob had started to build. That trust. That companionship. "I want him back." More than the shop, more than anything. "I want him back and I don't know what to do." He hiccupped for air and fought against the need to sob.

"Have you tried calling?" Len's voice was quiet, but clear. A lifeline of sense and caring in the cacophony of self-loathing that were his emotions. "Bri?"

"I did. Texted, too. But—I think he may have blocked me."

A hiss. "Shit. What did you say to the dude?"

What *had* he said? Some parts of that afternoon were so clear in his head. Others—not as much. "I—think—I told him to shut the fuck up and get the hell out of my shop." He cringed. "And I may have accused his company of using child labor."

Len groaned. "Fuck. Yeah, he probably did block you. In the same situation, I would've."

Brian squirmed and heat flooded to his face. "Thanks a lot." He rubbed the bridge of his nose, tears contained for now. "So, what do I do?"

"Go talk to him."

As if it were that easy. "I *can't*, Len. He's *blocked* me!"

On the other end, there was a thump and a huff. "Bri, there's more to life than cell phones. You know where he lives and you know where he works. You go—physically—and talk to him."

"You're saying I should go and—I can't just go to his company and ask to see him!" Could he? The thought echoed in his brain, unlocking the tension in his back.

Len laughed. "Of course you can. What do you have to lose?"

Nothing. He had already lost Rob. He might lose the shop, if things kept heading south. Crazy-ass idea, but there wasn't any other option.

"What if he says no?" He'd never tried to get back with someone after a breakup. Never wanted to. But he'd also never loved anyone like he loved Rob.

He *loved* Rob. Brian rubbed his eyes. Still. Missed him. Wanted him. He needed to see that smile and hear that voice. Feel those fingers on his skin, Rob's lips on his.

Len spoke the other side of the coin. "What if he says yes?"

Brian's heart thumped heavy and hard in his chest, and a painful stab of hope ached through his body. "I don't know." Whispered words.

Something creaked on the other end—probably Len on his hotel bed. "You need to figure out what's important to you." Despite the mundane background noises, Len sounded like some old sage. Fucking older brothers. They had a habit of being *right*.

Still, he protested. "I've spent *years* building up the shop." Not quite ten, but man, he was getting close. He blinked back tears again. If Grounds N'at closed, he'd lose a good chunk of his life.

"And you've known Rob for a few months," Len said.

Time that felt so much longer. From the moment Rob had stepped into Brian's life, he'd become part of his bones and blood. He'd never believed in love at first sight—but man, *something* had happened that day. A connection. A bonding. They'd built and built on that foundation, working toward something utterly beautiful. Then he'd torn it all down to ruin with his anger and insecurity.

"Are you saying Rob should come second to the shop?" That wasn't like Len. Especially when he'd cautioned Brian about working too many hours and burning out.

"No." Annoyance there. "I'm saying you need to figure out what's important to you. Rob or the shop?"

"They're both important!" He wanted to lob his phone across the room. He stood instead and paced. "God, the shop's been my life, even before I owned it. And Rob—Rob is—" His friend. His lover. His partner. Or had been.

Brian's gaze fell on the photo of his family that sat next to his computer. One from a summer day, not so different from today, back when they were younger. His parents sat on the porch steps, arms over each other's shoulder, both grinning ear to ear. They were flanked by Brian and Len, with Zoe on the steps below them.

His mom and dad had worked damn hard for years—but always put family above everything. His mom worked third shift to be there when they got home from school. Dad worked days to get them up and out. Sacrificed for what mattered most, especially when Len had gotten into trouble. The money for attorneys. Therapy.

The heart of family is the people you love. Brian. When everything else is gone, they're still there for you.

Rob. He exhaled. "I know what's important."

Len's voice was warm. "I had a feeling you did. Bet you know what to do now, too."

Yeah. The haze and noise in his head were gone. "I owe you one."

Len chuckled. "I'll put that IOU with the others."

Brian laughed, and for once, it didn't sound like a sob.

"Hey," Len said, "I should catch some sleep. I have an early morning flight to the West Coast."

"God, Len, I'm so glad you called."

"Hey, what are big brothers for?"

Apparently talking sense into him. "Let me know when you're back in town. We can catch a beer together."

"My treat," Len said.

"We can fight over it." Probably would, too. They said their good-byes, and Brian hung up and slid the phone onto his desk.

His heart wasn't pounding. Maybe this was the eye of the hurricane—calm and centered. If the shop fell down, he'd survive. Hell, he'd survive if Rob didn't want to get back together. Be horribly heartbroken, yes. Probably for years.

But he'd never forgive himself if he didn't try.

Time to see if he could clean up the mess he'd made. How and when, he didn't know. The schedule had him working every day from now until eternity, including all day tomorrow. Alone.

Brian stared at the photo of his family. *Family. Love.*

He closed his eyes. Time to take a chance.

Brian unlocked Grounds N'at the next morning, disabled the alarm, and relocked the door. He hadn't slept, his head too full of Rob and the conversation he'd had with his brother. When his alarm blared out at six thirty, he'd shut it off and gone through his normal routine with all the things he wanted to say to Rob tumbling through his head.

He should wait for Saturday, since he wasn't working in the morning and neither was Rob. He could go down to Rob's house, ring the bell, and apologize in person, though he wasn't sure he had the right words to say.

I fucked up. I'm an asshole. I love you. Please take me back. Yeah, that would go over well. Sure.

But two days from now, that was the plan.

He stood in his shop, scanning the darkened space, and his heart sank straight to his feet. The thought of coffee made his stomach roil even though he knew he needed the caffeine.

Given the shaking in his hands and the buzzing in his blood that sent spikes up his spine with every step, he wouldn't survive the day. Not when his heart was full of regret and his brain churning.

His stomach was a mess. His mind. Heart. Everything. Verging on tears if he thought too much—which he couldn't stop doing.

Brian took a deep breath. There was no one to call to fill his shifts—that's why he was working them, after all. He rubbed his hands against his jeans and glanced at his watch. Still thirty minutes before the shop opened.

He had bills to pay and he needed to take a good hard look at the menu and see if he could cut anything. Figure out how to entice people back.

Except without Rob in his life, he wasn't sure fighting to

save Grounds N'at was worth it. Wouldn't help if he kept the shop but lost his heart.

He pushed a hand through his hair. Family and love were what Anita had wanted from him. He couldn't give that to her and she'd found someone else who could.

Before Rob, he'd never thought about a time after Grounds N'at. He couldn't run the shop forever. Someday he'd retire. Who'd he spend his days with? Who'd help him make pasta? Watch old movies? Go on long walks?

He bit back a sob. Better if he let Rob go. When his chest tightened and eyes watered, he gulped air. Nope. Wasn't an option. Saturday then.

Or— Today. He could go apologize *today*. Head down to CirroBot like Len had suggested and talk to Rob. Get this all worked out now. Today.

Maybe then his head would be in a better place to solve the issues with the shop. Or he could close the damn place once and for all before it killed him.

Brian headed into the back. Paper. A Sharpie.

He wrote the date, then wrote in big block letters:

CLOSED TODAY DUE TO PERSONAL EMERGENCY

After grabbing a roll of tape, he stuck the sign up on the front door. He could do this... he was the owner, after all. The world would survive one day without Grounds N'at.

Though the edges of fatigue nibbled at him, he didn't make a drink for himself, just reset the alarm, locked the door, and headed back to his apartment.

Too early to head down to CirroBot. He'd have to wait a couple of hours—but better that than two days.

Rob was far more important than Grounds N'at.

CHAPTER TWENTY-THREE

The lobby of CirroBot was huge. Bigger than the entirety of Grounds N'at, even when Brian included the back room. Its vast space, sparse layout, and chrome-and-glass accents made Brian feel entirely out of place. Everything screamed high-tech, not earthy coffee shop.

This was the place Rob had built. So different from the one Brian had crafted. He pressed his lips together. Maybe this hadn't been the best plan. Still, here he was.

A receptionist sat behind a large desk plunked down in the middle of the space. A little farther back, near the elevators, sat a security guard.

Pretty obvious you needed to work here to get to the elevators, which made sense, but also meant Brian couldn't just wander up—even if he had any inkling of where Rob's office was.

Receptionist it was, then. He squared his shoulders and headed to the desk.

She had short black hair, dark eyes, and a friendly but professional expression. A tiny red rose tattoo on the side of her neck matched the color of her lipstick. “May I help you?”

“I hope so. I’d like to see Robert Ancroft, please.”

The friendliness vanished. “Do you have an appointment?” From the sounds of it, she already knew the answer.

Of *course* it wouldn’t be that easy. He took a breath. “No, I don’t. I—It’s a personal matter.”

“I’m sorry, sir. You’ll have to make an appointment with Mr. Ancroft’s personal assistant. Or contact Mr. Ancroft himself.” She paused. “If this is a personal matter.”

He would have, had Rob answered the voice mails or texts he’d sent. He leaned in a little. “Could you just... call him?”

She pushed away from the desk a fraction. “I’m sorry sir, but no. I’m going to have to ask you to leave.”

“But I—” Maybe it was the tone of his voice or whatever expression he had on his face, but the security guard slid off his chair by the elevators and headed toward them.

“Sir.”

He held up both hands and backed away. “Sorry. I’ll get an appointment.” After hell froze over, maybe. He turned away before the frustration made it to his face or loosened the tears in his eyes and stumbled toward the door.

God, he was such an utter failure. His vision blurred, he rammed into some one, and lost his balance. *Fuck.*

“Whoa, easy there.” Hands steadied him and a familiar voice brushed over him. “Brian?”

He blinked and looked up. Dark brown hair. Blue eyes. Fond of espresso shots. “Todd?” Fazil’s husband. He had a messenger bag slung over his shoulder.

“Hey.” Todd relaxed his grip on Brian, but didn’t let go.

He flicked a glance over Brian's shoulder, then focused on him. "What are you doing here?"

"I was trying to see Rob. Robert. Ancroft. He's—" His voice cracked. Boyfriend. Lover. Ex. *Oh God.* Brian gritted his teeth and tried to stop the shakes.

Todd's voice was gentle. "I know who he is." He pulled Brian over to the left. "Why don't we go over here and we can sit and talk."

They ended up at a small cluster of chairs, artfully arranged around a table with glossy magazines spouting all kinds of headlines that made no sense in Brian's blurred and jumbled vision. He was *not* crying. He blinked a few times and his sight focused.

Todd let him go at one of the chairs, and pulled another over closer, breaking the symmetry of the arrangement. Brian cringed at the scrape of metal on marble, and sank down to its hard black leather surface.

He met Todd's worried gaze. "Thanks."

"No problem." Todd slipped his bag off and lowered it next to his chair. "They're not going to let you up to see him, you know."

Fazil must have told Todd about him and Rob. Or maybe Rob had. Wasn't a surprise. Pittsburgh. Biggest small town in existence.

"Now I know that." Brian tried laughing, but it came out as a choking sound as pathetic as he felt. "I'm an ass."

"Nah, you're not. I've been there, man. I know how it goes." He cocked his head. "I take it you've called."

"Yeah. And texted. No response." He studied his hands.

A grunt. "How bad was it? The fight?"

Brian slumped deeper into the chair. "Take a guess." He gestured at the reception desk. "Truth is, I *am* an ass. And a hole as well."

That garnered a laugh from Todd.

"I have no idea what to do now. I guess I'll wait until the weekend and try to get up the nerve to go to his house."

Todd shrugged and pulled out his cell. "So, when I started working here, they gave me this phone. Pain in the ass sometimes, 'cause I can't help but look at the e-mails. Fazil has to take the damn thing from me at night." He tapped on the screen.

Brian bit his tongue. He had no idea where Todd was going with this, but Todd's sly smile kept Brian from interrupting.

"On the plus side, I have the entire CirroBot phone directory at my fingertips." He grinned. "Give me a minute." With that, he rose and stepped away, the phone at his ear.

Oh God. He was calling Rob. Brian's fingertips itched. If this worked, he owed Todd—and Fazil—big-time.

Please, please let this work.

THE RINGING FROM HIS LAPTOP STARTLED ROB OUT OF reading a design document for one of their next generation of medical robots. He glanced down at the corner of his screen and studied the incoming call indicator. *Todd?* He reached for his headset.

That was unusual. Most of the engineers knocked on his door or sent a chat message.

Still, he accepted the call. "Hi, Todd."

There was a pause. "Oh, I guess it tells you who's calling." Todd sounded a bit taken aback.

He chuckled. "It does, yes. What can I help you with?" This must be about one of the upcoming software releases.

An inhale. “Well, I’m down in the lobby… and Brian Keppler is here.”

Like a punch to the chest. All the air was gone from his lungs and his limbs numbed. “I—” Brian here? Why? How? He struggled to speak. “Can… you please tell him to leave?” He’d only started getting over that horrid Saturday. Couldn’t be a punching bag for Brian’s frustration or watch him work himself into a heart attack.

“I could.” Todd’s words were soft. “And I will, if that’s what you want.”

What he wanted was the Brian he first met that bright spring day.

“But I think you should come down and talk to him. He’s—” There was a crackle on the line for a moment, maybe Todd shifting his phone. “Well, let’s just say I’ve been where he is.”

“Sitting in the lobby of your ex’s workplace?” Somehow his voice sounded normal.

“Well, Eli’s office. But, yeah.”

Oh. Rob pressed against the back of his chair. He’d forgotten Todd had moved here to reunite with Fazil. That meeting must have gone well, given that they were married now.

That said something, but he pushed away that glint of hope. They were different people from Fazil and Todd.

He shouldn’t ask… he *knew* he shouldn’t ask. “How is he?”

Todd’s hollow laugh cut through Rob and Todd didn’t have to say *anything*. “Okay. I’ll come down.” Maybe if they cleared the air, they both could get on with their lives. A better break, one not born of anger and resentment.

“I’ll let him know,” Todd said.

They hung up. Rob took off the headset, placed it on his desk, and stared at his screen.

How was he going to do this? Well, like everything else —he'd figure it out as he went. He headed for the elevator.

The ride down to the lobby seemed both inordinately long and far too short. He blinked when the doors slid open —the lobby was bright—more so on sunny days like today.

Todd and Brian were easy to spot over at one of the seating areas. Both Richard, the guard, and Meena, the receptionist, started and wore worried expressions. He gave them a wave—one that meant *it's fine*—and headed over to the occupied chairs.

Todd rose and nodded to him. "I'll head upstairs." He gave Brian a quick smile. "Good to see you, Brian."

"Thanks." Brian's voice was cracked and rough and skittered along every one of Rob's nerves.

Brian looked up and met his gaze. *Oh, Bri. What have you done to yourself?* Red-rimmed eyes and a face drawn and thin. Rob sank into the chair Todd had vacated. "You wanted to see me?" Despite the ache in his heart, he kept himself in check. Part of him wanted a reunion—the other part remembered Saturday all too well.

"Yeah." Brian swallowed and wrung his hands. "I wanted to apologize. For being such a jerk to you. I was— Well, it doesn't matter. I shouldn't have treated you like that."

The ache under his ribs grew. Nearly *two weeks* and he was only coming to say this now? "Finally found the time? Had the day off?" Unexpected heat colored his voice. Still second fiddle to the fucking shop.

Brian flinched. "You never answered my calls or texts. I had a twelve-hour shift today." He met Rob's gaze, his face a mess of emotions. Hope, pain, anger, longing. "I closed Grounds N'at."

What? For the second time that day, words punched a hole through Rob's chest. Brian *closed* Grounds N'at? To come to see him? He found enough air to whisper. "For today? Or..."

A slight tremble ran through Brian and colored his voice. His eyes were far too wet. "Don't know yet. Haven't decided."

Shit. Rob rubbed his mouth and chin. Closing the shop spoke volumes, probably more than Brian could put into words. "Do you want to talk?" They needed to hash this all out.

"Yeah." Brian's Adam's apple bounced when he swallowed. "Lots of things I shouldn't have said... and lots of things I should've." Tears in those eyes, though none fell.

Rob felt his own burning at the back of his throat. He wanted to be more than an afterthought, but hadn't wanted Brian to kill Grounds N'at in the process. Just find balance. He studied his hands. "I'm not entirely innocent, either." The lobby was the wrong place for this. Too exposed, too public. "We should get out of here."

Brian rubbed his temple and grunted. "I could use some coffee."

A glance at his watch told Rob it was about ten thirty. On a normal day, Brian would have been on his third cup by now.

This day was shaping up to be anything but. Brian wore a frailty and sadness that dug deep into Rob and broke apart most of the resentment he'd felt. Brian had come here for *him*.

"Give me a minute." He dug out his phone and called Mallory. "Hey, Mal, something personal has come up. I need to cancel all my meetings for the rest of the day." He paused. Brian stared at his hands again, but the trembling had stopped. "Maybe tomorrow, too. Let's put those down as tentative."

Tapping on the other end, and she replied, "You have a phone call with the board this afternoon."

"It can wait." He still owned more than half the company.

She snorted. "They won't be happy."

"They never are. And you're a saint, Mal."

A chuckle. "I hope everything works out for you."

He studied Brian. "Me too. Thanks." He ended the call and tucked his phone back into his suit jacket. "Did you drive or..."

"Rode my bike down. It's locked up out front." Brian sounded better. "You didn't have to cancel your whole day for me."

Rob reached out, tentatively, and touched Brian's knee. "Yes, I did."

Almost as slowly, Brian covered Rob's hand with his own. "Rob, I—" His voice cracked to pieces.

Time to get out of here. "My bike's in the bike room." He nodded toward the door. "Let's go."

They both rose—Brian less steady than he should have been, but given everything, that was to be expected.

He was *here*. He'd closed the shop. Boggled Rob's mind, that. Maybe—maybe they could patch things up. "If you need coffee, there's several places we could go. Or—" He bit off the suggestion. They reached the bike room, and he pressed the badge in his wallet against the pad to unlock the door.

"Or?" Brian sounded more like himself, even if he looked shaken up and frayed at the edges.

Rob pulled his bike from its rack and steered it toward the door Brian held open. "Well, I don't live that far away."

Brian nodded but didn't say anything until they reached his bike at the rack outside. "I'd really like to talk about *everything*. You and me. The shop. What went wrong... I don't think I can do that in public." He unlocked his bike. "So if you don't mind your house..."

Rob unclipped his helmet from around the seat and strapped it on. "I don't mind. I've just never done this before, so I don't know the rules..."

"That makes two of us," Brian said. He shrugged, though it was close to a wince. "Guess we make it up as we go?"

Kind of like everything else. He gripped Brian's shoulder for a second. "Better than giving up."

That teased part of the smile Rob loved so much from Brian. "Much." That grin fell away. "You really ride in a *suit*? Your dry cleaning bills must be hellish."

Heat to his cheeks. "It's not *that* bad." Though, thinking about it, it was. "Come on."

They set off down Penn Avenue, toward Bloomfield, Brian in the lead, as if he knew the way. But then, he did. This place, the city Rob had chosen as home, was Brian's to the core.

What he really wanted was for Pittsburgh to be *theirs*. They still had quite a few things to hash out before that could be a possibility. There were events Rob never wanted replayed—and he needed assurances they never would be.

Then, only then, could he think about a future with Brian.

CHAPTER TWENTY-FOUR

Whenever Brian came to Rob's house, there was a tingle of surreality, his past overlaid with the present. Now there was also the agony of what might never be and that left him a breathless, more than he should have been from the ride over.

Despite the suit and the warmth of the day, Rob wasn't winded at all. They hauled their bikes into the house. Once stowed, Rob tore off his jacket and tossed it onto a chair. His tie followed. "Would you like some coffee?"

"Love some." That deep lack-of-caffeine headache was creeping through his skull. Might explain his inability to keep it together. "I don't suppose you have an espresso maker hidden somewhere?"

Rob chuckled. "Still only the drip maker and the French press. Pick your poison." He headed toward the kitchen, rolling up his shirtsleeves as he went.

Brian followed. "You joining me in drinking?"

"Yeah. I need something better than the stuff we have at work." Rob dug a bag of coffee beans out of his cabinet and handed it over. "Hope this will do."

Not from Grounds N'at, but from a good local roaster. Single origin. Expensive stuff. "More than." He headed over to the grinder. In the few steps he took, it occurred to him how fast he and Rob had fallen back into their normal routine. They fit so *perfectly*. He put the beans down and pressed his hands against the edge of the counter. "We—we need to talk."

"I know." Weight and a touch of heat in Rob's voice. "Believe me, I *know*."

Of course he did. After all, they were in his house during the day on a *Thursday* when they both should have been working.

Brian opened the beans and poured some into the grinder, eyeballing it. After all these years, he knew exactly how much coffee he'd need for a pot for two. "Drip maker. I could drink an entire press's worth of coffee myself."

A grunt. Rob rooted around in a cabinet above the machine and pulled out a pack of paper filters. Unbleached, thank goodness. Brian ran the grinder while Rob filled the carafe with water. "Ten cups?"

"Reading my mind."

A hollow laugh. "If only..." Soft words.

Yeah, that might have helped them both. He wasn't bad with communication, just with talking about the stuff he... didn't want to talk about.

Okay, so he was shit with communication.

Fuck. Tears returned to ring his eyes and he blinked them away. Together they finished setting up the coffee and started it brewing.

Rob gestured to the back porch. "It's nice out. And private enough."

Outside, they settled onto Rob's chaise lounge.

Brian stared out at the garden his father had planted for

Rob. Time to start working on the whole communication thing. "Truth is, you were right. The shop is falling apart."

Rob nodded, his face tinged with sadness.

"And I was a complete ass to you because I didn't want to see that." Brian dug his fingers into the cloth beneath his thighs, his chest aching. "I shouldn't have been snide. I shouldn't have thrown all my paperwork at you. And I certainly shouldn't have..."

He swallowed and met Rob's stare. The pain from the lump in his stomach—the one he'd had for days—was unbearable. "I shouldn't have broken up with you."

"Not like *that*, anyway." Amazing how soft Rob's words could sound while still cutting harder than diamond.

"Not at all," Brian said.

Rob gazed away, his hands twisting in his lap and his jawline so very hard. "Took you quite a while to realize that."

Not even an inch, Rob? "Yes... and no."

When Rob looked over, there was pain there. "I was trying to *help*, Bri. Because I fucking care. And you kicked me in the teeth for it."

Couldn't help the flinch. Wouldn't deny what Rob said.

A moment later, Rob softened. "I mean, I could have been kinder, too. But it's been damned hard watching you drive yourself to exhaustion. You have no time for *you*, let alone me. That's no way to live."

He nodded. This conversation he knew well. Same one he'd had with his parents. And Len. And Zoe. "I know. Well, *now* I know."

Rob furrowed his brows. "Now?"

From the kitchen came the glorious sound of the coffee maker finishing with a whoosh and a gurgle.

"Coffee?"

They spoke at the same time. Rob laughed at that, all teeth and dimples and Brian's heart soared until it cracked open completely and the pain was unbearable. He'd lost this. Might still lose this.

"Oh God, Rob. The things I said. I'm sorry. I'm—" He choked on the rest of it. This time, he couldn't hold back the tears. They strangled him, blotted his sight, and took his speech. He could only bend over and let go.

Fucking fool. Too wrapped up in himself to see how much Rob cared, how much he wanted to help. He'd been ugly and horrible and torn everything apart rather than face his own fears and problems.

Rob gripped his shoulders. "Hey, hey." Fingers in his hair. "It's going to be okay. I'm here. You're here. That's more than yesterday."

He grasped hold of that thought and looked up and there were tears in Rob's eyes, too.

"God, we're a bloody mess aren't we?" Rob stroked a thumb over Brian's cheek. "Let's have some coffee. Figure it out."

He croaked out a laugh. "Always solving problems."

Another caress. "It's what I do best." Rob blinked a few times. "When I can."

Rob's problem-solving when it came to the shop grated on every last one of Brian's nerves—but he appreciated it so much right now. Rob rubbed his shoulder. "I'll get you a cup."

He did, rising and returning with two mugs that steamed even in the hot June day. Rob's had a touch of milk, but he'd brought Brian one that was gloriously black.

With shaking hands, he took a sip. Bold and bright, nutty with a hint of citrus and caramel. He let the coffee slide down his throat and sighed. "Oh, that's good."

Rob had a weird little grin.

"What?"

"You. Us. Coffee." His humor faded. "Are you truly thinking about closing Grounds N'at?"

"Yeah." It was an option, and one he needed to look at. "I don't want to." He wrapped his hands around the mug, despite how hot it was. Better to feel something than nothing—he'd spent too much time being numb. "But I don't know what to do to fix things anymore. Hiring people isn't working, at least not fast enough."

A look of consternation in Rob, then his whole body relaxed into defeat. "I can't help you." Pain in those hazel eyes. "You were right about a few things, too. I don't know the first thing about owning a coffee shop, I only know you're running yourself into the ground." He paused. "Or grinding yourself up."

Brian choked on his coffee. "You didn't just pun during this conversation. Tell me you didn't just..."

Rob shrugged and his smile was that wonderful mix of sheepish and devilish that made Brian forget about everything. "I did, yeah." His expression softened to something more complicated. "It's either laugh or cry."

Brian contemplated his coffee before drinking. Laughing was better. "I thought I could manage the stress, that things would improve." He sipped. "I know you were trying to help, but the articles you read are... simplistic. Yeah, I could cut costs. Problem is, it's not about the bottom line. Never has been. I want to keep things in the black so I can keep going." He leaned back against the lounge. "When I created Grounds N'at, I wanted a place with *heart*. Local and ethical suppliers. Pay a living wage. Make a place *everyone* could come to and hang out. Like a neighborhood bar, but where all ages were welcome."

"A safe harbor."

He nodded. "Except I fucked it up, and now it's not." He hadn't seen Ev, Dan, and Jan in ages.

"There *has* to be a way back to that."

"God, I hope so." He wiped at his eyes and looked out into the yard. "You know, this is the first time we've really talked about work." He paused. "Well, my work."

Rob snorted. "Mine's boring."

It was a part of Rob as much as the shop was a part of him. "But who do you vent to? Who do you tell when you have exciting news?"

Rob blinked and sat back. "I don't." A quiet laugh. "I see what you're getting at." He took a swallow of coffee. "You'd think by our age we'd have all this shit figured out, eh? Relationships. Talking."

"God, the older I get, the less I know about everything."

Rob snorted. "Truth is that none of my other partners wanted to know about my work, not unless it involved how much cash was in it for them." Rob's brow furrowed. "You've never cared about the money."

"I've never even thought about it, to be honest." Brian finished his mug and felt a hell of a lot better. "Money's never been the important part of you."

Rob set his mug down on the table and faced Brian. "What is?"

"You." Brian clutched his mug like a talisman. "Being with you. This, now. The bike rides. Hiking. Photography. The way you smile. Your hands. Your freckles. Your voice. You. *All* of you."

Oh, that had broken some barrier of calm in Rob. He swallowed hard, eyes rimmed in red. "Me?"

Brian nodded. "If I can't figure out how to get Grounds N'at back on track *and* have a life outside of it, I'll close it.

I'd rather lose the shop than lose you." Brian swallowed, then whispered. "I love *you*."

There was that look again, the one that hinted of cracks and worry and tears, then Rob wrapped a hand around the back of Brian's neck, pulled him close, and their mouths met.

Oh God, he'd needed that. More than coffee. More than air. Brian gripped Rob's shirt and erased the distance between them. The kiss wasn't forceful, or demanding, but it melted Brian all the same, the way Rob's lips moved over his, the teasing of his tongue. Brian whispered between Rob's nibbles. "Coffee and cream."

He felt Rob's smile, then lost his breath when Rob deepened the kiss to wanton.

Couldn't help the moan, and Rob chuckled. "Slightly overroasted American."

Yeah, exactly that. He pressed his face against Rob's shoulder. "Please tell me I won't lose you."

Fingers in his hair, smoothing, settling. "I don't need to be the entirety of your life, Brian. The sole focus. But I want to be an important part, not an afterthought for when you have nothing better."

"I know. And you *are*." He lifted his head. "I know I need to prove that to you."

A soft smile. "But you have." He claimed Brian's mouth again, a deep but quick kiss that left Brian breathless, hard, and desperately wanting more.

Rob cupped Brian's face. "You haven't lost me. I adore you, except when you're being a fucking git." Thumbs skimmed over Brian's cheeks and Rob stared at him. "Please don't *ever* speak to me like that again."

He swallowed. "I—sometimes say things before I think."

"Mmm. I've noticed." Rob let him go, but they were

close now and the heat of Rob's body warmed him even more than the June air. "Honestly, so do I sometimes." He chuckled. "What we need is a phrase or word or something we can shout when we're getting stuck in one of those stupid arguments again."

"You mean like a safe word for conversations?"

Rob nodded. "Like 'Rutabaga' or some such thing."

A way to step back instead of blazing forward to burn the world down. "That's... not a bad idea." He stole a kiss of his own, then picked up his mug. "More coffee?"

"Please." Rob handed him the other mug.

This time, Brian rose and headed into the kitchen to fill the cups, adding a bit of milk to Rob's. He handed the mug back and reclaimed his spot on the lounge. "Too bad we can't solve the issues at the shop with a safe word."

Rob chuckled, but there was a hollowness to it. "I'm sorry you're having such a rough go with it."

"It's not the first time." Hadn't exactly been the same situation, but he'd been short-staffed—and short-tempered due to taking on too many shifts before. "Though this is worse. I didn't have the pricing problems. Or customers not coming back."

Rob sipped his coffee. "Not as simple as hiring Justin, then."

"No." That had been serendipity. He'd not quite believed the résumé the punk-rock wannabe had handed him, but once Justin opened his mouth, he'd seen the intelligence and work ethic there. "Even if I could hire Justin again, I don't think he could solve this."

Rob froze and had the strangest look on his face.

"What?"

Those hazel eyes focused on him and Rob looked as if

he'd been hit by a brick. Or inspiration. One of the two. "You absolutely should hire Justin White."

"I—" He stared at Rob. "I *can't*." God, he'd love to, but he'd moved on to better things. "Justin works for *Sam*. He's not a barista anymore."

Rob's grin was amazing. "Not as a *barista*, as a consultant."

The words made no sense, and then they *did*. Holy fuck. Air left Brian's lungs and he set down his mug. Justin White, a problem-solver who knew the ins and outs of his shop. Who knew business—better than Brian did.

It was *perfect*, but for one thing. "Sam saves high-tech firms. Not..." He waved his hand. "Tiny community coffee shops."

"But you're *his* tiny community coffee shop," Rob said. "And I have a feeling he'll jump at the chance to let Justin take on a project."

Hope bubbled—boiled—in his chest, so much that it was as painful as the heartache had been. There was another hitch with this idea. "I can't afford it." He had savings, but between being in the red and—well, he suspected Sam Anderson's consulting services didn't come cheap.

Rob took his hand. "Trust me on this one. I have a feeling Sam will be accommodating."

"I... don't know." God, it was such a long shot.

A squeeze of fingers. "There's no harm in asking, is there?"

Just the ruination of his pride, but that had been nothing but trouble anyway. "Okay. I'll see what he says." He had no idea how to even broach the conversation. "It's the best idea anyone's had in a while."

"See? I can help." Rob's grin was huge and he vibrated with enthusiasm.

Beautiful, perfect man. Brian pulled him into a desperate and deep kiss that said everything he couldn't put into words.

I love you. I can't live without you. I need you in my life.

Rob yanked Brian onto his lap, cupping Brian's ass and kneading the muscles there. The warmth of the day only intensified the heat radiating from Rob.

Brian kissed down Rob's neck, relishing in Rob's little huffs of breath, and the way Rob pressed against him. Somehow, he'd ended up straddling Rob. Breathless, he started on the buttons of Rob's shirt. Too many layers of clothes between them. "I should thank you."

Rob stroked his back and ass. "You should, but perhaps not on my back porch." He nipped at Brian's neck. "The neighbors might not enjoy the show."

Oh. Yeah. There was that. Especially since some of those neighbors knew Brian. He rocked against Rob. "You know, my brother was worried I'd broken up with you because you're a guy. He was relieved it was merely due to me being an asshole."

Rob huffed a laugh, then sobered. "I was under the impression he didn't doubt your sexuality at all."

"He doesn't. He thought I might have gotten cold feet because you're my first guy." He couldn't resist leaning down for another kiss. Rob arched into it, cock hard against Brian's.

"I think you've embraced your bisexuality quite nicely," he murmured before tangling his fingers in Brian's hair and claiming Brian's mouth, breath, and heart.

God, yeah. He had. And of all the people he'd dated, it was Rob who had made him contemplate a life outside of Grounds N'at. A future other than the shop.

Though right now, he wanted less shirt in the way of his

fingers. He skimmed a hand over Rob's pec and teased his nipple through the fabric.

Rob broke the kiss and sucked in a breath. "Fuck."

"Should we embrace my bisexuality inside?"

"Yes. Let's."

Brian had never quite understood the whole "light dancing in eyes" thing until he'd seen Rob smile. Because damn, his eyes danced and made Brian's mouth water and fingers itch to explore every inch of him. He rose from Rob's lap, but as soon as Rob stood, they reached for one another. "Bedroom." He spoke against Rob's lips. "Now."

"In due time," Rob said. He pulled Brian into the house. "After all, you owe me."

Yeah, he did. So, so, so much.

Rob yanked Brian from the kitchen into the living room. Damn good thing he'd canceled the rest of his day, because he intended to spend it tangled up with a contrite, sorrowful, hopeful Brian.

The man who would give up his business to save their relationship. He wanted Brian against him, wanted to feel that skin, hear his moans. Bring them both to the height of pleasure.

While there were flat surfaces aplenty in the kitchen, none of them were all that comfortable. The couch in the living room, however? Quite.

He pushed Brian onto the cushions and followed him down. "You're wearing too much." Tugging his shirt up exposed his stomach and part of his chest.

"Wait, let me..." Brian pulled the shirt off and tossed it out of the way.

Good. Perfect. Rob descended on Brian's torso, pinching one of his nipples, and mouthing the other. Got his reward. An arched back, a lovely moan, fingers in his hair, and Brian's hard shaft pressing against his.

"God, I missed you." Brian's voice was all air. "Should've—" His breath hitched and Rob met his gaze. Tears in those brown eyes. "You deserve better than I've been."

Rob wouldn't wave Brian's mistakes away, but he wasn't *horrible*, not when he'd recognized his faults and started to change things. He nipped hard at the flesh over Brian's ribs and his gasp was mouthwatering. "True," Rob murmured against skin. "But you closed your shop and you're here." He moved lower and bit Brian again. "Underneath me." Same lovely effect, this time with Brian's hands tightening in Rob's hair.

"God, Rob." Brian trembled.

"You enjoy that?" He licked at Brian's abs.

A moan, then a whisper. "Yeah." Deep breaths. "So much."

Good, because those whimpers were ambrosia. Rob nipped and bit his way across Brian's stomach until he was squirming, his jean-covered shaft hard against Rob's chest.

He'd never had makeup sex, never made it that far in a relationship. He pressed a kiss just above the top of Brian's jeans. "I think I'll keep you."

A sigh and Brian melted into the couch. "Please do. You can have anything you want."

So *much* he wanted. "That's a dangerous offer." He sat up. "What if I have a whole closet full of whips and chains and leather masks?"

A little shudder. "Do you?" Apprehension there, but also a glint of interest in his eyes.

Well, how about that. "No. It's two drawers and it's scarves, ropes, some dildos and plugs."

"Didn't you mention cock rings before?" Brian was flushed from his neck down to his jeans.

Rob touched the little red marks his teeth had left on that expanse of skin. "I did. You want to give them a try?"

Brian wore embarrassment *so* well. "Yeah, I wanted to try before, but... Well, I was an asshole and broke up with you." He took a breath and exhaled. "But I want right now to *last*."

Oh, it would. Rob palmed Brian's cock, relishing in the heat and hardness and the shudder that slid through Brian. "We have all day and all night to catch up."

"It's not just the sex. It's everything." Desperation there, and not just for getting off.

"I know, believe me. I'm not going anywhere." He undid the button of Brian's jeans and unzipped his fly. "But right now, if you don't mind, I want your dick in my mouth." He pulled jeans and underwear out of the way and freed Brian's cock. Hard. Beautiful.

Brian's stomach trembled and huffs of breath escaped as Rob stroked him.

"And when you're good and close, we'll talk more about my little drawer of goodies." Rob closed his mouth over the tip and gloried in Brian's long moan.

God, he'd missed Brian, too. And no, it wasn't just the sex, though there was something delicious about the way he moved under Rob. The thrusts, the sounds, the helplessness, and the demands. Fingers scraped against Rob's scalp and tugged at his hair, urging him on.

The taste of salt slid down Rob's throat and Brian thrust his silky hard shaft between Rob's lips. He ran his tongue along the sides and over the veins, humming with pleasure.

"Oh God, you're going to make me come." Brian's words were all moan and whisper.

That was the idea and he had no qualms about getting Brian right to the edge, as he'd promised. He didn't stop—and neither did Brian's hips. Groaning, sucking, thrusting, licking. When the grip on his hair tightened and Brian's moans turned to curses, Rob backed off.

Brian gasped and whimpered. "You—oh God, I was nearly there!"

He lifted his head and licked the taste of Brian off his lips. "Figured I should tell you that cock rings should only be put on when you're soft."

Brian sank against the couch and spoke through his teeth while rocking his hips. "There's a solution to that problem..."

Rob chuckled. "So what you're saying is you want my dick in your mouth, too?" He was just as hard, and damned if Brian would be the only one playing with rings tonight.

The look on Brian was pure lust. "I'd love that, but..." He gestured to the couch. "Not the best place."

True. They *could* manage, but there was a nice huge bed upstairs. He slid off of Brian, stood, and offered his hand. "Bedroom *now*."

Oh, that lit an inferno in Brian. His pants were off before they hit the stairs. At the top of the landing, Rob found himself pressed up against the wall, Brian's knee between his legs. He rocked his shaft against Brian's thigh.

Rob tilted his head back and grinned. "Someone wants something."

"You naked." Brian worked the buttons of Rob's shirt open and pushed it to his shoulders.

Soft, hot lips nipped his collarbone and Rob arched against Brian. "Want more, take me to bed," Rob said.

"With pleasure." Brian swung him around and pushed him into the bedroom. On his way to the bed, Rob stripped the rest of his clothes off and they fell in a tangle of limbs and groans and kisses. Rob rotated and crawled down Brian's body until that hard cock was between his lips again.

A moment later, Brian took him into his slick hot mouth, and Rob moaned around Brian's shaft. That tongue could take away Rob's mind.

Neither of them was going to last long. Too keyed up. Too hot for each other and oh, Brian's mouth and tongue were a fucking wonder of nature. He stroked Brian's dick. "Fuck, Bri. Where did you learn to suck cock like that?"

He felt the chuckle all the way up his spine, then warm breath against his balls. "Right here, in your bed."

Damn right he had. Rob went down on Brian's shaft again, relishing in the moans he felt around his own cock.

Brian caressed Rob's balls, sending his pulse and desire skyward.

No way he was coming first. He slicked his finger with spit, then found Brian's hole and circled it, all the while sucking and licking at Brian's lovely cock.

A groan that vibrated the whole bed. "Oh my God." Brian gasped for air. "Rob, I'm gonna—"

Then Brian closed his lips on him again, pumping and sucking his dick until all Rob could do was hold on and try to match the wicked rhythm Brian had set. Couldn't even thrust, not with the way Brian held his arse.

Still wasn't gonna lose. He slipped a finger inside Brian and thrust hard.

Brian uttered a strangled curse, his cock thickened, and hot salt hit Rob's tongue.

Yes. So *fucking* good. He licked and sucked until Brian shivered and cursed. "You—bastard."

"Your mouth may be magic, but I have years of practice."

"Guess I need more, then." Brian rolled him onto his back, then that gorgeous mouth was on his cock again.

Rob gripped the sheets and thrust up into Brian's heat, and gave himself over completely. "Yes. Fuck. Like—that!"

Brian flicked his tongue against Rob's crown and engulfed what he could. Perfect. Fire flowed through Rob as he fucked Brian's lovely tight mouth, light building behind his eyelids. His moans and curses bounced off the ceiling and back into his ears.

God, there wasn't anything better than this. Pleasured by Rob, any way he could have his sometimes bitter, burned-out lover.

When Brian stroked Rob's balls and pressed his tongue under his cockhead, Rob couldn't hold back. Light scattered in his vision, heat shot through every vein, he thrust into Brian's mouth and spilled every last drop of his seed.

Like every time before, Brian swallowed. Amazing. Unexpected.

When Rob could see clearly and breathe without gasping, he joined Brian at the top of the bed and kissed him.

Always a delight to taste himself in Brian's mouth. "Cream in my Americano."

Brian rolled his eyes. "Really?" But there was a smile there, and he pulled Rob in for another kiss. "In you, too."

"A lot of guys don't swallow." He stroked Brian's cheek. "I like that you do."

Brian's eyebrows hit his hairline. "Really? I mean, I get it with porn. You're there for the money shot. But in real life?"

Rob shrugged. "Semen turns a lot of guys off."

"Huh." Brian eyed the ceiling, as if in thought. "Then again, lots of guys won't go down on a woman for the same reason."

"I bet you did." He stroked Brian's ruddy chest. They both had worked up a sweat.

Brian rolled closer. "Oh, God, yeah. There's nothing better than making a woman come like that." He chuckled. "Though, I guess I won't be doing that anymore. I get to drive you wild instead." Brian laced his fingers between Rob's.

"Yeah. I'm hopelessly monogamous." Rob planted a kiss on Brian's nose.

"Well, so am I, so it works out." Perspiration gleamed along Brian's hairline and his grin was *wicked*. "Didn't you say something about toys?"

Rob's pulse ticked up. "Would you like to come into my closet?"

A little pout. "But I just came out of the closet a few months ago!"

"Brat." He mock punched Brian in the arm and stood. "I'll show you all my goodies."

"With an invitation like that, how could I refuse?" Brian rose and followed him into the large walk-in.

He'd had custom cabinetry made. A unit of drawers in the middle held his ties, underwear, and socks, along with other small items like cuff links and pocket squares. The drawers on the bottom were reserved for a host of *other* items. He stooped and pulled one open.

An intake of breath. "That *is* a goodie drawer."

The most prominent items were the large blue dildo and the two butt plugs. There were also two bundles of rope. Several folded sashes. A set of silicone cock rings of various sizes, and a leather and velcro one. "It's pretty vanilla."

Brian knelt down next to him and fingered one of the sashes. "Now what did I tell you about vanilla?"

Heat from Rob's head to his toes. That night was entrenched in his memory. His brain superimposed Brian wrapping the lovely purple sash he was stroking around Rob's wrists before he fucked him.

Rob cleared his throat. "Noted, but—" He waved at the drawer. "Not particularly kinky, on a scale of one to ten."

A sheepish smile on Brian's flushed face. "It's all new to me."

"I suppose one person's vanilla is another person's orange zest." Rob drew out the leather cock ring with the velcro closure and one of the silicone ones that fit him.

"Did you just make *another* pun?"

Rob sat back on his heels. "Technically, it was a metaphor." He held up the cock rings. "Need some zest, Americano?"

He thought Brian might choke on his laughter, but when he caught his breath, his grin was so wide. "Oh my God, I love you."

A different warmth. This man—this was the man he wanted to spend the rest of his life with. Indomitable. Stubborn. Hardworking. An arse at times, but thoughtful at others. "You truly want to be with me," Rob murmured.

The grin vanished. "Yes," Brian whispered. "If I could go back and erase that day—walk in and kick myself in the head for being so *stupid*, I would." He took a breath. "I don't know how to say I'm sorry."

"But you do." Rob fingered the cock rings. "You have." He met Brian's gaze.

The smile came back. "And yeah, I want some zest. Or at least to *try*." He eyed the rings. "Walk me through this."

Rob snorted. "There's not much to tell." He set down the silicone ring. "It's all about blood flow. Constrict the flow going back from the dick, and you stay harder longer. Bigger orgasm."

"And it works?" He was still eyeing the length of leather.

"Does for me, but everyone's different." He opened the ring with a little pull. "For you, since it's adjustable and easy to remove. If it hurts or you don't like it..."

"Rip." Brian mimicked pulling.

"Exactly."

Brian nodded. "Okay, but the other... how do you... put it on?"

Ah, well, he could show that. He handed the leather strap to Brian and picked up the other ring. Took a second to slip it down his soft shaft. "The next part is why you really shouldn't be hard." One at a time, he fed his balls through, and settled the ring against his belly.

"Well, shit." He eyed Rob's dick. "That's pretty damn hot."

"Mmm-hmm. Let's see how this looks on you." He plucked the leather band from Brian's fingers, then lifted his package to wrap it around behind his balls. Firm, but not too tight. "How's that?"

Brian was hardening, and his cheeks flush. "Uh. Fine." He swallowed. "Sexy?"

"Is that a question?" Rob caressed Brian's neck and drew him in for his answer—A hard kiss that had Brian moaning and melting. Surrender in some ways, but their tongues dueled until they were both breathless.

Brian broke the kiss. "God, that feels strange."

They were both hard. Rob took Brian's shaft in hand and stroked. "Good or bad?"

His eyelid's flickered and the answer was a moan. "Good. So good."

Perfect. Rob eyed the sash Brian had been playing with earlier. "Mind if I tied you up and fucked you?"

Wide open eyes now. "I—I'm game for that."

Rob drew the sash out from the drawer and rose. "Let's see if you deem this vanilla or orange when I'm done with you."

A little swallow and Brian looked up.

On his knees and with such desperation in his eyes, for a moment Rob considered fucking Brian right in the closet. But the bed was far more comfortable and he could tie Brian down.

He offered his hand, Brian took it, and he pulled him up into his arms. "I love you as well, you know." He kissed Brian's neck and enjoyed the tremble. "That's why I was so mad at you."

A grunt and a whisper. "Tie me up and fuck me, and I promise I'll never do it again."

Their dicks pressed against each other, and Rob walked them backward out of the closet, brushing past suits and shirts, the trappings of his business, until they were into the bedroom. "Promise me you'll not do it again, and I'll tie you up and fuck you."

Serious eyes. "Deal. Never. I Promise."

They reached the bed and Rob nudged Brian down onto the sheets.

"Now I see why you have a slatted headboard." Brian tipped his head back, lengthening his neck.

He couldn't resist kissing that throat. "Decorative *and* practical." He climbed on top of Brian, drew his wrists up above his head, tied them together, then tied the sash to the headboard.

Like with the cock ring, everything was firm but not too tight. "I suspect you could get out of that if you tried."

Brian wiggled his wrists. "Yeah, maybe." He grinned up at Rob and rolled his hips. "But I don't want to."

Rob chuckled and got the condoms and lube from his nightstand and ripped the foil open. "Do say something if you need me to stop."

"Like 'rutabaga'?" Sexy wicked grin.

"That works." He rolled the condom on and slid down Brian, far enough that he could suck the head of Brian's cock into his mouth.

Beneath him, Brian quivered. "Oh fuck."

"Don't mind if I do," Rob murmured against his hot, hard shaft. He sat back, grabbed the lube, and prepped himself. One slick finger inside Brian told him Brian was more than ready from the way he bucked to the long groan.

"Tease." Brian's arms strained as he gripped the sash. So lovely, that muscle and sinew, those damn shoulders.

"Not really." Rob pressed his cock against Brian and slid inside, inch by inch. Like each time before, the heat and tightness took his breath away. So did Brian's content moan.

They worked so well in bed. He rocked back and thrust in deeper, delighting in the grunt from Brian. "Yeah—that's —" The rest vanished in a huff when Rob plunged in again, and Brian moved with him. "God, you feel so good."

Rob spoke before claiming Brian's mouth. "So do you." Perfect. Hot. His. Just what he needed.

Couldn't get much movement kissing Brian like this—but Rob wanted *this* to last—frantic fucking could come later. For now, it was everything to feel all of Brian, taste his lips and swallow his whimpers, and move slowly inside him.

Rob slid his hands up Brian's arms, feeling the tension there, loving the trust. He'd no doubt Brian would keep his promise. The hard work—admitting the issue—had been done.

Brian was *his*. In return, Rob was Brian's. Their jobs were second to that—as they should have been all along. "I believe you," he whispered against Brian's lips.

A hiccup or a sob, Rob couldn't tell which. "Everything I have."

"Ah, but I don't need everything." He kissed Brian's throat and pushed in as deep as he could. "Only a part." Enough to know he mattered.

Brian arched underneath him. "God. I missed you." Spots of moisture, both on his brow and lurking at the corners of his eyes. "Missed us."

So had he. He *understood* Brian, more than he had any other man. The drive, the need to create, the need for control and to let go. The deep need to be loved for who he was.

They'd figure it out. He had no doubts.

Beneath him, Brian shuddered. "Fuck, this feels incredible." Those sweet brown eyes flickered open. "You feel—" He rolled his head back, rocked his hips, and stole Rob's breath.

Yeah, that was about right. He moaned against Brian. Spine-meltingly amazing. He was grateful for the cock ring and the earlier orgasm. Even now, heat and fire flashed up his spine with every stroke.

"More," Brian whispered. "Need more."

He could do that, with pleasure. Rob rose up to gain more leverage and drove into Brian. Again and again.

"Fuck!" Brian pulled against the sash even as he tried to match Rob's rhythm with his own. "Yes, like—that!"

Such a beautiful sight, that. Straining arms, helpless cries. He could get used to this. Rob gripped Brian's hips and fucked him with short, swift strokes.

"Oh my God!" Brian twisted beneath him. "I can't... I need..." He pulled at the cloth that trapped his hands, and tossed his head back against the pillow. "Don't stop. Please, please, please... don't..."

Rob didn't. Instead, he wrapped his hand around Brian's dick and stroked him in time with his fucking. Hard, fast, brutal. "More?"

"Yes!" Brian panted out the word and rocked underneath him. "Yes!" The word became a chant that fell from Brian's lips, then turned into a deep cry as Brian tightened around Rob and stole every thought. Hot semen spilled over his hand and onto Brian's chest, and that was the last he saw because his own orgasm took him in a blinding shower of sparks and fire. He drove deep into Brian until he couldn't move for the pleasure and the heat. Couldn't tell which of them was moaning, where their skin ended, whose breath gasped or whose heart beat so, so, so wildly.

Only that they were together. Twined. Joined. They remained that way until the light and the fire faded, until Brian shifted under him.

"You—you okay?" Brian's voice, nudging at his brain.

"Yeah." His own was rough, like dried leaves in fall. He swallowed. "Let me..."

They both whimpered a little when he pulled out. Rob reached up and tugged the sash holding Brian's hands free from the headboard, then loosened the loops around his wrists. "Was that—was it okay? The ring? The sash?"

A breathless laugh. "Oh my God, Rob." He gasped, his

grin wide, but there was an air of astonishment. "Never felt like that before. It was like—a trip."

Yeah, for him, too. "Better than weed?"

A longer laugh this time. "Much. So much better."

Rob propped himself up on his elbow. "Better than coffee?"

The smile melted into seriousness. "Yes," he said. "Always."

Now wasn't that something. "You're not going to be able to brew me and sell me." He slipped the condom off and wrapped it in a tissue, then cleaned his hand as best he could.

"No, I'll just blow you, fuck you, and keep you." A little grin. "All to myself."

"That sounds ideal." He rolled onto his back. "I need to throw this out, but I can barely move."

"Tell me about it." Brian shifted on the bed, then velcro ripped. "Fuck!"

"Are you hurt?"

He groaned. "No. Damn thing pulled a pube."

God, this was the best thing ever. Forty years old, in bed with his lover, and they were like giddy schoolboys. He laughed. "Be grateful you're not wearing the one I'm wearing."

"How are you getting that off anyway?"

"Same way I got it on." He was softer now. "But I'll use lube, too."

Silence for a bit. "God, we still have all night." There was amazement there, and a bit of fear.

That was showing their age. He felt both thrill and trepidation, too. "We don't *have* to do anything more."

A grunt. "You ever been fucked like that?" Brian sat up, and there was that sexy-ass glint.

"Tied up?"

Brian nodded, his grin cocky and devilish. Rob shivered, remembering the earlier image he had flashing through his head. "Once or twice."

"Want to make it two or three times?"

Oh hell, yes. He grinned back at Brian. "How about I cook you dinner, and we see how we feel?"

"Deal."

No doubt in his mind he'd be flat on his back and begging Brian to make him come in a few hours. None at all.

In the end, he was right. They didn't bother with the rings again, not after tearing each other's clothes off once more. The sash was wound around Rob's wrists—and he couldn't have gotten out, even if he'd wanted to.

Which he didn't. Not when Brian looked at him like he would spend the night devouring him whole.

Brian leaned down and took his mouth in a kiss that curled his toes. When he was a moaning mess, Brian relented.

"Thank you for coming downstairs." Tears in those eyes.

In Rob's eyes, too. "You closed your shop and came to me." Hope and gratitude twined with desire. "I'd have been a fool not to." He'd nearly been.

A more gentle kiss this time. One that led to heat and moans and Brian moving inside him, and the best night of Rob's life.

When they'd spent themselves again, cleaned up, and collapsed like the older men they were, when he wrapped himself around Brian and kissed his shoulder, realization zipped through Rob like the shock after a sudden clap of thunder.

He'd never come this far through the veil of forgiveness with *anyone* before. Not his former lovers, not his parents, not even *himself*. But they'd fought and they'd parted, and they'd returned and here they were.

If that wasn't love, then nothing in the world was. Rob closed his eyes and pulled Brian closer.

He had everything he ever wanted after all.

CHAPTER TWENTY-FIVE

OPENING GROUNDS N'AT FRIDAY MORNING WAS BOTH the same and utterly different for Brian. Everything had changed. His priorities, his plans, his life. He hadn't lied to Rob—he'd close the shop if it got between him and Rob again, but he hoped he could work something out with Sam. Maybe Justin could make magic a second time.

Brian pulled down the sign he'd taped to the door. A couple years ago, he'd have balked at asking for help, but now? Having a business plan—a real one—would be a good thing, especially if it meant a future that wasn't more of the past: Failed relationships. Stress. Heartache.

As he went through the motions of preparing to open, he realized Beth had closed the shop perfectly on Wednesday. Counters, tables, and machines gleamed. All the supplies neat and organized. She'd done a great job. He'd have to thank her for that. And give her that key on a more permanent basis.

For the first time in ages, he wasn't anxious, stressed, or exhausted, despite the physicality of the sex he'd had with Rob, both yesterday and this morning.

That hammered home how much he'd needed a break from Grounds N'at, and how much he'd needed to make things right in his life.

Whatever happened—shop open or closed—he'd survive. Thrive.

Just before eight, he unlocked the door. As normal, one of the first people to walk through the door was Sam, who looked distinctly relieved. "Good morning." There was a question hidden between those two words.

"Morning, Sam. The usual?"

Sam nodded and fiddled with the cuff of his shirt.

While Brian worked on a cappuccino, Sam asked what had been written on his face. "You doing okay?"

He finished frothing milk and poured the top onto Sam's drink. "I am now. But I wasn't yesterday—and I still have some things to work out."

Sam nodded, a furrow between his brow. "If there's anything I can do to help..."

Well if *that* wasn't an opening. "Um, actually..." He handed over Sam's coffee and took his card. No one else had come in yet, which was both good and bad. "I was wondering how I'd go about hiring you guys for some consulting. I need advice or a new business plan." He gestured to the shop. "It's not been going all that great lately."

The line between his brows deepened. "I—we don't—"

The bell on the door rang and Sam's face smoothed over, but the customers that entered were two more familiar faces from upstairs—Eli and Justin.

At least he hadn't chased away *all* of his regulars. A spike of pain, but he quelled that. Hopefully he'd fix the situation.

The first words out of Justin's mouth were, "Dude, what happened? Are you okay?"

Sam turned sideways and glanced at Justin—then faced Brian, his focus laser sharp. "Oh, I see." A sly smile. "Yes, maybe we can help. Are you free this afternoon?"

Brian nodded. "Miranda has the evening shift." He rang up the sale. The confusion that had been on Sam transferred to Justin. Eli stood back in his usual thinking pose—hands on his cane. He met Brian's gaze and nodded, but didn't say a word.

"Stop up at three, and let's talk." Sam picked up his coffee and took his card back.

"Will do."

Sam saluted him, and headed for the door. Justin took his place, with Eli a step behind. "Okay, what's going on?" This was the no-nonsense Justin. Same one who'd pulled him into the back room.

He answered Justin's first question. "I'm fine. I took your advice and talked to Rob." He paused. "Two shot caramel latte and an Americano with room for cream?"

Justin swept his fuchsia bangs from his eyes. "And that?" He pointed at the path Sam had taken.

"A cappuccino." He smiled as sweetly as he could.

In a strange reversal, it was Eli who laughed loud and long. He placed a hand against Justin's back and slid up next to him. "You deserved that." He grinned at Brian. "And yes. The usual. And the caramel latte will be fine for him."

Justin didn't look pleased. "I like knowing what's going on."

"Of course you do. I do as well." He tugged at some part of Justin's clothing—maybe a belt loop and pulled Justin closer to him. "We'll find out soon enough."

Brian hid his amusement by turning away to start their drinks. "I'm sure Sam will explain."

"Mmm-hmm." Eli's voice.

Justin inhaled in a way that was too familiar from his own breathlessness with Rob.

He didn't even bother to turn around. "Family establishment, gentlemen."

Another chuckle from Eli. "I'm not doing anything untoward."

He frothed the milk for Justin's drink, and finished both off. Despite Eli's remark, Justin was blushing furiously when Brian turned around and placed the drinks on the counter.

Still, he gave a sheepish shrug. "He's telling the truth." He picked up both drinks while Eli handed over his credit card.

Brian snorted and rang them up. "See you at three."

As they wandered out of the shop, Brian leaned back against the counter and took out his phone. His frantic texts to Rob from the previous day were still there. Well, at least that was in the past—and remained a caution for the future. He typed out a new text.

Spoke to Sam. We're talking at 3. I think this might work.

The look in Sam when Justin had walked in—Brian was sure Sam already understood what Brian needed and wanted. But then, Sam was a master of his business.

His phone buzzed. Two texts in rapid succession. The block must be off.

Good to hear.

How are you doing otherwise?

Brian glanced up, but no one else looked like they might walk into his shop.

Doing better than I have in a long time. Thank you. For yesterday. For everything.

He had hope and that was something he'd been lacking for a long time—since before he'd met Rob, if he were being honest with himself.

Someday, he ought to apologize to Anita for being such a shit. They'd not been right for each other, but he hadn't really handled it well, in retrospect.

You're welcome. A simple reply. Brian could almost hear Rob's voice.

He typed rapidly on the phone. I love you, you know.

I do know. And I you.

The bell on the door rang. Customers.

Take good care of them.

He nodded and shoved the phone into his pocket. Back to basics. He pushed off the counter, and the smile came naturally. "Hi, what can I get started for you?"

A LITTLE AFTER THREE O'CLOCK, BRIAN FOUND himself sitting in a chair in Sam Anderson's office. Justin sat next to him and Sam across the desk. He'd never felt more out of place in his *life*.

Despite Justin's t-shirt, jeans, and bright pink hair tips, the way he sat spoke of business and an edge he'd not seen in the coffee shop. This was as much Justin's domain as Sam's.

"So," Sam said, "you're looking for a business plan."

No surprise in Justin. Likely he had talked to Sam.

"Or something." Brian fiddled with the edge of his shirt. "The margins have always been tight, but now they're gone and I can't turn things around."

"And you're stressing yourself—and everyone else—out trying." Soft words from Justin.

He didn't even flinch. "Pretty much." He leaned back. "I can't keep doing what I'm doing."

Sam tented his hands. "Plus, you have more reasons not to be at the shop all the damn time."

His cheeks heated. "There's that, too." He paused. "So how does this work?"

Sam flattened his hands against his desk. "We're going to figure that out."

"I have some ideas." Justin grinned.

Forty-five minutes later, Brian rubbed his temples and stared at his former barista. Even back when he'd hired Justin, he'd seen his penchant for business—after all, he'd been an MBA student. But now? "This is—something else."

"Well," Justin said, "you wanted a plan."

"Or something," Sam said. For all the world, it looked as if Sam were trying not to grin from ear to ear. "Good work, J."

Sketched out on a pad in front of Justin were notes and suggestions, most of which had poured out of him. Ways to study Brian's business, his competition. What was trending in shops around the country. "I think you already have most of the pieces," Justin had said. "Just add a few, file down the rough spots, and put them all together."

Ambitious. Crazy. Wonderful. There was only one small problem. "You guys must charge a fortune for this kind of thing."

Sam nodded. "We do."

Brian's heart sank. "Shit."

Sam waved the curse away. "This isn't a normal situation. You're not high-tech, you're tiny, and you're our neighbor."

"I make you a damn fine cup of coffee."

Sam laughed. "You make me an exceptionally fine cup of coffee. And I stole away your best employee."

Justin shifted in his seat. "Hey, I applied to *you*."

Sam's lips twitched upward, but he ignored Justin. "Plus, someone's been pestering me for a project of his own."

"*Pestering* is a strong word," Justin said. "I've been asking politely."

This time, Sam couldn't contain the grin. "This seems like the perfect opportunity."

"This has to cost me *something*." Sam might be a fantastic customer and a decent guy, but he was also a smart businessman. You didn't give everything away for free.

"How about a year's worth of your exceptional coffee for all of my employees?"

Brian's breath caught. He let it out slowly. Because that much free coffee did add up to a decent sum. Doubtless, it was far, far, *far* less than what Sam normally charged.

"No blender drinks," Justin said.

Sam lifted an eyebrow. "Whose side are you on?"

"Both." Justin crossed one leg over the other. "I want

this to succeed. Do you have any idea how much of a pain in the ass those drinks are? You'll kill morale."

Brian chuckled. "It's true. Customers love them, but they're the *worst*."

Sam held up his hand. "Fine. Done." He paused. "Well, done if you accept."

"You're not planning on hiring twenty people or something? Right?"

Sam laughed. "No. We're at the size we're going to be for a while."

Seven people. An entire year. "Three-drink-a-day limit?"

"Four." There was a gleam in Sam's eye. "I think that's fair."

Justin was quiet. On both sides, indeed.

Brian did a quick calculation in his head—probably similar to the one Sam had done in his. A tidy sum, both a nice bonus for his employees and a price for Brian. It would be neatly spread out over the year and, if Justin's plan worked, well worth the cost. He nodded. "Okay."

Both men relaxed and Justin uncrossed his legs. "Eli's going to have kittens with the accounting on *that* contract."

"Eh, Eli needs a challenge." Sam looked downright gleeful.

"Please don't make Eli cranky with me. His is usually the easiest damn drink in the world."

"Oh," Justin said, "leave Eli to me."

Sam chuckled, but focused on Brian. "I'll have more formal paperwork drawn up, but do we have a deal?"

"Yes." He held out his hand, and they shook over Sam's desk. Brian turned to Justin. "It'll be good working with you again."

"You say that now." Justin leaned back in his chair. "I should warn you that I've become a pain in the ass."

He'd take that if it meant Grounds N'at surviving. "Apparently that's what I need."

Sam rose, and they all followed suit. "I'll stop by in a few days with the paperwork."

Justin saw him to the front door. When they passed into the reception area, he spoke. "This isn't going to be a cakewalk, you know."

"It hasn't been so far." He faced Justin. "And I'm not exactly looking forward to you picking apart everything I do. But, it's necessary. I'm too close."

The grin was gone, replaced with thoughtfulness. "Good." A pause. "Um. You and Rob? Things are better?"

He exhaled. "Yeah. I mean, I still have a lot of work to do there, too. But yeah."

"Good." He clapped Brian on the shoulder. "We'll make this work."

Words Brian believed. He gave Justin a grin, then headed back down to the coffee shop.

As soon as he walked through the door, he stopped in his tracks. Miranda was laughing with a customer sitting at the counter, one in a business suit and sporting a very familiar head of ginger hair.

Not even five yet. Warmth from his head to his toes. Miranda met his gaze. "And here's your man now."

Rob turned and his smile was summer and light. Oh yeah—he was Rob's entirely. Somehow, he crossed the distance on feet made of air and sat down next to Rob. "You're off early."

"The boss likes me."

Damn those eyes and dimples and... "*My* boss is an ass."

Rob slid a hand up Brian's thigh. "Only sometimes."

God. He really didn't need a raging hard-on in his own store. Brian laced his fingers between Rob's and drew Rob's hand back down to his knee. "Family establishment," he murmured.

There was Rob's pretty blush. "Sorry." He cleared his throat. "So, how'd it go?"

"Good. Really good." But he didn't want to talk about plans to save Grounds N'at while sitting *in* the shop. "How about I tell you over dinner?"

"How about I cook you dinner and you tell me?"

Miranda laughed. "You two are adorable. Get out of here."

They didn't have to be told twice. Once outside, Brian pulled Rob close and kissed him. "I'm glad your boss likes you."

Rob laughed against Brian's lips. "Thing is, he's got a horrible crush on you and wants to make sure you're fed, de-stressed, and really well fucked."

Brian shivered. "You're the best thing that's ever happened to me."

"Same." Rob stole another kiss. "My brilliant Americano."

He didn't quite believe *that*—but Rob had been right about everything else, so he let it go.

Sometimes, you had to take a chance.

EPILOGUE

Three months later

On a Saturday afternoon, at a table by the window in Grounds N'at, Brian studied a map on the laptop before him.

Rob leaned back in his chair. "I think it'll be fine. We've been biking all summer, and the weather will be cooler."

"I'm worried about it being too cool in the mountains." The Great Allegheny Passage's grade wasn't more than 1 percent. The C&O Towpath had steeper parts, but they'd been riding the hills in Pittsburgh. Nothing either path tossed at them should be too hard. Still, in the mountains it was bound to get cold during the first week of October.

Rob caressed the back of Brian's neck. "We've the lodging worked out. The bikes are in good shape. It's going to be fine."

He nibbled on his fingernail.

Rob slid his hand down to Brian's shoulder. "Don't make me rutabaga you in public." Amusement in his voice.

Okay, maybe he *was* being silly. "I've never done

anything like this before." A week's worth of biking. A few days in DC to see some sites, then a train ride home. Exciting, but also terrifying.

It meant two weeks away from Grounds N'at. He took a breath. "I've never been *away* this long." Not since owning the shop.

Rob softened. "I know. That'll be fine, too. You *know* it'll be."

He did. Between some hard work, hard choices, and Justin's tough love—they'd set the shop back on track. The coffee he owed Sam? He was making more than enough to cover that now.

The shop was running better than ever.

They'd rejiggered the menu and the ordering and the scheduling. Added some theme evenings once a month. Justin suggested Brian start crafting beverages again, a special drink each month.

He'd completely *forgotten* how well those went over. Too stressed to see beyond the schedule and the books to find solutions.

Hell, Justin had even tracked down Ev, Dan, and Jan and brought them back in. They'd finished high school and they'd all stayed close to home. Ev had ended up at the University of Pittsburgh—and taken a job at the shop.

Zie and Lamont were on tonight, with Lamont training and closing. While Brian always thought he'd end up promoting Miranda, with her schedule, he couldn't. Her grandmom was better, but still required a decent amount of care.

Lamont had taken on more and more responsibility and risen to every occasion. Brian really didn't see any reason *not* to make him assistant manager. All the other baristas agreed. Including Miranda.

Perfect solution.

"All right. I'll stop worrying." He closed the laptop.

Rob caught his hand and kissed it. "No, you won't. But don't let it keep you from enjoying this."

Life happened, whether he worried or not. He gave Rob's hand a squeeze. "I'm sure you'll help keep me in check."

"You can count on it." Rob's smile was wicked, though his kiss was on the chaste side—a peck that was a promise of more when they weren't in the shop.

The chimes on the door clanked against the frame, and brought a familiar face into Grounds N'at. Anita focused on the counter and her smile fell away. "Oh, damn it! He's not working? He's always working! The one time..."

Brian had to laugh, even if it contained the bitter sting of regret. Lots of lost hours with family and friends.

Rob patted his knee, as if he knew where Brian's brain had turned. Maybe he did—they'd talked a bit about Anita and his breakup with her a few times. After a moment, Rob pulled his hand away.

Ev pointed at Brian. "He's not working. But he's over there."

Anita swung around. "Wow. For a moment, I thought I was in some alternate universe." She grinned and came over.

"Well, I *am* off, but I'm also in the middle of packing my apartment—and we needed table space to plan our trip and —" He gestured at the table.

She eyed him and Rob. "Wait, you're taking a vacation?"

Brian nodded, not bothering to hide his grin.

"Maybe I *have* entered a different dimension." Her

smile drifted to horror. “Please don’t tell me this trip is at the end of October.”

“Beginning. Why?”

She dug into her purse and pulled out an envelope. Thick. Nice paper. “Because I have this.” She handed it to Brian, and there was his full name: Brian Galileo Keppler.

Rob stared at the envelope. “Your middle name is *Galileo*?” Loud. Loud enough that the entire shop heard.

Heat to his face. That was one of the very last things he told people. Anita had only pried it out of him after too much tequila and too many tacos. “Um. My parents thought it would be amusing—and it’s Italian. They figured if I was already named after one astronomer…”

Rob’s lopsided grin took away the pain. “Your parents are the fucking *best*.”

Anita looked utterly confused. She glanced between Rob and him.

Brian carefully opened the envelope, though he had a good idea what it contained. He pulled out the gorgeous and gilded wedding invitation for the last Saturday in October. “Congratulations,” he murmured, and meant it.

“Thanks.” Color touched her cheeks. “I said I’d invite you. And it’s plus one. I didn’t know if you were seeing anyone.”

Rob shifted in his seat and Brian’s stomach tumbled. He’d kept his bisexuality tighter to his chest with Anita than his middle name. He read through the rest of the invitation and glanced at the RSVP card to stall for time, then tucked everything back into the envelope. “Actually—Anita, I’d like you to meet Rob Ancroft. Rob, this is Anita Carrillo, my ex-girlfriend.”

Rob held out his hand and Anita took it. She wore

surprise, but not of horror, which was good. "Pleased to meet you," Rob's voice was soft, friendly. British.

Anita met Brian's gaze and he took a breath. "Rob's my boyfriend."

"Wow." She puffed out a breath. "So you're bi or pan? I mean, I shouldn't assume you're not gay, but..." She waved her hand at herself and her cheeks flushed. "Um. Well..."

Yeah, they'd enjoyed themselves in bed. A *lot.* He nodded. "Bi."

She glanced at the closed laptop. "You're planning a vacation together?"

He nodded again.

"How long?"

Rob gave her his best smile, the one that turned Brian inside out. "Two weeks."

A huge grin spread across her face. "I *need* to know how you two met." She grabbed a chair from another table and pulled it over. "If you're dragging him from this shop for two weeks, this is seriously *serious*."

The heat on Brian's cheeks returned. "He... breezed in one day and swept me off my feet."

Rob snorted. "You wooed me with coffee and puns about cream, then licked ice cream off my hand."

Oh God. He buried his face in his hands. "Rob..."

Anita laughed. "You *have* to invite me to the wedding."

Wedding. His breath caught and he lowered his hands. "We're not even engaged."

"Yet," Rob said, all teeth and dimples and love.

Sitting there was his present and his future. His life and love. Rob.

Brian reached for Rob's hand and they twined fingers. "We'll send you an invitation."

THANKS FOR READING!

Dear Reader,

Thank you for reading *Daily Grind*! I hope you enjoyed Brian and Rob's story. I apologize for all the coffee puns.

When Brian first appeared in *Just Business*, I knew he'd eventually get a book of his own. He's a hometown Pittsburgh boy with deep roots, and this book, more than any other, showcases some of what makes Pittsburgh special to me.

If you enjoyed the coffee theme of this book, I suggest checking out my book *Cinnamon Roll*, and the other books in the multi-author series Bold Brew, which is centered around a coffee shop in a western Pennsylvania town.

To find out more about all my books and new releases, you can follow me on BookBub, join my facebook group or sign up for my newsletter.

Thank you so much!

-Anna

ACKNOWLEDGMENTS

Those who know me know my love of coffee, but it wasn't always so. I owe a debt to my dear friend Lynne Glowacki for buying me my first café mocha so many years ago. It's her fault I drink coffee, and I love her for it.

I also owe several cuppas to Elyse Springer for her barista knowledge. While I've sat in countless coffee shops, I've never worked in one.

As always, I owe Lori Witt for her unending support and optimism that I could do this thing when I was sure I could not. Thank you for everything. Again. Always.

I also owe thanks to Jennifer Udden, and to my hardworking editor, Kristine Swartz, both of whom make my writing shine.

While Grounds N'at is entirely fictitious, there are many fine independent coffee shops in the Pittsburgh area upon which Grounds N'at is based, including my neighborhood shop, The Coffee Buddha. Grounds N'at is my love letter to all of them.

There's a certain freedom to being older, as Brian

discovers. This book is also for my fellow bisexuals of any age. It's truly okay to be bi.

ALSO BY ANNA ZABO

Close Quarter

Close Quarter

Slow Waltz (a Close Quarter short story)

Takeover

Takeover

Just Business

Due Diligence

Daily Grind

Twisted Wishes

Syncopation

Counterpoint

Reverb

Standalone Works

CTRL Me

Outside the Lines

Weave the Dark, Weave the Light

Cinnamon Roll

ABOUT THE AUTHOR

Anna Zabo writes contemporary and paranormal romance for all colors of the rainbow. They live and work in Pittsburgh, Pennsylvania, which isn't nearly as boring as most people think.

They can be easily plied with coffee or a chance to see the Pittsburgh Penguins.

Anna has an MFA in Writing Popular Fiction from Seton Hill University, where they fell in with a roving band of romance writers and never looked back. They also have a BA in Creative Writing from Carnegie Mellon University.

Anna uses they/them pronouns and prefers Mx. Zabo as an honorific. They can be found online at annazabo.com.

twitter.com/amergina

instagram.com/amergina

bookbub.com/authors/anna-zabo

amazon.com/Anna-Zabo/e/B00A7LA6OC

www.ingramcontent.com/pod-product-compliance
Lightning Source LLC
La Vergne TN
LVHW041102080826
845145LV00007B/1657

* 9 7 8 1 9 4 7 5 5 0 0 8 7 *